SNOW SANCTUARY

BY

LEE HALL DELFAUSSE

the PeppertreePress
Sarasota, Florida

This is a work of fiction. Except for well-known actual people, events and venues, the names, characters, places, and incidents are the product of the author's imagination or are used fictitiously, and any resemblance to actual persons, living or dead, businesses, companies, events, or locales is purely coincidental.

www.snowsanctuary.com

DEDICATION

To all those who love the mountains and skiing

"*I am younger each year at the first snowflake.*
While I see it, suddenly, in the air, all little and white
and moving, then I am in love again and very young
and I believe everything."

—Anne Sexton,
letter to W. D. Snodgrass

"*Snowflakes are such ephemeral things, but look what*
they can do when they stick together."

—Becky Langer

CHAPTER 1

Damien

I'd never felt such cold, balancing on my skis in the starting gate, dressed only in a thin racing jacket and stretch pants, shivering, waiting. I cringed at the lack of snow on the mountain racecourse. I wondered how the Eastern Ski Association could make me—us—practice for the downhill championships with so many stumps mushrooming from the icy trail? At this moment, all I wished for was my feather comforter over my head instead of my silver crash helmet, a fiberglass bucket that afforded little protection from the 10 degree February morning here on Sugarloaf Mountain in Maine.

"Lia, I'll ski first. I know you'll be slower," said Damien, taunting me with his devilish grin, his Colgate-white teeth, his cheeks growing frost-feathers on his teenage fuzz. Seeing my expression, he became serious, "You look a little scared." He paused and closed his eyes. "Remember, courage isn't the absence of fear—it's doing your best despite it."

I laughed, "Ha! Speak for yourself. You look like a snowman." Trying to reassure myself, I continued, "Watch out or I'll catch you on the first fall-away turn, just above the birch grove." He turned toward the course, so I yelled again to his hunched back, "Don't forget your pre-jump. Remember Marsha is ahead of you."

The wind muffled my words as it blew the inch of powder away from the makeshift starting gate. Damien poled out of the start, his skis rattling on the boiler-plate ice. When he hit the first turn, his skis scratched the crust, creating a sound like fingernails scraping a chalkboard. He tried to skate in order to pick up speed

1

for the first artificial bump. He looked like a baby bird attempting its first flight, arms and legs askew. Then, silence.

I counted to thirty in order to give him a lead, in case he had trouble. A blast of loose snow delayed my leap out of the gate. On course, I hit a tuck, head to knees in a perfect aerodynamic egg position, to get speed for the bump. The bump came sooner than I expected, indicating the course was faster than before. Three gates down, I had to start my turn for the fall-away gate much earlier than I had planned. As I set my edge on the dusting of wind-blown snow, I saw a track below me, headed for the woods.

Out from the woods ran my friend, Marsha, frantically waving her arms as if she were a policewoman trying to stop cars. She struggled for balance in her effort to stop me. "Come quickly, Damien tried to pass me, lost control and went into the birches," she screamed, trying to be heard over the moaning wind.

I threw my skis sideways, clicked out of my bindings, and ran toward the largest birch tree. Pressed against the white bark, Damien's head tilted at a right angle. Unmoving, he resembled a chickadee lying in the snow, neck broken, after flying into a window. When I knelt by his head, I saw a red spot on the snow. His ski helmet dangled from his face. His skull was split open. I tried to brush away the trickle of blood flowing across his cheek. Unseeing, his dilated, blue eye stared at me. In my stupor, I barely heard Marsha yell, "Go for help. I'll stay with him." She pushed me away crying, "Oh my God!"

I ran back to my skis, struggling to find them through my tears. In a daze, I skied the rest of the course, standing up, missing most of the control gates. At the finish line, I saw my father, Stan, and yelled to him, "Send help up to gate 4. Damien went off course." I waved uncontrollably up the hill.

News about Damien's death spread quickly after the directors closed the course and canceled the downhill race. Not one of the junior skiers wanted to race again, yet the coaches demanded some sort of result in order to pick the team for the up-coming Junior Nationals in March. For this reason, the race officials re-organized the downhill race into a slower giant slalom to be held the next day.

I knew that in order to make the team, I needed to have a solid result to complement my third in the slalom two days before, yet my heart cried out at the injustice of having to race when I only wanted to stay in bed and think about my friend Damien. On the other hand, I also knew that he would want me to race—not to give up on our dream.

Years before, Damien and I had made a pact: for three winters we had worked to make the team to Junior Nationals. Although he was from a town in New Hampshire, every weekend from December to April, he would travel north to my Vermont home-town and practice with me. We would borrow slalom poles from the ski patrol at Mad River Glen ski area and set up short courses. For fast downhill training, we would get to the mountain early, before the recreational skiers, and practice tucking the intermedi-ate trail called the Porcupine. We both agreed that if we worked harder than the pampered racers in organized programs, we could achieve our dreams of being on the US Ski Team and, just maybe, the Olympic Team of 1972.

He was my first boyfriend.

Now one day after Damien's death, once again I stood in the starting gate. I caught the eyes of the head race-official, John Boast, who stood below me, his thick, dirty-blonde hair, tanned face, and powder-blue parka making him look like a model from *SKI Magazine*. He was the one who had demanded that the race be held, because ambitiously he wanted to coach the Junior National Team headed for Montana.

My anger at him caused my breath to quicken. I looked down to make sure my boots weren't touching the electric wand across the start. I extended my poles over the trip rod. My adrenaline made me forget everything as I stood charged, ready to fly. "Racer ready," yelled the starter. I jiggled my goggles to clear the fog off the lens and looked down again. That's when I saw it on my blue stretch pants—a dried, white crust from Damien's brain. "Five, four, three, two … " I bent low, my heart jumped. "One … " I drove my poles outward, kicked my boots back, launched my body over the baton, as every one hundredth of a second counted. "Go." My body sprang off the pad before my boots tripped the wand.

On course, I had to ski a perfect race for both of us. I took a deep breath as I pushed out into the line of red and blue flags. I was in a trance, my skis dancing left to right, slicing the icy track, my knees pulsating, my weight driving forward to each gate, my knuckles knocking the giant slalom poles aside. I felt as if a fresh wind were pushing me on. Now I understood—yes, ski racing would still be my life. This dance with the snow and the challenge of the gates transported me into a zone beyond words, into a world of light, texture, and balance.

The wind-snapping flags led me down the course like Buddhist prayer banners, just like the ones my mother used to fly in our yard—my mother, who also had died.

CHAPTER 2

Bend, Oregon

Two months later in April, I jumped off the school bus and raced across the dirt road to my rusted mailbox. I'd done this every day since I applied to Middlebury College. Stuffed in the back were two letters; one from Middlebury and one from the United States Ski Team.

My hands shook as I carried both into my living room. First ripping open the smaller letter from the ski team, I held my breath as I read and then reread the words.

Dear Lia Erickson,

Congratulations on your 1st and 4th place finish at the Junior Nationals in March. On behalf of the US Ski Team, I would like to invite you to a US Ski Team training camp in Bend, Oregon, from July 6-14, 1970. You will be joining fifteen of the top racers in the country.

All your expenses will be paid by the ski team.

Please respond immediately.
Sincerely,
John Boast, Coach US Alpine Ski Team

I sat down on the blue couch, called my dog Sheba over to cuddle with me, reread the letter aloud to her, and then jumped up on the soft pillows and screamed, "The US Ski Team!"

Slowly, I opened the second letter from Middlebury that also began with congratulations, I'd been accepted into the class of 1974. Now my dream of racing for a college would be realized.

Yes, I could have both dreams: trying out for the US Ski Team in the west this summer and then racing for Middlebury College.

In July after my graduation from Waitsfield High School, I flew out to Bend, Oregon, where Coach Boast, surrounded by two athletic, smiling girls, awaited my arrival inside the small terminal. "Welcome, Lia," he said, his grizzly-bear hair spiking in the light as he extended his oversized hand. "I'd like to introduce you to two of your teammates." At this point, a muscular, dark-haired girl stepped forward and grabbed my hand. "Hi, I'm Becky Langer from Monmouth, California. Coach Boast has told me wonderful things about you." I gasped when I saw her large, thunder-thighs.

The other girl barely looked me in the eye and tried to hide behind Boast as she said, "And I'm Tracy Languile from Eugene, Oregon." Her petite legs, pointed nose, and short-brown hair reminded me of the British model, Twiggy, not a ski racer.

When the station wagon arrived at the Mountain Bachelor base lodge, Becky helped me with my skis while Tracy disappeared into the building behind Coach Boast. Eagerly, Becky said, "Hey, Lia, you'll room with me for the next two weeks." She winked. "I can't wait for you to meet my friends from the Monmouth ski team."

I immediately relaxed, smiling, "Thanks for making me feel comfortable. I ... I've been very nervous about all this." Becky shouldered my ski bag, while I dragged my suitcase into the base lodge. The sweet odor of hot ski-wax mingling with the pungent smell of new pine boards reminded me of my local ski lodge.

As we started up the stairs to the dorm rooms, Becky dropped my ski bag at the bottom.

"Not to worry," she said. "You're not alone here. There are fifteen skiers here from all over the country. Most don't know each other." She nodded, running her hand slowly through her wavy hair. She laughed, "Yup, soon you'll get to know the seven girls and eight boys." She continued in a more serious tone, "To the point, we get up at 6 a.m. and are in the snow-cat headed up the slopes by 6:30. We need to complete our slalom training by 11 before the hot sun turns the ice sheet into slush. In the afternoon we have dry land training." She waited to see my reaction to this demanding schedule.

"Whoa, I've been running the mountains in Vermont, but this sounds even more rigorous," I answered with a quiver. "Will I be able to keep up at this altitude?"

"Take it slowly at first, because you'll get headaches," said Becky as she gently placed my suitcase on a twin bed.

"So who are the other racers and where're they from?"

"As you saw in the letter, Boast has chosen the top junior racers in the country to train together. He hopes to prepare us for the 1972 Olympic team. You definitely must be one of the best. I saw your results at Junior Nationals."

"Thanks."

"In fact, you fit the image he has for the team. Blonde, dark eyes, hard-working."

"What? What do my looks have to do with my skiing?"

"Oh, yeah, you're so naïve—marketing. He needs money for the team. The ski companies such as Kneissl and Head love to have poster children and do they ever pay!"

"Money—who gets the money?"

"Guess who, Lia—there's big bucks in ski racing. Sometimes, in fact, the parents of the young racers will do anything to get their kids on the team. Yup, even slip money under the table." She looked around the pine-boarded room and toward the door before whispering, "The perfect storm for an ambitious coach."

"Holy cow, this is a whole new game for me. My dad's just a school teacher. He doesn't have any extra money for this."

Becky ignored my remark and continued. "Coach Boast loves the young skiers. They can be easily manipulated, much more than the veterans from the '68 Olympic team. Remember Joan Taylor who won a bronze medal," said Becky as she wrinkled her nose in disdain.

"Wow, will Joan be here at the camp? She's one of my heroes." I held out my hands in respect.

"Nope, Joan's decided to stop racing. She never liked Boast's authoritarian way of coaching. It is either his way or the highway. He tried to change her style from Arlberg to the modern technique of using both hands together around the poles," said Becky, pushing her two fists forward toward my nose. She nodded her head in the direction of the dining hall. "Time to get some chow." The smell of hamburgers cooking on the outside grill reminded me that I hadn't had a solid meal since I'd left the East twelve hours before.

The next morning, Becky woke me at six by throwing a pillow at my head. I threw it back in playfulness. In the communal bathroom, I stood side-by-side with Tracy who grunted a good morning. Brushing my straight, blonde hair, I noticed Tracy staring at me in the mirror.

"Wow, would I love to have your hair. It's so full, so blonde and so smooth. Mine is gnarly, dark, and way too thin," said Tracy.

"Hey, take what you get. Remember this is about skiing, not looks," I said in a firm, yet challenging voice.

At breakfast, Becky nodded for me to join her table of three. Juggling my tray of scrambled eggs and English muffins, I slid onto the wooden bench seat.

"Hey, Lia, these are my other friends from Monmouth Mountain in California. Carla Kluckner and Wren Mumford," Becky said in a sing-song tone.

"What's this place Monmouth that you keep mentioning?" I asked, squinting at the bright sun reflecting through the plate glass. Carla and Wren looked like apparitions.

Carla, her face as tanned as the pine boards, smiled as she

announced assertively, "The most beautiful mountain in the world, owned by Justin McElvey. He's our coach, mentor, and patron." Her large Roman nose wrinkled. "You … you should come down one day."

"In my wildest dreams," I said, my eyes darting to each skier.

Wren put her hand out to me. "Nice to meet you. Becky says you're very cool, that you'd fit in well with us at Monmouth."

I immediately took a liking to Wren whose round, snowman-face lit up every time she spoke. I looked directly at her and asked, "Tell me more about this Coach McElvey."

"Well," said Wren, leaning over so as to avoid eavesdroppers. "Justin has a dream. He wants to give a few hardworking racers an opportunity to become the best in the world."

Wrinkling my brow, I asked, "How does this differ from Coach Boast?"

I heard a giggle before Becky, her eyes darting around the room like a bee searching for pollen, took over the conversation. "In reality, Boast has a separate agenda that includes his own career as a coach. McElvey, who owns Monmouth Mountain, is a self-made man who just wants to give racers a chance to fulfill their dreams. He never had the opportunity to ski race, because he grew up in a poor neighborhood in Los Angeles."

Carla put up her hand as a way to interject. "Wait a minute … McElvey also has an agenda, he's not totally selfless. Remember, he has three kids—two boys and one girl— and he wants us to be role models for them. He thinks we can push his kids to aspire to the Olympic dream that we have," she said, looking out the window up to the volcanic peak called Mount Bachelor.

"This is getting way too complicated—Boast, McElvey?" I asked, "Do these two get along?" All three girls, Carla, Wren, and Becky, smirked.

A bass voice from the other side of the room stopped all conversations. The sound of forks dropping on the metal trays told me Boast had supreme authority. He announced, "Can I have your attention, please? Quiet." He waited for the rumble of voices to settle. "You've fifteen minutes until the snowcats leave for the upper slopes. Grab your skis and meet me in front of the lodge." All fifteen racers and three coaches jumped up and started for the door as though a fire drill had been called.

Outside, Becky guided me to the snowcat where my new friends had slid in next to each other on the padded back seat. Tracy Languile hopped into the front next to Coach Boast, our driver. Turning on the diesel engine, he gave Tracy a flirtatious wink.

I squished into the back next to Becky and stared out the window just as the yellow, mechanical-cat began creeping up the pumice slopes like a mountain lion inching toward its prey. It shook and groaned, belching black smoke all the way to the snowfields at 8,000 feet.

When it lurched to a stop, I held my breath to avoid breathing the fumes and jumped down to the icy surface. The sun-pocked snow looked like it had been sprayed with buckshot, while the high-altitude sun, glinting off the glacier, blinded me. I felt as if I'd left earth and landed on a cloud.

I thought of Damien and how he would've loved this.

CHAPTER 3

Juniper Lake

In the afternoon, all seven of us girls tested ourselves running, lifting weights, and stretching as part of the dry land training. I loved this challenge, knowing that I could work harder than most. Overseeing our workout, Coach Boast, always one for aphorisms, would yell, "When the going gets tough, the tough get going!"

On the lodge sundeck, before the endurance run up the Three Sisters Mountain, Boast set up an obstacle course on the floor that included bench jumping, situps, pushups, and leg squats. Every racer had to complete the course three times, mastering each segment in less than five minutes.

Today, eager to start, I lined up behind Becky. The Monmouth girls, Becky, Carla, and Wren, formed their own support group during these tests. Fortunately, they'd accepted me as one of theirs. Tracy Languile, slighted that she had to get behind us, whined, "Lia, get to the back. I had this place behind Becky." She shoved past me, tripping over her own feet and tumbling to the deck. Her ugly, tight red shorts glared like a stoplight beneath me.

Laughing, I stepped back trying to avoid confrontation, but Coach Boast saw me. He moved over, assessed the situation and gave Tracy a hand up. Narrowing his eyebrows and puffing his shoulders under his tee shirt, he scowled, "Take it easy, Tracy. This isn't a contest." I raised my hands, trying to show I'd done nothing.

As each girl took her place at the start, Boast slapped her butt, his style of encouragement to work hard, before he said, "Push yourself, we have to beat the Europeans this year."

When Tracy's turn came, she giggled at Boast's intimate

touch. Behind her, I moved away from Boast so that he couldn't touch me. His acne-scarred face reddening, he said with a sardonic smile, "Hey, Lia, are you afraid of me?" I rolled my eyes, trying to focus on the bench jumping that started the course, a task that always unnerved me, yet also gave me an adrenaline rush.

I pulled my legs up ten times left to right, my knees hitting my chest as if I were jumping side-to-side over a brook. I knew that these jumps were an important part of downhill training. Each jump represented a pre-jump on a race course, the difference between taking air and keeping the skis on the snow. Also, in a fall-away turn, the balance would help me keep my skis pressed on the snow, making it easier to hold my line into the next gate.

The situps created a tight abdomen, necessary for the un-weighting of my skis during the gravity-defying part of the turn. My abs burned after each series, but I knew I was getting stronger.

Next came the pushups to build my upper-body strength for that all important drive out of the starting gate and poling to the first turn.

The final leg squat, air-sitting, my back against the building with my legs bent in a ninety-degree angle, prepared my quads for the seemingly interminable tuck at the end of a two-mile downhill course. Even though most races didn't last longer than two minutes, I knew the four-minute squat would give me extra confidence when I was tested. I had learned that the end of a downhill race was the time a racer could lose her focus, mostly because of poor fitness. I dreaded the exhaustion coming after these repetitions, yet I always made sure not to show my fatigue.

I followed Tracy through the course, noticing that she shorted herself on the situps and pushups. However, whenever Boast looked over, she picked up the pace. Becky, always the role model, encouraged us, "Keep it up. We all want to be at our best in the first World Cup race in Germany." Hearing these words, Tracy smiled at Boast.

After three repetitions, all seven of us lay down on the redwood deck. I loved the feeling of the hot sun radiating into my tired body. The warmth from the wood relaxed my back. I felt like a grilled cheese sandwich toasting on the top and bottom. My eyes wandered up to the 8,000 foot mountain where I noticed a storm building—huge black clouds mushrooming off the top.

"Hey, Becky, we may have some weather this afternoon," I said, sitting up and pointing nervously.

"Wow, that looks like a summer lightning storm." said Becky, her voice quivering. She looked over to Coach Boast.

Tracy, giggling, said, "Maybe we won't have to go for our run this afternoon." She sighed in relief.

Upon hearing this, Becky, Carla, Wren, and I looked at each other. Simultaneously we whispered, a soft "tsss," cementing our mutual disdain.

In a confrontational tone, I said, "A little rain will feel good after our three-mile run." I stood up, dusting off my blue shorts, as if getting ready to go.

Coach Boast motioned for us to circle around him. He tried to avoid looking at Tracy when he said, "Some of you need to work harder during these training sessions. Remember, even though the Olympic team is selected on FIS points, I do take into consideration each person's work ethic." His wink at Tracy belied his statement. "Now go hop into the vans. Coach Ryan and I'll drive you to the Three Sisters trail. Uh, don't worry about the storm— it's not supposed to come in until tonight."

I waited my turn to get in, but made sure to sit next to Becky. The smell of sweat pervaded the narrow cabin, an odor of old laundry. Tracy gagged as she climbed over me. "God, everyone smells rotten," she said, purposefully letting her red shorts brush against my face.

"Speak for yourself," said Becky. Carla and Wren nudged each other while I tried to smother a giggle.

Coach Boast poked his head in, smiling like the Cheshire cat in *Alice in Wonderland*. His white-capped teeth beamed just as they did on the TV sports show that he sometimes hosted about the US Ski Team. *What a showman,* I thought.

He said, "I'll follow in the Jeep with the others. Tracy, do you want to come with me?" Tracy got up and pushed passed me again. This time I reached up and pinched her butt. I'm not sure she knew who did it.

The high desert road passed over dry creek beds, through Ponderosa pine forests, then junipers, and finally dwarf scrub pine. The smell of dust choked us as if someone had begun beating rugs in this small space. The roar of the engine, combined with the creaking of the springs, made conversation impossible; however, the closeness of my friends relaxed me. Soon I fell into a short catnap, letting my head fall against Becky's shoulder.

"Jump out!" demanded Coach Ryan. I shook my head, bringing my thoughts back to the task ahead. "The storm is coming in faster than expected. I want you to run up to Juniper Lake and back instead of the base of the Three Sisters."

Each of us took off as soon as our feet hit the sandy soil. I quickly passed Tracy, in order to join Becky and Carla up the boulder-strewn trail. The unevenness of the path reminded me of the many miles I had spent boulder-hopping up Scrag Mountain behind my Vermont home. I used to run the two mile trail, all two thousand vertical feet, weekly in the summers. My trail, a worn creekbed, the soil long ago washed down the mountain, held different-sized boulders for me to dodge and jump over. On a good day I could complete the up-hill run in forty minutes—on a rainy day fifty.

On the trail up to the lake, we quickly spread out. Each of us had a different style. I found my balance by running up the sides of the larger rocks, then jumping to the next bare spot on the ground. I imagined I was running a slalom course where I had to jump from gate to gate. In order not to sprain an ankle, I made sure to look ahead, preparing my airborne foot to settle on a smooth spot even as I launched. Years of sprained ankles had taught me this skipping-stone technique.

Becky, Carla, and Wren had had little experience with this style of running, so they asked me to lead. Working together, they counted on my foot agility to find safe landing spots, then each would sequentially follow. Becky stayed right behind me, always cautious to run around the larger stones. Carla, on the other hand, would walk over the larger stones, placing her feet carefully next to the loose stones. Wren, knowing she was not as in good shape as the rest, brought up the rear. She felt pressured to keep up, often taking chances and jumping from the smooth rocks without locating a safe landing.

Most of the time I gasped for breath at the high altitude. Finally stopping, I asked Becky, "Did you all pass Tracy back down the trail?"

Becky said with derision, "Oh, she had already stopped at the first steep pitch."

Carla trotted up slowly and said, "She looked like a bedraggled dog. I think she'll walk the rest of the trail."

"What will Boast say about her effort tonight?"asked Wren, still wheezing to catch her breath.

"I'll bet he doesn't even make note of her lack of effort" I said, throwing up my hands in disgust. At the last uphill, we decided to run as hard as our weary bodies would let us. Sweat poured down my eyes, a salt-river springing from my forehead. The pain in my thighs felt as if I had a hundred-pound weight on each.

When I rounded the last bend, the lake jumped into view. The aquamarine-glacial tarn became a mirror, reflecting the snow-covered peak. For a second, I thought there were two mountains. Once again, I gasped at the beauty; an image I'd only seen in *National Geographic* was now mine. *If only Damien could see this,* I thought.

Carla looked at my slack jaw and taunted me, "Hey, Lia, bet you don't dare to jump in."

Loving a challenge, I looked back at her, stepped up to the tip of a boulder, stripped off my tee shirt, and launched into the Edenic double image. Hitting the thirty-two degree water, I screamed. My echo was still reverberating through the mountain amphitheater when my head came out of the water.

I dogpaddled back to the rock where Becky extended her hand, "You fool! You sure do like to take risks." My feet slipped on the rock, but I found a handhold, quickly grabbing my tee shirt in a show of modesty. Becky added, shaking her head, "No more challenges for Lia. She's too much of a risk-taker."

I smiled at her, "Yeah and you're not. You're the downhiller who loves going sixty miles an hour."

"My risks are calculated and practiced …"

" … Enough," said Wren softly. "Hold it, you two. I don't like seeing you arguing." She turned to me. "Lia, I guess you're one of us now."

Just as we turned to start back down, two others came panting up the trail. First Pammy, the wannabe Bonnie Belle model, flashing her perfect teeth and summer blonde hair, her stomach rippling in her halter top, and then Kate, a tomboy with short dark hair, so shy she hid her body in baggy sweats.

I asked in a curious tone, trying to project innocence, "Has anyone seen Tracy?"

"No," said Kate, obviously affronted that I would imply that she was responsible for Tracy.

After a moment of silence, Pammy said, "She stopped about a quarter of the way up. Claimed that she had twisted her ankle and would wait for us there." She mimicked a limp.

"Ha, I never could've guessed," I said in my most sardonic tone. "Well, then, let's head down," I bounded off the rock, my shorts dripping with water. I yelled back to the group, "The storm clouds are building on the peak. They look like giant mushrooms."

"Take it easy on the way down," cautioned Becky. "No sprained ankles today."

With this, the six of us headed down the trail, with me in the lead. The route back was easier because I had memorized every boulder and step. I bounded like a deer through a pasture. On our way down, I remembered the story my father always told about the Iroquois Indians who had once inhabited my valley. He described their traveling through the mountains, creating what they called a song-line, memorizing the natural markers of the trail. They only had to sing their way back down the trail. I'd often used that trick hiking along the Long Trail in my beloved Green Mountains. Now I taught this method to Becky and the others, singing our way back down single file. "Flat boulder to gravel landing. Jump the root and dodge the tree." At each turn, I expected to see Tracy.

Finally, just before the last half-mile flat stretch, I saw a pair of red shorts dart from the woods. Sure enough Tracy had waited until we appeared, and then she took off. Sensing that she would beat us to the finish where Boast and Ryan waited, I picked up my legs as if running hurdles. As I shot passed Tracy, I felt a jab in my side. I lost my balance, unable to get my feet in front of my falling body. Not retaining my balance, I stubbed a root and fell flat on my face. The fall came so quickly that I'd no time to protect my face. My forehead slammed into the ground as if I were a boulder cascading over a cliff. With my nose planted in the sand and trying to decide what hurt, I felt Tracy jump over me and dash toward the last two turns in the trail.

When Becky and the other four girls rounded the bend, they stopped to help me. Gently, Becky lifted me, dazed, to a sitting position. "What happened?" she said, squinting as if ready to cry. Her hand rested on my shoulder in an effort to support my head.

"Are you hurt anywhere?" said Carla as she knelt to touch my bruised forehead.

17

"No, I'm angry," I said. "Help me up and let's finish the run. I'll tell you what happened when we get back." The six of us jogged slowly to the van with me in the rear, struggling not to show my injury. I didn't want to give Tracy the pleasure of knowing that she'd hurt me.

Resting against the yellow van, Tracy stood with the two coaches. "How the heck did you get here ahead of us?" demanded Becky.

"Oh, I took a short cut," said Tracy, winking at Boast who stood with his arm around her like a proud father or worse, a boyfriend.

At that moment the clouds let loose sheets of rain. I pushed passed Tracy into the van, thinking to myself that somehow there would be justice.

CHAPTER 4

The Invitation

The last day of summer camp brought back the cloudless, azure skies and early-morning 30 degree still air. I now looked forward to returning home and beginning college at Middlebury.

At breakfast, Becky motioned for me to sit with her and my new friends. Never having been part of a team before, I marveled at how comfortable and supported I felt. No competition, just collaboration. "Hi, Coach," said Becky, looking past my shoulder. "How was the drive from Monmouth?" I turned to see a tanned, statuesque, fifty-year-old man walk toward our table. His broad jaw, light brown hair and muscular shoulders made him appear like John Wayne—even his body seemed to tilt to one side in the style of a gunslinger.

"Greetings, Becky," he said, exuding a self-assured grin, "Great ride. I saw the most magnificent elk crossing Route 395." He laughed, "Not to mention numerous dead rodents." He paused to see how she would react to the latter before he continued. "What a face. Anyhow how's the training going?" He looked to each one of us individually. "Are you girls making me proud, representing Monmouth well?" He put his rough hand on Wren's shoulder and looked down at Carla. "Listening to Coach Boast?"

The silence from Becky spoke for her discontent about Boast's coaching.

"Okay, let me rephrase my question. "What have you learned from this experience?" he said, shaking his head in concern.

Becky, looking up from her plate of eggs, chose to dismiss this question. "Not much. Hey, Coach, I want you to meet my new friend, Lia, from the East. She's fearless. Lia, this is coach McElvey, our Monmouth coach and patron. The one I've been telling you about."

He enthusiastically extended his hand, making me put down my tray of pancakes and orange juice. "Nice to meet you, Coach," I said with a slight blush. "I've heard from Becky, Carla, and Wren about your exciting program at Monmouth."

He said firmly, "Oh, I hope it was all good. We do have a most unusual setup. These three girls certainly do take advantage of the opportunity. Where're you from exactly?"

"Oh," I answered shyly, "as Becky said, I'm an eastern skier. I train at a small area called Mad River Glen. It's certainly not a Monmouth." I looked into his blue eyes to see if he knew what I was talking about. He nodded. I continued, "We specialize in ice back home." I nervously let my sneakers slide on the wooden floor.

"That must account for your outstanding runs in all the time trials. Coach Boast told me you've often set the standard for the other racers."

I winced. I'd not even known this fact, because Coach Boast had never shared the results of the time trials with any of us. He preferred that the racers focus on his new racing techniques.

From the front of the room came a loud voice. "Time to leave for the last day of training," announced Coach Boast over the clanging of porcelain plates and clumping of ski boots. "Make sure to say hi to Coach Justin McElvey who just arrived from Monmouth. He's already been up on the hill, setting a challenging slalom course for you." He paused before ending with another of his platitudes, "Remember, preparation determines destination."

Wow, had I grown tired of these clichés! The sweet smell of butter and maple syrup whetted my appetite, so I stayed to finish my meal after the others got up.

Becky turned to me as she grabbed her tray, "See you outside.

I'll save you a seat in the snowcat." I appreciated how she always looked after me.

Outside the first light rays backlit Mt. Bachelor, yellow, pink, purple sun-streamers rode over the upper cornice and colored the snow field. I followed Becky and McElvey to the yellow Bombardier, a two runner centipede with heavy metal tracks like a bulldozer. Already I was fascinated with this mountain man, who walked with the long strides of an elk. I struggled to keep up with him, hoping to ask him more questions. With my skis bouncing over my shoulders, I almost walked into the teeth-like treads of the machine parked behind a Ponderosa pine. Before loading my skis into the mesh rack, I stopped to breathe in the crisp morning air, feeling it bite into my lungs, and then looked up to the glowing snowfields. On the top, I saw a thin line of smoke rising from the horizon as if the extinct volcano were breathing.

Carefully placing my skis into the ski rack, I jumped on the backseat with Becky, Carla, and Wren. Tracy, McElvey, and Coach Boast had already snagged the front seat. Over the roar of the engine, I said, "Hey, the mountain looks as if it's smoking today. What's this about? I ... "

McElvey turned and stopped me, saying, " ... Don't ever go near any of those gas vents." "What you see is a fumarole, an opening in the volcano that allows the pent-up gases to escape. The carbon dioxide, carbon monoxide, and sulfur can kill anyone who falls in."

"Whoa, I knew skiing was dangerous, but this is a new ... " I said hesitantly.

He continued, " ... furthermore, the edges of these fumaroles are unstable. The hole can be ten feet deep and is often concealed by a thin layer of snow. We have many on Monmouth Mountain." His voice slowed in a fatherly tone.

Tracy giggled uncomfortably as she snuggled next to Coach Boast. Boldly I asked, "Has anyone ever fallen into one at Monmouth?"

McElvey stopped talking and looked out the small, frosted window toward the Three Sisters Mountains. An uneasy silence fell over everyone, letting the grinding of the vehicle fill the cabin.

Finally, Becky yelled over the noise. "Hey, Coach, the other girls and I would like to ask you if Lia could come to Monmouth this fall and winter to train with us?"

He broke out of his uncomfortable reverie and focused back on the four of us scrunched in the back seat. He looked from Becky to Tracy to Coach Boast. "From what I've heard, Lia would fit in perfectly." He paused, weighing the seriousness of his next offer. "I would welcome her into our program. But I'll need to talk to her parents about the arrangements," he said.

Coach Boast looked back and glowered. His eyes appeared to go from brown to red as he listened to my answer. "Wow, you mean I could spend a winter in the High Sierras training with my new friends!" I exclaimed.

"Absolutely, and furthermore, you would be my guest as part of the Monmouth team," McElvey added. "As long as you follow the rules and work hard, you'll be welcome."

An image of a high, snow-covered peak with untracked powder, granite outcroppings, and steep couloirs flashed into my thoughts. "Of course, I'd have to ask permission from my father. You know I'd planned to attend Middlebury College in the fall. Not sure how he'll feel. He's been very lonely since my mother died three years ago," I said, trying to hide my emotions. A silence fell over the cabin as the snowcat ground into the pumice of the upper slope like a cougar advancing on its prey.

That morning in the time trials, I never worked harder. Unlike the courses Boast had set, I loved the rhythm of McElvey's course: the flushes, hairpin turns, and closed gates created a dance on the mountain. After each run, I sought him out for tips about my technique. "Try to be more relaxed with your hands, Lia. Let them lead you naturally," he said. "You don't have to steer yourself."

"But Boast wants me to use my hands as if I were driving a car," I answered, puzzled that the two coaches could be teaching such different styles.

McElvey looked up the mountain to where Boast stood before he answered. Picking his words cautiously, he said, "Do what feels comfortable. You can't force your style. The mountain will teach you if you let yourself relax. I like the way you initiate your turn on your uphill ski."

I welcomed his gentle way of coaching. As a ski visionary, he sensed that I had a different style, one that I had learned not from running gates, but from free skiing on the narrow trails of Mad River Glen. I pushed off toward the T-bar feeling free, eager to complete at least three more runs. Finally, I knew I had found a coach who appreciated my unique eastern style.

In my next practice run, I decided to try to clip the slalom poles and see if I could cut the radius of my turn. If I succeeded, I could shave seconds from my run. In the first turn, I realized that I carried more speed than usual into the three-gate flush. Instinctively, I started early into the blue gate. Stepping quickly from edge to edge like an ice skater, I clipped the poles and finished the sequence in complete control. With confidence, I blasted through the rest of the twenty gates and tucked to the finish line. Stopping, I looked up the hill with pride. My blonde bangs fell across my eyes, my sunburnt nose tingled, and my legs were weak like wet noodles. Yet, I felt invincible. I herring-boned back up to the finish line to get feedback on my run from Coach Boast, as I knew I'd punched it.

Boast looked down to me and yelled as he checked his stop watch, "Fastest run of the day by two seconds. Lia, what got into you?"

CHAPTER 5

Monmouth

Back in Waitsfield, I worked for three months, painting my neighbor's red barn and white farmhouse to earn money for my flight to Monmouth that would leave just before Thanksgiving. I longed to be independent of my father, so what I earned would cover my flight to Reno, 200 dollars, and still leave me some spending money. I couldn't believe that Coach McElvey had offered to cover all my expenses while at Monmouth and at the races. I would now be on a team, the Monmouth team.

While painting, I passed the time memorizing poems, my favorites being Frost's "The Road Not Taken" and "Swinger of Birches." Free, I would become a swinger of birches and launch myself into a life I'd only dreamed about.

During my plane trip across the country, in *SKI Magazine* I read about Monmouth, a volcanic cone, resting in a gap of the Sierra Nevada Mountains, just south of Yosemite. The 11,000 foot monolith created its own weather. The seasonal snowfall exceeded 365 inches, or in New England terms thirty feet of white fluff—enough to bury my small cape-style home in Vermont. During the previous winter of 1970, Monmouth Mountain had held a storm for five days as it deposited ten feet of snow. A photo in the magazine showed white mounds completely covering the cars in the parking lot, surrounded by twenty-foot snow banks. The article described how, during these mega-storms, the mountain, called Inyo by the local Paiute Indians, often became isolated from the town of Monmouth Falls.

After landing in Reno, I took a taxi into town to catch the bus south. The carnival-like atmosphere of this gambling town scared me: casinos, neon lights, billboards, wedding chapels, pawn shops, gun shops, divorce clinics, drunks, prostitutes—a hell on earth. Even though the outside temperature was thirty-two degrees, Harrah's casino, across the street from the bus station, kept its doors wide open, excreting sounds of jackpot bells, music, and laughter. At the station, a homeless man, wrapped in a blanket, pressed an outstretched hand toward my ski bag, asking if he could carry it for me. He didn't look strong enough to lift my ski boots, so I reached into my purse and gave him a dollar instead. I really didn't want anything to happen to my equipment—so far from home, I felt vulnerable and confused.

During the three-hour bus ride south on Route 395, I became even more nervous. *Would my new friends Becky Langer, Wren Mumford, and Carla Kluckner meet me at the isolated log outpost that substituted for a bus stop below Deadman Summit?* I tried quieting my fears by pressing my nose to the window, feeling my breath crystallize on the cold glass, and watching the fiery sun drop behind the uninhabited front range. A fresh snow had fallen, so I imagined myself climbing into the treeless snowfields and skiing the steep couloirs.

When the bus stopped at Deadman's Pass, I stepped down into Becky's extended arms. "Welcome to our world," she said, moving forward to embrace me. Wren and Carla followed, checking out my black parka and tan chinos.

"So, how was your flight?" asked Carla, ever the buffoon, flapping her arms like a bird.

"Long," I said, trying to hide my nervousness with a yawn. "Wow, you guys, this is a world unto itself. Where are the houses and stores?"

Becky looked puzzled before she answered, "Welcome to Monmouth Falls—you know, just a town of three hundred before the skiers arrive." She put my one suitcase in the back of the station wagon and then effortlessly lifted my ski bag to the roof rack. Taking the wheel of the car, she added, "We live five miles up on the mountain along with thirty staff."

The drive to the base lodge in McElvey's Ford station wagon was unsettling, even though I shared the comfort of my new friends. This strange land of Ponderosa pines, lava outcroppings, and rustic log buildings contrasted with my warm world of white New England farm houses and red barns. The evening sun jumped between the mountain peaks at each turn of the serpentine mountain road. I thought about how in this strange land I was hoping to follow my dream, the same one Damien and I had once shared.

"Lia, at times you become so quiet. Are you worried?" asked Becky. I let my thoughts return to my new friends, each bundled in her puffed powder-blue Monmouth parka.

"Is this your Monmouth team jacket?" I asked, touching Wren's red stripe running down the sleeve.

"Yup, McElvey will give you one tomorrow," said Carla, her grin warming her Italian complexion. "Welcome to our world. Here we ski as much as we want. Yup, do what we want as long as we follow McElvey's rules." She scrunched up her nose as though she were not completely happy with his authority.

Wren added, trying to be part of the conversation, "You know he expects us to be ready to train at 7:30 every morning—like first on the lift."

I thought for a second. "Do you mean we can get first tracks if it snows?"

Becky nodded, "Many times. Face shots when the snow is real light."

As the station wagon rounded the last bend, the base lodge came into view, a concrete fortress built to withstand a thirty-foot avalanche. The ski trails flowed like threads down into this, my new home, a castle for staff and racers. Looking up to the bald head of the mountain, the white behemoth that guarded this outpost, I sucked in my breath.

As the four of us sauntered into the cafeteria, I immediately spotted McElvey. He stood up, beckoned me over to his family table. The noise of the workers scraping their chairs on the floor, the smell of roast beef and potatoes, and the crackle of the pine fire all reminded me of the numerous Vermont ski lodges that I'd stayed in, only this one was four times as big. Pine timbers lifted a twenty-foot ceiling, wooden tables and benches lined the rough-hewn floor, and posters of powder skiing and blue skies festooned the walls.

"Welcome to Monmouth," said McElvey, extending his hand while his blue eyes probed deep into mine, as if trying to read my mind. "You look exhausted." He paused and turned to the kids at his table. "Let me introduce you to my family: my wife Rose, Dave, Steve, and little Stephanie." At this introduction, Stephanie, looking no older than sixteen, turned her head with a sneer. The kids did not stand up, but instead waved gratuitously. My cheeks flushed as though I'd been standing in front of a fire.

I'd no idea that McElvey's family was so large. To ease the introduction, I did just as my father had always told me, walking around the table to shake each person's hand. A silence spread through the room, so I turned to see that the rest of the diners had stopped talking and were looking at me. McElvey turned to the group, "Now everyone, please welcome Lia from Vermont." Trying to be self-confident, I looked over the large post-and-beam room and waved to the others. At that point, the mixed group of workers and skiers broke into applause. I realized that they'd been told I was coming. I felt at home.

After getting my food, I couldn't resist the pastries. Becky led me over to a seat next to a rugged, middle-aged man wearing a ski instructor's sweater. She warned me, "Hey, Lia, be careful with the pastries. You'll wear them faster than you can eat them." She smiled, continuing, "Meet Guy," said Becky. "He's head of the ski school."

"Hi," I said, looking down at my shoes. I'd never seen such a handsome man; his weather-beaten face, high cheekbones, dark eyes, and broad shoulders framed his white-toothed smile.

Becky added, "You'll want to get to know Guy. He helped McElvey build the area in 1957. Yup, he left his home in Austria to bring the modern alpine technique to America." The four of us, Becky, Carla, Wren, and I settled comfortably around him. He seemed to relish the attention.

Carla spoke up as she touched Guy's shoulder, "You know that Guy was in the 1956 Olympics before he came to California."

"Golly," I said. "The first Olympian I've ever met."

Waving his hand humbly, Guy reached over to me, "Welcome, Lia. We all heard you were coming." Turning to Becky and adding in his heavy German accent, he said, "So, Becky, I haven't had a chance to talk with any of you since you returned from training camp in Bend. How did you enjoy your time with—ah—Coach Boast?" His wink implied that he knew about the rift over ski techniques between McElvey and Boast.

"C'mon, Guy, you know that's an unfair question. In reality, I'll get in trouble if I tell you the truth—it might get back to the wrong people," Becky said, nervously playing with her brown pony tail. She continued, leaning forward toward me, "Even at Monmouth, no one feels safe. The ski-racing world is a microcosm. Everyone knows everyone. Allegiances are strong. Vindictiveness is part of the game." I shivered, hearing the warning in Becky's voice.

Turning toward Guy, I said cautiously, "Guy, I know I'm the new kid on the block, but I felt the coaching from Boast was regimented and impractical. He never left room for individual style."

Wren, frowning, shifted her seat and said, "You know, like I've never felt so inferior, as I did in Bend." She ran her hand through her short brown hair. "Boast hand-picks his protégés. He gives them his complete attention." Looking around for support, she saw Becky, Carla, and me nodding in agreement. "Did you see how he hit on Tracy?"

The conversation then turned to Boast's suspected improprieties. Wren, not resisting the gossip, said, "Who saw him after hours with Tracy?" Carla and I giggled, but Becky remained imperturbable.

I thought for a moment, softly adding, "I'm not sure Tracy likes me."

"Why?" said Carla.

" 'cause I had two run-ins with her," I said, pointing to the thigh I'd bruised in my fall.

"Wow, I know about her pushing you down during the run from the Three Sisters, but what else happened?" asked Wren, innocently.

"Well, I never mentioned it, but once in the bathroom, she made comments about my looks," I said.

Trying to diffuse the situation, Becky said, "Ok Lia, you know she's jealous of you, because you're the perfect poster girl for the ski team. Look at you, you're blonde, skinny, bubbly. " She paused before adding, "I think she's jealous and worried that Coach Boast will start paying more attention to you."

I sat back in amazement; I hadn't realized that the dynamics of the ski team could become so petty.

The smell of fresh coffee and apple pie, combined with the laughter and talk from the tired workers in the dining hall, reminded me of a family Thanksgiving gathering, complete with aunts, uncles, and cousins, all before my mother died.

After dinner, the four of us got up to find our rooms. I felt our common bonds—not only did we love the sport of skiing, but together we had found two mutual adversaries.

CHAPTER 6

Bill

The days at Monmouth passed quickly as I eagerly awaited the opening snows. I loved the mornings of dryland training which included a four-mile run from Monmouth Falls to the base lodge. After that, we—both guys and girls—did calisthenics with McElvey, ate lunch, and then did chores. This included painting the inside walls of the base hut—our deal to help out until we started skiing. In addition to that, the guys—a small crew of adolescents who'd come to Monmouth to train—had to maintain their night cafeteria jobs all season. Sometimes they complained it wasn't fair, but we just batted our eyelashes and smiled.

At this time I befriended one of these night workers, Bill Emerson, a 20-year-old racer from Concord, Massachusetts. I identified with his New England accent, values, and work ethic more than with the California surfer-dudes. He spoke with a slow New England drawl, a heavy accent that turned his "R's" into "H's." Always a little aloof, he acted wiser than his years—I soon discovered why.

He'd left his college studies at the University of Wyoming in order to train at Monmouth. Unfortunately his draft number in Massachusetts had been picked, so he'd spent September and October in basic training with the army near San Antonio. Coach Boast, who seemed to have connections in high places, had arranged a deferment for him until after the first few races in December. After that, if Bill qualified for the US Ski Team, Coach Boast had promised him he would get him an assignment to race on the team, representing the US Army. Like a god, Boast had the power of life and death.

In the evenings following dinner, Bill and I meet secretly to share another common interest: literature. Since first grade, I'd loved reading, and while in high school, I had some inspiring teachers such as Miss Young, a spinster, who taught American literature and even took our class to Concord, Massachusetts, to see the homes of the Transcendentalists. Until my invitation to Monmouth, I'd hoped to major in English at Middlebury College, a plan that I'd deferred for this opportunity.

One evening I caught Bill in the ski room, where he often spent alone-time filing and waxing his skis. As I entered, the hot, acrid smell of burning Toko wax made me cough. I tried to sneak up on him, but slipped on the wax peelings. He grabbed my arm, "Hey, be careful. I've got a hot iron here."

"Oh, sorry, I thought I'd surprise you." I looked down in embarrassment.

"You always surprise me." He set the iron down on the workbench, his heavy accent making him sound like President Kennedy.

"Hey, you've waxed and re-waxed your skis three times this week. Do you think it will snow soon?" I asked, sidling up to him while trying to make conversation.

He stepped back. "Well, you know I don't want to miss one turn in the fresh powder when it comes." His dimpled smile and strong chin made my heart race. "You know, I don't have much time." He winked and went to work scraping the bottom of his ski.

"Hey, Bill, I've been thinking. You said you're from Concord, Massachusetts, and your name is Emerson. Is there any chance you could be related to the great Ralph Waldo Emerson?" I raised my chin, stood up straight and tried to look scholarly.

He gave me a little shove. "How clever of you, Lia. Emerson, Emerson. Concord, Massachusetts. Concord, Massachusetts. Hmmm."

"C'mon, stop fooling around. Tell me straight."

"Well, yeah, my father tells me I'm related to him through my grandfather's brother. I'm not sure exactly, but I've grown up in his legacy." He put his ski down and vaulted his butt up on the workbench in a casual manner, as if he were going to tell me a secret. "To tell the truth, I've become more interested in Emerson's writings, because he and Thoreau were so anti-war." He looked toward the door as if to make sure no one could hear him, softly adding, "I do love Emerson's ideas, even though his writing can be obtuse. Have you ever read any of his essays, especially *Nature*?"

As he spoke, I noticed his resemblance to the picture of Emerson I'd seen in my high school textbook. His long aristocratic nose, wavy brown hair, and creamy skin gave him a patrician appearance. His lanky body, barely supporting his blue jeans, attested to a young boy, almost man, who had just finished a growth spurt without the supporting muscles. *Awkward*, I thought.

Trying to impress him, I paused, putting my hand to my chin. "Well, let me see. I did read excerpts from his writing during my junior year ... yes, with Miss Young in English class." Letting my thoughts wander back to my shy years, remembering blushing when called on. She demanded that students have a quote memorized for each class, and she would randomly pick us to recite it. One quote in particular I remembered, because I'd used it for my college admissions essay. Before I knew it, I was saying it to Bill, "Standing on the bare ground, my head bathed by the blithe air and uplifted into infinite space, all mean egotism vanishes."

Bill interrupted, " ... I become a transparent eyeball—I am nothing. I see all." We both stopped, looking into each other's eyes, and said together, "The currents of the Universal Being circulate through me."

Drawing in a breath, we continued together, "I am part or parcel of God." I felt my legs go weak, my heart race.

He broke the silence. "Whoa, you must have gone to a good school."

I nodded, thinking about how much I'd loved learning and decided to test his knowledge more. After all, he was an Emerson. "So, what do you make of his transparent eyeball?"

Bill laughed, "He seems to be on some sort of drug trip." Hopping down, he moved closer to me.

I squirmed. I thought Bill might be asking whether I did drugs. I had an aversion to any form of hallucinogenic, mainly because I'd seen too many friends become dependent on marijuana and uppers. I said, "I'm … I'm not sure, but I do love the idea that nature can teach us moral lessons. I like the idea that we can learn absolute truths. Didn't Emerson use the words 'intuit these truths?' "

Bill seemed caught off guard. He jerked back, almost burning his hand with the hot iron that balanced next to his ski. "Hey Lia, how about this? Let's each find an essay by Emerson and share it."

I loved the idea, and so began my first friendship with a boy since I'd lost Damien. I was happy that Bill didn't seem to want a romantic relationship. In our evening talks, he told me that he feared developing an intimate friendship, because soon he might be leaving for Vietnam. Moreover, he had to focus on his skiing, if there were any chance of deferring from the draft.

During the morning jogs from Monmouth Falls back to the base lodge, the two of us would run together. I loved chasing him through the tall, white pines—we were like two squirrels, sometimes even circling a tree. We often left the rest of the pack, finding new trails up the pumice slope. The sand sometimes slid away, so we had to duck walk with our sneakers to get purchase.

Unlike in New England woods, the volcanic slopes had no undergrowth. The hard winters on the old volcano, complicated by the lack of summer rain, allowed only the sturdiest trees to survive. They became towering trees, with eight foot trunks, which rose over the forest floor sometimes sixty feet, erect as stately ministers holding their pine cones like Bibles.

On one run I picked up a cone, tossing it at Bill's cute butt. He turned and grabbed my ankles, making me to fall sideways next to a large rock. Opening my eyes, I looked into a deep volcanic fracture in the hard granite, an abyss of blackness and nothingness. For an instant, I felt my usual playfulness wash from me like an outgoing tide. I shivered. I pushed back from the gap and heard the sound of sand and rocks sliding into the pit, a clicking sound as though the devil were throwing dice.

Bill pulled me back, saying apologetically, "Jeez, I'm sorry. Close call. Be careful. That must be a cleft from an old earthquake. Remember, we're on a volcano. This place is like a time capsule. I think this mountain last erupted about 700 years ago and became the rounded lava dome it is now."

"Seriously, how do you know all this?" I asked, nervously brushing pumice from my lips.

"Well, I've been reading about volcanoes since I came to this area. They fascinate me, because they're so primitive." He paused. "And so violent. You know, compared to New England, this area is young geologically."

"Will it erupt again?" I asked, easing back from the crack.

"Well, no one knows, but we do know that there are occasional earthquakes in the area."

"Oh, do you mean that Monmouth will no longer exist one day?"

"Hey, silly, we're such a small part of the history of the earth. Of course," sweeping his hand across the skyline, he continued slowly, "all this will all be gone one day." He looked meditatively to the distant horizon.

I sat down on a rock, felt the coldness run through my shorts into my butt, dug my feet into the grainy pumice, and cowered at the rawness of all this. Trying to think of what to say, I stood up to confront Bill and said slowly, "Well then, what we do now, here, had better be done well and yes, honestly, because that may be all we have."

Bill nodded, smiling with a sardonic twist of his lips as if he knew more. Immediately, he turned and ran up the hill. I heard him mutter, "You're so bloody naïve."

CHAPTER 7

Sierra Crest

My eyes followed the shaft of morning light to the pink, lenticular cloud covering Monmouth—November 15th and still no skiing. I laughed, thinking the veil looked like an oversized shower cap, maybe one that would bring snow to the ashen slopes, soon to be my crystal playground. Curling up in my down comforter, warm and cozy, I made folds in the white cotton material and traced ski runs down the flanks, over the cornices, and through the gullies, all the while basking in the homey smell of bacon, eggs, cranberry muffins, hash browns, coffee, and fresh bread coming from Stefan's kitchen. I loved the solitude of the morning and the sense of beginnings. A sharp rapping startled me.

"Hey, Lia, McElvey wants to take us on a hike today. He wants to check out the backside of Monmouth along the John Muir Trail," said Becky with an eagerness in her voice that I rarely heard.

"What?" I said, rubbing the sandman from my eyes.

"I said get your butt out of bed. We have a chance to do some hiking with McElvey."

"When are ... are we leaving?"

"Get your hiking boots on and bring some warm clothes. We'll leave right after breakfast around eight," said Becky, obviously growing impatient with my questions.

"Who's goin'?"

"The usual—you, me, Carla, Wren, Stephanie, Bill, and Brandy.

"What about the other guys?"

"Nope, McElvey needs them to attach some chairs to #3 lift," said Becky. "Always the optimist, he thinks the snows will be coming this week."

I couldn't believe that I'd a chance to hike on the Sierra crest near the John Muir trail. My father had just sent me Muir's book, *My First Summer in the Sierra.* Now I would get to experience the high Sierra ridge with McElvey, a mountain man who'd roamed these peaks for twenty-four years.

I saw my compatriots at our favorite table by the window that framed the summit of Monmouth. My eyes glanced around and settled on Stephanie, who didn't look up when I sat down, sliding my tray next to hers. I tried to get her attention. "Hey, Steph, are you coming on the hike?"

Still looking down, eating a pastry and Cheerios, she said, "Yeah, my dad is making me," Her voice had the solemnity of one announcing a terminal illness. "Like I really love hiking in the back country," she grimaced.

I didn't know how to answer, so I winked at Becky and started eating. We all knew that Stephanie didn't share our commitment to dry-land training. She participated in the exercises in order to please her dad, who dreamed that one of his children would make an Olympic team.

The room quieted when McElvey walked in after completing two hours of work on the mountain where he had organized the lift crews so he could take the day off. Every day he wore the same outfit—a collared shirt, grease-stained chinos, and tan leather work boots. His brown hair, swept to the side, gave him a wise look, not the look of a book-learned man, but the look of a student of nature, the look of Daniel Boone or Davy Crockett. His hands were as dirty as his hardest working mechanic.

McElvey came up behind me and I blushed. Smelling of oil and sweat, he said, "I'll meet everyone at the station wagon in twenty minutes. Stefan has packed a sandwich and drink for each of you. Make sure to grab a bag before coming outside," Pausing, he backed up, realizing his clothes smelled, and continued, "Oh yes, bring a parka and hat because the weather can turn. We'll be hiking for ten miles." Business-like, he immediately walked away, so that he didn't have to listen to his racers' comments or Stephanie's groan.

"Wow, he must be upset about something," said Carla, looking worried.

"Do you think he knows about our night meetings downstairs?" whispered Brandy, his Korean eyes squinting into the sun. He looked at Carla and then me, and I nodded in complicity.

"Shh, not everyone knows," said Carla.

"Oh, come on, guys, he just wants to touch base with all of us before the snows come," said Becky. "Remember he's sponsoring us. Right. We have a free ride. The only stipulation is that we work hard." She emphasized the word "hard" and looked straight at Stephanie, asserting her leadership like a disgruntled school marm, hands akimbo, feet askew.

I tried to break the tension. "Hey, everyone, I'm excited to spend some time with McElvey and learn more about his life story." I scraped the last of the scrambled eggs onto my fork.

"You'll be lucky to get three words from him unless he has a lesson to teach," said Becky. "He's a man of action, not words."

Bill and I made sure to get our sandwiches first, so that we could pile into the back seat of the Chrysler station wagon. I loved feeling his strong, tanned body next to mine. Brandy and Carla also squished into the back seat, leaving Becky and Wren to climb into the luggage compartment where they could stretch their legs out while resting their backs against the side windows. Stephanie reluctantly climbed into the front seat next to her dad, who drove, of course.

The thirty-five minute trip took us north on highway 395 to Abraham Mountain where we would ride the chairlift up to begin the hike. McElvey drove the winding road as if racing the Indy

500. He cut the corners and pushed the pedal to the floor over Deadman Summit.

Bill took this moment to explain the area to me. He pointed to Lookout Mountain with the Long Valley to the right and the Inyo craters to the left. He said softly, "These new craters were formed from a volcanic eruption 600 years ago. Ground water came in contact with a rising magma flow, became superheated, and the steam blew a hole in the ground. The one on the left is 200 feet deep."

"How long ago did you say?" I said, cowering at the thought of such violence in the earth and remembering the fissure I'd almost slid into.

"You heard, 600. Hey, Miss Julie Andrews, everything you see here is raw nature. You've been so sheltered in the East. The Green Mountains are geologically so much older and definitely much tamer," said Bill in a scolding fashion. "Look to your right. "As he pointed, his arm brushed against my breast. "Oops, excuse me." I giggled. "See the 8,000 foot Lookout Mountain. Well, this is what is called a resurgent dome. When the Long Valley caldera first collapsed over 700,000 years ago, this mountain rose up. Very strange." Bill started speaking louder, realizing he had the attention of everyone in the car, including McElvey. He continued, "Notice the slopes are mostly pumice, like the pumice on Monmouth. Pumice is created when magma is explosively ejected. The lava is filled with tiny air bubbles that make the stone very light." I felt myself gasp, listening to his words. I thought, *This whole place is one big sandbox or worse—a bed of quicksand, ready to explode.*

McElvey spoke from the front, releasing his hand from the wheel and waving it across the horizon. "Well, Bill, you certainly know your geology. How'd you learn all this?"

"I've books downstairs in my room," said Bill. "You know, I would love to minor in geology, if I ever get back to college." He retreated into his thoughts. "Hey, everyone is welcome to come down and borrow them."

McElvey turned his head and said, "Not on your life, especially Lia. You know the rules: girls are not allowed in the boys' rooms. Remember." Carla and Brandy giggled and poked each other, while I blushed at being singled out.

To break the silence, McElvey decided to add to the conversation. "You probably wonder why they call this Deadman Summit," he said matter-of-factly. "Well, the story goes that William Hayes, a local mailman in 1940, got stuck on the pass in a pre-season five-foot snowfall. A group of rescuers took three days to reach his stranded wagon. He had frozen to death."

"Whoa," I said, sitting up to hear more of the story. "When the snows come, they come fast here."

McElvey continued, "Yep, the snows are late this year; however, our local weatherman expects a bigger than usual winter." He smiled. "He says the elk and deer have already left the high country for Red's Meadow—we could get as much as forty to fifty feet of snow over the winter."

I felt warm and comfortable, snuggling against Bill's blue flannel shirt, smelling his Old Spice deodorant. The Beatles "Can't Buy Me Love" played on the radio. Brandy sat to my right with Carla practically on his lap, his hands pulling her tight to his body. Wren and Becky started singing along and all six dreamers joined in unison. Only McElvey and Stephanie held back.

At the fork to Abraham Lake, McElvey turned off the radio and lowered his voice. "Okay, kids, just a few rules for the hike. We need to stay within earshot of each other, as the trail is not always well-marked. If you come to a fork in the path, wait. We'll stop by Agnew Dam for lunch."

At the base of the chairlift, our party of eight piled out of the station wagon. Doug Ross, the new manager of Abraham Lake Ski Area, welcomed McElvey with a hug. The two obviously had respect for each other, even though they were rivals in the ski business.

"Oh, man, looks like you'll have a clear day for a hike," said Doug. "Be careful. The word is that a bear and cub were recently sighted up near the dam." He instinctively let his hand fall to his side where I noticed a bulge and the handle of a pistol.

The noise of the chairlift drowned out the rest of Doug's cautionary words, but I felt comfortable with McElvey as guide. However, I noticed that his usual welcoming smile had changed; his head nodded in response to the rest of Doug's story, and then he retreated into thought. I wondered what he knew.

Once off the chairlift, we started with a fast walk, each vying for a place behind McElvey, who led. I stepped in behind Bill, so I could follow each of his steps, soon learning I had to take two steps to his one. The thin air at 9,000 feet caused me to breathe harder than usual; I hoped this pace would slow soon.

The group rounded the first bend where the high ridge of the Sierras rose from behind a stand of Jeffrey pines. I stumbled as I looked up at the ragged mountains. Never had I seen such wilderness, such savage beauty: the serrated Minarets and the pointed Mt. Ritter, the mountain I'd just read about in Muir's memoirs. In his journal, he wrote about his epiphany in 1872 while climbing the Minarets. He decided that if he could conquer these jagged peaks, he could overcome any adversity in life.

In my mind, I imagined these peaks, dressed in what Muir called "enduring" snowfields, to be a battalion of medieval knights, balancing pointed helmets while they circled to protect the Holy Grail. I slowed my pace in order to step cautiously around a sheer drop-off, the backside of Abraham Mountain that sloughed toward Red's Meadow. Two stones broke loose and banged their way down the sixty-degree slope.

McElvey stopped next to a whitebark pine, a tree dwarfed by the lack of oxygen and bent southward by the north winds. He took a deep breath and said, "Okay, kids, now you can see the magnificence, yet the danger of this area. To the west and north are hundreds of miles of wilderness and to the southeast is Monmouth and beyond is the highest peak in California—Mt. Whitney at 14,000 feet."

I gasped as his hand swept along the ridgeline; these peaks were three times as high as my Green Mountains. He continued, "Now the trail will narrow and become very rocky as we drop to the dam. Please slow down and watch your steps." I relaxed in the authority of his voice.

Becky broke the silence of the group saying, "Is this the famous Muir Trail?"

"Not exactly," said McElvey, "although we've now entered the Muir wilderness area. We should be fine. The weather is clear." He motioned for all of us to gather around him in a semicircle. "However, if you do see a bear, stop and stand as large as you can." He stood tall and raised his arms above his head. "Do not run. I've got a pistol on my belt for protection, but the bear will usually walk away if you make enough noise. She doesn't want to engage us."

I felt Bill's wing-like arm across my shoulder, so I pressed against him, his warmth flowing into me. The group took off again, following a well-marked path that smelled of pack horses and fresh dung, one more obstacle to tiptoe around. The crisp air, warming sunlight and trail dust flowed into my lungs, causing me to cough. No one talked, because the pace kept us struggling for air.

Our group pressed on in silence for an hour. I listened to the sounds of our boots scraping the hard rocks, my thoughts turning to the many weekends of hiking in the Green Mountains with my father. How he loved to find new trails, new approaches to the well-worn peaks. I think he used these hikes to forget the pain of his marriage and the death of my mother. During these trips, I never asked him any questions. Instead, I just became his silent hiking companion.

In contrast to the East, I noticed the lack of clouds in the Sierra sky—rarely did we have a cloudless day in Vermont. Interestingly, because McElvey didn't talk, the rest of us remained silent. I looked for the lesson in the quiet. Gradually, I felt my other senses become more acute, especially my sense of smell: the musk from the plants mingled with the sweet odor of the lodgepole pines. A breeze carried the scent of campfires in Red's Meadow.

At the sound of a screaming bird, McElvey put up his hand, forcing the group to stumble into each other like dominoes. No one moved until all had caught up, even Stephanie and Wren. Again, silence. A gentle wind blew the sweat from my face.

"Do you hear that bird?" said McElvey, looking around slowly. Everyone nodded, but no one broke the uneasy hush. "That's a Clark's nutcracker. Something's up." McElvey's body stood stiff and alert like a hunting dog on point. His blue eyes darted up and down the trail. "The birds act like a radar in the mountains," he continued softly.

His eyes searched for what had upset the mountain bird in the nearby pine. I tried following his eyes, to see what he saw. Then, he stared at a brown stick across the trail—the answer. A rattlesnake lounged in the sun with a half-swallowed, gray bird in its mouth. The snake had obviously captured the nutcracker's mate.

McElvey waited without moving until he felt sure the snake wouldn't attack. He relaxed, letting his shoulders drop as his hand moved from his holster. He gave out a sigh and said, "One can never be too cautious. Stay alert. The answers are always out there. Right." Slowly, he led us off the trail into the sagebrush, moving in a wide circle away from the rattler. He stopped, making sure that each of us had passed safely.

He strided on with unhurried, measured steps. Again, a communal silence, pumice clogging my nose. Using his keen sense of hearing, he stopped and pointing up, he asked, "Did you hear that bird in the whitebark pine?" No one responded, all shaking from the sight of the rattler.

Feeling someone should answer, I said, "Yes."

"Well, there's a lesson to be learned from the bird and the tree," said McElvey. "Sit down for a moment and rest." *Now*, I thought, *we'll get to hear from our own mountain man.*

The seven of us found either a log or a granite boulder to sit on. I drank from my bottle, enjoying the cold water that washed the dust from my throat. McElvey moved into the center of the circle, squatted, and said, "The pine and the nutcracker have a unique relationship." He paused to make sure each one of us was listening. "In scientific terms it is called mutualism. The whitebark pine nuts provide an important food supply for the nutcracker. Meanwhile, the bird buries many of the nuts in caches to be used later. Of course, as the nuts are dispersed, they become new trees."

I felt as if I understood what he wanted to teach us. Here was an Emersonian moment, a truth intuited from nature. I raised my hand, as if in school.

"Yes, Lia," said McElvey, looking annoyed that I'd interrupted him.

I said eagerly, "Are you trying to tell us that we all need each other?"

"Well, Lia, that's one way to interpret this. Remember, all of you are heading into the most challenging year of your lives. You'll be traveling together, supporting each other, yet competing against each other. Some will make the Olympic team. Some will not. In the end, you alone are responsible for what happens." He looked carefully into the eyes of each one of us, making sure we understood.

Then, each of us looked from one to the other, not sure how to respond. In silence, McElvey motioned for us to get up and start walking.

CHAPTER 8

More Lessons

"Hey, coach, I think we're going too fast for Stephanie," I yelled ahead, stumbling over a rock as I looked up. The sun stood high in the sky, so our shadows had all but disappeared. I looked behind to see Stephanie and Wren slipping behind a small cinder cone.

McElvey looked back in frustration, saying, "We'll wait for them at the dam. It's just two turns down the trail." He smiled, "They probably have to make a pit stop."

Now I understood that each had to be responsible for her own well-being. The group would not slow for the weakest. Stephanie and Wren would have to find the energy to push themselves. I knew that the thin air of the Sierras demanded extraordinary conditioning unlike the oxygen-rich air in my Green Mountains. I could only imagine how easy my breathing would be in the upcoming races at the lower altitudes, such as in Vail. This explained why the racers from Monmouth had an edge over the other American skiers. Our bodies had been forced to grow enriched, oxygen-carrying red blood cells that made us super women.

At the dam, McElvey stopped the group for lunch and to await the arrival of the stragglers. When we assembled around him, he took the time to tell us the story of the dam and Mono Lake. Off to the east through a gap in the mountains, I could see the outline of the lake set into the hardscrabble. A salt crust framed the aqua-blue water, sparkling like diamonds around a sapphire. The lone island in the middle had salt pillars, reminding me of the Biblical story of Sodom and Gomorrah and Lot's wife who had turned into a salt statue when, disobeying God, she looked back in empathy for her friends. I thought, *How should I feel for my two friends who are struggling behind us?*

I turned to listen to McElvey begin his tale. "In 1941, the Los Angeles Department of Water and Power acquired the rights to divert the tributaries to Mono Lake. The authorities built a dam and tunnels to supply the growing water needs of Los Angeles." He groaned in disgust. "The mayor of Bishop negotiated a deal that, to this day, no one understands. Everyone assumes that money passed hands. The acquisition of the water supply put an end to the fruit farming around the towns of Bishop and Lee Vining just below Monmouth." He paused and let his eyes roam out to Mono Lake. "With no inlet or outlet, they made the lake into a dead sea."

Upon hearing this story, I couldn't refrain from interrupting. "How can they just take the water from an area? That's not fair."

"Lia, you'll learn that not everything in life will be fair. Those in power can buy or coerce others to get what they want," he said, pointing his finger to accentuate his message. I heard the others whispering, so I slid from my rock and moved next to Bill, as if to ask for his help in my argument.

Bill shook his head and said "Oh, you innocent one. One day you'll understand."

I poked him, "Maybe I'll be the one to stand up and fight."

He shook his head, "If you do, you'll get crushed."

To break the tension Becky stood up. "Hey, let's have some fun. Does anyone know the song, *Oops, there goes a billion kilo-watt dam?* Oh, I mean, *another rubber tree plant?*" She started singing and waving her arms as if conducting an orchestra.

> Next time you're found with your chin on the ground
> There's a lot to be learned so look around

McElvey leaned up against a glacier-polished rock, put his feet over a log, settled his hands behind his head, and closed his eyes. He obviously loved this moment of unity with his skiers.

At this point I stood up next to Becky and joined in, knowing exactly where Becky wanted to go with the song. Becky continued in her angelic, soprano voice, I in my alto part.

> Once there was a little ol' ant
> Thought he'd move a rubber tree plant.
> Just what makes that little ole ant
> Think he'll move that rubber tree plant?
> Anyone knows an ant can't
> Move a rubber tree plant

Carla and Brandy stood up and started dancing as they blended their voices.

> But he's got hi-i-igh hopes, he's got hi-i-igh hopes
> He's got high apple pi-i-ie-in-the-sk-y-y hopes
> So, any time you're gettin' low, 'stead of lettin' go,
> just remember that ant.
> Oops, there goes another rubber tree
> Oops, there goes another rubber tree
> Oops, there goes another rubber tree plant.

Bill sat alone now, letting his eyes drift out east toward the gutted Mono Lake. He shifted uncomfortably and frowned. This made me sing even louder.

> When troubles call and your back's to the wall
> There a lot to be learned that wall could fall

Then Becky took on the next verse by herself.

> Once there was a silly old ram
> Thought he'd punch a hole in a dam
> No one could make that ram scram
> He kept buttin' that dam

At this point Bill got up, put his two index fingers to his head and mimicked a ram butting his head. Joyously, we were all dancing as if we didn't have a care in the world. We held hands and started circling McElvey like a carousel—the dust made him cough.

'cause he had hi-i-igh hopes, he had hi-i-igh hopes
He had high apple pi-i-ie-in-the-sk-y-y hopes
So, any time you're feelin' bad, 'stead of feelin' sad,
just remember that ram.
Oops, there goes a billion-kilowatt.
Oops, there goes a billion-kilowatt.
Oops, there goes a billion-kilowatt dam.

Then Becky sang.

A problem's just a toy balloon, they'll be bursted soon
They're just bound to go pop "Pop!"

She clapped her hands to accentuate the pop. We finished the song by falling to our knees still in a circle.

Oops, there goes another problem ker
Oops, there goes another problem ker
Oops, there goes another problem ker-plop
Ker...

"Help!" A scream interrupted the singing. McElvey jumped to his feet, recognizing Stephanie's voice. Grabbing his pack, he ran back up the trail. Bill and I followed but couldn't keep up.

When I rounded the last turn, I stopped as if I'd run into an invisible wall. There in front of me stood McElvey, his jaw clenched, his gun raised in the atavistic pose of a man protecting his family. Standing on its haunches, human-like, six-feet tall, stood a bear, her teeth bared at Stephanie and Wren, who cowered behind a small rock outcropping. The sun glinted off the bear's black coat and her extended claws shown like polished nails. Her growl echoed throughout the peaks, loud as a strong wind funneling through a canyon. I froze behind McElvey.

He yelled to the two unprotected girls, "Stand up, spread your arms, yell." Then he fired his gun into the air. The bear turned to see what caused the noise. As the animal dropped to all fours, she squared toward McElvey.

Frozen, fighting back my tears, I grabbed Bill who stood next to me. For an instant that seemed like ten minutes, no one moved. Then, the bear, recognizing that she was out-manned, jumped down the side of the trail onto a ledge. Her last snarl reverberated off the rocky wall as she disappeared. Then out from under the ledge crawled a small cub, swaggering like a rag doll. The two creatures nuzzled each other before sliding down the steep slope toward the valley.

McElvey ran to his daughter and Wren, carefully lowering his pistol to his side. He put his arms around both in a loving gesture and then backed off, scolding them. "I told you to keep up with us. Holy cow, you obviously frightened the bear who only wanted to protect her cub." He shook his head with a look of concern. "She should have started hibernating by now. It's been way too warm this fall." He let his reprimand sink into the silence of the mountains. Thoughtfully, he concluded in a soft Solomonic voice, "The mountains have their own code. We're the outsiders. Remember this." Each word seemed tipped with barbs.

I tried to calm my two crying friends on our walk back to the others, while McElvey and Bill followed, deep in conversation. Sensing McElvey's impatience, I tried to convince the girls that they needed to absorb the lesson. No one said a word throughout the rest of the lunch until McElvey announced that the group would slow the pace and that all must stay together for the rest of the hike.

Now as I looked toward Monmouth Mountain and Mt. Ritter, like Muir, I saw not only the purity of what he called "the coruscating snowfields," I felt a meaning in the dark shadows under the volcanic outcroppings.

CHAPTER 9

First Snows

The snows finally came. By mid-November, the dustings started to accumulate. At night the top of the Monmouth cone became a white leviathan and each morning the sun reflected off the summit. Then it hit—the first major storm of the season—snow that's measured in feet, not inches, snow that buries cars, trees, roads, and houses.

The November 21st storm set in at 5 p.m. and lasted for six days. Now I understood why the base hut had a six-foot thick concrete wall facing the mountain. Such deep snows could easily avalanche, sliding 1,000 feet before slamming a wall of snow twenty feet deep into the lodge. Fortunately, the living quarters of the lodge rested a secure thirty feet above the ground.

To get outside during the blizzard, I would wander out on my balcony that overlooked the mountain and catch the falling snow on my tongue. Sadly, no skiers were allowed on the mountain while the storm dumped three feet a day. The lifts did not open even for us, because McElvey didn't want any of his racers out until the ski patrol had blasted the top cornice with cannons, releasing any potential avalanches. Most of the time, the mountain remained enshrouded in clouds. Cabin fever set in.

To pass the time, after our chores of painting and cleaning, Bill and I sat around the fire, reading Emerson's essays. I grew to love his Boston accent, his lack of "r's", his slow methodical way of dissecting the material. Often he stopped just to reflect on a passage. "Hey, Lia, do you agree that 'a foolish consistency is the hobgoblin of little minds'?" he asked with a wink.

"Nope, unless you think I have a little mind." I looked to see his reaction. "You know, I like to be consistent. I like to keep true to my set of values."

"Okay, Miss Priss. What are these values?"

"Hey, that's not fair." I giggled and continued. "I do believe you share some of these—for example, hard work, honesty, kindness, education, and family."

"Whoa, sounds as if you've bought into the Puritan ethic hook, line, and sinker."

"Hey come on, you grew up with these, too."

"Really, well, what if these values aren't working for you?" He looked down, silently withdrew without moving a muscle. The fire sputtered and dimmed.

I realized that something had been festering in his mind. "Give me an example of this?"

"Let's see, what if you believe that you must never cheat, yet cheating might get you what you want?"

"Never."

He thought for a moment. "Let me give you an example. What if I were to purposely get hurt skiing in order to get out of the draft?"

"Oh, I see where you're going. Well, I couldn't do that, but, of course, that's your choice."

He looked pained and kept reading. I realized that he was in a Catch-22. If he raced well, but still didn't make the team, then the army got him. If he got hurt, I mean really hurt on purpose, then he wouldn't make the team, but also he wouldn't have to go into the army.

That evening in the wax room, we joined the other racers as they finished their ski preparations. I'd just received six pairs of skis from Kneissl: three slalom and two giant slalom, and a pair of downhill skis, all thanks to Coach Boast who'd submitted my name to the pool of ski companies that sponsored the most promising racers. My favorite event, slalom, demanded a different flex ski for different types of courses, so I ordered three pair. After Damien's death, I grew to dislike downhill, so I only asked for one pair of the longer skis. Bill helped me mount them with Marker bindings and then he waxed and sharpened their edges.

When the storm broke on the seventh day, leaving a total of eleven feet of snow, Bill, Brandy, Becky, Wren, Carla, and I agreed to meet at Chair One at 7:30 for the milk run with the ski patrol. We planned to spend the day powder skiing in preparation for race training in two days. There were only three weeks left before the Monmouth team would have to drive east to Vail for the 1970 Christmas downhill camp, sponsored by none other than Coach Boast, who was head of the US Ski Team.

"I'll race you to the chair," said Bill as he skated around the corner of the base hut.

I felt the competitive thrill. I wanted to beat this guy. I kicked my feet into my bindings, compulsively putting left before right, and took off. Poling, skating, I struggled to stay ahead of him. However, when he slid alongside me, he stuck his pole in between my skis. I fell hard into his powder-blue ski pants, knocking him down, and crumpling on top of him. We became a writhing spider with eight legs. The smell of his cologne, the feel of his hard body caused a warm swelling throughout my body.

Just then, I heard a stern voice from above. I looked up to see McElvey, dressed in his navy-blue ski pants and jacket, staring out of his goggles. He spoke with the voice of a commanding officer, "Lia, Bill. You could've hurt yourselves." A slight smile curled his lips. "We've just begun a long season of training and racing. No injuries, please." His laugh told me he hadn't forgotten the child-joy that the first snowfall brought. After such a long wait for the snow, the many days of dry-land training, the nights of work and ski preparation, I felt like a kid in a wonderland.

I settled into the metal chairlift with Bill at my side. He casually drew me to him, using his expansive arm. The wind whipped the fresh snow up from the ground into our faces. Once on the lift, a singing started from Wren and Becky in the chair behind us.

> In this white world that reaches the sky,
> I found a future for me.
> Standing high on a mountainside,
> I am the ruler of all I see.

I remembered the words from my days of skiing with Damien. Joining in the next verse, I turned toward Bill in a flirtatious manner.

> The snow is my lover,
> The sun is his kiss,
> The wind sings a love song to me.
> With the wind,
> and the sun and a vast powder run,
> just like an eagle, I'm free.

Laughing, Bill and I turned back to Becky and Wren as we hollered the refrain.

> For my skis are the things that give me my wings
> just like an eagle on high.

In the chair ahead, Carla and Brandy joined us on the next verse.

> If you see a track in the powder-
> white snow etched beneath the sky,
> a man soaring down the mountain,
> flying through the trees,
> racing the wind rushing by,
> look for the skier whose heart's in the clouds,
> the song in his heart tells you why.
> For I am a skier with my spirit fulfilled,
> an eagle who must ever reach for the sky.

Finally even louder, we finished:

> For my skis are the things that give me my wings,
> Just like an eagle on high.

I relaxed into the warming chair, feeling a new contentment. This was the moment I'd awaited. As our chair passed the final lift tower, I knew I'd found my bliss: a boyfriend, a ski team, and a snow-covered, treeless mountain.

Sliding down the off-ramp, Bill looked up to the cornice, a sheer outcropping of ice. He pointed out where the ski patrol had completed its job—two small slides had come down the right gully and stopped at the bottom of the ramp. Bill and I took a moment to stamp down the loose snow. We knew that the lift crew would appreciate the help. Excitedly, we took off side-by-side down St Anton's run.

Becky and Wren cruised by us, laughing. "Ha, we'll get the first tracks," yelled Wren, looking over her shoulder. Carla and Brandy pulled up beside us. Bill poled harder and let his skis run straight to catch them. I poled after him.

The six of us skied abreast in perfect synchronized "s" turns down the untracked slope. We adjusted to each other's pace the way a flock of starlings murmurate, shifting direction in the air. Powder shot up into my face as if I were standing in a waterfall. I could barely breathe, much less see through the snow-plumage; however, I sensed Bill to my left and Becky and Wren to my right. The first drop-off caused me to shorten my turns. Wren didn't adjust, so her skis crossed mine, and she fell into me, and I into Becky. The three of us ended in a pile of fresh powder, while Bill stopped above us and sent down even more confection to cover us. Brandy and Carla stopped above Bill, trying to cover him with a sheet of white.

Above us, I heard a strange crack, a gunshot. I looked up to see a slab fracture from the cornice. In slow motion, the whole upper slope started to move, a wall of death building toward us. I'd never seen or heard an avalanche before and froze.

"Get up. Get up," yelled Bill. "Ski off to the side of the gully now." I stood and poled toward a rock pile on the side. The wind in front of the roiling snow blasted my face; its roar, the sound of a fast moving train. I couldn't believe the force of the snow as it rumbled past me, a wave of frozen crystals. I struggled to keep my balance as it passed, a living, breathing monster.

When it stopped, the silence of the mountains returned. I looked around for my friends. Bill and Becky stood behind me, and Carla and Brandy had skied to the other side of the gully. But nowhere could I find Wren. My heart leapt, I adjusted my goggles to get a better look. I pleaded to Becky, "Can you see Wren?"

Panicked, I started walking to the encrusted remains of the avalanche, a hard pack of cement, screaming, "Wren." In one instance the soft powder had turned into concrete. I wondered how one could ever dig out a buried person. As my heart pounded in my ears, I heard a small voice call from behind the rock. "Here I am, Lia. Don't worry."

"Oh, my God! I didn't know what to do," I screamed in furious joy.

At that moment, Bill skied over to me, shook his pole, and in a stern voice said, "So, now you know. Nothing is consistent or predictable in the mountains." He laughed, "You little hobgoblin."

CHAPTER 10

Evening Activities with *King Lear*

By the end of November, all the racers, both boys and girls, had grown comfortable with each other, so after training, we spent the long nights entertaining ourselves with songs and card games. Bored with these, Becky asked me what I thought about reading a play together, even trying some impromptu acting. She said she'd loved her senior drama class during her last year at her Los Angeles high school.

That night, after my favorite dinner of roast chicken, mashed potatoes, peas, and apple strudel, the group gathered around the fireplace for the evening activities, and Becky announced, "What about finding a copy of a Shakespeare play to read together?"

Puzzled, I asked, "Have you always been this much of a type A? Shakespeare?"

Carla giggled, "Yup, she was always a superstar in high school. The teacher's pet." She looked at Becky with envy, "Straight A's, right." Becky nodded with a smirk.

Wren dragged her chair closer to us, feeling left out and said, "Hey, guys, I read a Shakespeare play in school, too. 'Sleep no more, Macbeth doth murder sleep.' " She staggered up from her chair as if sleep-walking, her arms stretched out front.

Becky laughed, saying, "Let's find a play that has many women in it. I hate all the ones about murder and men."

"Good luck," I said with a sneer, remembering I'd read *Romeo and Juliet, Hamlet, Macbeth,* and *Julius Caesar*—one each year in high school.

Becky must have read my mind. "Okay, what about *King Lear.*

If I remember right, there are three sisters in the play," she said.

"Perfect," answered Wren. "Who'll play the guy's parts?"

I smiled, saying, "I know we can count on Bill, because he's such a literature freak,"

Becky looked at me with a smile, "Yep, and Brandy will make a perfect fool. He is always goofing around. Remember when he came out with the clown costume?" she said.

"Hey, that's not fair." said Carla. All knew Carla had a crush on Brandy.

After agreeing on the choice of play, Becky and I decided to take the next afternoon off from free skiing and drive to Bishop. McElvey, always generous, let us use the company station wagon during our free time. We had called ahead to the bookstore and ordered eight copies of *King Lear*.

The next evening after dinner, we gathered around the fire to divide up the parts. Becky, dressed in jeans and a white turtleneck, stood in front of the fire, a soft glow lit her face as she assumed the role of director. "Okay, Lia, you absolutely have to take the part of Cordelia. Just like her, you're so naïve, so trusting," she said with a smidgen of derision. "Plus your name sounds like hers."

I laughed, but secretly felt hurt—now both Bill and Becky had made fun of my innocence.

Looking down the list of characters, I retaliated. "Okay, but then you have to be Goneril. Gotcha. What a gross name."

Taking charge again, Becky looked at Wren, "Wren, will you play Regan? You and I can be the conniving sisters together."

"I don't know the play, so what can I say," said Wren, moving nervously in her chair. She must have sensed the tension in the room.

"Hey, what do I get to do?" said Carla.

"You can play some of the men," said Becky. "You like to be tough, right. And you just cut your hair short, like a boy's."

"Hey, don't knock my hair. I hate the hat-hair I get from skiing all day." She rubbed her hand through her two-inch long hair. "So, I cut it short." She moved her fingers like scissors. "Watch out. I'll cut your pageboy, too. Just think, then you can get rid of all the blow-drying in the morning and evening."

I felt the sarcasm growing and broke in, "Enough about hair. We all have hair problems when we're skiing. Who has time to keep it up? Even so, I'm not cutting mine." I shook my hair back and forth to tease Carla. "I like my long, blonde hair. At night I just pull it back in a ponytail anyway—no hat hair. As for the male parts, what about Bill?"

Becky laughed and said, "I had him picked for King Lear. Do you think he'll do it?" She spoke with authority, knowing Bill had no choice.

Now our days felt complete. Free skiing in the morning, race practice in the afternoon, ski preparations after dinner, followed by an hour of play reading before bed. Brandy and Bill would join us and then leave to complete their evening chores of dishwashing and cleaning. At times, I felt guilty that they worked so hard for their room and board compared to the girls' carefree life.

Becky assigned the scenes ahead of time, so we could practice. Also, this helped the guys plan their work schedule, depending on whether they had to read or not. I never wanted to miss a moment, so I always settled by the fire before the others. And I secretly hoped Bill would sit beside me.

Soon we had an audience of the other workers. To identify our roles, we decided to add costumes. Rummaging through the lost and found, I found some old skirts for the girls as well as a few funny-looking ski hats. The one I found for Brandy, the fool, had three flowing tassels and a floppy peak. Bill decided that his gold racing helmet would make the perfect crown for King Lear.

At times Carla had trouble understanding the dialogue, so Becky would stop us to explain the words. I hated the break in the action but understood that the word play often went over all our heads.

Carla asked, "What does 'Fairest Cordelia, that art most rich, being poor; / Most choice, forsaken; and most lov'd, despis'd' mean?"

Becky did her best to explain what a paradox was. "Carla, it's like irony. Saying one thing and meaning another. Or appearance versus reality."

Carla, still looking confused, said "Oh you mean when Coach Boast says he's impartial and then favors Tracy?"

"Right, you've got the idea. In this play, nothing will be as it appears," said Becky, looking at me to see if I caught her warning. I squirmed, tried to laugh, but sensed that I'd been left out of a bigger secret.

By the time we got to the end of Act I, scene 1, I'd gotten over my reservations about Cordelia and read with conviction, often acting out my lines. I put my shawl over my hair and read slowly, now understanding Cordielia's role as the truthsayer. "Time shall unfold what plighted cunning hides. / Who cover faults, at last shame them derides." Silently, I reread the lines and wondered: *Is this a prophecy? Why me—why I am I saying these lines?*

The next night, by the time we got to Act I, scene 4, Bill, wearing his gold racing helmet that drooped to one side, spoke regally in his Boston accent; while Brandy, balancing his tri-colored, tasseled ski-hat and brandishing his work broom like a misshapen scepter, recited his lines haltingly, attempting a British accent, he said,

> Mark it, nuncle.
> Have more than thou showest
> Speak less than thou knowest,

He put his fingers to his lips.

> Lend less than thou owest,
> Ride more than thou goest,

He pretended to gallop on a horse, hands in front holding the reigns, knees posting.

> Learn more than thou trowest,
> Set less than thou throwest;

He threw the broom down.

> Leave thy drink and thy whore,
> And keep in-a-door,
> And thou shalt have more
> Than two tens to a score.

Now he was in full stride prancing back and forth, his hat flopping from side to side, his Asian eyes, just narrow slits.

All five of us broke into such contagious giggles that I had to cross my legs to avoid wetting my pants. Brandy was a natural. He gesticulated, he waved his arms, he stumbled like a mad man. My laughter caused me to gasp like a drowning swimmer, so I didn't realize that the others had stopped.

Looking up, I saw a stern figure standing in the doorway, casting a long shadow into the room, one arm pointing in the direction of us. His face resembled an angry father or worse an outraged principal. "I'd no idea that all of you were such scholars," said McElvey, shaking his finger. I'd never heard him so angry. "Don't you think all of you should get to bed?" He stepped toward the guttering firelight, squinting to each of us.

Carla, trying to break the tension, said, "Why does thou think we be so silly/When all around lies abound willy-nilly." She was definitely getting into it.

I saw that McElvey neither appreciated, nor understood, the playfulness. His face glowered, red from the firelight, as he strode closer to us. Becky stood up to defuse the situation, saying, "I'm … I'm so sorry, Coach. We've been having fun reading *King Lear.*"

McElvey didn't respond. His blanket-silence disapproval smothered us. As he turned to leave, I heard him mutter, "Kids, will they ever understand?"

In the ensuing void, all I heard was the crackling of the pine logs. No one dared to say anything until McElvey's dark silhouette moved beyond the doorway. Becky then spoke up, "Okay, you need to know that Coach has a one-track mind for us: ski racing."

Carla protested, "But—but we have to have fun."

"Well," said Becky, choosing her words carefully, "he thinks our fun should be on the ski slope. Night should be for work or sleep."

"Okay," I broke in, leaning forward so all could hear me. "But doesn't he understand that we all like to learn, too?"

Becky glared at me and said, "Okay, Miss Scholar, not everyone has had the advantages you've had—a good high school education and acceptance to a great college."

"What do you mean?" I asked, frustrated.

"Just that. McElvey never even finished high school. He had to go to work to support his mother. I think he worked in the fields of southern California, picking vegetables."

"So?" I said, still not sure of her point.

"So, Miss Smarty Pants, he does for us what he never had. He supports us, so we can fulfill our dreams of racing. He expects us to focus just on this."

"Hey, we're kids," I answered.

"Not anymore," responded Becky, shaking her head and frowning. "You'll see."

I had to get the last word in, so I said under my breath, "At least he had a mother."

Becky glared and answered, "What did you say?"

Angrily, I said loudly, "At least he had a mother."

She rolled her eyes and said, "We'll talk later."

Bill saw that I was getting upset, "Hold it, calm down. Let's be grateful. I'll talk to him tomorrow. I'm sure he'll understand. I need to ask him about the letter that I got today anyway." Stumbling on the next words, he continued, "from Coach Boast."

CHAPTER 11

Bill

The lack of trees above 9,000 feet allowed us unfettered skiing in the virgin powder. Bill and I spent each morning searching for new slopes to conquer.

The light snow, untouched by the wind, gave me the feeling of surfing, particularly when the snow, fluffy as eiderdown, roiled in my face. By sitting back on my heels, I could get the tips of my skis to ride on top of the untracked snow. With just a slight unweighting, my skis would create "s" doodles. At times, Bill would cross my tracks in symmetrical figure eights, the equivalent of riding the perfect wave. These were the moments that I'd dreamed about in Vermont and I could now share them with my new friend.

In the afternoons after slalom practice, Bill and I, along with the others, would help Coach McElvey make the final preparations for the season. He usually had us shovel snow at the top of each chair lift or set up ropes, fencing off dangerous cliffs. I quickly learned to respect the 11,000 foot monolith called Monmouth, a creature that changed with each snowfall—the gullies filled in, the spiny ridges grew mottled, the cornice rose higher, and the trees shortened in the heavy snowfall. To the west as the gray-brown pumice disappeared, Mt. Ritter and Banner resembled white teeth protruding into a blue sky. Bill told me that the measure of a place's greatness is how much it makes one forget the rest of the world. I soon learned why he said this with such resignation.

One afternoon at the top of Chair Three, as Bill and I were assigned fencing in the down-ramp, I asked him, "Hey, Bill, you've never really told me what brought you to Monmouth?"

"Do you want the long story?" he said.

"I've got the rest of the afternoon. Go ahead."

"Well, Uncle Sam decided that because I'd dropped out of college to ski race, I should serve in the army. I received 1A status in the draft. Since most of the kids from my hometown of Concord, Massachusetts, remained in college, I was given a low draft number. This meant I'd be first pick for Uncle Sam. To avoid going in as a recruit, I enlisted in officer training."

"Why'd you drop out of college?"

"I wanted to change my major from pre-med to English at the University of Wyoming. I needed some time off to figure out what I really wanted to do. I guess I played the roulette game and lost."

"So where did you do your first Army training?"

"The army shipped me to San Antonio for four months of basic."

"Whoa, so now are you waiting for your orders?"

"In a way. During basic training, I wrote to John Boast—you know—the coach of the ski team, to see if I could get into his special training program. The army had given him four spots for nationally talented racers. He was able to hand pick the ones who could ski on the US Ski team, instead of being deployed."

"Oh, I see. Is this the same Boast that ran the ski camp in Bend?"

"Yup. He wrote back that if I could get my international FIS points low enough at the Christmas training camp in Vail, he might consider me."

"Do you trust him?"

"I've no choice. Then, I wrote to McElvey, knowing he'd a reputation of helping out aspiring racers. He liked my background of college racing and agreed to give me a job, working at night and training with his Monmouth team during the day."

"So here you are?"

"Yes, and loving every minute, especially because many of my friends have already received their orders for Vietnam. But ..." as he looked away up toward the mountain peak, his lips quivered.

I gulped, remembering my two friends from Waitsfield, Vermont, who were now serving in Vietnam. I remembered reading the letters they'd sent home that spoke of horrors beyond belief. One friend, David, when on leave, had sneaked back some photos. One in particular I'll never forget. It showed recruits standing in front of a tent, smiling, shouldering their guns, while behind them human skulls, bleached white by the sun, hung from the center post. I shuddered at the thought of what this distant war had done to my friends, to my generation, and now maybe to Bill.

Just as we placed the last safety rope, protecting the unloading skiers from the cliff to the left, Stephanie, McElvey's daughter, skied off the lift. She was a striking figure dressed in tight, powder-blue Monmouth pants, a red-stripped parka, flashing a blonde ponytail that flowed down her back. With no sunglasses or goggles, her tanned face shown like a bronze bell. In a taunting voice, she called out as she stopped below us. "Hey, Bill, my dad wants you to join him at the bottom of Chair Two to finish shoveling the off-ramp. He knows you want to talk to him—something about a letter from Coach Boast. I'll ski over with you." Then she turned to me, "Lia, Dad wants you to finish the ropes here."

I snarled, feeling a sense of jealousy. Not only did she not have to work, she was now taking Bill away from me.

I turned to see Bill's expression and asked him, "What letter?" He started to ski off and shrugged, "Later."

In frustration, I glared at Stephanie. "What does Coach want me to do after I finish here?"

She laughed. "Since it's 3:45, do what you want." Her strange hyena-cackle made me shiver. "Just remember serious training begins tomorrow. We've only two weeks until the Vail Christmas Camp." I watched with envy as she skied figure eights over Bill's track.

CHAPTER 12

The Bristlecone Pine

"One hundred Viet Cong killed. Three Americans died," announced Walter Cronkite on the black and white TV. A fuzz came across the screen, so I got up to move the rabbit ears that brought us reception. Fritz, the bachelor accountant at Monmouth, occasionally invited us to his apartment to watch the only TV in the building. This was the way we could keep in touch with the outside world, especially the war, as no newspapers were delivered to the lodge.

This statistic of both American and North Vietnamese deaths sent chills up my spine. My friends Becky and Wren cheered, believing we were winning the war; whereas, I thought, *Who were the three Americans today? Could one be my friend, Peter, from Waitsfield?*

To pass the time, we had continued reciting *King Lear*, but before bed, Becky, Carla, Wren, and I felt we needed to know more about Vietnam, considering that Bill might get drafted. Fritz, an awkward small man, enjoyed our company, after all who wouldn't want four trim, athletic girls to help pass the long nights?

Pragmatically, he felt we were both financial and marketing assets to the ski area. If we did well on the ski circuit, this would rocket Monmouth into national prominence among skiers. Slowly, I began to accept that in the end, it's always about money.

Cronkite continued, "The NLF offensive has been stopped, and the Americans have regained control of the Da Nang Province."

I wondered what the NLF was. It sounded like a football team. And where was Da Nang? Why was our government sending my generation there to die? My only other knowledge about these events was the weekly letters from my father who ardently supported the war. He argued that the United States needed to stop the spread of Communism in the southern tip of Asia or other countries could start falling under communist control—a domino effect, an idea almost universally accepted.

As a follow up, Cronkite then shifted to the antiwar resistance at the Pentagon. "700 young men and women protested the war in Washington." The camera zoomed to a crowd—wild-looking, unkempt group of hippies shouting, "Hey, hey, Nixon, how many men did you kill today?"

Suddenly, there was an uneven rapping on the door, followed by a plaintiff plea, "Is Lia in there?"

Recognizing Bill's voice, I jumped up to open the door. His face looked as though he'd just confronted a Sierra mountain lion. "What ... what's the problem?" I asked, my knees weakening.

"Please come down to the cafeteria. I'll meet you by the fireplace," he said as he turned to leave. I'd never see him so disheveled, so distressed.

I knew that McElvey wouldn't allow his female racers to visit the boy's rooms, the cave below the girl's apartments, so I wondered what he had in mind. I turned to my friends, saying, "I'll see you in the morning. Don't wait up for me." I excused myself just as Walter Cronkite signed off. "And that is the way it was on December 10th, 1970."

I found Bill huddled in a chair by the fire, his knees curled to his chest. He didn't look like my self-confident friend, but rather like King Lear who had lost everything on the heath.

"What's wrong? You look like someone stole your skis," I said.

"In a way, someone did."

"What do you mean?"

"Remember I told you that John Boast said I could try out for his elite team and avoid the draft to Vietnam?

"Yeah."

"Well, a few days ago I received a letter from him."

"So?"

"He withdrew his offer, because he'd already selected four skiers from his college team—skiers he knows." His lips trembled as he finished. "To include ..."

" ... Wait a minute. Didn't he say that the spots would be chosen *after* the Vail training camp and based on FIS points?" Moving closer to Bill, I put my arm around his shoulder. The glow from the fire embraced us silently as the finality of Boast's decision burned into my brain, images of dead soldiers flashing before my closed eyes. I moved my hand around his neck, feeling his tension. His body started to heave, his legs to quiver, his hands to shake. The heat from the fire blasted my face—I had to turn away.

I held him in the silence of the large timbered room. The fire burned the last log of a lodgepole pine, while I counted the snapping of the dying sparks, like a ticking time bomb. I thought about Cronkite and the evening news. *Would Bill be in Vietnam soon?*

Angrily, I jumped up in front of him with my hands on my hips, and yelled, "This isn't fair! He can't go back on his word. Maybe McElvey can speak to him?"

Lowering his head, he said, "I've already spoken to coach. He called Boast for me. He has no leverage." Wiping a tear from his cheek, he swallowed hard. "No one can question John Boast. He's the authority in US skiing now. I'm just a pawn in his game."

Shaking my head, I stepped between Bill and the fire. "What are your choices then?"

In a resigned voice, he said, "Vietnam or Canada."

"What do you mean? Canada?"

"I can catch a bus over the border before I receive my active duty orders and sit out the war in Canada."

"Then what?" I said.

"Then, when the war is over, maybe—just maybe—I can come back to the US."

It took me an instant to organize my thoughts into words. "What about refusing the draft and going to jail like Henry David Thoreau? You're always quoting the Transcendentalists to me." I put up my fists as if doing battle with an imaginary enemy.

"Lia, my parents wouldn't accept jail or Canada."

"So, you're going to go to Vietnam and become another number?" I yelled, afraid to hear his response.

"I've got few choices."

"Damn John Boast—damn his promises. I'll bet the racers who are exempt paid him money"

"We'll never know. Promise me that you'll continue with your dreams of the 1972 Olympic team. One of us has to make the team."

With that comment, I felt a slight breeze pass by me—perhaps a draft from the fire? Remembering Damien, his dreams for the Olympics, I thought, *Yes, in all this man-made insanity, there has to be something to believe in, an ideal beyond all the pettiness. For me, I had hoped it would be the Olympics.*

Bill broke my thoughts, "Hey, you, sometimes you get so distant. Would you climb to the top of Monmouth with me tonight? I know you start training tomorrow, but I just need to get away and think." His face puckered. "I need a friend right now."

Agreeing to meet on the back veranda, I returned to my room to get my parka, winter boots, snow pants and goggles. The blue sheen of the full moon on the snow would light our way to the top.

I waited for Bill outside, enjoying the moon rising over the crest of Monmouth. With fear, yet anticipation, I sat on a bench, watching the winds whip the snow into a plume over the cornice, wagging like the tail on an unknown animal spirit.

"What brings you out here, my friend?" a stern voice asked. I jumped even though I recognized McElvey's deep, confident words. Rarely did any of us see him after dinner, because he usually went out to the mechanic's sheds to supervise the night crew as they prepared the snow-cats for the night-grooming.

"Wow, you scared me! I was just waiting for Bill. We plan to hike to the top of Chair Three tonight."

"Is that a good idea the night before we begin serious training?" he said in a patronizing voice.

"I … I, that is, Bill has just received some distressing news," I said.

"And what, pray tell, might that be? The hesitancy in his voice made me feel that he was testing my knowledge of the situation.

"Ah, he said he'd already spoken to you about it."

Before he could respond, he turned to see Bill walking out the door. Bill looked handsome in his Monmouth blue parka, even though his slumped shoulders indicated resignation. He spoke hesitantly, "Lia, who are you talking to?"

McElvey stepped out of the shadow, blocking the moon's rays that shone on Bill. Looking at coach's profile, I was reminded of the Old Man of the Mountain who watched over the New Hampshire Presidential range, so constant, so stern.

Bill turned, "Oh, hello, Coach. I'm surprised to see you here. Lia and I were just planning to hike to the top of Chair Three tonight."

"Don't you think that might be a little dangerous and foolish the night before you begin training?" he repeated.

"Well, sir, to tell you the truth, after I spoke with you, I'm undecided whether to follow orders and report to Ft. Devens next week or go to Canada," he said, nervously fumbling with his mittens.

McElvey said in a raised voice, "I'm so sorry, Bill. You know I called Boast, because he'd promised me he wouldn't pick the team until after the Vail camp. I thought you'd have a chance."

"Well, he promised me the same," said Bill, lowering his voice with each word.

No one spoke. Bill could be on his way to Vietnam within two weeks as a second lieutenant. Finally, breaking the moonlit-silence, McElvey whispered, "Now I understand why you want to climb the mountain—to say goodbye."

"Yes, sir," said Bill, looking up to the white, inscrutable peak, its blunted snout straining toward the moon.

"I'll tell you what. I've wanted to check out the bull-wheel on the top of Chair Three before the lift starts tomorrow. What if I drive the two of you to the top of the lift? Then you can have fun sliding down," he said with an impish grin.

At that moment, I wanted to hear from McElvey who must have faced a similar decision during WWII. "Coach, what would you do if you were Bill?"

McElvey answered with a beckoning motion. "Follow me. Let's go to the tractor shed. I want to take you somewhere."

The three of us walked slowly over the crusty snow to the outlying wooden sheds that housed the mountain equipment. No one spoke. McElvey indicated with his hand for Bill and me to wait outside.

I heard the roar of a snow-cat; a two-tracked, yellow cabin emerging from the shed, lights blazing into my eyes. For a moment I felt as if I were about to be abducted by aliens. McElvey opened the side door, yelling over the engine, "Hop in. I want to take you to a special place on the mountain."

I climbed up the studded tread and twisted into the cab. Bill slid in next to me, putting his padded arm around my shoulder. McElvey spun the snow-cat toward the west where a winding road led up the ridge above Red's Meadow. No one tried to talk over the grinding of the engine. McElvey turned the headlights off; the moon's glow lit the edges of the trail. The cat had no shock absorbers—every bump became a jolt, every turn pushed me into either Bill or McElvey. The overhanging branches on the trees defined the road; snow slid from their limbs onto the windshield. McElvey turned on the wipers, the slap, slap adding to the cacophony.

Just below a cliff, next to a granite outcropping, McElvey turned off the engine.

"Jump out. I want to show you something," he said.

I twisted my ankle as I dropped the four feet to the ground. Fortunately, Bill held my parka and restrained my fall. McElvey led the two of us toward a barren tree barely poking out of the crusted snow. Another awkward silence ensued. Kneeling down, he used gentle, caressing strokes to brush the snow from around the trunk of a gangly, stunted pine. Over his shoulder, I noticed the blackened outline of the serrated ridge-line of the Minarets. I felt awe at how McElvey melded into the setting as though he'd been born out of this mountain. Bill shuffled his feet, waiting for McElvey to speak.

"Do either of you recognize this tree?" said McElvey.

"No sir," said Bill, obviously uncomfortable with McElvey's stern tone.

I sensed that this would not be an ordinary lesson. At 9 p.m. with the Milky Way spreading over my head, I imagined I was on a Star Trek voyage to outer space. *Would there be a moral in this experience similar to a lesson taught by Captain Kirk?*

"What an awkward looking tree," I said.

"Yes, awkward, yet enduring," said McElvey, touching it gently. "Has either of you heard of a Bristlecone pine?"

Bill and I answered together, "Yup." But I couldn't remember what I knew about the tree.

"Take a closer look at the bark," said McElvey, digging around the trunk.

Bill knelt down as if in prayer and I leaned over his back for support. The creased wood reminded me of the face of a hundred-year old man. Only two green branches grew from the trunk.

"This tree is 4,400 years old," announced McElvey. His obvious reverence for this stunted miracle sent shivers through me. I saw him caress the flaking bark the way a child might caress a dying parent. "I found the tree in 1942 while I was exploring this region. At the time, I knew that one day I would want to put a ski lift on this mountain."

"Wow, you had plans way back then? I thought you'd built the area in the mid-fifties," said Bill.

"Yes, World War II delayed my plans." He pointed to some hatch marks on the trunk.

I leaned closer. The year 1942 could barely be read through the darkened wood. "Why did you put this date here?" I asked.

"I had to decide whether to go to war or stay stateside and work in the defense industry. At the time, I already had two children," said McElvey. Then I understood why he had brought Bill to this spot. Just as Bill had a decision about Vietnam, McElvey had made his decision about WWII.

"Oh, and what did you decide?" asked Bill, fearfully looking up.

"I spent the night on this mountain next to this tree and the answer came easily," he said. "At times, one must do more than serve one's own dreams. I chose to go into the 10th Mountain Division, the ski troops."

"Did you regret it?" said Bill, looking down as though hoping he wouldn't get an answer.

"No, but I carry the wounds from the battle on Mt. Belvedere in Italy," said McElvey, pointing to his leg. "So, Bill, you have a major decision to make. I brought you here so you could spend time in this spot. When you're ready, just walk down the cat-track. I know Lia will be waiting up for you at the base lodge."

I began tearing up, realizing that Bill needed to determine his own fate. Would he join the army or become a draft-dodger in Canada?

McElvey put his hand on Bill's shoulder to help lift himself away from the tree. Putting his arm around me, he led me back to the snow-rover, his slight limp causing pressure on my shoulder. Just before getting into the yellow cab, I looked back at Bill who had taken his place next to the survivalist tree.

Stoically, I looked to the skies: one star, a falling-western star, stood out from the others; the rest resembled sniper fire, shooting at Bill's darkened image.

CHAPTER 13

Waiting for Bill—Brandy's Story

A Sierra storm woke me at 1 a.m., thudding against the window, rattling the roof, grating like a train crossing a trestle bridge. To get back to sleep, I tried reading the book my father had sent me, John Muir's, *My First Summer in the Sierra,* but I couldn't keep my mind off Bill, so alone on the mountain, so cold and wet. I needed to find Brandy, my Korean pal, who was also Bill's dear friend, and who might go up on the mountain to find Bill.

On my way down to the boy's dormitory, I tripped on a dirty pile of long johns and turtleneck sweaters. A smell of body odor caused me to pause and curse the boys' laziness—they never did their wash. I jumped over two steps. The thud of my landing woke Brandy.

"Who's there? What the hell are you doing at this time of night?" he yelled.

Peeking into his room, I whispered, "It's me—Lia. I'm scared and lonely, and Bill's in trouble. Can you come up to the fire in the main room?" I turned away for fear of rejection. Brandy had always indicated he'd be my friend, yet I'd never reached out to him like this. I worried he might think I was making a sexual advance.

"Lia, we have to start training in the morning. Go back to bed." His anger intensified my fear.

"No, no," I pleaded, "you don't understand. Bill's up on the mountain. He needs our help."

"What're you talking about?" He moaned and yawned.

"Please come up. I'll explain everything."

I heard Brandy's feet scraping on the floor and then the rustle of clothes as he dressed himself, realizing he must sleep in the nude.

When he poked his head out the doorway, his tousled black hair made him look like Tom O'Bedlam. Struggling to follow me through the darkened stairway, he didn't help his image by singing in a monotone:

> He that has and a little tiny wit-
> With hey, ho, the wind and the rain-
> Must make content with his fortunes fit,
> For the rain it raineth every day.

"Okay, stop the Shakespeare and stop making fun of me. Get serious," I said. "I need to talk to you. Bill's in trouble."

"No, I'm not making fun of you, just Bill, especially if he's fool enough, like King Lear, to be on the mountain when a storm's coming in." Walking into the café and stepping in front of me, he continued, "Whoa, do you look like a mess. What's up?"

"Wait until you hear what's happening."

Brandy threw some logs on the hot coals, before we settled next to each other in the Adirondack chairs. The growing heat from the eight-foot opening hit our faces. Brandy pushed his chair back from the fire, but I welcomed the warmth, the sweet smell of the burning white pine.

"Okay, why's Bill on the mountain?" he asked. I followed his eyes as he looked out the large window into a curtain of white. The wind howled, pushed the sleet-ice into the window, making the sound of a swarm of insects—rat, tat, tat.

I took my time explaining Bill's situation, realizing he hadn't told Brandy any of it: about the army draft, his basic training at San Antonio, his break before deployment, Boast's broken promise, and whether to serve in the army or flee to Canada. Brandy's eyes opened wider at each revelation. His mouth drew tight, his skin reddened. I couldn't tell whether he was feeling the heat from the fire or just getting angry.

"Damn. I never liked that creep," said Brandy.

"Who?"

"Boast. I met him last year when he came to Monmouth to check out our race program. I could tell he was jealous of McElvey."

He stopped speaking. I heard nothing but the snapping of the fire. Closing my eyes, I imagined the whole world on fire.

"He's mad that trusts in the tameness of a wolf, / a horse's health, a boy's love, or a whore's oath," whispered Brandy.

"What did you say?" I raised my voice in frustration.

"Oh, more lines I remember from *King Lear*."

"What's your point?" I felt my anger growing, wondering if he'd even listened to me.

"Let me tell you a story about a young boy who had to face a war. Then you'll understand why I see war as madness."

"I'm confused." I threw up my hands.

"Just listen for once, Miss Know-It-All. Please." He stopped, gave a long look into the fire, and sighed, as though trying to find strength for what he was about say. "What do you know about the Korean War?"

"Not much. My father said it was a result of the Cold War with Russia—maybe around 1954."

Brandy began his story. His accent changed to a high-pitched Asian twang, which caused his voice to rise at the end of each sentence. I struggled to keep my mind from shifting to Bill caught in the storm, facing his difficult decision.

Brandy's face turned from buffoon to victim as he described his life in Korea in 1950. "My family had to leave a small village near No Gun Ri, because of the advancing North Korean troops. You know, I was only five years old, yet I still remember my umma, my dear mother, carrying me on her back in a handmade, swaddling sling." He paused, swallowing. I could tell this was a painful memory. He continued, "My older sister Li, just ten, struggled to keep up with my mother. So sad, my father had stayed behind, stupidly to try to protect the village."

"Wow, I'd no idea you came from somewhere else. I thought you were American."

"Well, I am now. Just listen, please. As the three of us drew near the trestle bridge over the local river, we heard machine gun fire." He pointed his fingers like a gun, "Tat, tat, tat. My umma put my sister and I down in the bushes, telling us to remain quiet."

I cringed at his misuse of the pronoun but didn't interrupt him. He continued, "Oh, how I tried to quiet my breathing, hoping to remain hidden from the soldiers with guns. My sister covered my face with her body. Then, I heard more strafing of machine guns and the roar of airplanes. When the noise stopped, we both waited for our umma." He stopped as if he were reliving the moment.

"Wow, what a brave sister. Go on," I said, leaning closer to him.

He squinted and shivered. "The cold night forced us to cocoon each other, covering ourselves with the swaddling blanket. By morning, my sister realized that we'd need help. She told me to stay put for one more night while she went for help.

"When I began getting hungry, I started eating the grasses next to the river bank. This just gave me more pain in my stomach. After three days and nights of terror, I knew I had to find help. I crawled down to the river and followed the clear, running water to a large rock. Cold and hungry, I decided to stretch out in the sun on the smooth boulder. I can still remember the warmth, pushing the chills from my body. Soon, I heard a voice asking a question in a strange language. I tried to crawl behind the rock. An American soldier came around the side and pointed a gun in my face. I curled into a ball and didn't look up until I felt the caress from his gloved hand, a hand that smelled of tobacco and gunpowder."

He stopped for a minute, staring into the fire. I broke the strained silence. "Please tell me how you got to America."

"Slow down. You need to learn from this story." He drew a breath and continued, "I remember the soldier carrying me to a truck and a bumpy journey to an orphanage, where I received my first full meal in over a week. During my time in that sanctuary, I didn't speak to anyone and cried each night for my mother and sister. After six months in the orphanage, a priest called Padre arranged for my departure to a US Air Force base. I remember to this day the roaring of the engines, the banking of the plane, and the view from my window of just ocean. From the base, I was flown to Bakersfield, California, to the home of my military rescuer, Josh Trudeau." Brandy said the name as though it were a prayer.

"I never saw Josh again. Three months later he, my savior, was killed in Korea. His parents raised me and introduced me to ski racing at Monmouth in 1958. Coach McElvey took notice of me when my parents entered me in the racing program. I was twelve. I guess, um, he liked my work ethic. After I finished high school, McElvey invited me, you know, to stay at Monmouth to work and train. That's why I'm here. One day, yup, one day I would like to race in the Olympics, yes, and represent my country, South Korea." He smiled with the widening grin of one who had just finished a perfect ski run, his oriental eyes growing narrower.

I could barely blink by the end of the story. My eyes burned from the heat of the fire, my tears stung my cheek. "Why are you telling me this story?" I whispered.

"I want you to know that war isn't just about soldiers, guns, and glory."

"Hey, I know that."

"Yes, but have you ever met an innocent victim of war? A child-survivor, an orphan?"

I thought for a minute, shifting my position in the chair, realizing I'd not moved for fifteen minutes. Before I could answer, Brandy stood up in front of me and said in a defiant voice, his eyes glowing in the firelight, "I hope Bill decides to go to Canada. War's stupid and unjust. No one wins." He put his hands on his hips, stood tall, and stomped his foot.

We both stopped, turning our heads toward a screeching sound at the main door to the cafeteria, an ear-piercing noise, resembling an untuned violin that announced the opening of the heavy pine door. Bill entered looking like an old man, his cheeks speckled with hoar frost, his efflorescent hair snow-stiffened.

CHAPTER 14

Bill

Bill stomped his feet to drop the snow from his boots and then shook his head, causing a cascade of snow to cover the floor. The snapping of the logs in the fire matched the pounding of my heart against my rib cage. He resembled the abominable snow man, a creature resigned to a haunted, hunted, lonely life in the mountains. His heavy footsteps echoed through the empty cafeteria as he approached us. I knew by the slump of his head that he'd made a decision.

Brandy, sensing that Bill and I needed to be alone, said, "Guys, I think I'll be heading to bed. I'll see you in the morning." He pushed his Adirondack chair back, stood up and gently rested his hand on my shoulder.

Bill and I waited for Brandy to disappear behind the kitchen stove before we reached out to hug each other. I felt his cold, wet arms around my turtleneck. As I strained upward to see his expression, he pushed his lips to mine and held them there until all the ice had melted down into my shirt. I tasted his breath, his fear, felt his clasp like a drowning swimmer trying to stay afloat.

Never before had I felt such emotion— his hard body enfolding mine, the hunger of his lips. When Bill tried to speak, I put my fingers to his lips and stopped him. Shaking my head, I guided him to the chair by the fire.

"Let me take off your boots. Please warm yourself by the fire before you say anything," I whispered. I didn't want to hear his final decision, because either way I would be losing him. I knelt in front of him, pulled off his heavy winter boots, straining against the tightness, until one broke free and sent me backwards toward the fire. "Yikes," I screamed. "That was close." I took his wet left foot into my hands and began to rub it. The wool steamed, the wetness smelling like mold and perspiration.

Finally Bill relaxed, staring into the fire as if wanting to disappear into the flames. The glow reflected in his wind-reddened eyes. He broke the silence. "Lia, I've reached my decision. I know you won't approve." I nodded. "McElvey did the right thing, taking me to the old pine. I spent three hours just listening to the wind sculpt the top of Monmouth. After a while I truly did become egoless. I felt as if I were part of the mountain." I continued to rub his frozen toes, hoping that I could bring more emotion into his voice. I heard the word—"Fate. This is my fate. I must serve my country. I've been called."

I gasped, realizing what he was saying. The hot air from the fire seared my lungs, yet I welcomed the pain that distracted me from my thoughts.

"Yes, I've decided I'll not argue with Boast, that I'll not desert and go to Canada. I'll join my training buddies and go wherever the military wants me. This is the honorable and right thing to do."

Remembering Brandy's story, I blurted, "But war is stupid. No one wins. It's about the military making money."

"Lia, it's not about winning or losing. It's about making my parents proud of me, about honoring my fellow trainees who'll be shipped overseas," answered Bill in a resigned tone. "It's not definite I'll go to Vietnam. Remember some are being sent to Korea."

"Korea,! Ask Brandy about Korea," I said, jumping to my feet and running into the kitchen. The tears slid over my checks—I actually bumped into the cash register and slumped down. The coins in the machine jingled.

Bill shuffled over and knelt down next to me on the floor. We held each other without saying a word. I felt him relax in my arms and whispered into his ear, "Bill, follow me." He got up and we walked side by side toward my apartment, our hands clutched to the point of pain.

Bill, sensing where we were headed, pulled back, "Hey you, I can't come to your room. McElvey will kick me and maybe you out of the program if he finds that I came in."

"Guess what? You're leaving anyway, and no one will tell on me." I said, half sarcastically, half resigned.

Bill nodded. We both knew this might be his last night at Monmouth.

"Bill, come in quietly. Carla's upstairs. She won't mind. She's already asked me if she could have Brandy stay here."

Bill followed me into my part of the apartment under the stairs. Bumping into a dresser next to my bed, he caused my father's picture to fall to the floor. A soft voice called from upstairs. "Lia, what're you doing up so late?" asked Carla.

"Shh, I'll tell you in the morning. You owe me one," I answered.

Gently, I took Bill's hand and led him to my bed where we snuggled in our clothes, pulling the down comforter over our enfolded bodies. I could feel his tears dampen the pillow as I kissed his cheeks, lips, and neck. He grabbed my hand, leading it slowly to his crotch where I felt his hard bulge.

I whispered softly, "No, I can't have sex with you. I don't want to get pregnant. Remember, I'm going to make it to the Olympics for both of us and for Damien."

"Damien?" whispered Bill.

"Yes, a friend of mine who died at Sugarloaf Mountain last winter."

"I knew a Damien from my early days in racing in New England. What happened to him?"

A tightness hit my chest as though an avalanche had just buried me. I choked up, sobbing. "He was killed in a downhill in the Eastern Championships. I'll tell you later." I pushed my head into his chest.

I felt Bill moan, "Damn."

Neither of us talked after this, but neither did we sleep. We held each other quietly, fearing we might wake Carla. The storm roared outside while we nestled, breathed together, hearts in sync. Slowly, I relaxed, losing all sense of time and individuality.

CHAPTER 15

Carla

I panicked at the sound of Carla's feet stepping out of bed above us. Hoping to distract her as she came downstairs, I sat up in my bed, pulling the comforter over Bill. Barely seeing through my dangled wisps of blonde hair, I demanded, "Who's there?"

"Excuse me, Lia, this is my room too," said Carla. "Time to get up, get ready for training."

"Oh, I didn't sleep well." My hand moved to cover the top of Bill's head. "I kept worrying about Bill," I answered.

"Hey, who's in your bed?" asked Carla, moving closer.

"Okay, I fess up. Bill spent the night with me." Fearing that she would be mad, I quickly added, "He's decided to go to Vietnam."

At the sound of the word Vietnam, Bill sat up in bed, struggling to understand where he was.

"What? What's going on?" he said confused.

Trying to defuse the situation, Carla pounced on Bill and me in bed and the three of us tussled for the top position like puppy dogs in a pen. Just like the old days, we started tickling each other until Carla jumped out of bed.

"Okay, you guys. Explain. You know you've broken McElvey's rule number two. No co-mingling in apartments," said Carla.

Bill stood up and raised his arms in the form of a cross as if he were a referee separating two boxers in the ring. "Don't worry Carla, we didn't do anything. Lia's upset because I've decided not to fight my army deployment." With no shirt on, he stood tall, lean, his muscular body overshadowing both of us. The machine-gun splatter of snow pricked the window. I felt weak as I looked at the size of his pecs and his smooth, hairless chest. He continued, "I'll be going downstairs to my room now. You two get ready for some serious training. I'm going to organize, make some calls, and then join you."

He left the two of us sitting on the side of the bed, watching him tiptoe out the room. His form became a shadow in the hall light and then a blur. As I began to sob, Carla put her arm around my shoulder. My body shook in slow shudders, then larger ones, like the first tremors of an earthquake.

"I'm so sorry, Lia," said Carla. "War sucks, no one wins."

I gasped, "That's what Brandy told me, too."

"Oh, did Brandy tell you his story about his escape from the Korean War?"

"Yup, last night while we were waiting for Bill to come down from the mountain, I heard his frightening tale," I said, trying to rub the pain from my face.

"Did Brandy tell you my story, too?" said Carla, nervously running her fingers through her closely cropped hair.

"What do you mean?"

"One thing that brought us together is our experience with war." said Carla, stiffening her back against my arm. She looked down, her face becoming younger, more vulnerable, not the sarcastic, funny Carla I knew.

"What war?" I demanded.

"World War II, dummy. Let me tell you my story," said Carla, placing a pillow against the wall and leaning back. I pushed back with her and helped her pull the white comforter over our legs.

"Well, where to begin," she said slowly. "I guess the beginning. You probably know that I'm Italian."

"Not exactly. I thought you grew up in California."

"Well, you know I was born in 1948. But what you don't know is that I was born in Italy. Yup, that's why I've straight black hair and a funny Roman nose."

"Hey, I've never made fun of your nose."

"Okay, before the war, before I was born, my parents were farmers who struggled to make a living. They worked picking crops, mostly potatoes, to support their first-born son, my brother, Roberto."

"Oh, that's the brother you always talk about."

"Hey, you, don't interrupt. Anyway when the war came, Mussolini's army tried to draft my father, but he had an injured leg. A tractor accident. So he stayed in our village to help with the crops. Then my mother, Victoria, became pregnant again."

"Okay, was that you?"

"Yup. She continued to work in the fields, because even though the war had ended, there still wasn't enough food in the village. I was born in May and she took to bed right away with a fever. There were no doctors in the village. They'd all gone into service and not returned. She died when I was two months old."

"Oh, I'm so sorry."

"With little food, no jobs, my father couldn't care for us, so he sent us to a Catholic orphanage. He left the nuns with one request—that Roberto and I be adopted together."

A silence ensued, broken only by the sound of the snow pelting the window. I looked across the room to my dresser to the picture of my dead mother.

"Hey, do you want to hear this story?" she asked.

"Of course, I was just looking at the picture of my dead mother."

"So I guess we don't know that much about each other even though we've been rooming together for two months. Neither of us has a mother."

"Yup, but please finish. This is your story."

"Right on. Well, since Roberto was four years older than me, he took care of me in the orphanage and made sure I had enough food." She paused as if a painful memory had ripped through her thoughts. "Often giving me part of his small evening dinner. Well, in about six months, a couple from Colorado inquired about adopting a boy. They had discovered the orphanage through the Catholic charities. They picked Roberto, and when it came time for him to go, he clung to me and said he wouldn't leave without me."

"Holy cow. How brave. So he won out."

"Yeah, so the two of us flew back to Colorado where I learned to ski. Skiing became my freedom, but my brother chose to become a student and go to college."

"Hey, I'd like to meet him some day. Does he look like you? Where's he now?"

"Slow down. In medical school, studying to be a doctor. Plus, as you know this keeps him from being drafted."

"So, how'd you get to Monmouth?"

"The same way you did. Coach McElvey saw me ski at Bend and invited me here. That was the year before he saw you, or he would've probably picked you over me. Who knows?"

"Come on. Right now, you have a better racing record than I do. Maybe we'll both make the Olympics." I let my words trail into a prayer-whisper.

"Hope so. Because one reason I want to make the Olympics is so I can get over to Europe to find my biological family." She hesitated and whispered, "If they remember me. My American parents never wanted me to contact my father or anyone else in Italy. I'll have to find the orphanage first."

"What a story," I said as Carla got up from the bed. "I can understand why you want to find your real family one day." I thought how simple my life had been in comparison. However, we did share two common bonds, our longing for our dead mothers and our dream of the Olympics.

She slipped upstairs, opened her dresser drawer, and brought down the picture of a dark-haired, oval-eyed, high-cheeked woman standing next to a rugged, broad-shouldered man. I immediately noticed that the tired beauty in her mother's face matched the pain in Carla's.

I touched the picture as I said, "What a beautiful woman. Of course, everyone in the village will remember her." I felt Carla touch my shoulder as I said this. I realized she probably hadn't told many people her sad tale. I was honored that she trusted me.

A silence filled the room like the quiet before a gentle snowfall. The clanging of pots in the kitchen broke our reverie. Stefan had started breakfast.

"I'll tell you what," I said, jumping up from the bed. "I'll help you write a letter to the orphanage. We can send a copy of the picture. Maybe the nuns can help you."

"But my parents will be mad," said Carla in a whisper.

"You don't have to tell them anything unless we find out more," I said. "It will be our secret."

Becoming very quiet, I looked at her mother's picture once more, thought about Bill and Brandy, and angrily spoke the words of Carl Sandburg, "Someday they'll give a war and nobody will come."

Like two conspirators, we vowed not to tell anyone of Carla's project as I threw on my ski pants and smiled, thinking of our morning ahead of powder skiing, followed by slalom training. I needed to get lost in the new snow, to forget what was happening to my friends, to our innocent Monmouth world.

CHAPTER 16

Training

By the first week of December, the pace of our training had changed. McElvey had decided we needed to begin time trials. He knew that at the Vail training camp, each run would be judged and logged by Coach Boast—from these results the European World Cup team would be picked.

I still loved the free skiing that McElvey allowed us before he set the gates for training. Each morning he'd lead the pack of us down the slopes. Each skier would vie for the opportunity to follow right behind him, trying to match him turn for turn, struggling to mimic his unpredictability. When my turn came, I made my legs pump instinctively, hopping trampoline-like from right to left. I had to look ahead in order to anticipate his turns or I'd run into him, an unforgiveable sin. Just like in racing, my peripheral vision followed the snow and my eyes led me to the next turn. I had to stay loose, balanced, and sensitive to the edge of my skis on the snow, as McElvey changed the rhythm to force us off balance. The same could happen in a slalom race, where a patch of ice could change my line. He taught us how to dance, edge to edge, thereby gaining speed after each turn.

After the third run down the face of Chair Three, he stopped us and said, "I'll go over to set up a slalom course on Chair One now. Please meet Guy at the top of Chair Three. He wants to take some photos of you before you all leave for Vail. We might be able to use these for publicity."

"Wow, do you mean we might be on a poster for Monmouth?" I asked. Instantly, I thought of the pride my father would feel.

"Hey, Lia, with your rice-blonde hair and snow tan, you could be a poster for a surfing magazine," said Stephanie with a sneer.

McElvey stepped forward and raised his hand. "Enough of this, please. Guy's looking for pictures of skiers, not models." Stephanie shook her dirty-blonde hair like a horse flicking its mane as a way to defuse her father's reprimand.

At the top of Chair Three, Guy waited for our party of seven. His Nikon camera hung unprotected, swinging like a flask around his neck. "Please kindly line up against the rock, so I can get a group picture with the cornice in the background. Uhh, Coach McElvey will let me have you for only thirty minutes," he said in a stern, professional manner.

In the group photo shoot, I nestled between Bill and Becky, knowing one day I would cherish this picture. My six friends, the white untracked snows of Monmouth, and the cerulean-blue sky burned into my mind like a nuclear flash.

After the camera clicked ten times, Guy pointed toward the steep slopes below the cornice, asking, "Could you all ski over to that slope and climb up toward the overhang at the top?"

I loved the feeling of throwing my skis on my right shoulder, anticipating each boot kick up the steep slope through the two feet of powder. I made sure to follow Bill's footsteps for ease as breaking track was hell. "Hey, Bill, did you ever climb Mt. Washington back East?" I asked.

Bill stopped, looked down, grimacing before he said, "Wow, do I ever remember trips up there. My family used to make a weekend of climbing on skis up the Sherburne trail to the base of Hillman's Highway."

"Hmm, I wonder if we were ever skiing on Mt. Washington at the same time," I said. My thoughts flashed to a warm spring day with my mother and father standing together just below the Headwall on Mt. Washington. In happier days, they loved to ski together.

"Well, since I'm older than you by three years, I doubt it," he paused, reflecting. "Do you remember the story of the young man who died by falling over the Headwall and into the crevasse? I think it was 1962."

"I'm not sure which year it was, but I was only 10 years old then and my parents wouldn't tell me everything that happened. You know, they thought it would scare me. Mmm, but did I ever love those special ski trips with them ... I was often the youngest on the mountain."

"Same for me. I, too, liked those early days of skiing without lifts. Such innocence. Anyway, we need to be careful here as we climb up, because sometimes a crevasse can form." He pointed up to the overhanging lip. "Watch carefully and step in my footsteps."

In the shadow of the cornice, the group's single line traversed up the 45 degree slope, resembling a snake slithering toward its prey. We had to kick twice into the loose snow on the steeping slope. The powder, above our knees at this point, made each step more difficult. Soon I had to turn my skis sideways across my shoulders, parallel to the slope, in order to progress up. Otherwise, my ski tips would bump into the rising slope.

From below, Guy's disembodied voice said, "Okay, don't try to go over the cornice. Stop below it and get ready to make some fresh tracks. Please leave time between skiers, so I can prepare the camera."

I snapped into my bindings as Becky said, "Oldest first." She pushed off to the right, making the most perfect turns I'd ever seen. Her powder-blue snow pants pushed the snow to the side, spraying like a water skier.

Carla jumped in behind, crossing Becky's track with figure eights. Wren took off her goggles and hat in an attempt at vanity, her short brown hair flowing behind, and said, "Watch this—I'm going to head toward the rock on the right and hit it with speed. I'll bet I can get some air for my picture."

Stepping in front of Stephanie, I said, "Remember I'm older, so I get to go before you."

"Why do I always have to be last?" whined Stephanie, also removing her hat and sun glasses.

"No, Bill and Brandy will be last. Ladies before gentlemen." I laughed and looked up into Bill's blue eyes.

He winked, saying, "Okay, you can go before me, but remember to leave some fresh snow for me."

Stephanie jumped in front of me and took off toward the rock outcropping where she found a place to launch herself, copying Carla. She crossed her skis in mid-air and landed face first. I realized I'd have to forgo my turn at a picture in order to help Stephanie out of the deep snow. I skied over to her and pulled on her arm. As she lifted her snow-covered head, I heard a yell from above the cornice, a war-whoop that echoed through the U-shaped valley of Canyon Run.

"Catch this one, Guy!" yelled Bill. I turned to see Bill and Brandy propel themselves off the ten-foot cornice into the fresh powder. The two daredevils looked like the Blue Angel jets, dangling contrails of snow behind them. Both of their arms were extended from their bodies as they tried balancing to gain extra buoyancy. Bill's ecstatic grin reminded me of the enigmatic smile of a Buddha statue: pure bliss. Landing, their knees thumped into their chests, slowing them a bit, before they picked up speed and made three screaming C's down the broad face of the mountain. I took a deep breath, realizing that their risk-taking mentality was embedded in both ski racers and soldiers alike.

When our group of free spirits reassembled at the bottom near Guy, he said. "Now take off to the top of Chair One. I'm going down to get these pictures developed. I will try to have the pictures before you leave for Vail in four days."

Bill led the group down to the top of the racecourse where McElvey stood—his stop-watch in hand. "Okay, I hope you had fun. Please catch your breath before taking your training runs. I'll go to the bottom and signal when you should start."

Feeling worried, I asked, "Do these times mean anything?"

"No, Lia, not yet. Today, you can try different lines to see which will be fastest," he said, moving his hands as if tracing a course. Then, demonstrating, his elegant, muscular body took off into rhythmic, perfectly matched turns.

Leaning forward, poles under my armpits, I watched Becky, Wren, and Carla ski off one at a time. I compared their lines on the course, realizing I could hold a tighter line if I began the first turn by stepping uphill.

Bill saw me hesitate. "Hey, Lia, try to cut gate #4 early and lift your legs before the bump. You'll be able to hold a tighter turn," he said, his tone patronizing. I smiled at him with an air of confidence. To taunt me, he stepped in front and took off ahead of me. I saw he had a litheness, a balance, a fluidity to his skiing, which would make him a top racer for the US, if only he could have a chance. He looked like a coyote running in the tall grass dodging bullets from a farmer's 22 rifle.

Quickly, Stephanie stepped up to the start. "Is it okay if I take off before you?" she said.

"Be my guest," I said, bowing as if to the queen, "I'm still studying my line." I moved my hand in front of my eyes to trace a perfect run before I actually jumped onto the course. Closing my eyes, I felt a fresh breeze caress my cheek. When I opened them, I noticed Stephanie hadn't waited for her father's signal to start. In fact, she jumped the signal by at least a second. I thought, *That's an easy way to get a faster time.*

When my turn came, I prepared carefully for McElvey's signal to start. Looking down, I shivered nervously. I squatted, planted my poles in front of my tips, and bounded into the course, gaining confidence as I discovered a faster, shorter line than the others. I had the strength, the acumen, and the ability to carry more speed through each gate. I planted my pole in the fall-line before each turn, rolled my ankles, dropped my hip, clipped the underside of the gates with my hands, absorbed the ruts and relaxed. To start each turn, I stepped uphill, gaining an extra foot of vertical before I dove into the next gate. Each turn flowed flawlessly into the next, just as when I had skied behind McElvey on the open slope. My springy legs followed the terrain; I hugged the poles and like a race car, accelerated out of every turn.

At the finish, McElvey yelled across to me, "Lia, great run. How on earth did you hold your line through the last flush with all that speed? You beat Stephanie by two seconds; she had the fastest time for the girls.

"Thanks, I really worked to shorten the radius of my turns. Bill taught me this."

Bill, skiing over to me and putting his arm around me, said, "Lia, you have it. You can go as far as you want."

"Yeah, but I want you to be with me," I said, looking longingly into his dark blue eyes.

"No, I've other obligations; you know that," he said slowly. "In fact, I've not told you yet, but I'll … " he stammered, " … I'll not be going to Vail with you." He looked down at his boots, hiding the pain in his face. "I've just received a letter saying that I have to report to Fort Devens on December 15th."

"Not fair! That's the day we leave for Vail," I said stamping my skis into the snow.

"I guess that my destiny will be different from yours," he said. "However, I'll live vicariously through you. I know you'll write as often as you can." He skied off toward the lift.

I didn't know whether to feel excitement about my fast time trial or anger at a world that seemed to take away those closest to me. I slapped my ski pole on the ground and the gun-shot snap of the aluminum shaft made me jump.

CHAPTER 17

Guy

My stress doubled now that I was in a countdown for Bill's deployment and my trip to the Vail training camp. The lack of new snow made the mountain an icy, wind-packed bobsled run. The skiing became dangerous. McElvey decided to limit our free skiing and had us train slalom in the morning and giant slalom in the afternoons. Often I struggled to leave my cozy bed, especially when the temperatures dropped to 10 degrees.

One evening, Bill and I met in the laundry room to wash and sort clothes. We cuddled against the pulsating machine, imagining a time when we might truly share our bodies. The warm heat from the dryer, the smell of Tide detergent, and our isolation helped me forget the future for an instant.

"Hey, Bill, do you think I'll need any dressy clothes for Vail?" I said, bending over to open the dryer door.

The door banged against the side, emphasizing Bill's answer. "Uhh, dressy clothes. No, in fact right now I'd like to imagine you without any clothes."

I slammed the dryer door closed and turned to him with my mouth open. "Is that all you guys ever think about?"

"Well at this moment, yes. I don't want to think about the future."

"Okay, okay. You made your decision to go to war. Now live with it," I said angrily. Moving toward him, I threw my arms around his shaking body. "I'm sorry. We're both feeling the stress of your leaving."

"I'm angry, Lia. You're packing for a future spot on the Olympic team. I am packing for ..." At which point his voice trailed off.

To diffuse the tension in the room, I changed the subject. "Hey, I know. Let's see if we can find Guy tomorrow to get the pictures he took." Pausing before slowly adding, "Then we can each carry a memory of our carefree times here at Monmouth."

"Good idea," said Bill, lowering his head, "It's been almost three days since he took all those shots on the cornice." Looking toward the mountain, he continued, "I would love to have that shot of Brandy and me exploding over the lip and, the group picture as well. And, of course, one of you, your blonde hair, pug nose, and bronze skin all set against Pacific-blue sky."

"Okay, let's ask McElvey whether we can borrow the company station wagon to drive up to Guy's house. I think it's on the Old Monmouth Road near Pierce's Lake." I giggled, imagining the two of us driving the narrow, winding road up to Guy's small cabin, probably perched over the cliffs. The two of us alone.

"Oops, I forgot I promised McElvey I'd shovel the back deck after training tomorrow."

The next morning I jumped out of bed early, hoping to catch McElvey before he left for the snow-cat sheds. Running through the grand room to get to his apartment on the other side of the building, I passed the fire still glowing from the numerous logs Bill and I had piled on late into the night. I smiled, thinking how close the two of us had become in the last few days. I saw McElvey heading down the back stairs, lost in thought. "Eh ... eh, excuse me, Coach," I said.

"Lia, what are you doing up so early?" said McElvey, adjusting his collared shirt.

"I'm having trouble sleeping now that we've only one day left before we head to Vail."

"Well, I hope you're packed and have your skis sharpened and waxed."

"Of course. Will you be coming to Vail with us?"

"Absolutely. I wouldn't miss this training camp for the world. With the times you, Stephanie, Wren, and Becky have been posting, all of you should make the team to Europe this winter."

"What about Carla?"

"She's not been working very hard recently; I'm afraid that Coach Boast will consider this when making his decision." Looking me straight in the eyes, he added, "Has she been distracted by something?"

I didn't want to jeopardize her stay at Monmouth, so I chose my words carefully before saying, "Well, maybe it's her time of month."

He blushed and said, "Oh ..."

"Anyway, I wanted to ask if you've seen Guy recently. He promised he'd bring the pictures of the photo shoot before we left." Looking down, I realized I was still in my pajamas. "I wanted to make sure that Bill had some to take with him to ... "

Before I could finish, he interrupted, " ... to Vietnam? I know what you're thinking. No, I haven't seen Guy, but that's not unusual. Often he stays up in his cabin for days ... he's a strange one."

"Okay, could I borrow the station wagon this afternoon and drive up to find him?"

"Of course, but don't skip out early on training."

"Never. I wouldn't miss our last day of practice."

"Also, be careful on the way up to Guy's place. The road narrows, and there are no guard rails along the drop-off."

"See you at practice," I said, turning and prancing back to my room.

In the main dining room, a stream of morning sun broke through the plate glass window, spotlighting the two gray Adirondack chairs facing the fire place. The smell of Stefan's freshly baked sweet rolls made me realize how early I'd gotten up.

At 3:30 after our practice, I ran down to the office to get the company station wagon's keys. I hadn't told Becky, Carla, or Wren about my plans, because selfishly I wanted to drive alone to Guy's cabin.

Fritz, the accountant, opened the door to the office and said in surprise, "Well, well, why are you down here rather than getting organized for your trip to Vail tomorrow?" This loveable, short German had been with McElvey since the inception of Monmouth; many claimed he was the financial brains behind its success. He always treated us as if we were his nieces.

"Oh, excuse me, Fritz, McElvey told me I could borrow the car to go to Guy's cabin to retrieve some pictures," I said, nervously brushing my hair away from my eyes.

Standing up with his shoulders barely above the desktop, he scolded, "To Guy's cabin? Are you aware of how dangerous that could be? The road is rarely plowed that far out. The cliffs drop off with no retaining walls."

"Oh, I've been there before," I said, my lie causing me to blush.

"Okay, but I'll bet you've never been out there after a snowfall."

"Okay, okay. I'll be careful," I reached for the keys.

The tan station wagon, nestled near the far snow bank in the parking lot, looked like a toy car against the 10-foot snow drift. I shivered, my heart pounding, as I unlocked the driver's door. I'd not driven for months—in fact not since I'd left Vermont.

Driving down from Monmouth Mountain toward town, I felt the car skid twice when I braked on the hairpin turns. I remembered my father had taught me to pump the brakes in a slide and to steer into the direction of the skid to regain control. I thrived on the adrenaline rush that turned my fear to confidence; just like in a downhill race.

In town, I passed the doctor's office and the company gas station, all owned by McElvey, who had built this burgeoning ski town. The Old Monmouth Road turned right and swept uphill along the rounded back of the mountain. Just a mile out of town, the buildings stopped, the snow banks grew higher, and the road narrowed. The snow no longer piled up on the left side of the one-lane road, because there was no edge to the road, just a drop-off to the valley below.

Slowing the car to a crawl, I opened the window to listen to the sound of my tires on the snow-covered road. Again, my father had taught me that the spinning noise would tell me whether the car was slipping. The crunching noise assured me I'd good traction.

Ahead lay a most frightening sight: the lava cauldron, which had produced the Monmouth cinder cone, was darkening in the fading afternoon sun. Wisps of snow, dancing like dragon's tongues, flew into the air from the surrounding peaks. The plug in the middle made the crater resemble the umbilicus of the earth. Scared, I imagined that I was witnessing the formation of the earth in all its violence: the lava fires, the smoke, the burning pumice. *Why had Guy built his cabin overhanging this hellish scene?* I wondered.

Just as the road narrowed to impassible, Guy's cabin appeared on the left, perching on the cliff's edge as if guarding this gate to the underworld. His black pickup blocked the entrance to the house, so I had to leave my car in the road. There were no wires leading into his house—Guy probably lived without electricity or telephone.

Because the path to the front door hadn't been shoveled, my only choice to get in was to push around the truck and follow a narrow path to the back deck. On tip-toe, glancing down between the deck boards into the canyon, I couldn't imagine how he'd ever built his house over the cliff's edge.

Turning the corner toward the back door, I realized that the three picture-windows along the deck gave him an unobstructed view of the center of the old volcano. The distant peaks, lit by the setting sun, were reflected in the windows. Superimposed over this surrealistic image, my reflection startled me. My shadow darkened the snow. Holding my breath, passing the first picture window, I saw a small form jump from the couch inside. *Did Guy have a cat?* I stopped to look in the window, but didn't want to get too close. I worried about being rude if Guy were in the room. Gasping, I saw five more cats jump from behind the couch.

Approaching the redwood door, I heard only the sound of the wind rushing up between the boards. The strong gust forced me back, warning me not to enter. I knocked three times. No answer. I called Guy's name. Three times the name echoed off the rock cliff. After waiting for any response, I tried the door. The knob turned easily. *Should I open the door and call again?* The squeaking door made a cat hiss.

I poked my head in, glancing around the paper-strewn living room. Guy had only three wooden chairs, a table and a couch. Like Thoreau, this Austrian bachelor had few visitors. Two more cats glided around the couch. Their black tails caught my eye just before I saw him or rather his cowboy boots, poking straight up from the floor, partially covered by the hem of his torn, faded jeans. A strange smell of decaying hamburger made me want to leave.

I hesitated for a second, *Should I go in or return to my car and get help?* I called his name once more before crossing the pine floor. My after-ski boots scuffling broke the silence in the room. Slowly stepping around the corduroy couch, I gasped when three cats jumped away from Guy's face. I screamed, horrified as he had no face. The cats had eaten the flesh from his cheeks and chin, revealing bone and red sinew. One lidless eye stared blankly toward the ceiling. Blood had congealed in a pool on the floor.

Turning, I ran toward the door, slamming it behind me, so the cats couldn't follow me, and jumped into the company car. Driving away, I no longer feared the drop-off to my right. The tires skidded, but I pumped the brakes, hugging the rock wall on my left.

In town, I stopped at Doctor Seaton's office. Not bothering to turn off the engine, I rushed into the office. "Doctor Seaton. Help. Guy ... is dead." Collapsing on the floor in tears, I was vaguely aware of the nurse's comforting arm around my quivering body.

CHAPTER 18

Departure

The next morning, I woke to Carla prodding me, "Hey, Lia, get up. We'll be packing the car this morning and leaving for Vail by noon." I couldn't remember how I'd gotten back to my apartment and my bed.

"What … what's happening?" I said, feeling as if I were descending from a cotton cloud, dizzy and light-headed.

Carla sat on the bed and caressed my hair. "You don't remember now, but Dr. Seaton brought you back here yesterday afternoon and gave you a pill—250 milligrams of Noctec, I think he said."

"What's that?"

"A sleeping pill. You were in a state. He felt you needed to sleep off the nightmare."

I sat up, rubbed my eyes and shuttered. The image of Guy's ghoulish face flashed through my thoughts, then Damien's crushed skull followed. Carla tried to hold me as I broke into uncontrollable sobs.

"Oh, Carla, you won't believe what I saw."

"Yup. Last night Dr. Seaton explained everything to us. You couldn't have done anything for Guy. He died of a heart attack."

"It's so awful. I was … "

"… Shh, try not to talk about it now. Let's get up and finish packing for Vail. We can talk in the car during our two-day drive. I'm sure someone will tell you Guy's story if you ask."

A soft rapping on the door startled me. Becky poked her head in and joined our huddle. Wren followed; although reluctant to get on the bed, she put her arms around the three of us. I never felt closer to my three friends. We held each other in this strange bond of solidarity, a friendship that only adversity can create.

The smell of bacon and eggs made Becky take charge. "Lia, Carla, Wren, can you get organized now? We need to get the station wagon packed," she said. Realizing maybe she'd not shown enough sympathy, she added, "Lia, I'm so sorry for what happened to you. We'll talk about everything when we get into the car." She looked frustrated, but then she smiled. "You know we'll support you. Remember, there's no 'I' in team." She gently patted the top of my head.

My sobbing made the group draw closer together. Bill's voice came through the door, breaking our huddle, "Hey, everyone, I can't come in. Could you meet me for breakfast right away? I want to see Lia."

Remembering I needed to get packed, I jumped up. Not only did I have to get my belongings sorted, I had to say good-bye to Bill, who soon would be catching the Reno-bound bus and then his flight to Fort Devens. Fortunately, I'd already laid out most of my clothes on my dresser. I hoped we would have a laundry in Vail, as in no way did I have enough underwear and socks for two weeks.

After breakfast, I dragged my allotted two bags, a backpack and boot bag, toward McElvey, already waiting in the parking lot to load the station wagon. Always the engineer, he knew how to fill every corner of the car. He lashed the six ski bags to the roof rack, each containing three pairs of skis.

By the time Stephanie came out of the lodge, Becky, Wren, Carla, and I had already loaded our belongings into the car. McElvey stepped down from the floorboard and stomping his boots in disgust, he scolded, "Steph, I told you that you could only bring one suitcase."

"Come on, Dad, like I've too much stuff. Remember, unlike the others, you know, I still have to bring my school books." She sneered at us.

"Okay, we'll have to put your book bag on the passenger's floor. We're already overloaded with three of us in the front and three in the back," he said, scratching his head.

Bill then put his arm around me and said pleading, "Coach, I forgot to ask if you could fit me in just as far as the bus station below Deadman Summit? I've only got a small duffle bag. I've already shipped my skis and clothes home to Concord, Mass."

McElvey stood up straight and looked at our beleaguered group huddled around the car, "Okay, okay. What a day. We go to Vail and you leave for the Army. All of you go get a few snacks from Stefan in the kitchen. Meet me here in fifteen." He smiled, pointing toward the front door of the main lodge.

Carla took off first and Stephanie jumped ahead, saying, "I'll beat you there."

Becky shook her head in disbelief. "Always competitive."

Wren followed, humming to herself. "Climb every mountain."

Bill and I walked side by side, trying to match each other's stride—left, right, left, right. Entering the great room and striding past our Adirondack chairs, we must have been quite a sight, dressed in our matching red sweaters with blue stripes on the sleeves. The fire crackled next to a little girl who looked up adoringly at Bill and me and gave us the thumbs up. "Good luck, racers." I guess she knew the Monmouth team was off to the training camp.

I was drawn to the smell of Stefan's cooking, especially his schnitzel, pasta, and fresh bread, and now realized that I would be leaving this for a while. Breathing deeply, I savored the aromas. If I made the team to Europe, I wouldn't return to Monmouth until March—almost three months. We walked past the line of skiers who'd come in for lunch, the combined smell of their wet, wool hats and wood smoke making me sneeze.

I led Bill down the pastry aisle—the smell of the apple sticky-rolls reminded me of the cider that my father used to make from our apple trees. I stopped and grabbed one.

Bill took my hand, "Hey, how're you going to pack that in the car. Besides that's not good for training." Chastised, I put the soft pastry back.

We continued past the fresh bread, the rolls piled like snowballs, and finally the pasta bar. The smell of garlic made my mouth water. Today the cook had planned to serve chicken alfredo, my favorite. Wow, was I ever going to miss these delicacies. I realized how lucky I'd been for the last two months to have such delicious food, better than any home cooking I'd known. Next came the hamburger bar, an array of meat sizzling on the burner. The steam hit my eyes in an overheated cloud. Beyond was my favorite, the salad bar, resting behind a glass barrier. I'd always loved making a fresh salad for lunch: piles of lettuce, sliced tomatoes, diced peppers, crumbly feta cheese, minced onions, whole pickles, and diced cucumbers. The homemade balsamic vinegar dressing gave the lettuce a bittersweet taste. The colorful mix of reds, greens, yellows stood out like a tropical garden, a contrast to the sterile white of our winter world.

Finally, I came to the dessert rack. Here Stefan had placed his famous cherry tortes, blueberry cheesecake, and chocolate mousse. Stopping, I put my nose close to the tray, wishing I could sample a small bite. "Uh, uh," said Bill again. "Remember, training, discipline."

So, I wasn't to have any of this. Stefan signaled to me to follow him to the back of the kitchen, next to the freezer. The paying customers in line looked angry that they had to wait. I shrugged apologetically, and passing them, I joined the other racers in a semi-circle outside the metallic freezer door. Stefan stepped forward. "Well, girls, we'll miss you here," he laughed, "especially when you raid my custard and ice cream at night." Turning toward the freezer door, he continued, "Ja vohl. I've prepared a small treat for you to take in the car."

I looked at Becky, who smiled with the telling look that she knew exactly what was about to happen. After all, she'd made this trip before. The metal door opened, a burst of frozen air pushed me back, and out sprang Fritz, Brandy, and three other staff members. Each had a paper bag in hand. In unison, they said. "Good luck! Make us proud of you." They launched into what had become our team song, "My skis are the things that give me my wings." Fritz stepped forward, stood on tiptoes, and kissed me on the cheek before handing me a brown lunch bag. I blushed.

Becky stepped up and spoke, "Thanks for thinking of us. We'll spread the name Monmouth Mountain across America and Europe this season." I nodded and grabbed Bill's hand—I felt I was saying goodbye to my family, to what had become my new home.

Carla stepped over to me, whispering, "Could you stall the group for about ten minutes? I want to say good-bye to Brandy."

"Try to hurry. I don't want to get in trouble," I said, "What's up?"

"I'll tell you in the car. Brandy's in big trouble."

I ran outside to the car, panicked that the rest had gotten there ahead of me. McElvey leaned against the overloaded station wagon and said impatiently, "Okay, what's going on?"

"Uh ... uh, Carla needs a few minutes to say good-bye to Brandy," I said, looking down to avoid his glare.

His silence made me realize I didn't understand the depth of the problem between Carla and Brandy. Before I could ask, Carla came running out, slipping on the icy path. She crashed into McElvey and me before hitting the car. In a stern, thunderous voice, McElvey said, "Okay, get in. We've much to talk about on the trip to Vail ... yup, all two days."

No one spoke on the descent from Monmouth. Stephanie and Becky sat in the front seat next to coach. Wren, Carla, and Bill squished in the back while I sat on his lap, snuggling into his chest and smelling his cologne. The roar of the engine filled an awkward void.

"Enough silence," said Bill. "This isn't the end of the world. Yes, I'm leaving for the army. My choice. You're going to Vail. Your choice. Let's all do our best and keep in touch."

McElvey, sensing the tension, said, "Bill, I'm proud of you for your decision. You'll always have a home here at Monmouth when you return." His voice trailed off as though he doubted what he was saying.

I gave Bill a hug, saying, "I'll write you every day from Vail."

At the bus stop, a primitive shelter, Bill lifted me from his lap, jumped out, grabbing his duffel bag. Aware of the awkwardness of the moment, he said, "Don't get out. Everything will fall down. See you in a year."

As I turned to wave, squinting into the sun, my last image of him reminded me of a shimmering impressionist painting. The cornice of Monmouth created a halo over his head and the two snowy couloirs, falling behind each of his shoulders, resembled wings. I whispered to myself, "Good night, sweet prince."

CHAPTER 19

The Desert

We drove into the wild west—no stop signs, no speed limits, no gas stations, and, of course, no houses. Route 6 east of Elko, Nevada, and the Great Basin was a straight line until it came to a ridge of hills. I'd only seen pictures in *National Geographic* of this high eastern desert, an ancient ocean where dinosaurs once roamed.

I poked Becky in the front seat, asking, "How … how do people make a living out here in Nevahdah?"

Carla laughed, "Did you say Nevahdah? You can't even pronounce it right. We say Ne-vadd-a."

Becky answered in her condescending tone, "Hey, you Easterner, welcome to the real West. Remember, this land has only been settled for about ninety years." She pointed out the window. "Duh, didn't you ever study how the miners broke trail through here in 1878? So dangerous, many died on their way to the silver mines in Bodie, even Monmouth. For us Californians, we studied this in elementary school; meanwhile, you Easterners, well, you probably learned about your pampered Transcendentalists, your transparent eyeballs. Same time period. Different folks." She grinned, thinking she'd one-upped me.

I hated being singled out as the only Easterner. I sighed, once again missing Bill, my Eastern support. "Oh yeah," I paused, closing my eyes before continuing, "I remember … I saw a few of those mines on my way to Guy's cabin." My voice trailed off as I regretted bringing up the subject. I felt an awkward shift of position, followed by the sound of shuffling feet.

Becky took charge, turning her head toward the back seat, "Okay, Lia, since you mentioned Guy, do you want to hear how he got to Monmouth?" I nodded. Quickly, turning to McElvey driving beside her, she asked, "Coach, will you tell us how you met Guy?"

McElvey pushed the accelerator to 80 miles per hour; the road straightened, the sagebrush flew by. He said, "Before I tell you his story," he paused, "Do something for me. Each of you put your head out the window ... I want you to know what 80 mph feels like on your face."

When my turn came, I crawled over Wren and stuck my blonde head out and felt the blast rip my hair backwards. The wind distorted my mouth and lips and pressed my eyes closed. For an instant, I felt as though my face would rip off.

"Holy cow," I said, bumping my chin as I brought my head inside, "I'm sure glad we wear goggles when we ski at that speed!"

McElvey laughed, "You probably won't hit more than 60 mph. The FIS rules state that girls shouldn't exceed that speed in the downhills."

I didn't find this reassuring. Straightening up, he raised his chin, "Okay, sit back and I'll tell you about Guy and how we met." His voice lowered as if speaking a eulogy. "To the point, in Austria, Guy was a famous racer. He arrived in Monmouth in 1956 just after the Olympics. They were held in Cortina, Italy, you know. He'd captured a silver in the slalom and was confident he could make good money as a ski instructor in America. You probably don't know that these were the first Olympics to be televised. Well, since the New England ski areas already had their Olympic ski legends such as the Austrian Hannes Schneider, Guy decided to strike out West, just like the silver miners you mentioned."

He slowed the car, finding his words carefully. "I think he took a train to Los Angeles and hitchhiked his way up to Monmouth. I'd just built Chair One and Two and needed a ski-school director." He paused, remembering a scene he didn't want to talk about. "Unfortunately, Guy wanted to take control not just of the ski school but the mountain as well. After three years, I had to let him go, but I allowed him to stay on as a photographer and instructor … "

Becky, wanting more information, broke in, " … I always sensed a rift between you and Guy"

McElvey put his hand to his mouth. "Let's not get into it. Let's say we respected each other, but he wouldn't accept my leadership. So he started to undermine my authority with the employees. In fact, I almost lost control of the mountain."

"But Dad, why on earth did you let him stay at all?" asked Stephanie as though she had never heard this story before.

McElvey swallowed and continued, "Because your mother didn't want me to fire him. She liked him and he'd no family or home to return to. I guess I was a little jealous of him, so I limited his time at Monmouth. As you know, Guy often spent days in his cabin."

"How did he earn money?" I asked innocently.

"Well, I made sure he had a small monthly wage and he always had free meals in the lodge with the rest of us. As you know, he built his cabin all by himself."

I looked out the window into the unending sand, shivering at the barrenness of this uncivilized land, of Guy's lonely death. The endless blinking of the dotted yellow line flickered in my eyes. A heaviness settled on me. Slowly, closing my eyes, I let the thumping of the tires put me to sleep.

I woke with Carla shoving me. The car had stopped. "Hey you sleepy head, we've been traveling for five hours. McElvey wants us to get out and stretch our legs by running up that sand hill."

"What the heck?" I said covering my yawn. Carla opened the door. And a blast of cold air hit me.

Becky, Wren, and Stephanie had already jumped out and started up the hill. "Get going," yelled McElvey. "You can catch them!" He waved his hands in the direction of a small cinder cone.

I realized this was a way for us to make a pit stop in the desert, but before we could pee, we had to run straight up the 500-foot dirt mound. Stepping into the loose sand, I learned that each stride would take a double effort, similar to running up an ocean dune. If I did a duck walk, my feet held. Also, by zigzagging I was able to find the roots of the brown sage plants where the footing improved. The smell of crushed sage tingled my nose as sweat dripped from my brow, relieving some of the dryness of my lips, and my arms swung apelike. I laughed to myself thinking, *how stupid I looked.*

At the top, Stephanie, Carla, Wren and Becky gave me high-fives and encouraged me to sit on a wind-sculpted rock. "Great job," said Becky, "you just passed the test. McElvey sometimes throws out the most absurd requests, but we do them because we respect him. He knows we need to stay in shape during these two days of travel. Hey, did you notice how much stronger you feel at this lower altitude? That's the way you'll feel skiing at Vail." Smirking she added, "And while we're here, we all need to go to the bathroom."

Each took a turn going behind a granite outcropping. While waiting, I leaned against the cold boulder, feeling my heart pounding and listening to the wind rustle across the grains of sand. There was no vegetation here except a few spotty patches of brown sage and greasewood. How strange not to see trees, even telephone poles, to measure distance. To the west, the Sierra Mountains were dark waves, rolling in a haze of dust. Below, across the dry basin, small dirt roads branched like slug trails, to where I couldn't guess. There were no buildings any-where—I felt small, unimportant.

"Who would want to live here, even drive out here?" I asked Wren, who waited her turn to go behind the rock.

She responded, "First, this is the only road east. Second, the cattle ranchers use this land for free-range grazing. You'll rarely see animals, but occasionally you'll see the windmills pumping water from under the ground for them. Right, I know because I've been to my uncle's ranch just east of Ely."

I stared into the distance, wondering what the original settlers who pulled wagon trains must have felt as they struggled to survive in this place. I asked, "Is this where the Donner party crossed? Where they first saw the Sierra Mountains?" Looking to the west, I continued, "What a horrible death awaited them."

Wren groaned, "Oh, so you've read about their tales of cannibalism."

Surprised, I answered, "Of course, this tale is a part of American history, all school children study them—even in the east." I rolled my eyes.

"Beat you down!" yelled Stephanie as she took off toward the station wagon, eager to win her dad's approval.

I jumped behind the rock to relieve myself. Lowered my jeans and squatting, I let my eyes traced the straight line of the black road we'd just traveled. The skin-splitting dryness of the wind chafed my butt. How I wanted to be done with this place, this waterless ocean. For the first time, I truly missed New England, our lush fields and forests. I squinted in the brightness of the unfiltered sun. Silence, emptiness, loneliness.

I pushed my finger through the sand, trying to write Bill's name, but before I could finish the wind came up and erased each letter. I shivered. Faintly, from below I heard my name called. Reaching for my underwear, I saw a red spot in the crotch. *Damn,* I thought. *I'm not supposed to get my period for another week. This'll definitely complicate the training at Vail.* I grabbed a Kleenex from my pocket and stuffed it in my underwear.

Bounding down the hill, flailing my arms and legs, I struggled for balance. My feet rocked left and right like a clock's pendulum while my eyes stayed straight. I leapt off a rock, flew ten feet in the air, and did a 360 turn.

The fifteen minute run to the top had turned into a 50 second downhill race back to the comfort of my friends, to my moveable home.

CHAPTER 20

Belonging

Once I was safely settled back into the car, in my same seat, Becky turned to me, a cloth bag dangling from her fingers. "Take this; find the knitting needles that you want. On our past trips, each of us has knitted a hat for a friend. It helps pass the time."

I picked out a skein of blue yarn, and Carla gave me a pair of round, plastic needles. She showed me how to cast stitches on the needle before beginning the rhythmic process of knitting. Watching my clumsiness, she put her hand on the wool to stop me, "If you are going to knit this for Bill, you'll need to start with 100 stitches."

"How did you know?" I said softly.

"Just guessed. I'm going to knit mine for Brandy."

"Good idea. What's going on with him anyway?" I asked, whispering in her ear, not sure I wanted to hear the answer.

Timidly broaching the subject, she asked McElvey, "Coach, do ... do you want to tell ... tell Lia about Brandy or can I?" She struggled with each word.

Everyone stopped knitting, the awkward silence amplifying the roar of the engine. "Well, go ahead, Carla, I'd like to hear how you explain this," said McElvey in a fatherly tone.

Carla began, "Okay, you probably don't know that Brandy has been asked to leave Monmouth." She trailed her words at the end, while running her fingers through her bangs in an attempt to cover her eyes.

"Why?' I said, raising my hands naïvely

"Well, he was caught with Mary Jane." said Carla.

"With whom?"

The group of girls giggled. McElvey slowed the car to make sure he could hear Carla's answer.

Wren interrupted, trying to diffuse the awkwardness, "Hey, stupid! Don't you know about drugs?"

My jaw dropped as I realized my naïveté. "Okay, okay. You mean he had some marijuana?"

"Duh," said Becky. "You know the rules: no drinking, no smoking, if you want to be a part of the Monmouth team." McElvey smiled and nodded. I remembered the tacit agreement between us and him: he'd pay all our bills if we worked hard and lived up to his high standards.

He broke in, "Yes, and when you get to Vail, you'll be under the supervision of Coach Boast. He's just been made the official head of the whole US Ski Team organization." He waved his finger, accentuating his warning. "Ah, but once there, you'll learn that his male racers don't follow the same rules as I expect from you. Don't be swayed. Remember, you're going to Vail for one reason only— to make the team to Europe and then to the 1972 Olympics." He stopped and squinted, and said very slowly, "There'll always be those who will try to distract you."

No one spoke as we absorbed this caveat. One by one we picked up our knitting, the unison clicking of the needles, affirming the cohesiveness of our group, of this skein of friends.

CHAPTER 21

Vail

McElvey spun the California station wagon off Route 70, skidding into the snowbound parking lot of Vail on December 19. I gasped with wonder. The lights of the Vail Inn reflected up the steep slopes, turning the snow into a white sheen and the building into a cruise ship adrift on a foamy sea.

Christmas decorations—red, green and white lights—hung from every pole and balcony. A massive spruce tree, also festooned with lights, welcomed us to this neo-Tyrolean village.

Holding my breath, I poked Carla next to me. "Oh, my gosh, look, look!" I gasped, now aware that I had awakened Becky, Wren, and Stephanie, too. McElvey stopped the car so the headlights pointed up the groomed trail behind the inn. Red and blue, rectangular downhill-flags snaked down the slope, the distance between them telling me this would be a very fast race. Tightness seized my stomach.

The course ended right in the village. Bleachers surrounded the roped-in finish area, which was surrounded by banners advertising Bouton goggles, Scott poles, and Kneissl skis. With an air of authority, McElvey turned to us, "Yup, this is the real deal here—the snow show or as some called it, The White Circus."

Carla sat up with a start. "What the heck! I never thought that Vail would be so built up. It certainly is different from Monmouth."

"Look at all the shops," said Stephanie, pointing past her father's chest. "I could have some fun here." She purposely avoided her father's frown.

"I'll bet there are great night clubs and music in town," said Carla, humming *It's Been a Hard Day's Night*.

Becky raised her hand from the front seat in a slow, cautionary tone, saying, "Hey, you all, enough." Pausing to get the group's attention, she added, "Welcome to the big time! Remember I was here last year for this training camp. You know that Vail is now the second biggest ski area in the country. Don't let the glitter distract you. We've come for these reasons: to train on the downhill, to race, and to qualify for the team going to Europe."

McElvey nodded, adding, "Well said, Becky." He turned the car left through the parking lot toward a small, dimly lit inn and stopped before a wooden sign that read "Poor Simon's Hostel." The pine lodge wore a mantle of white snow. He looked hard at Carla, "One more time. You'll follow my strict rules about evening activities: dinner at six p.m., ski-sharpening and waxing after, and lights out at nine p.m. You'll be together in one bunkroom, so if one breaks the rules, all will know."

Stephanie and Carla looked at each other, sharing a smirk. He continued, "Now let's unpack and head over to dinner at the Gatehouse." He ended in his commanding voice, "Coach Boast has called a meeting for the racers at seven."

As a group following McElvey, we entered the Formica-sterile cafeteria, where I let my eyes roam from one white table to the next—obviously, a place where the Vail workers ate—certainly not the high-paying guests. I recognized a handful of boys from the Bend training camp, but the rest of the fifty racers, boys and girls, were new to me, and probably from the other USSA sections, top racers from all over the country. As we trooped in, heads turned from each table. We made a commanding entrance, each wearing the red Monmouth sweater with the thin, blue sleeve-stripe. Limping slightly, McElvey strode with the authority of a commander leading his troops to battle.

To my left, I heard a few snide comments: "Hey, look at the cute blonde. Who wants her? What about the thunder thighs on the brunette?"

Feeling like a cow going to market, I turned, confronting the offenders, and noticed that Coach Boast sat at the head of their table. He appeared to be giggling and commenting along with the seven male skiers. Blushing, I saw a short, dark-haired girl next to Boast. I stepped out of the procession to take a closer look—the girl was none other than Tracy Languile. Trying to avoid a confrontation, I sidled back to my friends, who had cued up in the food corral. The smell of hamburgers, French fries, and fresh-baked bread took away my anger.

Balancing our trays, Becky, Wren, Stephanie, Carla, and I walked to a side table, while McElvey went over to the coaches' table at the head of the room. Boast immediately got up and came over to us. As he bent over to be at our height, a strong scent of Old Spice and liquor made me sneeze. "Welcome," he said. "I'd begun to get worried about you. I'm sure McElvey found your dorm and got you situated."

He rose, moving to a lectern in the front of the room. He tapped the microphone, put it to his lips, ran his fingers through his dirty blonde hair, lighter than I remembered, and smiled, glowing through his artificial tan. Dressed in a collared shirt and blue sports jacket, he had the suave appearance of a TV announcer. In a western drawl, stopping after every few words, he began, "Welcome USSA racers. Most of you know me. I am Coach John Boast. I'm the new head of the US Ski Team." He paused as a slight applause, beginning at his former table, rippled around the room. "We've invited fifty of the top racers from around the country to participate in this, the fourth annual Vail Christmas training camp. Each of you earned your place here, because of your outstanding results in your section last year." He let his eyes shift toward Tracy Languile, who blushed at the extra attention.

Raising his voice, he continued, sternly, "Your coaches and I expect that you'll follow all the rules of the camp, as outlined in your welcome packet. If you look at the schedule, you'll see your day will begin early: breakfast at seven sharp." A slight moan rose from the boys' table. "We expect you to be dressed and ready to go, so you can catch the first ride up to the start of the downhill training. We only have the Lodgepole Trail closed for three hours in the morning. You'll need to make good use of your practice time." He looked around the room to his boys' table. "After lunch, you can free ski or train slalom on a course that will be set up on Slopeside Trail. Dinner at six—that's six sharp. The wax room will remain open for your ski tuning until nine." Again, pausing, he looked at the boys from his table. "You'll be expected to be in your dorms by ten every night."

I looked toward McElvey and put my hand to my mouth, realizing that already Boast's rules were different from his. McElvey smiled, nodding.

Boast pointed to a chart behind him, continuing, "Please note that your downhill pre-run will take place in three days on Thursday. The downhill race will follow the next day. Saturday we'll have a giant slalom race on the lower part of the downhill course. Finally, the camp will end with a two-run slalom race on Sunday. The team for Europe will be chosen from the results of these three race results. Good luck."

At first, a silence followed, as if all the oxygen had been sucked out of the room. Then, a slow applause grew, starting from the coaches' table. I noticed McElvey wasn't clapping.

I'd never seen Boast so direct and unemotional. As he walked back to his table, he stopped to greet McElvey, who had stood up in order to stand eye-to-eye with him. Actually, McElvey was the taller. Even in their exchange of a few perfunctory pleasantries, I saw a tension in McElvey's face, as if he'd just confronted the devil.

I picked at my dinner of hamburger, fries, and peas, wishing for Stefan's cooking. Giggling, I joked with Carla about the formality of the introduction. Turning to Becky, who seemed the most comfortable with the seriousness of the first meeting, I said,

"Hey, Becky, who are those old men at the far table in the back? They look as serious as undertakers."

Becky looked before saying, "Guess what, Lia? Those are the journalists. They were here last year, too."

"Journalists—what journalists?" I asked.

"Well, I see Lem from *The New York Times*, John from *SKI Magazine*, and Pierre from *Paris Match* for starters. Remember, this camp is a big deal both here in the US and in Europe. The Europeans want to scout the competition—they're beginning to respect US skiing, now that the program has solidified with a head coach. One, I might add, who is backed by major funding from the ski companies."

"Impressive," I stammered, pointing to the other corner.

"If you look over to the left, you'll see all the ski reps from Head, Alais, Kneissl, and Dynastar. Oh, and there's Atomic. I'll bet you think he's cute," she said with a hint of jealousy.

For the first time, I sensed the weight of the expectations placed on me. I was no longer a little-known racer from New England! I couldn't wait to call my father after dinner and explain my new-found pride—a pride tinged with pressure: a pressure I knew I could rise to.

Back in the dorm, I picked my bunk, telling Wren I didn't mind being on the top above her, because I rarely needed to get up in the middle of the night. Stephanie wanted the single cot next to the window. Becky chose the lower bed on the second bunk, leaving Carla to climb to the loft above her.

In her matter-a-fact fashion, asking for no response, Becky said, "Let's unpack quickly and lay out our ski clothes for the morning. After we take our equipment to the wax room, we can roam the village for a while."

I'd gotten used to this routine, making a home away from home, because of my years of racing and traveling in the East. I carefully laid out my racing clothes in one pile and my evening pants, turtle necks and underwear in another, and then stored them in a dresser next to my bed. My PJs always went under my pillow. Discretely, I put John Muir's book about the Sierras on a shelf next to my bed and hid my journal, toiletries, and Tampax under my clothes, but Stephanie saw me, "Oh, oh, guess who just got her period," she said smirking.

I put my finger to my lips and blushed, "Shh! It's none of your business."

"Yeah, but you know how it works, once one gets it, we all get it. Hormones they say." If I'd been a guy, I would have punched her.

I struggled to lift my heavy ski bag into the basement where McElvey awaited us. The familiar fragrance of fire, melting ski wax, and perspiration filled the room. A shrill noise from an automatic grindstone made conversation impossible, so I set my skis in a rack and quickly turned to leave. McElvey took Becky aside and appeared to be giving her instructions.

Once outside the five of us ran toward the village under a canvas of stars. The bright night sky foretold a cold spell—below zero always came under a clear full moon. A sharp bite of air burned my cheek; the frozen snow crunched under my feet like shards of glass; and my breath froze in front of my face, cloud-like. Vail would definitely be colder than Monmouth. I shivered, thinking about the downhill training tomorrow, when I'd have to run the course in just my one-piece, skin-tight racing suit.

Stephanie, taking the lead, waved us toward a dimly lit alley, where a narrow stairwell led toward a wooden sign, The Beer Garden. The Beatles song "Eight Days a Week," thundered from a darkened door. Around a corner to my left came five boys who seemed to be expecting us. Stephanie ran to the cute blonde wearing a Wyoming University ski parka. "What's going on?" I asked.

Carla said, "Shh, Stephanie has made arrangements for us to meet some boys here." She looked around to see if anyone was watching us. She pushed past me, following Stephanie into the beer den. I grabbed Becky's arm in an effort to get her attention, but Becky waved me off, saying, "Let them go. It's harmless fun. You, Wren, and I can have fun walking around town, exploring. I want to show you some outrageous stores. The show window at Gorsuch's shop has the most amazing Bogner outfits, trimmed with fur, and designed just for snow bunnies."

The three of us forgot about our other compatriots and let our eyes roam the narrow streets lit by Christmas lights. A tinkling of Christmas bells played from a carillon. The moon, reflecting off the mountain peaks, created a backdrop for *The Sound of Music*. As if reading my thoughts, Wren broke into "The hills are alive with the sound of music."

Becky and I joined in, marching down the street arm in arm, "With songs they have sung for a thousand years. / The hills fill my heart with the sound of music/and my heart wants to sing every song it hears."

We stopped in front of Gorsuch's ski shop to laugh at the frilly outfits. I poked Wren, "Wow, you'd look cute in that. All five feet of you."

Wren laughed, "Well, if you curled your hair and put on the light-blue outfit like that one, you'd look like a Hollywood celebrity trying to be a skier. Oh, except for your broad shoulders."

Becky couldn't resist adding, "Yup, and both of you could be groupies for the boys' team."

Wren put on her silliest girl-talk, sounding as though she didn't have a brain in her head. "Oh, you mean those cute guys with the WU uniforms. I'll bet I can catch one before you." She wiggled her butt.

Just then, three tall girls wearing skin-tight ski pants, fur-trimmed boots, and rabbit-fur hats came around the corner. I stepped back to let them pass.

Wren broke the silence, addressing the tallest one. "Hi, we love your outfits." She exaggerated the word love, causing me to break into laughter. "By the way, do you know anything about the races here at Vail. We heard there are some cute guys."

The tall one stopped and looked down at Wren. "Cute. Why they're sooo handsome! That's why we've come to Vail. We heard they were hot, rich, and easy to catch."

I joined the charade. "Yeah, and I hear that the girl racers are a bunch of nuns."

The tallest one laughed, "Yup, no competition for us. The guys say they're all single-minded jocks."

I barely smothered my laughter, but wanting to goad her more, said, "Have you heard about their head coach? He's the hottest of all. I'd love to see one of you catch him." Carla stepped off the curb, doubling over.

To one-up me, the brunette with the pink parka stepped forward, saying, "No problem, I already did," she paused, "Last night before the racers arrived. He couldn't stop bragging about his new position and all the money he's making. He sure is aggressive."

Incredulously, I continued, "Oh, you don't say. Then, you must know his name."

The brunette thought for a moment, looked into the lights, struggling to find the answer, and said, "Ah, I think he said his name was J … John."

"And," I asked, "his last name?"

She closed her eyes, trying to pull her energy into her one brain cell. "Um, let me see, he said it rhymed with most. Um, oh yeah—Boast."

CHAPTER 22

Training

Carla tossed a pillow in the direction of the 6:30 alarm, "Who the hell set the clock?" she yelled.

Stephanie groaned, "Shut up. Just get up. I want to catch a little more shut eye."

"Enough you two," I said, starting to crawl down from the top bunk.

Becky took charge again, "Okay, let's make a plan. Only two of us can use the bathroom at a time. Carla and Lia, you go first since you're both on the top bunks. After, Wren and I'll wash up. I guess that leaves her highness to the bathroom by herself."

"Okay, I get the point, but let me get some more sleep," said Stephanie smashing her pillow over her head.

Wren sat up when I stepped on her and immediately starting singing, "Rain drops on roses, and whiskers on kittens," knowing that this would annoy Stephanie. Almost yelling to Stephanie, she said, "If you and Carla had gotten in before eleven, we wouldn't be bothering you. Come on, guys, you can't stay out that late and expect to be at your best in the morning."

I looked at Becky, who put her finger to her lips and said, "I'll handle this."

After breakfast, I returned to the wax room to retrieve my downhill skis. McElvey stood next to them, his face tired with bags under his eyes. Placing his hands squarely on his hips, he said, "I just changed your wax to Toko Blue, because the zero-degree temp will make your skis run too slowly. The new wax should help you carry your speed over the flats this morning. Get your scrapers and shave off the excess before you buff them with your hand."

I hated this part of skiing, because I didn't understand the chemistry of waxing. Also, I disliked the feel of the wax-shavings in my fingernails and how they clung to my stretch suit. However, all five of us thanked him for getting up early to help us.

Before leaving the room, he said, "I'll meet you at the start of the course in twenty minutes. I want to side-slip it with all of you, so that we can go over the lines you'll be taking this morning. There's one nasty bump Coach Boast has built into the hill that we need to look at carefully. It could be very dangerous, if you don't carry enough speed into it." He raised his hand simulating a lift-off.

At the double chairlift, Carla and Stephanie decided to ride up together, probably to reminisce about their evening's adventures. I offered to ride alone, so Becky and Wren could have some time together. Just as I slid up to the chairlift, a young man wearing a red Wyoming University parka jumped on next to me.

I felt his warm, muscular leg next to mine, as we both reached to pull down the safety bar. "Hi, my name's Pete. I'm a friend of Bill Emerson's. I've wanted to meet you."

"Hi, how'd you know who I was?"

"Oh, Stephanie pointed you out to me. I met her last night. Also, Bill told me about you. Remember he went to WU."

"What? When have you talked to Bill? I thought he was out of touch,in basic training somewhere."

"Oh, I guess you haven't heard."

"Heard what?" I said, wincing as I anticipated the answer.

Pete stopped for a moment, trying to find the right words to break the news. A gust of cold arctic air hit, taking my breath away. My nose instantly froze; I put my mitten up to my face, bumping my goggles.

"Well, I talked to Bill last night. He told me you'd be at this training camp. He'll be deployed to Vietnam in a week. He didn't know how to call you, so he asked me to find you and tell you the news."

I'd expected to get this news one day, but not like this. I closed my eyes, trying to pretend that this hadn't been said, yet the word Vietnam echoed in my helmet. I looked up to the mountaintop and saw the snow blowing off a distant peak, felt a biting cold, right out of a Jack London tale, slapped my cheek, and shivered with the fear of the upcoming downhill training and Bill's deployment. Afraid, I sensed a threat that had no face—death.

Trying to say something to Pete, I couldn't find my voice. He saw my pain and put his arm around me. I laid my head on his shoulder and let the creaking of the lift towers and the rattling of the chairs fill my emptiness. As our chair crested the summit tower, I looked into the backside of Vail. Mountains upon mountains filled the horizon. At my feet a bowl of white, untracked powder beckoned.

Pete sensed my desire to ski off away from the training course. "No, Lia, remember you and I are training on the downhill this morning. We can't free ski until this afternoon. Please turn to the right. I believe McElvey's waiting for you at the start of the downhill," he said, sliding out of his chair and skating out of sight.

I skied over to McElvey, making sure to stop below Becky, Wren, Stephanie, and Carla as I'd been taught.

He motioned for the five of us to follow him. Reminiscent of our days of training, we mirrored him down the course, carving slow turns around the red and blue flags. In contrast to slalom and giant slalom, the rules let us practice our turns in the downhill course. The freshly-groomed snow creaked from the cold, moaning as though a ghost were buried beneath.

After three turns, McElvey stopped. He pointed up the trail. "Okay, the first three turns are self-evident. Keep a high line and begin your turns early. Now look down into the fourth turn. You can't see the gate. There's a blind gate below and you'll need to find a marker in order to establish your line. Depending on your speed, your marker will change. To begin, let's pick the tall pine as your reference point." He pointed up to a tree on the side. "Aim for that and then begin your turn when you come to the rock on your right. Push hard on your downhill ski as the side-hill will try to pull you into the rocks." He lifted one ski to model. "Once around, step quickly uphill and slide around the red flag. If you hit this high, you should be able to carry most of your speed onto the flat."

I tried to see the pine and the rocks, but a cold gust of snow hit my face. "What if we're blinded as we go into this turn?" I asked cautiously.

Looking very serious, McElvey answered, "As you practice, try to gauge the amount of time it takes from when you first see the pine to when you need to begin your turn. After a while, it'll become second nature to you." He looked straight at Wren. "Are you listening? Pay attention! This is a dangerous course."

Not waiting for an answer, he took off with Stephanie, Carla, Becky, and Wren on his heels. I waited a minute, hoping to see when they initiated their turn into the blind gate. I followed, trying to skate and catch up to them. Then I bent into a tuck with my head down between my legs, my body curled into an egg-shape. To pick up speed, I kept my weight on the tails of my skis after the blind gate.

Below, McElvey threw his skis sideways and motioned for us to stop. Wren crossed her skis and fell forward toward him, forcing him to step back in frustration. Beyond him, I saw the bump, the most deadly kind, because the landing would be flat, hard, and icy. I couldn't believe someone would have created such an obstacle, two mounds divided by a ditch between the liftoff and the landing. It resembled a pillow that had been cut in two. Between the two swellings, a dark crevice stretched twenty feet.

"What's this?" said Becky, trying to be heard above the roar of the wind.

McElvey raised his hand in caution, saying, "This—this is the toughest part of the course, except for the final pitch. Boast had the snow groomer build these two bumps. To safely clear the gap, you must actually launch from the first, lift your knees, and let your momentum carry you smoothly over the second lip. If you don't carry enough speed, approximately 60 mph from the last turn, you won't clear the second bump. Then, heaven help you." He made a "tsk" sound.

McElvey stopped talking and looked at our reactions. My mouth was open. Here in one quick lesson lay all the challenge of downhill racing—how to carry your speed safely and maneuver under extreme circumstances. Since Damien's death, I'd never liked downhill; however, I was required to race all three events: slalom, giant slalom, and downhill.

McElvey took off again, avoiding the bump, and tucked most of the flat. He stood up before he approached the final pitch, stretched out his arms, and let the oncoming wind slow him down. He stopped at the top where a cliff dropped directly into the village. The tops of the buildings looked like a barricade of army tents, the narrow streets meandering between the roofs. The constant grind of the bull-wheel at the base added an ominous note to this village scene.

Once again he reminded us to memorize where we wanted to initiate our turn, a crucial move before gliding into the final steep and the last two turns. A wide banner was stretched across the finish and beyond it, a flat area encircled by red fences. Shaking, I realized this course would be long and demanding, two minutes of leg-burning hell.

Seeing my concern, Wren took off first, laughing as she poled away from the group. I envied her fearlessness, her fluidity as she pressed to gain speed over the last bump where she tucked her legs, lifted ten feet in the air, did a spread eagle, and landed just before the finish line.

As I took my turn and poled to the blue gate on the knoll, a ghoulish image flashed across my mind: a tree, a split skull, Sugarloaf.

CHAPTER 23

Wren

Downhill training began at nine. The Arctic cold had brought cloudless skies punctuated by rime-ice on the trees, a study in white on blue. The cliffs glimmered between the gargoyle-like treetops that stooped from the weight of the snow. The only colors on the mountain were the blue and red downhill flags. I felt grateful that I'd one more chance to review the course with McElvey before being on my own to experiment with lines, tucks, skating steps, and pre-jumps for the final non-stop run.

This morning I made sure to put on two pairs of long underwear and socks. During this last practice run, I'd be skiing without my parka and warm-up pants at 60 mph in my skin-tight racing suit, a polyester skin that gave little protection from the knife-wind.

Now the time for tunnel vision had come. Our group, Wren, Becky, Carla, Stephanie, and I, clutching our freshly waxed skis, jumped up and down at the base of the course in an effort to stay warm. McElvey, in his typical silent, self-confident manner, nodded and pointed his finger, signaling for us to pole over to the lift. I made sure to push hard, so I could catch the ride up the double chair with him, perhaps getting a few more tips about the course.

"Morning," I said as I slid my butt next to his, wincing as the metallic chair shot cold spikes up my spine.

He smiled under his dark goggles and patted my shoulder. "Well, young lady, are you ready for this test?"

"Yup, but I've got a few questions."

"Go ahead."

"How'll I know my speed heading into the first blind turn?"

"As I said yesterday, take each run with caution, start slowly." He paused, looking up the chairlift. "As you begin to judge your speed, you can adjust your line. You know, make sure to note where you start your turn so that you can have a reference point for race day." He paused to look down at the course between his skis. "Each day the conditions will be different."

I couldn't see his eyes through his goggles, but I felt the concern in his voice.

I said slowly, "Yeah, but I'm also worried about the two bumps on the flat." I looked up the hill to the bumps. "How do I know if I've enough speed to clear the second one?"

"The problem is not speed, but lift." He made a gesture with his right glove sliding over his left. "Start with a solid pre-jump to see how much air you can get. Remember, you'll have to keep your knees up until you've cleared the second lip." He kept his right hand hovering over his left. "Then immediately press your boots down and try to touch the snow as soon as possible." He looked into my eyes and smiled. "Make sure your skis kiss the snow. You're always faster on the ground than in the air—you know, air resistance. I'll be standing near the bump. Stop at the bottom of the course. I'll ski down after all of you've completed your run. At that time, I'll give you feedback."

My breath had begun freezing on the outside of my goggles. Unbuckling the strap from my helmet, I removed my goggles, fumbling because of the padding in my down mittens. I carefully placed the lenses inside my parka to warm them. A silence followed. I couldn't hold back any longer. "Hey, Coach, did you hear about Bill?"

"Yes, but I didn't know if you had. His parents called me—I didn't want to worry you."

"Is it really just a week before he leaves?" I held my breath, anticipating his answer.

"Yup."

Closing my eyes, I tried to refocus on the course, to imagine making a perfect run down the course. Each bump, gate, and flat unfurled in slow motion. McElvey nudged me as the chair approached the top tower. "Stay loose," he said as he lifted the gate and skied off toward the start.

All his racers gathered above the starting gate, a flock of sparrows on a telephone wire, poised, silent, and wary. McElvey stood in front of us, gesticulating with his arms. He looked as though he were directing traffic while he discussed our lines on the course. A familiar voice from above caught me by surprise, "Can we go ahead of you?" I looked up to see Peter Timmons with his cadre of WU boys, handsome in their dark-blue racing suits. "We want to cruise the course at top speed," he said, skating past us to get into the start.

"Of course. Be our guests," said Becky, with a slight scowl. Turning to us, she whispered, "They always think they have priority over the girls."

McElvey ignored the boys by turning his back and said to us, "Remember the rules of pre-running. Leave at least a minute between racers. Stop if you see someone flagging you down. I've arranged for another coach to bring down your parkas after all of you have gone. Wait at the finish line for me." His unemotional voice worried me.

After the adrenalin-charged boys had rocketed out of the gate, Becky stepped up between the two start poles. She threw her parka off to the left, indicating that the rest of the Monmouth girls should follow suit. Wren side-stepped down to her and rubbed her back, as she hunkered over her ski poles to get more leverage. "Make a good line for us," whispered Wren in a prayerful voice.

I trembled, bending over to buckle my boots. I felt a stare from a man up the hill, a stare that lasted too long. Looking up, I saw Coach Boast, all decked out in his new dark blue US Ski Team parka embroidered with the team's yellow insignia. His face was half-lit by the sun, which gave him a menacing look. His over-sized, warm-up pants accordioned at his ankles, reminding me of the Michelin man. Turning away from him, I struggled to clip the final frozen buckle. Now I wished I hadn't kept my boots loose until the last minute in an attempt to get more circulation into my toes. I'd frostbitten my toes so many times that they'd freeze as soon as I tightened the top buckle. I dreaded the ankle pain that came with the last snap. Snug in my boots, I stood up to stare back at Boast.

Becky took off down the course, while Carla counted to sixty before jumping in behind her. "Try to catch me," she said to Wren, "I'm the gingerbread man!"

Wren slid in next, since I'd made no effort to move, saying, "Okay, I'll go, but leave more space for me, because I don't plan to hit the bump with much speed the first time." I heard some sarcasm in her voice.

I tried warning her to keep her speed up, but the wind muffled my words.

I knew I was the next to go, because Stephanie, still dressed in her parka, stood unmoving on the slope above me. "Are you going to ski with all your warm-ups on?" I asked.

Stephanie nodded, "You know I hate downhill. I just do this to please my dad."

Sneering, I answered, "I wish I could keep my stuff on, but I want to make sure I have a feeling for the course. You can't get that if you ski like a sailor with his jib flying." I immediately turned to focus on the course. The first red flag snapped in a cold blast from the north. I counted down and poled hard out of the gate. Hitting my tuck, I rested my forearms on my knees, my head pressing be-tween my legs. With a deep breath, as though trying to put myself into a trance, I felt my skis pick up speed. I rolled my ankles to find a flatter glide.

One hundred feet above the first gate, I rose from my tuck and let my skis flow out to the side. As my edges grabbed the snow, I heard a scraping sound. *Damn,* I thought, *there's boilerplate underneath.* The next series of gates came faster than expected, so I started my turns sooner. I liked the bite my edges made in the snow; I felt like a dancer as I rocked between the tighter gates. Then came the blind, side-hill gate. I aimed for the pine tree, checked the rocks to my right, took one skating step uphill and fell into the fall-away turn. Easy. No sound, just snow, cold air, and a bright sun that transformed the course into a ribbon of white velvet. My body relaxed; the laws of time and space stopped—the course unfurled in slow motion.

I knew I had enough speed for the split bump, so I relaxed back into my tuck. I rolled my knees to the outside, as I'd been taught, to flatten the bottoms, causing them to run freely on the snow, and then pressed my weight back on my tails. Just before the first bump, even from my crouch, I saw a blue arm and ski pole flapping above the snowline. For a moment I couldn't register what was happening. A group was gathered around a body that was spread out on the snow just below the bump looking like a bird that had fallen wingless from the sky. I threw my skis sideways. Snow blasted into my goggles, blocking my vision; the wetness of the fresh flakes stung my lips.

Struggling to catch my breath and clear my goggles, I heard McElvey's cry. "Oh my God! Call for help!" I scrambled to get off the course, in case another racer was coming. Twenty feet below me lay Wren, not moving.

Soon, with red crosses on their backs, ski patrollers, like wolves to their prey, descended on Wren's prostrate body. McElvey motioned for me to ski to the bottom just as a toboggan pushed past me.

I knew I couldn't help her, but still I skied near her body. One patrolman knelt over her face as though he were giving her mouth to mouth resuscitation. Her unnaturally twisted legs imprinted in my mind.

McElvey yelled to me again, "Lia, head on down to the bottom … now!"

Looking up the hill to ensure no one was on course, I jumped back into the fall line below the bump. I wanted to finish the course, because I'd have only two more practice runs today. The final six gates presented little challenge, since I didn't carry very much speed from the flat.

Becky and Carla were waiting in the finish corral, gesturing with their hands above their heads, mocking my lack of effort. I threw my skis sideways, blasted snow into their faces, and said. "Hey, you guys. Stop it. Wren got hurt on the bump. McElvey wants us to go inside and wait for him." Becky started toward the lift, so I yelled again. "No, the patrol is bringing Wren down. He wants to meet us in the cafe. Stephanie should be right behind me."

Inside the empty cafeteria, the four of us bought hot chocolate and waited. After prying off our frozen boots, we huddled together on the bench seats, not saying a word. I could feel tears begin to flow down my cheeks; their warmth caused my frozen skin to tingle. Finally, Becky broke the silence, "So what did you see?"

Before I could answer, Stephanie spoke up with authority. "Dad said Wren had hurt her back and that they were going to put her on a backboard before they brought her down. It'll take some time. He doesn't want us to go anywhere until he gets down."

I closed my eyes, feeling the hot chocolate trickle down my throat, and tried to keep my mind quiet. My body felt as weak as a blade of grass. I'd been here before.

CHAPTER 24

Free Skiing

"Okay, Becky, what do we poach first?" I said, jumping onto the chairlift next to her, my baggy warm-ups catching on the sidebar. We had the afternoon off for free-skiing because McElvey had taken a helicopter with Wren to Denver General and Boast wanted to work on the bump.

"Right. Always like you, looking for the forbidden. Look to your left. Let's head over to Riva Ridge. I hear there's some mint glade skiing," she said, resting her arm on my shoulder in order to point to the ridge of lodgepole pines. The afternoon sun glinted off an ice fall. Narrow strips of snow plummeted down walls of granite, swirling white on black.

I smiled, poked her, and said, "Maybe we could huck a cliff?"

The still-cold bore down on me like a weight, a force that could take the breath from any living creature. No other skiers were on the lift or slopes, because it was so late in the afternoon. To gain warmth, I snuggled next to Becky's blue, Monmouth parka. I felt free now that I'd traded my racing helmet for my red knit hat. My down pants kept my legs and butt toasty like a loaf of bread in the oven. Only my feet and hands hurt, but I'd grown used to this discomfort—a small trade-off for an afternoon of gravity–induced bliss.

Stephanie and Carla had gone into town to find pastries, and perhaps boys, their form of distraction from their fears about Wren. I had little money, plus no desire to be indoors shopping, when I could be doing what I loved best. Fortunately, Becky felt the same way.

The chairlift crossed over the downhill course on Lodgepole trail where a yellow snow-cat was grinding down the bump right at the spot that Wren had fallen; its front blade pushed chunks of ice to the side; the engine groaning like a dying bull. Pointing to the ground, I yelled to Becky over the noise "Hey, why do you think they're bulldozing the bump?" I shook my head with the authority of one who already knows the answer.

"Duh, I heard that Boast got in trouble with the other coaches. Some have been complaining about the bump from the first." She smirked, adding, "Who knows, maybe someone has threatened a lawsuit against him?"

"You know, I've heard other racers complaining about his style of coaching. No one likes the way he plays favorites with the racers," I said, trying to stifle my anger.

Becky nodded in agreement. "You're right. Worse, some coaches feel he's not qualified to be the head of the US Ski Team. Rumor has it that he was a hockey coach before he became a ski coach." She paused and added softly, "For sure, he has very little experience with world-class ski racing."

"So, why'd they let him set this course?"

"Who knows? He always gets his way. I've heard the European press has been writing very negative reports about this training camp." Giggling, she continued, "They've called him an elephant in the elite world of ski racing. Others say, the Hannibal of America."

"Who?"

"Oh, you, I forgot Miss English Major. Maybe you should learn some history. Someone said, 'If you don't know history, you are bound to repeat it.' "

"Okay, but Twain said, 'History doesn't repeat itself, instead it rhymes.' Anyway, Miss Smarty-pants, who was Hannibal?"

"Oh some general who tried to defeat the Romans with elephants."

"With elephants in Europe? Sounds dumb."

"Yup. And he eventually lost."

"Wow, wouldn't it be fun if we made the team to Europe, then together we could learn more about the history over there." I nodded as if in a dream.

"Right, I'm not sure you have any more room in your bag for books." She giggled, "You might have to leave some of your poetry books."

"Never."

"Well, Boast has strict weight limits"

"On bags or girls?" I said, puffing up my cheeks to look fat. "Funny, do you think he'll go to Europe with the team?"

"Duh, he's the head coach … this'll be his moment of glory."

"Maybe the powers that be won't let him go because of Wren's accident," I said, shaking my head.

"Sorry, like he's the power that be now," concluded Becky, rolling her brown eyes and making a slicing motion with her hand across her throat, indicating that it was time to cut short the small talk. "Remember we promised not to talk about Wren all afternoon. Let's go have some fun."

At the top of the lift, I felt my giant-slalom skis settle onto the smooth surface of the run-out. Sliding down the ramp, I shifted my poles from under my arms and into my hands, easing the leather hand strap around my wrists, and poled hard to get speed. I still couldn't catch Becky, who'd already started down the trail. The froth from her turns told me that no one had been on this trail for a while. The loose powder made my turns effortless. I crisscrossed Becky's line in perfect C-shaped arcs, creating the infinity sign down the trail, my snow calligraphy. My frozen breath rose in a smoke-cloud, as if an inner fire burned in me. The silence, my fast pulse, and the sparkle of the afternoon sun transported me into a world of no pain, no feeling, no thought—just raw energy.

Becky stopped at the beginning of a chute, which broke from the main trail. A sign read CLOSED in large black letters with an *X* below. She didn't say a word, just pointed with her ski pole. Looking down the 30-degree slope of untracked powder, I nodded my assent, ducked under the rope that crossed the trail, and let my skis pick up speed in order to ride to the surface of the three feet of virgin powder.

Flexing, floating, gliding, soaring in untracked crystals, my legs pulsated as though I were bouncing on a trampoline. I didn't want to stop to check out what lay ahead; however, as the trail banked to the right, Becky, now leading, threw her skis sideways. Losing her balance, she fell face first into the snow.

Immediately, I had to pull a hockey stop to avoid running my skis over her hand. In slow motion, I fell downhill onto her. Bundled together in the snow like a pile of discarded clothes, we both broke into uncontrollable laughter. "Was that the best ever?" I said, spitting snow.

"Best," said Becky as she put her hand up for a high-five. "Let's never forget why we take all these risks on the race course. This is what skiing's really about. I sure hope both of us make the team to Europe, so we can spend every afternoon dancing in the Alps. God, I love this sport."

"Boy, would Wren … "

Becky raised her hand, stopping me, "Remember our promise."

Slowly, we, two snow-lovers, emerged from our winter co-coon. Realizing I'd lost a ski, I dug it out, placed it uphill and kicked my boot back into the Marker bindings. This effort actually took my breath, making me aware that I was still at 9,000 feet. Becky reached up to brush the snow from my hat. "You look beautiful when covered with snow, like … like an angel," she said softly.

I smiled, realizing that our friendship had just grown to a new level. To avoid more talk, I pointed to a rock outcropping on the left. "Let's take some air together. I'll stay left, you stay right. If we get enough speed, we should be able to clear the rocks and land on the downhill slope," I said, feeling drunk—drunk with joy.

Becky nodded in agreement, and simultaneously we flipped our skis downhill and skied as if tethered through the untracked snow toward the lip of the outcropping. I didn't realize that the drop below was six feet, not two feet. Instinctively, pulling my knees to my chest, I floated like an eagle on an updraft. I loved that gravity-defying moment. Becky chose to push her skis out to the side in a spread eagle. In my mind, I prayed, *Don't let this ever stop.* I looked down for my landing, watching my shadow rise to join my skis.

Becky landed first, checked her speed with two quick turns and pulled up. I landed beyond and did a screaming *C* on the open slope before stopping. Looking up the slope toward Becky and the icy abutment above, I felt invincible. We could ski anything. We would be unstoppable.

The rest of the run took us through yellow-white aspen trees. Because the snow covered the underbrush, we had a clear path, which allowed us to ski ten feet apart—a perfect dual slalom course through the skinny trees. My eyes flowed three turns ahead, helping me avoid the immoveable trunks. My hands and poles pumped rhythmically, snow flew behind me like gossamer threads. After creating a trail where none had existed, I pulled up under a small spruce tree and indicated to Becky to stop.

"Hey, I remember from eastern skiing that we should take off our wrist straps in case our poles snag on a branch. That way, only the pole will be pulled from our hands."

Pointing to a ten-foot trench surrounding the spruce, she added, "Oh, yeah, and you Easterner who's never seen this much snow, don't forget to steer clear of the larger spruces and pines that have tree-wells. You know, where their branches stop the snow from filling in around the base. To the point, I've heard of skiers falling into these holes and freezing to death, because they couldn't crawl out." I looked down below the branches of the spruce and saw a black hole with rocks on the bottom. I thought,

What a lonely death.

We took off, dove into the wooded glade, bashed through the low-hanging branches, jumped in the air to make turns, chasing each other the way squirrels spiral down a tree. The low lemon light led us to the warmth of our dorm.

✻　✻　✻

Secure inside the rustic building, we left our skis in the wax room, so we could work on them after supper. In our bunk room, we heard Carla's insistent voice, "Hey, where've you guys been?"

"Well, we told you we were going free skiing," said Becky, rolling her eyes. A tension built in the silence. I sat on Wren's bed, waiting for the standoff to break.

Finally Carla said, "Well, we've been trying to get in touch with you. Did Coach Boast speak to you?"

"No, we saw no one on the mountain," answered Becky, now not as confident.

Again, a silence spoke to everyone. Breaking the awkward emptiness, I said, "So ... so what's going on?"

Carla and Stephanie looked at each other. Stephanie pointed to Carla to speak. Struggling to find the words, Carla said, "Well, McElvey called from Denver. Wren's seriously hurt. Her back may be broken." Choking on her words, she continued, "At the moment, she can't move her legs."

No one spoke as the four of us walked forward with our arms out and hugged each other. Muffled by our rustling parkas, a whisper came from Becky, "Dear God, no." I let my eyes wander from the huddled group, out the window, to the last rays of sun which pulled a black curtain up Vail Mountain.

CHAPTER 25

Pre-run

To get a psychological head start on my teammates, I started my pre-run rituals at 6:30 the next morning, first my sunrise jog. I carefully slid out of bed, avoiding stepping on Wren's sheets, even though I realized she wasn't there and wouldn't return. Feeling empty, I grabbed my running shoes and sweat suit, before tiptoeing to the bathroom to dress. This sacred time, the silence, the peacefulness, helped me regroup and lessen my pre-race jitters.

Once outside I noticed that the sun had yet to slide over the Rocky Mountains. A reddish streak glowed above the peaks, stretching like fingers from an unknown spirit. The fresh dusting of snow had erased most of the car tracks—it was a new world. For thirty minutes, Vail would be mine.

Running down toward Highway 5, I heard the morning sounds—the scraping of palettes with fresh vegetables and fruit being unloaded, the clanging of trash cans, and a few "Guten morgen" greetings from the Austrian bakers. A confectionery smell from Pepi's bakery told me that the cooks were already hard at work on brioche, tarts, Linzer torte, and I hoped my favorite— Traunkirchner cake.

On icy Bridge Street, I ran slowly, at times slipping like a car without snow tires. Turning left, I headed up a steep incline toward the private chalets of the wealthy—not a single light shown from these faux Austrian mansions. I sprinted uphill until my breathing became labored and my legs ached. Stopping in front of a large, brown chalet carved into the hillside, I spotted a white station wagon with the red, white, and blue logo of the US Ski Team.

Looking closer, I realized it was Boast's car. A dog barked, letting me know that I was the intruder in this playground of the rich. A door opened and a woman's voice called for the dog, so I dashed down the hill.

A half-hour later at breakfast, Coach Boast sat down with me and my three friends. "Morning. Looks like McElvey hasn't returned from Denver. So he asked me to look after you during the morning pre-run." He smiled like a man who had just received a secret toy. "Meet me on the top of the course at 8:30, okay? I'm allowing you to complete two practice runs before your pre-run at 10:30. The boys'll start their training at 11. Make sure by then that you are clear of the course." His face reddened; his voice grew more commanding.

Becky, raising her hand as if in school, spoke for our stunned group. "Ahh, any more word on Wren?"

"Nope, but I'll let you know if I hear anything. Her parents are arriving today from LA." He stared at Becky with a scowl that indicated no more questions.

"Who'll take our parkas down after the pre-run?" asked Carla.

"Oh, it's warmer. Don't worry too much," he said. Realizing he needed to tell us more, he added, "Okay, I'll get my assistant Dan to bring your parkas to the bottom of the lift. Do try to get a good clean run, preferably non-stop," he said with a smirk.

I interrupted, "We haven't waxed, because McElvey wanted to do that."

"McElvey, everything is McElvey. Well, I'm in charge now. No worries. You don't need wax today. I'll make sure you get some wax for the race tomorrow," he said and abruptly got up to return to his coaches' table.

I waited for him to get out of earshot before saying to my group, "What an a-hole. Do you think he cares about us at all?"

Leaning toward me, trying to feel part our group, Stephanie added, "Like are you kidding? He just wants as many of his WU girls to make the team to Europe, including Tracy and Susan."

Carla slapped her hand on the table, "Well, let's try to change that! He can only take five girls this year, and we can be four of them." She then rubbed her hands together as if washing them. "Like would that ever make McElvey proud of us."

Unaware that others might be watching, the four of us placed our hands on top of each other's in a pact of solidarity. "Time to go," said Becky, nodding to each one of us. "This'll be our day."

I looked back at Boast to make sure he couldn't hear what I said next, "Hey, guys—guess what I saw on my morning run?"

At this non-sequitur, my three friends looked quizzical. Becky sighed, "What's this got to do with today? We need to go."

Offended, I said, "Well, I thought you might be interested. It might have to do with today."

"Okay, give it up," said Becky impatiently.

Now with everyone's attention, I said, "I saw Boast's ski team wagon parked at the top of the hill, you know in the land of the rich and famous. Yup, in the driveway of the largest chalet."

Becky blanched and sat down, "Say that again, please."

"You know, if you go up Hillside Road, at the top is a terraced chalet. His car was parked there at six-thirty this morning," I said more confidently.

"You mean the house with an American flag on the side and the barking dog," she paused to see my nod. "Guess who owns that chalet?" she said as if she had just learned the answer to a school exam.

"Who?" said all three of us at the same time.

"Not sure what all this means," said Becky. "Well, Dr. Languile, Tracy's dad does." No one spoke, realizing the implications of this discovery.

✳ ✳ ✳

Once on the hill, I completed my two practice runs without waiting for the others. I wanted to focus on the course, get a feel for the snow and the speed of the course. The two bumps had been shaved down, so I could easily clear the second without worrying about a jolt. Although I hated downhill, this course skied like a field of fresh powder, so the speed didn't worry me. It might be a different story on race day, when I would be racing at the end of the girls' event. I didn't get a good start number.

At 10:30 I joined Becky, Carla, and Stephanie at the start. All forty racers wore bibs indicating their order for the final pre-run. Becky, the best downhiller among us, wore bib #10, while Carla got #20, Stephanie #27 and I had #30—what bad luck. This would also be my race order for tomorrow.

The start was buzzing with excitement as some racers climbed uphill and attempted a few short turns. Some stretched to loosen their muscles. To relax, I slid away from the group, closed my eyes, and visualized a perfect run, tracing the course with my hand. When I opened them, I saw Tracy Languile in the start with bib #1.

When number #29 left the gate, I side-slipped into the start. I tried ignoring Coach Boast who waved from the first gate to get my attention. "Hey, Lia, you looked good on your two practice runs. See if you can beat Tracy's time."

I snarled and didn't respond. Slowly, I edged my ski tips into the start so that my ankles were resting against the starting wand and my ski poles were draped over. A fresh breeze blew up the trail, a dusting of cool snow wet my lips. At the sound of "Go," I kicked up my heels to get leverage on the wand and maybe save a hundredth of a second. I poled twice, skated twice, and settled into my tuck. My legs relaxed on the flat. I held my line through the tight turns, pre-jumped the double bump, remained in my tuck over the second bump, shifted my weight back on the last flat, and felt my speed increase. Standing up, I cruised through the final gates, because I didn't want to give away my actual time, knowing that Boast was timing the pre-run. "Hey, Lia, why did you finish like a snow bunny?" yelled Carla as my spray hit her face.

"My secret," I said, turning my head up the hill to wait for the last runners. In the back of the finish corral, I saw Tracy standing with her group of six racers from the University of Wyoming. The group appeared to be congratulating her.

"What's going on over there?" I said, turning back to Becky.

"Oh, I just heard that Coach Boast has been running times on the racers and Tracy had a fast time," said Becky.

I smiled, realizing that Boast must have thought I had a bad pre-run.

Misreading my expression, Becky said, "Hey, it doesn't matter. We already have our start order. This is just a psychological game of Boast's."

CHAPTER 26

Celebration

The four of us turned in our bibs, picked up our parkas, and shouldered our skis for the walk back to the dorm, where we would call McElvey at the hospital. As we sauntered through the narrow streets of Vail, I felt proud, even sexy in my skin-tight race suit. A smell of fresh donuts made us stop in front of Pepi's pastry shop.

"What about a little treat?" said Carla, eyeing a strawberry croissant in the window.

"Yeah, a celebration that training is over and the races will begin," said Stephanie, always looking for an excuse to eat. "And that camp will soon be over."

The sweet smell of coffee and hot chocolate lured us to a table by the window. From here we could keep an eye on our skis leaning against the building, gossip about the tourists, and eat without being spotted by the coaches. The small, round, wooden table barely allowed room for our lithe bodies. I carefully placed my racing helmet and goggles under my feet so that no one would trip on them.

A tanned, dark-haired boy strode up to the table with four menus in hand. In a heavy Austrian accent he said, "You look lost. Would you care for lunch, ladies?"

I giggled, realizing that he didn't recognize us as racers. "Danke schön," I said, feeling very savvy. The others poked each other.

Carla ran her hand through her short, dark hair. "Yes, we'd love to have a menu, but we probably only want a snack. We want to explore Vail," she said, trying to keep up our pretense of being tourists, "but right now, we'd all like a hot chocolate."

145

"Take your time," said the young man, emphasizing his accent as he slid his order pad back into his belt, winked at Carla, and turned confidently toward the kitchen.

"Great job," I said, raising my thumb to show approval. "I love it when we can be incognito. Does anyone else get tired of being identified as ski racers?" All three nodded in agreement.

Stephanie flicked her blonde pony-tail back in order to catch our attention. "I get sooo tired of being a ski racer everywhere I go. Yup, just for one day, I'd like to see if I could be appreciated for being me. No background, no father as coach. In fact, sometimes I wonder who I'd be if I weren't a ski racer."

The three of us looked from one to the other at this outburst. One by one we nodded in agreement. Becky saw where this conversation was going and slowly said, "So you know that all any of us has ever done, yes since we learned to walk, is ski and race. For sure, we were good at this, so our parents have pushed us. But now, we're here because each one of us has chosen to accept this dream—right?"

A long silence ensued. I decided to break the tension, saying, "Yes, but we do have different motivations." I hesitated to see whether the others were following my train of thought. "We've never really talked openly about this. In fact, I feel as if this is my secret. Maybe we should play truth or consequences now?"

"I've an idea," said Carla, raising her napkin like a start flag. "Let's each say just one or two sentences about why we're ski racing. I'll start." She paused to catch her thoughts. "I've won every race since I was eight years old. My adoptive parents have spent a lot of money giving me this opportunity. I'm grateful. I do it for them, but I also hope to one day get to Europe and find my real family." From the look on the other's faces, I realized that they, too, knew Carla's story.

Becky waited for this to register and then said, "I'm racing, because McElvey saw early on that I had potential. He's supported me for ten years, allowing me to be in the racing program every weekend. I ski for him, but … I also love to ski."

Stephanie frowned uncomfortably. She picked up her hot chocolate and slurped the whipped cream before saying, "I do this, because my dad makes me. Like, I'd rather be playing tennis or riding my horses." A white mustache covered her lip.

I saw the tears well up in Stephanie's eyes and put my arm around her. "It's okay. We can be honest. No one'll tell." I reached over with my napkin to wipe the white fluff from her lip. I thought about Damien, Bill, and then said softly, "For me, I just love skiing, every aspect of this … " I paused, searching for just the right word. "It's my covenant with the snow, with the mountains. It's such freedom."

Before anyone could respond, the waiter returned. "Well, have you ladies decided what you want? You all look so serious for a group of women on vacation."

Seizing the opportunity to continue the charade, Carla said, "Yup, we're on vacation. What a beautiful place to relax." Pushing her bangs away from her face in a flirtatious manner, she added, "By the way, can you tell us why some of the trails are closed and there are flags set down the slope?"

The tanned waiter stood tall to speak with authority. "I guess you don't know. The best racers in America are here training before they go to the World Cup races in Europe. I've heard names like Becky Langer, Tracy Languile, and Pete Timmons, and that new hotshot from Wyoming, Pammy Siemans." I looked to see what Becky would say.

Becky, continuing the joke, leaned forward. "Wow, I think I read these names in SKI Magazine. You say they're here?"

"Ja, right here and staying at Poor Simon's," said the young man. He puffed up his chest. "What I would give to meet one of them."

All of us giggled, poked each other before Becky said, "Maybe you'll get lucky. Maybe they'll come here one day for hot chocolate."

I decided to order before someone broke in with the truth, "Oh, yes, we'd all love to have four strawberry croissants. We want to hurry back into town to see if we can watch those hotshot skiers on the course." Shaking my head, I added, "How could a girl have such courage?"

We looked from one to another, realizing we'd just gotten away with this duplicity. Looking back to the waiter, my eyes wandered out the window. Across the street, walking together in matched strides, came Coach Boast and Tracy Languile. They stopped in front of Gorsuch's Ski Shop. I couldn't tell whether they were admiring the fur-trimmed Bogner ski outfit in the store front or their own reflections.

Down the street from them, I saw a bedraggled young man in a WU parka walking toward them, carrying his skis uncomfortably over his shoulder. He staggered like a drunken flea, almost falling into Boast and Tracy, who reached out to support him. When he turned away from the display window, I realized it was Pete Timmons.

CHAPTER 27

End of Camp

Exhausted yet jubilant because all the races were over, I pranced down the narrow alleys of Vail Village toward the cafeteria where Boast had called a meeting to announce the results, award the trophies, and select the team for Europe. For a moment as the street lights came on, I felt giddy like a princess in a fairy tale off to meet her prince. My results over the last three days had made me a contender for the European-bound team.

Entering the bare cafeteria, I scanned the room for my friends, Carla, Becky, and Stephanie. To my left I spotted Tracy, Pammy Siemans, and Peter snuggled against the back wall. Pammy flirted with Peter, smiling up into his dark eyes, flicking her page-boy blonde hair, and even resting her head on his shoulder at times. Their intimacy implied they already knew something the rest of the group didn't.

I moved toward my group of friends, unmistakable in their Monmouth red sweaters, talking with McElvey. Sliding across the floor, almost tripping on a bench, I grabbed him from behind. "Welcome back, Coach. Wow, have we missed you."

He turned in surprise, pushed back, and in a fatherly manner patted me on the shoulder. "Great job, Lia. I knew you had the skills to put together three strong races." I blushed, realizing that he must've checked out everyone's results. My 5th in the downhill, 3rd in the giant slalom and 1st in the slalom had made the *Denver Post* and *The New York Times*.

Before I could ask about Wren, Boast took the podium and tapped the microphone. He wore a tie and jacket, his hair newly cut, his face smooth and tanned. Unlike in his previous speech at the beginning of camp, he seemed more confident and polished, taking his time with every word. "Welcome again, racers and coaches. We've just completed the fourth annual Christmas training camp at Vail." He paused, looked up, ran his hand through his thick, even blonder hair, smiled to the crowd, and waited for the applause from the exhausted participants. "I especially want to thank Pete Parker and all the employees here at Vail who've made this event so successful." He looked around and said to the back of the room, "And to all you racers: remember, if you can dream it, you can achieve it."

I let Boast's words fade into the background as I relived each race. The downhill had gone so smoothly that I felt, in time, I might enjoy the challenge. In fact, I'd lost my fear of the bump and even relished the speed. The giant slalom, my favorite event, had caused me some trouble, because I'd been over-confident. Needless to say, my two runs in the slalom course had been my best two slalom runs ever. The icy track had skied just like the eastern ice at Mad River Glen. The western racers had trouble releasing their edges on the turns, causing them to slide and lose speed, while I'd danced down the course like an Olympic skater, picking up speed after each turn. My edges had barely touched the snow before I'd released them into the next turn. I knew I'd turned in an outstanding second run because, for the first time ever, I'd heard the crowd roaring as I approached the finish line.

Boast's sonorous voice broke my reverie. "Now I'd like to award the trophies for each event." I felt Becky's hand on my shoulder, my stomach churning. I knew I'd have to go up in front of the whole room to receive two trophies. He called out, "Third in the women's downhill, Tracy Languile with a time of one minute 50 seconds." A small round of applause ushered Tracy to the front, blushing as she shook Boast's hand. I wondered if others saw the wink Boast gave her. "Second in the women's downhill, Pammy

Siemans with a time of one minute 49 seconds and two tenths."
Pammy trotted to the front, repeatedly flicking her coiffed, blonde
hair. A cheer, then cat calls, erupted from the back of the room
where ten Wyoming University male racers stood. "First in the
women's downhill, Becky Langer with a time of one minute 48
seconds." Our group of Monmouth girls jumped up, trying to out-
do the former cheers of the WU racers. Becky looked back toward
me, giving me a thumbs-up just before she reached for the silver
Revere bowl Coach Boast held out for her.

I didn't even hear the results of the men's downhill as I con-
gratulated Becky who had returned to us. Leaning over to touch
the trophy, I saw my smile reflected in the shiny bowl. She handed
it to me. "You'll be next," she said.

I didn't stop handling the smooth silver until I heard. "Third in
the women's giant slalom, Lia Erickson with a time of two minutes
5 seconds and 2/100ths." I felt my legs go limp as I tried to stand
up. I walked to the front to the applause from the WU corner and
from my own Monmouth corner. Boast leaned down to me and
placed a third place medal into my hand, whispering, "Well done,
Lia." It was then I noticed that his face was covered in a layer of tan
makeup, caked so thick that it cracked when he smiled.

Scanning the assembly of friends, rivals, and coaches, I shivered with excitement. Although I'd received numerous trophies
in the past, none compared to standing in front of the best racers
in the United States and being applauded. I wanted to savor this
moment, to bask in the warmth of friends, in the flashing of the
press bulbs, in the cheers from the crowd. Truly, I felt accepted
and yes, loved. Smiling toward McElvey, I mouthed the words,
"Thank you."

"Second in the women's giant slalom, Carla Kluckner with a
time of two minutes 4 seconds and one one-hundredth." Carla
jumped up and climbed up the podium next to me, barely looking
at Boast as he handed her a silver medal. She poked me and said,

"Here we go!"

Boast continued, "Finally, first in the women's giant slalom, Becky Langer with a time of two minutes 4 seconds." My eyes followed Becky as she sauntered toward the front of the room. I tried to imagine what a one hundredths of a second meant: a blink of an eye, a snap of a finger. Becky received her second silver bowl and turned to the roar of the crowd, holding her bowl over her head. As she took her place next to Carla, I looked across the line of three red Monmouth sweaters. *Would this be the team to Europe?* I wondered.

As I stepped down from the riser, I saw a tear in Stephanie's eyes. McElvey had put his arm around his daughter. An invisible curtain seemed to be drawn between Stephanie and the rest of us. Returning to the bench, I reached over to pat her shoulder, but she turned away. Worried about her, I barely heard Boast's voice announce the men's winners except when he announced, "And in first place, Peter Timmons with a time of one minute 51 seconds."

McElvey's hand touched my shoulder as I realized that the next results would bring me the greatest accolade of my skiing career. I closed my eyes, wishing that this moment would never end. Boast's voice jolted me back into the room, "Finally in the women's slalom in third place, Tracy Languile with a combined time for the two runs of two minutes and 10 seconds." Tracy, sneering in defiance, looked over her shoulder toward us Monmouth girls. As the applause settled down, he continued, "In second place Becky Langer with a time of two minutes 9 seconds and 2/10^{ths}."

Becky handed her silver bowl to Carla and whispered to me, "Here we go."

"And in first place Lia Erikson with the incredible combined time of two minutes 3 seconds." I moved forward but could barely see my way to the podium through my excitement, my heart thudding in my chest. How I wished Damien and Bill could be here to see me. A collective sigh rose from the crowd; then everyone stood up in a thunderous applause. I reached out for the silver bowl and turned toward the room. The flash bulbs from the press corner made me jump as if a bomb had exploded before me.

Becky grabbed my arm as we walked back toward our group. McElvey leaned toward the two of us, saying quietly, "You two earned this. Your next stop will be Europe."

I looked up in surprise, my mouth open. Becky nodded in agreement. Coach Boast finished the awards with the men's slalom results and then concluded, "Now the moment we have all been waiting for. The US Ski Team to Europe. Would the following racers please step forward? Becky Langer, Lia Erickson, Carla Kluckner, Tracy Languile, and Pammy Siemans."

Carla, Becky, and I linked arms as we slowly walked toward the podium. Like an incoming tide, the applause pushed us forward. Preparing to step on the riser, I felt a leg bump me as if to trip me. I looked up to see Tracy and Pammy, standing at my side, laughing. Coach Boast handed each of us a certificate and then turned toward the cheers of the crowd.

He smiled, staring straight into a large video camera, stenciled with the letters ABC Wide World of Sports. "Congratulations again to these outstanding skiers," he announced, "They have been picked to represent the United States in the first four World Cup races in Europe starting on January 5th, 1971."

Turning back toward our group of five, he said sternly, "Please make sure your passports are in order before we meet in New York in two days. I'll hold an informational meeting tomorrow morning at 8 a.m. Be there." He winked at Tracy.

I heard the word passport and stared directly into Coach Boast's eyes. My heart tightened, I had no passport!

CHAPTER 28

Leaving Vail

The flashbulbs continued to dance off the walls, blinding me as I stepped down from the dais. I felt Becky's arm around my waist, while Carla, behind me, put her hand on my shoulder. Pammy and Tracy lingered on the stage to talk to Boast. Blinking, eyes watering, I scanned the crowd for McElvey's smile. In the darkened corner where he had previously stood, I saw his blue parka resting over the back of a chair. No coach, no Stephanie.

The three of us walked toward the door, hoping to find him outside. As we stepped into the doorway, Boast's assistant coach, Dan Ryan, grabbed Becky's shoulder. Menacingly, he asked, "Where are you three going?" He stepped in our way.

Becky snapped, "To find our coach."

He laughed, "I'm your coach now." His eyebrows furrowed.

I froze. "What do you mean?"

He stepped forward close to my face, and said, "Oh, I guess you haven't heard. I'm going to be your coach in Europe. Yup, along with Boast." He waved his hand to dismiss us. "Oh, by the way, McElvey told me that he'd been called to the phone. I think in the hotel lobby. Uh, Stephanie went with him." He paused, looked down, before saying, "Something about Wren." I couldn't read the pseudo smile on his face—was it a grimace or a smirk? Hearing Wren's name, I panicked. Before I could say something to Becky, a metallic banging followed by a crescendoing applause stopped me. I turned toward the podium to see five young men, two with red parkas, bowing to the audience. Peter Timmons stood above the group, like a young Apollo, as the flash bulbs illuminated his baby face. For an instant I thought of Bill and the last time I saw him at Monmouth.

Becky motioned us to step outside. Carla jumped in front, saying, "Wait a min. Like you're always the one following the rules. Don't you think we should wait 'til the awards ceremony is over, to see who'll be on the men's team?"

"No," insisted Becky. "You can stay, but I'm worried about Wren."

I could feel the tension between them. Raising my hand, I said, "I agree. C'mon, let's just wait until the men's team is picked. It'll only take two minutes. It's only respectful."

Just as I finished speaking, Coach Boast announced in his loudest voice, "These five young men, who've been chosen to represent the United States in Europe, will be serving their country with as much honor as our soldiers who are fighting in Vietnam. Please put your hands together for Peter Timmons, Jason Lang, Scott Forman, Dennis Albright, and Tony Koch."

I looked at Becky, scowled, and raised my hand. Deliberately, I put one finger to my ear, slowly turning it in a circular manner and shook my head sideways. Becky pushed me out the door. We barely took two steps before I said what we were both thinking. "Did you hear that? The soldiers in Vietnam. I wonder what Bill would think about that?"

"Egad, speaking of Bill," said Becky, "Have you heard from him?"

"Nope," I said, pausing. "Except what Peter Timmons told me."

"What was that?" asked Becky, looking worried.

"Oh, you remember. That Bill had been deployed and was on his way back to active duty." I paused trying to remember where he'd gone first. "Through Massachusetts."

"Oh, yeah. So does that mean he'll be going to Vietnam?" Becky shook her head in disbelief.

"For all I know, he could be fighting in Vietnam now," I said, indicating with both hands that I didn't want to talk anymore.

Carla interrupted, her face red with anger, "Jeeze, you guys. You didn't even have the courtesy to stay to congratulate the guys' team. Like how self-centered can you get?"

Both Becky and I acknowledged our rudeness. Together we said, our heads down in mock remorse, "Sorry."

"Forgiven," said Carla. "Now let's go find Coach and Stephanie."

We went directly to the Vail Lodge where McElvey had been staying. We found him, bent over the main desk with a phone grasped tightly in his hand. Stephanie sat in a large, overstuffed couch next to a fire, smothering her face in her hands, obviously trying to hide her expression.

Becky settled in next to her, while Carla and I moved in front of the fire to warm our hands. "What's going on?" said Becky in a slow, concerned voice.

Through her sobs, Stephanie cried, "Dad just called the hospital ... Wren has taken a turn for the worse. She's having trouble breathing. They put her on a respirator."

"What about her legs?" asked Carla, rubbing her thighs to warm them up.

"No one knows for sure." said Stephanie. Looking frightened, she added, "Dad wants us to go back to the room and like—um— meet him in the morning. Well, of course, after your meeting with, ah, Coach Boast. I think he plans for us to drive to Denver to visit Wren."

Becky looked to McElvey, still on the phone, as he waved his hand to dismiss us. We left the warmth of the lobby for the street. A light snow started to fall in only the way a Colorado storm can—first large flakes, saucers spiraling down from the metallic sky—then the frozen hexagons growing smaller and increasing in number until I could no longer see through my lashes. Lifting my face to the sky, I let the crystals tickle my cheeks and heard them hiss as they hit my parka. I stuck out my tongue to taste their coldness.

At the footbridge that led to Poor Simon's, Carla said, "You three go on. I think I'll go back to congratulate the guys who made the team."

"That's not a good idea," said Becky, holding up her hand like a policeman stopping traffic. "You know they'll want to party."

"Duh. Like why do you think I'm going?" snapped Carla.

"Well, don't wake us when you get in," I said, turning my back on Carla.

✳ ✳ ✳

The next morning, Becky, Carla, and I went to the meeting in the cafeteria with the new US Ski Team: five girls and five boys. Coach Boast gave us each a glossy folder and went over the information inside. We would have two days off before meeting in New York to catch a Lufthansa flight to Geneva. Each of us needed to call the ski team office in Boulder to make arrangements for our flights to New York.

When I told Boast I didn't have a passport, he immediately said he would make arrangements for me to travel to New York ahead of the others, so I could get the necessary documents at the new office of Senator James Buckley.

Returning to the ski-tuning room, we found McElvey packing the wax kit. Stephanie was off in another corner, loading her black ski bag. One solitary, smoke-covered light highlighted McElvey's unkempt, dirty-blonde hair. I'd never seen him look so tired and old as he bent over. I breathed in the smell of wax, pytex, and metal filings, and closed my eyes, excited about making the team, yet conflicted about Wren's predicament.

"Morning, Coach. We're here," announced Becky, as if he had nothing else to worry about.

He dropped the black metal Monmouth wax-kit onto the box marked US Ski Team. A clang resounded through the room like two sabers clashing in battle. When he turned to face us, his cheeks grew red with anger. He slowly found the words to say. "Sit down, girls. I want to tell you what we're doing today."

I sat on a wax-covered bench, facing him as he spoke in the monotone of an executioner. He stood in front of us, his legs astride the two ski kits. His hands hung down at his sides in resignation. "Get your ski bags packed and be at the car in one hour. The three of you going to Europe need to organize your clothes and skis in two bags, one for Europe and one for Monmouth. Stephanie and I will take your extra clothes back with us."

Shocked by his emotionless voice, Carla asked, "What about Wren? I thought we were going to Denver to see her." I nodded in agreement as Stephanie came over to sit on the bench with us.

"Yup, we're all going to Denver," he said, now searching for his words. "I'm not sure we'll be able to see her, because she's gone back to the ICU. When I left her early yesterday morning, she'd been recovering in the orthopedic unit, her back and neck stabilized. That's when she experienced breathing issues … " He shook his head in frustration. He waited a moment for this information to register and to see how much we knew about her condition. No one said a word, so he continued. "… she has a fracture in her lower vertebrae. There's pressure on her spinal cord." Again he stopped as the four of us let out a communal gasp. "At this point she can't move her legs; however, … " A pause as he tried to sound convincing, "… this may be a temporary condition until the swelling subsides. I'm not sure why she's having trouble breathing." His voice trailed off.

Even Becky couldn't find any words to break the silence that ensued. I tried pushing away the frightening images that flooded my brain like a slide show: Wren in a neck brace, white sheets, fluorescent lights. Nurses in starched white uniforms. Doctors with green masks. Yellow linoleum floors. Disembodied voices over intercoms, "Paging Doctor Hirschberg."

Then came the image that made me shiver: my mother lying in a hospital bed after her car accident on the Appalachian Gap;

my mother with her neck in traction and her head bandaged, her black, swollen eyes trying to express her love for me even though she couldn't speak through her tracheotomy. Then, the final image of the minister standing over my mother's grave saying, "Father, we commend to you the soul of your daughter, Margaret Ford Erickson."

Carla nudged me to bring my thoughts back into the room. "Hey, stupid, what are you doing. Coach just left and we need to get packed."

I said, "Wow, I just had a total out-of-body experience! I missed everything that coach said after he told us about Wren."

Carla smiled, saying, "Not to worry, just pack your ski bag. Stephanie, Becky and I are going back to the room now to finish packing. We'll see you there. Be at the car at 10:00 a.m."

Shaking my head to free it from my daymare, I said, "I think I'll walk the long way around Vail just to be alone for a minute."

CHAPTER 29

Crossing the Divide

Emptiness greeted me when I returned to our bunk room. The others had already packed, and Wren's bed on the lower berth remained neat, while the rest of our beds had the sheets and blankets bundled on the mattresses. Grabbing my clothes from my dresser, I began arranging them in piles on Wren's untouched comforter. Although I'd been through this process many times, now I had to pack for five weeks—five weeks in a foreign land.

I wondered, *Would there be washing machines in Europe? What if I needed new toiletry articles? How much toothpaste should I bring?* Overwhelmed, I sat on the bed for a moment to quiet my mind.

Opening my rucksack, I started stuffing my clothes in, first my rolled underwear and bras, then four pair of pants—one black, one jean and two khaki, four turtlenecks, and three pairs of long johns. No one ever wore skirts at the race banquets, so I decided to send my dressy clothes back to Monmouth in my other bag. I definitely needed six pairs of ski socks, as they always got wet, and three pairs of regular socks. I separated my Monmouth ski gear—red sweater, parka, ski pants, warm-up pants, and racing jacket—all to go back with McElvey, because Boast had insisted that we should now wear the US Ski Team's uniform, which would be waiting in Denver.

When I discovered the yellow sweater that Wren had worn for the first night's dinner, I sat down wondering if I should take it to her or send it to Monmouth? I smelled the sweater to remember Wren's rose perfume, her looks with her short brown hair, pug nose, and squatty-body, bow-legged walk. *Would she ever walk again?* I decided to take the sweater to Denver.

Fortunately, I had to go to the bathroom or I'd have forgotten my toilet case. I placed my shampoo and hair spray into the Monmouth bag, hoping that the hotels in Europe would supply me with such basics. My European travel bag already overflowed. I had little room for my books, so reluctantly I packed my John Muir book, as well as Emerson's essays, with the Monmouth clothes. One of my small found-poems fell out, thoughts that I'd written after my afternoon of free-skiing with Becky:

> Everybody needs
> Beauty
> As well as bread.

> Everybody needs
> Places
> To play in, to pray in.

> Everybody needs
> Nature
> To strengthen body and soul.

Only Norton's *Anthology of Poems*, my journal and, of course, my pens would come with me. Someday I'd have fun sharing my writing with Bill. Also, in order to write letters to my dad and, maybe, to Bill, I grabbed notepaper and envelopes. Struggling, I could barely zip the overstuffed bag.

I dragged the two bags down to the station wagon where Becky, Carla, and Stephanie were waiting. McElvey's head peeked over the roof rack as he fastened the last of the ski bags on top.

"Hop in," he said. "Steph, you sit in front so you can direct me. Here's the map."

"Where are we staying in Denver?" I asked.

He said sternly, "Coach Boast has made arrangements for the three of you going to Europe to be guests of Jason Lang's family. I hear they're quite wealthy and you'll be very comfortable. Stephanie and I will stay at a motel near the hospital." He slid into the driver's seat.

No one spoke while the overloaded car groaned up the hairpin turns on Loveland Pass. Once again, I snuggled with my friends. My eyes traveled up the slopes to the black spine of the Rocky Mountains—the clear blue sky contrasting with the opalescent snowfields. Each bend brought another distant peak into view. On the uphill side, the snow banks rose ten feet above the car and higher where an avalanche had crossed the road.

At the top next to a sign that read *"Loveland Pass, 11,990 feet Atlantic – Pacific. The Continental Divide,"* McElvey pulled the car over to let pass the ten cars that had gathered behind us. Turning to our huddled group, he said, "I know you're scared about Wren. Your silence tells me everything. Let me remind you that when we get to the hospital, you'll need to be cheery. She needs positive feedback." Pausing, he let some emotion show. "Also, once we part ways in Denver, I'll no longer be your coach. Boast has let me know that he and Dan Ryan will take over. I'm to have minimal contact with you."

Becky tried to ask a question, "But … ?"

"Please let me finish, Becky." He sighed, gathering his thoughts. "And, I'll no longer be financially responsible for you. The US Ski Team will be paying for all costs—travel and racing."

Smiling, he reached into his pocket, pulled out his wallet and handed each of us a crisp new bill. "However, when you return from Europe …. " He hesitated at a loss for words. "Remember, Monmouth will always be your home." He grabbed the steering wheel, shifted into low and let the car crawl down the Continental Divide. I liked the fact that he spoke to communicate, not to discuss. Carefully, turning my bill, I saw a picture of Ben

Franklin— one hundred dollars! I'd never seen one before.

The bright sun reflected off the windblown crust, blinding me. I felt conflicted and scared about the future: to the east lay my home in Vermont, behind to the west lay Monmouth and all that I'd grown to love about western skiing. Way ahead lay Europe and the World Cup races.

In a small way I didn't want the car to sail forward—I felt as though I were losing my anchor.

CHAPTER 30

Denver

Jason Lang's modern house on 14th Avenue stood out like a mutated bug among the older Tudor homes, ugly with blank, plate-glass windows and a flat roof. Along the oak-covered boulevard, cars streamed by, honking, squealing, reminding me of how much I hated cities. As we pulled into the driveway, I looked back longingly over my shoulder toward the west and the Rocky Mountains, invisible because of smog.

Even before we came to a stop, the double-wide front door opened. A perfectly coiffed woman emerged. Her tight, tan pants emphasized her anorexic legs, and her white cotton sweater revealed two small knobs just below her pearl necklace. Becky and I poked each other, giggling. Before anyone was able to step out of the car, the woman's red nails grabbed Becky's door and jerked it open. Compared to my mom, who rarely dressed up, just jeans and tee shirts, this woman looked like a pampered princess. Her mascara-covered, Barbie-face poked in the car door.

I could barely hear her words as I gagged on the smell of her makeup, hair spray, and perfume. "Welcome, y'all. You must be tired. My son, Jason, has already told me about your races."

McElvey stepped out, extending his hand, "Thanks for hosting the girls. I'm Justin McElvey, their coach from Monmouth. You're very kind. Yes, they're exhausted." He, too, backed off once he smelled the perfume. Reflexively, his hand went up to his nose, stifling a sneeze. Again, I had to quash my laugh.

The woman replied, curtseying flirtatiously, "Ah, I've heard about you all and your program at Monmouth. Such a wise coach." She moved toward him, reaching to put her hand on his arm. "Jason has told me much about your support of the girls." She batted her lined eyelids.

Pulling his arm back, McElvey answered, "Why, thank you, but they deserve all the credit." He quickly moved toward the rear to begin unloading.

Becky jumped out first. "Hi, I'm Becky Langer from Los Angeles."

Carla tripped on her way out and said, "And I'm Carla Kluckner from Monmouth."

Awkwardly bumping my head on the door frame, I stepped into the bright light and smiled, "And I'm Lia Erickson from Vermont and Monmouth."

Hearing a noise behind me, I turned to the front of the car just as Stephanie's dirty-blonde head emerged. Slowly, her face appeared: drawn, baggy-eyed, looking as if she had been lost in the woods for days. "And I'm Stephanie McElvey."

Before I could ask the woman her name, an athletic boy came striding out the front door. His large shoulders moved slowly forward with the confidence of a weight lifter. "I suppose you all know my son, Jason," said the made-up woman. I looked into his gorgeous blue eyes and admired his aquiline nose.

Carla immediately stepped out in front of the group, tossed her dark hair to the side, and reached out her hand. "Hi, Jason, we met in the Ratskeller last night."

Jason smiled as if he remembered more than he was willing to tell. "Oh, yeah. You're the great dancer, if I remember right." He rocked his hips in a circular motion.

McElvey looked askance at Carla and said sternly," Okay, girls, grab your bags. Stephanie and I are heading to the hotel. I'm sure Mrs. Lang will make you comfortable. I'll call you in the morning after I've heard about Wren. Rest up and have fun."

He and Stephanie climbed back into the station wagon while

the three of us gathered our belongings. I'd gotten pretty good at strapping on my backpack before hoisting my ski bag over my shoulder. Without offering to help any of us, Jason indicated that we should take our skis to the garage.

Mrs. Lang took us upstairs and gave us each a separate bedroom. I felt lost in my oversized room with its king-size bed and private bath. Pink curtains matched the bedspread and over-stuffed chair. My bathroom, also pink, included a glass-enclosed, marble shower. I picked up and studied pictures of a blonde teenage girl in a high school cheerleader's outfit that had been carefully placed on top of the bureau.

After unpacking, I wandered into Becky's bedroom, decorated in a neutral tone. I noticed pictures of a baby-faced, thin boy with hippie length dark hair, standing on top of a rocky peak, a large backpack balanced on his shoulder.

Carla startled me when she walked into the room, towing Jason behind her like a toy dog. She looked very comfortable with him as she patted the bedspread and pulled him down to sit next to her. Enthusiastically, she said, "Hi, guys, like have you ever been in such a gorgeous house?"

Jason smiled, putting his hand on Carla's knee, and said, "So Becky, you're in my brother Sam's room. Lia, you're in my sister Tanya's room. Tanya's away at Radcliffe. Sam's home, waiting to go into the Peace Corps. He just graduated from the U of Denver." He rolled his eyes. "And you, Carla, you get the guest room next to mine." He clicked his tongue.

Just then, a lithe, long-haired boy stepped through the door, his tie-dye shirt hanging almost to his knees. "Hi, I'm Sam. So Becky, you get my room, okay. Mommie made me move in with Jason," he added, seemingly frustrated. "I've got only three days before I have to pack and go to New York to catch my final training." He stood taller and continued, "I'm headed to Uganda."

No one knew what to say, so finally Becky broke the

awkwardness. "Well, are you going to tell us why you're going to Uganda?"

Sam moved to the Barcalounger chair next to the window and said impatiently "Haven't you been following the news? Vietnam, the war, the draft." He looked disgusted, "Duh."

I raised my hand as if in school. "Of course, we know about it. We haven't been totally naïve. In fact, we've got a friend on his way to Vietnam right now." Then, frustrated, I said, "What's this have to do with you?"

Sam answered, "Okay, just joking. Don't get so upset. Like, you probably understand the choices that I faced when I graduated from the U of Denver. I got listed 1A at graduation and my chances of getting drafted were 100 percent. So, I signed up for Kennedy's Peace Corps." His face beamed with pride.

I broke in. "I haven't heard about the Peace Corps. What is it? Part of the military?"

Sam laughed at my confusion and said, "Not quite. Just the opposite. The Peace Corps is an alternative form of service for college graduates. If I serve two years as a teacher in Africa, I can't get drafted. I'm hoping by the time I'm done, the war will be over. If not, I'll re-up for another two years."

Becky noticed me getting angrier and broke in, "Wait a minute. Do you mean that you can avoid the military if you go work in Africa?"

"Yep, but you have to have graduated from college. In New York, I'll get three months of training in Swahili and lessons on the Ugandan culture," said Sam showing the assurance of someone who had beaten the system. "Then, I can be a teacher in a rural village in Africa."

I turned to Becky and asked, "Could Bill have done this?" She shrugged.

"Who's Bill?" said Sam.

"Oh, a racing friend of mine who just got drafted to Vietnam,"

I said angrily as though everyone knew about Bill's situation. "He trained at Monmouth with us, but when he got cut by Boast, you know, from the US team, he got his draft papers." Turning to Jason who appeared to be more interested in Carla, I continued, "By the way, Jason, how can you leave college and ski in Europe with us? Won't you get drafted?"

Jason looked very embarrassed and said, "I can't tell you the whole story. Let's just say that Coach Boast has connections. None of the guys on the team have to worry about either the draft or the war." He rubbed his fingers together in a gesture of money-exchanging.

I stood up, signaling to Becky and Carla that I was uncomfortable. "Let's go downstairs. Is there any food in the kitchen?" I asked, rubbing my stomach.

I ambled down the ornate stair case, sliding my hands along the curved, mahogany railing. A three-story rotunda, painted with a detailed fresco of four naked nymphs lounging in a field, rose over my head. Stepping delicately, almost tripping while looking up to the rounded bodies, I tried to figure out why anyone would want to have nubile girls hanging above their foyer.

In the kitchen, a dark-haired Mexican woman stood over a stainless-steel counter, preparing sandwiches. She turned, her pug nose twitching, and said, "Buenos dias," and then returned to work. Mrs. Lang looked up from a glass table in the breakfast nook, put down her glass of white wine, inhaled her cigarette, and drawled, "Ah, so y'all have unpacked. I hope you met my boys. They're sooo excited to have you here." She exhaled a large smoke circle. "This is Dolores, our maid. She's finishing some cucumber sandwiches for you. Please sit down. After you have a quick bite, I thought I'd drive you around and show you our Denver. It's not quite like Charleston where I'm from, but it has some interesting cowboy history." She paused, faking a yawn, "Of course, we can always go shopping if y'all get bored."

I'd never met such a stuck-up, prissy woman and felt really self-conscious as I sat down at the table that faced a formal backyard surrounded by shorn hedges and gravel paths. As Dolores served the crustless sandwiches and iced tea, Becky said formally, "Why thank you Mrs. Lang, you're so generous." She lifted the sandwich delicately between two fingers, making sure her pinkie curled as she turned to me with a smirk.

"No problem," said Mrs. Lang, dismissing Becky's comment with a wave of her hand. "But please call me Charlotte. We don't have to be so formal here."

I had trouble following the conversation because a television droned in the background. A reporter mentioned Vietnam, fifty American soldiers killed. Mrs. Lang raised her hand and said, "Shh, I do want to hear this wrap-up of the news."

All turned toward the large black and white TV in the corner next to the refrigerator. The announcer said, "To sum up the year, American troop levels have reached 334,600 with 6,081 confirmed deaths. Yesterday, President Nixon announced more bombing of Cambodia to bring about peace."

Mrs. Lang got up to turn off the TV. She shook her fist, "It's about time. Those damn commie bastards! I hope President Nixon blows them to smithereens."

I'd never experienced such hostility toward North Vietnam. Attempting to break the tension, I innocently said, "What about all the children, families?"

Charlotte Lang turned on me as though I'd dropped one of her favorite china plates. Shaking her finger, she said, "You don't understand. You've been off skiing in Vail and haven't been watching what the Viet Cong have been doing. Why, you're just like Sam—you're afraid of confronting evil. If the Viet Cong take over Vietnam, then the rest of Asia will fall to the Communists. We've got to stop the Commies now or, before you know it, we'll all be their servants."

Becky, sensing that this conversation was heating said, "Excuse me. Charlotte, I can see you support the war. We probably don't understand much. We only hear from our friends who're getting drafted."

"Well, girls, let me tell you a few things. My husband, John, works for Lockheed and he says that … "

Before she could finish, Sam walked into the doorway. He flicked his long hair off his face, and said, "Oh, Mommie, don't get going about the war again. Let's just enjoy our guests. I'm only going to be home for a few more days. Remember, we promised not to talk about politics." He leaned against the door frame, trying to look casual but didn't move farther into the room.

Charlotte waved her hand in acquiescence and said, "Dolores, could you clear the table? I think it's time to go shopping with the girls. I need to get some new shoes for our club's New Year's Eve party tonight"

Needing a break, I stood up, "Thanks again, but I think I'd rather go for a run this afternoon. Anyone want to join me?"

Becky jumped up and nodded in agreement. "You bet. I feel as if I need some exercise, too." She winked at me.

Carla, looking up at Jason as he entered the room, said, "Why I'd love to have a tour of Denver, especially if Jason comes, too."

Becky and I excused ourselves and went upstairs, put on our running shoes and sweat pants, and headed out into the cool December air. On the street, Carla, Charlotte, and Jason passed us in a black Mercedes sedan bearing the license plate Colorado 15. When the noise of the engine receded, I heard the cackles of crows, an indecipherable chatter, as though I had turned on a TV from another country.

CHAPTER 31

The Flight East

On New Year's Day, well rested, I woke early, so I could catch a run toward the east, past the Denver Tennis Club, where I might catch a glimpse of the Rockies and maybe a sunrise. I wanted to start 1971 fresh, excited that this would be my year, a chance to ski for the United States in World Cup races and earn enough points to make the Olympic team. Tiptoeing down the staircase, I tried not to wake my friends—I craved being alone.

My father had once told me that if you run with someone, you talk to your companion; if you run alone, you talk to the world. I needed time to sort out my emotions. So much had happened in the last couple of weeks that I felt I'd lived many lives in one: the dangers of racing, the joys of powder skiing, the frustrations with coaches, the pettiness of Tracy, the hysteria of Stephanie, the rebelliousness of Carla, the dominance of Becky, and finally, the uncertainty of Wren's injury.

I looked forward to seeing Wren this morning. During all these highs and lows, I'd no one to really talk to. Even when I tried to open up to Becky about my fears, she dismissed me, telling me just to focus on my own fitness and racing. She warned me that the background noise and petty issues would only get even more confusing in Europe, so I should just worry about myself, become more self-centered.

The brisk air and clear skies snapped me awake as I stepped from the curb and jogged up the boulevard. At the first rise in the road, I stopped, and looked back toward the Rockies, imagining the peaks to be a dragon's spine of black boulders mantled with white scales. I pinched myself—time past, present, and future melted into one. Continuing, one step in front of another, I felt in control again.

Returning to the house, I found the US Ski Team station wagon parked in the driveway next to Charlotte's Mercedes. *Who could be here so early?* My heart raced, my hands shook. Guardedly, I stepped into the foyer, calmed by the sweet smell of omelets and salsa. From the shadows on the right I heard, "Good morning, Lia. I was just unloading your team uniforms and dress clothes for Europe." Coach Ryan stepped forward, smiling and flexing his football-sized shoulders under his t-shirt.

"Wow, I'd no idea we'd be getting all these clothes," I said as I picked up a sapphire-blue parka with white stripes down its sleeves and a gold and red US Ski Team patch on the left front panel. I hugged the jacket to my chest, a glow of pride warmed my cheeks.

From the same shadow stepped Mrs. Lang, lifting her lace night gown from her toes, her hair teased high into a rat's nest. "You girls are so lucky to have us as benefactors for the team. I just completed a fundraising banquet to raise money for your uniforms. Y'all do need to look sharp when you land in Europe." She winked at Coach Ryan who nodded in agreement.

I blushed, realizing that Mrs. Lang seemed a little too comfortable around him as she stood in her thin negligee. To break the awkwardness, Coach Ryan said, "Now you see, Lia, I was just telling Charlotte ... ," he paused, smiling at her, "... that I'll pick you up this morning at eleven to catch a plane to New York."

Dropping the parka, I stepped back toward the door. "What? I didn't know we'd leave this soon," I said, panicking that I didn't have time to get organized or to see Wren.

Undaunted by my protests, he continued, "The rest of the team will join us in two days at New York airport. We'll fly KLM to Brussels and then Berlin. Believe it or not, your first race is in Oberstafen on January 6th."

I felt out of control, my thoughts circling like water going down a drain. No one had let me know the schedule. "But—but," I stammered. "The three of us had planned to go to the hospital with Coach McElvey to see … "

Emotionless, he stopped me. "Well, I doubt you can squeeze that in. I haven't talked to McElvey. Boast has given me orders to get you to Buckley's office in New York by 9 a.m. Jan 2, where the Senator will have a passport ready for you. I just do what I'm told." Before I could answer, he concluded, "As I said, I'll be here at 11 for our 12:30 flight. Please pack efficiently: one bag plus your ski and boot bags."

I ran up the stairs to find Becky without acknowledging his final caveat. Anger welled as I burst into her room. Becky sat up, pulling her covers to her chest in modesty and said, "What the heck's happening? You look as if you've just seen a ghost."

"You'll not believe what just happened. I—I can't go with you to see Wren."

"Why not?"

"Coach Ryan just stopped by with our uniforms and told me that I have to go with him to New York this morning."

"Ah, I see," she laughed, letting the covers fall to her knees. "Welcome to the US Ski Team. From now on your life's not your own. They make the rules—they tell you where to be, how to dress, what to eat, and where and how to ski."

"But, Becky, we'd all planned to see Wren today—McElvey promised."

"First of all, it's not guaranteed that we'll see Wren. It all depends on whether she's out of the ICU. Second, you don't have a passport and need to get one before we fly to Europe. I still don't understand how Boast can get you a passport in one day." Seeing me look away in modesty, she pulled the covers back up.

Relieved, I said, "Coach Ryan told me that Senator James Buckley's office was taking care of the matter. Apparently, if you have power, you can do anything."

"Well, yeah, make that power and money. So it's settled, you'll go to New York and we'll see Wren. Why don't you go shower and write Wren a little note before breakfast? I know you want to be a writer, so start there." She pretended to scribble with her hand. "You're always writing in your journal. I'll take it to her." Waving her hand to dismiss me, she settled back into her bed.

I calmed down in the shower. The warm water coursing down my back and between my legs felt like a liquid caress. Wrapped in a warm towel, I sat on my bed and began writing in my journal. My handwriting jumped around, but this exercise helped to quiet my thoughts before I jotted a note of encouragement to Wren.

Wren, sorry to miss you. Becky will explain. I think of you every day and will run every race for you. Get strong. Love, Lia. Frustrated with my lack of fluency, I tore the page from my journal. Then, I added a quote my father always used from Winston Churchill, *Never, never, never give up.*

Rereading my words, I felt helpless. Words, the words that I loved, couldn't express my pain for Wren, for her suffering. I tried to imagine Wren stretched out on a hospital bed, her head in a halo, her legs immobilized under the covers, her brown eyes pleading for a reprieve.

At breakfast, the phone rang while Dolores served us huevos rancheros. Charlotte, relaxing in front of the TV, yelled to Becky to take the call. When Becky returned, she said, "That was McElvey. He'll be here at 11:30 to take us to the hospital." Her eyes crinkled in a smile before she continued, "It looks as if Wren's out of ICU."

I dropped my fork. "That means I won't be able to see him either. To … to say good-bye."

Becky looked puzzled. "Who? Oh, you mean Coach. That's not the end of the world. Did you write the note to Wren? I'll take it. I doubt we'll be able to spend very much time with her anyway."

"Yes, I did, but it's not fair that I can't say good bye to McElvey,

Stephanie, or Wren," I whined, lowering my voice to a whisper.

Becky looked around the room before saying, "Hey, stupid, I was on the team to Europe last year and discovered what you're now learning. You can't make any plans. You're basically working for Boast and the team. Your time is not your own." She paused, lowered her head so as not to meet my eyes. "And forget the word 'fair.'"

Now angry, I shot back, "But, but what about *my* feelings, *my* needs? Isn't there someone I can talk to about this?"

"No," said Becky. "You've just discovered one of the paradoxes of ski racing. We work as a team, lose our identity to the coaches, yet ironically, we fight for individual points." She shook her head angrily just as Jason entered the room, his thick hair spiking like a porcupine's and his bare chest hairless. Carla gasped as though she had just seen Elvis Presley come in.

He laughed, "Hey, girls, why so sad? We're about to begin the adventure of a lifetime." Getting no response from Becky and me, he turned to Carla. "That was fun last night, right? Did you like the band?" He winked at Carla and tripped as he stepped toward her. "I'll admit I'm a little hungover."

Carla raised her finger to her lips, but not before Becky said, "Okay, Carla, I thought you went to bed when we did. Fess up. Did you decide to go celebrate New Year's Eve after all? Do you want me to tell Coach Boast?"

Jason laughed a hyena squeal to the point that he had to hold his stomach. "Tell Coach Boast. Are you kidding me? He was out partying with us."

Carla tried to laugh, too, but she realized that she'd broken the code of Monmouth girls. "Please, Becky, don't tell McElvey. He'd be disappointed in me."

Jason saw a fight coming as Becky stood up, hands on hips. He stepped into the middle of the room, "Calm down, girls. We all need a little fun. Besides, McElvey doesn't make the rules now. Boast is one of us and likes partying."

I excused myself to go pack.

At exactly 11 a.m. the US Team station wagon arrived with Coach Boast at the wheel and Coach Ryan riding shotgun. Grabbing my two bags by the door, I thanked Charlotte for her hospitality, hugged Becky, and waved to Carla. "See you all in New York."

"Beware of Coach Ryan," said Becky in jest.

✳ ✳ ✳

Once in flight, I didn't feel comfortable sitting next to Coach Ryan, his broad shoulder pushing intimately into my arm, so I kept my gaze trained out the window. I'd only flown three times previously and each time I had to hold my breath during takeoff. I would count to 100 as the plane left the ground. Someone had once told me that these were the most dangerous seconds of the flight, and I remembered reading about the crash of the Electra during takeoff in Boston. I think the plane went down in less than a minute because birds flew into the propellers.

Ironically, I feared crashing in a plane more than I feared a falling in a downhill. At least in a downhill, I had some control. The steady roar of the engines and the pressure in my eardrums reassured me that we were climbing quickly. I relaxed, letting my thoughts wander out into the clouds. *Air snow,* I thought. *The undulating kernels would make a perfect ski run.*

Once aloft, I grabbed my journal. A picture fell out into coach's lap. Picking it up from his crotch, he asked, "Who's this good-looking guy? I didn't know you had a boyfriend."

Looking down, I said, "He's not exactly a boyfriend. He's just a really good friend from Monmouth. He just got drafted and is on his way to Vietnam. Did you ever know Bill Emerson? He skied for Boast once, on the WU team."

"The name rings a bell, but I haven't worked for the team very long. Boast just hired me. I used to coach up at Crystal Mountain in Washington state. He just asked me to come along to Europe to help with the girls' team," he said, smirking as if he were the fox in charge of the chicken coop.

Annoyed at his smugness, I decided to stop the conversation and start writing in my journal. I erased, crossed out, scribbled my thoughts about Wren. I laughed to myself. *Where are my winged words?* Not long after, the purr of the engines put me to sleep.

A sharp bump from the plane and a quick loss of altitude woke me. At that moment I realized that coach's left shoulder had been rubbing against my breast. I jerked my head up and felt him pull away, but not before I noticed his right hand playing with his crotch. I moved quickly toward the window, pretending not to have seen what he had been doing.

CHAPTER 32

New York

New York City: I'd never been there or, in fact, to any cities, except once to Boston with my dad to visit the Museum of Science. I didn't think of Burlington, Vermont as a city, because it didn't have the big-city crime or the high-rises.

This evening the bleating of taxi cabs, the parade of pedestrians at stop lights, the glitter of streetlights, and the glow from the overhanging skyscrapers made me feel like a river stone dropped into a box of faux jewels. Fortunately, the sight of snow-covered Central Park across from the Plaza took the edge off my anxiety.

Coach Ryan grabbed my arm as we entered our hotel between the two columns and across the red carpet. A tall, dark porter tipped his top hat while opening the glass doors. I couldn't help but stare at his bulbous nose. He nodded, "Welcome to the Plaza, young lady." Stumbling, not knowing how to respond, I stepped onto the marble tile, only to be met by a funereal waft of lilies. Once more I looked over my shoulder at the park, dreaming I might catch a short run through the pseudo-forest the next morning before taking a taxi to Senator Buckley's office. Coach Ryan handed the porter a few bills, gesturing to our bags piled by the yellow cab. I felt uncomfortable and useless.

During dinner in the hotel's restaurant, I began to feel more at ease with Coach Ryan, who now asked me to call him Dan. He was even more handsome in his white turtleneck and hip-hugging blue jeans that accentuated his muscular quads. The dim lighting made his tanned face look younger than his 30 years. Authoritatively, he began, "So, Lia, we have no time to waste tomorrow morning—we've got an appointment at Senator Buckley's office at 8 a.m."

I settled back in my over-stuffed velvet chair. "How am I going to get a passport in one day?" I asked innocently.

He leaned forward, putting his hand up, "Not to let your little head worry about such details. Connections … we have connections. Isn't that how the world works?"

I let this information register before responding. "But how do they have all my information, such as my birth certificate?"

He smiled smugly, "Have you talked to your father recently?"

I recoiled, realizing that he must know more about my private life than I'd assumed. "No, I'd planned to call him after dinner."

"Well, Boast called him. Uh, he got all the important information. You'd be surprised at what Boast can do with his connections. It started when he became friends with the Kennedys. He was really good friends with Bobby Kennedy. How much do you know about the Kennedys?"

"Well," I said, looking away across the room toward the porter, not wanting to recall the loss of hope I'd felt at the President's assassination, "I remember the day President Kennedy was shot in Texas, November 22, 1963. I was in English class." For an instant, I remembered the cold of my school desk, the pile of notebooks, and my hands skimming my essay on Walt Whitman, while I read the teacher's comments. I said, recalling each detail, "My teacher was called out into the hallway. When she came back, she was pale, her hands shaking as she told my class the President had been shot, that he'd been taken to the hospital in Dallas. My heart snapped like a stick being cracked on a rock." I paused, and then asked, "Oh so, where were you?"

He looked as if he didn't expect this question. He thought for a moment, then smiled, "Well, you are quite the poet." He laughed, smirking, "With a girl."

A silence stopped the conversation. I felt relieved when the waitress came to ask for our orders. I noticed that Dan didn't look the young girl in the eye, rather at her breasts.

"Yes, thanks," he said and turning to me, "You'd better get a hamburger and fries here, as you won't get any in Europe."

The rest of the conversation revolved around how he had become a coach for the US Ski Team. I barely listened, simply waiting for him to finish. Finally, the waitress sauntered back. I noticed that her scooped-neck blouse exposed more of her cleavage. She looked directly at Dan, cocked her head to the side, and asked coyly, "Would anyone like dessert?"

Dan, unable to take his eyes from her rounded flesh, said, "No, thanks. Maybe later. We're in training." He made a motion for the bill with his fingers. You can go to your room, Lia. I'll see you for breakfast at 7." He continued, never looking at me, "After we get your passport work done, we'll have to head out to the airport, because at 5, we'll meet the rest of team. Our flight to Brussels leaves at 8."

My chair protested as I slid back from the table. Since he was preoccupied with the waitress, I, somewhat relieved, headed for the elevator and pushed the button for the fifth floor. My room, dominated by a queen-sized bed, piled high with gold-tasseled pillows and matching velvet curtains, adjoined Dan's room. I made sure the door between the two rooms was locked before I lay down on the mattress and made the collect call to my father. I had to be brief with him, because he hated to spend money on phone calls—in fact, he hated spending money on anything.

"Hi, Dad, I'm in New York now."

"Hi, honey, great to hear from you."

"I'm staying at the Plaza Hotel with a new coach, Dan Ryan. You probably know we're here to get my passport."

"Yes, dear, Coach Boast called me a day ago. I gave him all the information he needed. I still don't understand how he's able to expedite the process."

"I guess the ski team has connections with Senator James Buckley. I've got to go to his office tomorrow."

After a slight pause on the other line, my father said, "That would explain everything. Are you ready for Europe?"

"I think so, but I've got to say that I'm nervous about the travel. Also, I'm not sure whether I like the new coach, Dan Ryan."

"Uh, what do you mean?"

"Well, he flirts with every female he sees." I hesitated, remembering the awkward moment on the plane.

"Hon, this is the US Ski Team. I'm sure they hire only qualified coaches. I do hope you're being respectful to your coaches." He emphasized the "do."

"Well, they just don't seem as honest as McElvey."

"Uh, in what way?" My father sounded impatient.

"I don't exactly know. The coaches seem to pick favorites." I paused, trying to choose my words carefully. "They seem to be chauvinists."

"Hey, I don't want to hear such talk from you. Now, Lia, please be respectful of your coaches. I don't want to have to say this again."

"Okay, Dad, I hear you. At least I have my friends, Becky and Carla, on the team to talk to."

After a short pause, "Lia, do you need any money for Europe?"

I gasped, not used to such an offer. "No thanks, Dad. McElvey gave each of us $100 before we left." I tried to think of something to say and continued, "Have I received any mail from my friend, Bill? He's supposed to be deployed to Vietnam."

"Ah, that explains a letter that came with an APO address."

Excited, I squeezed the phone. "What did you do with it?"

"I forwarded it to Box 24 at Monmouth. Just like I always do."

I leaned back on my oversized pillow, letting a tear course

down my cheek. "Oh, well, I guess I won't know where he is until I return from the five weeks in Europe."

"So, good luck in Europe. Boast told me you'll be going to Oberstaufen, Germany; Grindelwald, Switzerland; Bad Gastein, Austria; and Maribor, Yugoslavia. What a dream trip! I'll try to follow your results in the New York Times."

I grasped the phone tightly, hoping he'd say "I love you" or "I'm proud of you." After a short silence, I concluded, "I'll call when I get back. Bye."

"Bye, good luck again." The phone clicked.

I always felt a churning in my stomach after talking to my dad. He made me feel as though I were imposing on him, but at least he'd offered me some money. Never feeling loved after our conversations, I much preferred to write to him. At times like this, I missed my mom, even if she'd been drunk half the times I talked with her on the phone.

Putting the phone down, I heard some giggles coming from the next room. I couldn't make out the words, but I did recognize Dan's low western drawl. Then, a waft of sweet smoke came under the door between the rooms. Turning on the radio next to my bed, I found a station that played rock and fell asleep to Nancy Sinatra's, These Boots Are Made for Walking.

CHAPTER 33

Senator Buckley's Office

A frizzy-headed, twenty-something blonde secretary greeted us at the Senator's office the next morning. She stood up and blushed as though in awe.

"Welcome. You certainly are prompt. I'm Julie Sawyer."

Dan reached out to shake her hand, but instead raised her fingers to his lips. "Thanks for arranging this. I assume Coach Boast sent you all the info."

"Yep, but you all will have to go down to Park Avenue to get a passport photo." Eyeing me like a hero-worshipping teenager, she continued. "So you're the famous Lia Erickson. I just read about you in *The New York Times*. Wow, like have you taken the ski world on by a storm!" I started, smiled, and then turned to Dan for an explanation.

"Okay, okay, Lia, I guess you didn't know that Boast had sent a press release to *The Times* along with your photo. He wanted to get some publicity for the team going to the World Cup races in Europe. He decided you should be the featured skier."

Sensing my confusion, Julie broke in. "Hey, would you all like to see the Senator's office? He's not back from his family Christmas vacation in Aspen."

She led us through the ten-foot mahogany door to a paneled room carpeted with oriental rugs and then over to the Senator's large, flat desk. Gesturing toward the pictures on the wall, Julie said, "Look around; I'll go get some paperwork for you to sign. After all, one doesn't often get to see a Senator's office."

Dan and I both moved toward the back wall where there hung

some black and white photos: one of President Nixon and the senator, another of the senator on a sailboat and then one of Buckley's family skiing in Aspen. For an instant, I felt overwhelmed to be in the presence of such power. I turned to find Dan, only to discover he'd left the room and was sitting on the edge of Julie's desk, his feet casually crossed at the ankles.

Dan and I spent the rest of the day taxiing back and forth from the passport building, the photo studio, and the senator's office, so by the time we arrived at Kennedy International Airport, I felt a mixture of tiredness and exhilaration, like the way I used to feel after climbing Camel's Hump in Vermont.

A reassuring hug from Becky and a pat on the shoulder from Carla put me at ease. Tracy and Pammy stood to the side, nodding to me. We all looked very impressive in our gray slacks and navy blue US Ski Team travel blazers, the red and gold, ski-team patch embroidered over our left breast, adding to the effect.

Becky seemed somber, "So how'd your day go? I mean did you get everything you need?" she said, moving to put her ski bags on a trolley that would carry them to the check-in.

"Hey, I've got a lot to tell you. Yup, I got my passport," I said, feeling that I could finally unburden myself of all my worries. Cautiously, I nodded toward the coaches and raised my finger to my lips. "Later. But first, please tell me about Wren."

"Okay, okay, I get it," said Becky with a wink. "After we get through check-in, I'll tell you about Wren. Don't worry."

Once at Pan American Gate 11, I sat between Becky and Carla. "Okay, guys. Tell me what's going on with Wren."

Carla looked to Becky as if to get permission to talk. "Well, like, we did get to see Wren. She's out of the ICU, but she's still in traction," said Carla, guarding every word.

I sensed nervousness in Carla's voice, and asked, "What do you mean, traction?"

"Well," Carla lowered her voice more. "Wren did break her

back. The doctors are stabilizing her, so that she can heal."

"Heal? What do you mean? Can she move around?" I asked, impatiently and then held my breath.

Becky, breaching her white-faced silence, interrupted. "Okay, quiet down. We can't hide from you the fact that, at this point, Wren can't move her legs. The doctors are hoping that if they stabilize her with a halo over her head and stop the swelling, she may get feeling back in her legs."

I cupped my hands around my face and turned toward Becky, pressing my nose right into her nose. "Just say it. Wren's paralyzed."

CHAPTER 34

Oberstaufen, Germany

By the time our rented van pulled into the parking lot of the Oberstaufen Hof, I realized that we'd not only flown fifteen hours from New York to Geneva with a stop in Brussels, but that we'd driven three hours in the van, three long hours of intermittent sleep broken by small conversations with Becky and Carla. Much of the time I'd rested my head against Becky's shoulder, her breathing rocking me to sleep. Carla, on my right, laid her head on my shoulder, reminding me of our Monmouth days, comfortable, safe, invincible. Not even the occasional stares from Tracy and Pammy from the front seat could bother me.

The white stucco Tyrolean building, accented by brown trusses and hand-carved balconies, resembled the pseudo-Alpen inns in my hometown of Waitsfield. Stepping out of the car, I breathed in the moist, crisp air and turned toward the ancient mountains glowing in a watermelon-dusk. I squeezed Carla's arm, "We're here, we're in Europe!"

Carla turned, giving me a pat on my shoulder, "Yes, and now the fun begins." We both giggled like two girls in a fairy tale.

Before we could enter the lodge, Coach Ryan stepped in front of the five of us. In his low, rasping voice he said, "Okay, this is where the show starts. I'll check you in. Lia and Becky will have one room and Pammy and Carla the other. Coach Boast wants Tracy in her own room. Please get unpacked and meet me for dinner in one hour, right." He stopped and wagged his finger at us. "Uh, it's imperative that you adjust to this time schedule. Even if you want to sleep, don't. We'll go over tomorrow's plans at dinner."

To demonstrate who was in command, he handed Becky three large medieval, metal room keys, embossed with a large O.

Becky took one key and handed the other two to Carla and Tracy. Taunting me, she said, "Hey Rapunzel, I'll beat you up the stairs." I fell down on the top step, bumping my chin on the hall rug. My pride wounded, I got up and saw that all of us had connecting, rooms number 2 and 3 and Tracy had 4. I took a breath and let my mind think of this as an omen. *Would we take a second, third, and fourth in the race?* Superstitiously, I loved to look for signs of success as though there were a destiny guiding me.

Inside the darkened room, I followed the smell of fresh linen to a down comforter on a single bed nestled beneath a trellised window. I pressed my face into a feather pillow, breathed in the pine scent, and threw it at Becky. "This is better than I could imagine." I flopped down into the billowing nest.

Becky caught the pillow and smothered me. We started wrestling on the bed when Carla came in, grabbed another pillow and covered both of us, stating, "Cool, I'm stronger than all of you. In fact, I'm going to whip your butts in the giant slalom race, for sure."

Becky raised her head and said, "Look who's talking, Miss Humble. Remember I'm the one with European experience. You're so naïve … this is a whole new ball game." She climbed out of the pile of contorted legs.

I jumped up, confused. "What're you guys talking about? Skiing and racing are the same everywhere, in every country." My eyes darted from Becky to Carla.

"Okay, Miss Know-It-All, let me educate you now," said Becky in a slow, patronizing drawl. "Sit down. I'm sure Coach Ryan will tell you the same tonight. I mean, Europe is different from the States: the food's different, the snow's different, the language is different, and the crowd's different. You'll find yourself overwhelmed for a while. It'll be hard to focus, for sure." She paused as if remembering something painful, "You'll need to acclimate."

Indignant, I answered, "Okay, fearless leader, how do you expect us to do that?"

Throwing another pillow at me, she added, "Just listen, please. We need to stay together, you know, eat together, train together, and basically support each other. Even though we're racing for individual FIS points, points that will put us on, yes, the Olympic team, each one needs to encourage the others. Remember a victory for one translates into a victory for all. This way each can produce their best."

I couldn't resist correcting Becky, "You mean her best."

"Oh, you English major, you know what I mean."

Carla broke in. "Like, do you mean that we need to support Tracy and Pammy, too?"

"Of course," said Becky, standing up, putting her hands on her hips. "There's no Monmouth versus the others now. It's the United States versus Europe. Of course in the end, it's about each of us individually. We've got a fine line to walk." I liked it when she got huffy.

After unpacking, Becky and I dressed in our gray team slacks and white turtlenecks and headed to the restaurant to meet Coach Ryan. At the top of the staircase, we met Pammy, Carla, and Tracy who'd decided to dress in tight black slacks and their own blouses. *A small statement,* I thought.

A rotund, ruddy-faced maître-d', stuffed into a gray felt Batzi jacket, trimmed with gold embroidery on the lapel, greeted us at the door and led us to a table for six, smack in the middle of the formal dining room. Heavy curtains covered the floor-to-ceiling windows and an oriental rug muffled the sound of our footsteps. Voices quieted, heads turned as we sat down, and a small, blonde girl pointed at us. The smell of fresh baked bread caused my mouth to water, making me realize that I hadn't eaten anything substantial since New York.

Looking like a model from *SKI Magazine,* Coach Ryan glowed in his gray flannels and white-collared shirt. He stood up and said, "My, don't we look beautiful." He turned directly to Pammy, pulled out a chair, and winked at her. "Please sit down and order. I believe there are two choices tonight, steak tartare or pasta alfredo."

I realized that the meals had been pre-arranged, probably to save money. "What's steak tartare?" I asked.

Becky broke in, "You probably don't want that. It's raw beef. Not cooked."

"Yuck," I replied.

A buxom, brunette waitress, squished into a tight blue-laced dirndl that pushed her breasts against the top panel, took our orders in a voice as taut as her bunned hair.

Dismissing her, Coach Ryan took over the conversation, "So four of you are new to European racing. Only Becky has previous experience. For this reason, I'm making her the captain." He scanned our group for a reaction and continued. "I mean, please check with her regularly about meeting times, eating times, waxing times, and debriefing times. You're expected to be on time everywhere." He winked at Tracy.

Becky winced, indicating this was the first time she'd heard about her new responsibility. After a pause, Coach Ryan continued. "I'll let you sleep in tomorrow, Sunday, so you can adjust to the time change. However … " He paused, looking at me. "Some of you might want to get up at your regular time to go for a run. Breakfast is always from 7-8:30 here. Let's plan to meet after lunch here to get in a few runs on the mountain. I'll leave your week ski passes at the front desk. Dinner will always be at 6, here. I expect all of you to be in bed by 9, right. Any questions?"

I looked at Becky and then at the rest for a response. No one spoke, so I took the initiative. "That sounds great. Could you go over the race schedule, please?"

Appearing angered by my question, Coach Ryan scowled, "Lia, I won't know anything until the coaches' meeting tomorrow."

Becky interjected, "Well, can you give us an overview? If I remember from last year, I think the giant slalom race is on Wednesday and the slalom's on Thursday. I know we don't have a downhill here, because the mountain's not big enough. Our first downhill will be in Grindelwald in a week. Right?"

Coach Ryan, reddening in frustration, said, "Oh, sorry, I didn't know that you were so unaware of the race schedule. I guess Boast never gave any of you an itinerary? I'll try to get one printed for you in the next few days." He reddened, continuing, "To tell you the truth, I'm new to this game, too."

In unison, all of us said with a hint of sarcasm, "Thanks."

"Now back to the races here," he said. "You're representing the United States. You must wear your uniform at all times when you're skiing. Need I add that you must act with courtesy at all times." He looked at each of us before continuing. "I don't need to remind you that you're not to drink at bars or go to any parties." He grinned. "Although there aren't any guys racing here, you'll have opportunities to meet local boys." I smiled, thinking of the pictures of the blonde European racers that I'd seen in the December issue of *SKI Magazine*, especially the French man, Henri Duvillard.

He continued, "Finally, you can come to me with any problems, but Becky may be more versed in female issues." He rolled his eyes, blushing. "Remember, you're a team and are to help each other. Becky, do you have anything to add?"

Becky seemed flustered, "I ... I guess I wasn't prepared to say anything." Pausing, she added, "Okay, remember that we're here to help each other even though we're trying to do our individual best. In a way a victory for one is a victory for all."

I noticed Tracy and Pammy winking at each other, as though they had made a pact long before. A silence crept over the table like a curtain of fog coming down the mountain.

✳   ✳   ✳

After dinner, Carla asked Becky and me whether we'd like to go for a walk around town. Becky declined, "I've got to get my skis in order."

I jumped at the chance, "We can get the skis ready tomorrow morning. Let's see what we can find open. It's only eight."

Outside, Carla and I both slipped on the ice, even though we had good treads on our sneakers. A light snow had started falling, obscuring the cobblestones and curbs. "Be careful," said Carla, grabbing my arm. "We don't want any injuries right away." I giggled at the irony of getting hurt while walking around town.

Heading toward the main street, we noticed that the small shops were closed; however, a group of people were walking deliberately in the same direction as if being pulled by a magnet. "Let's follow them," suggested Carla.

At the corner, we, like two lost pilgrims, stopped, confronted by a white-washed stone church the size of fifty whales. "Wow, have you ever seen such a … a, I guess you'd call it a cathedral!" I said, my eyes moving up and down like a searchlight. A sudden tolling of the bells made me jump back. The crowd we'd been following flowed up the stairs and through the large wooden doors: blonde children holding their parents' hands; ladies with scarves on their heads, balancing on canes; Germanic-jawed men bundled in wool coats helping them.

Bellowing out the door, organ music intoned the prelude, *Jesu Joy of Man's Desiring*, and Carla indicated she wanted to go in. "Hey, Lia, I was raised as a Catholic. Like, I'd love to go to Mass."

"Ahh, I don't have much experience with church. I went to the Congregational church in our town for a few years, but then ski racing stopped me," I said gleefully, remembering how happy I'd been to be outside skiing instead of inside sitting in a moldy church.

"Cool, same for me. I couldn't even get to Saturday Mass on weekends. C'mon. This'll be different." She grabbed my arm.

Into the cavernous stone sanctuary we wandered, but I quickly realized we wouldn't go unnoticed. Heads turned, fingers pointed, neighbors whispered to neighbors. A musty smell of warm wool, candle smoke and mildew made me sneeze. Carla put her finger to her lips and then pointed toward a group of young boys waving to us. Their cherubic faces couldn't have been more than twelve years old.

Carla slid into the wooden pew next to the tallest of the group while I took the aisle seat under a stone pillar. A life-size wooden statue of an apostle stared down at me, his hands folded in prayer. I shuddered to think he might fall on me if I moved.

The three boys to the right of Carla giggled. The older boy said, "Welcome. Are you part of the race?"

Carla took the initiative, "How'd you know?"

The tallest boy said, " 'cause you're new to town. Always, when the World Cup comes, we get new people who come to the church. Where are you from?"

"Guess," I said, leaning over Carla, trying to be included in the conversation.

He put his finger to his lips as if thinking, "Okay, America. I can tell your accent. No, just kidding, I see an American flag on your parka." All three of us giggled and blushed.

Carla leaned forward to see the boys, "Hey, how'd you get to have such good English? You can't be more than twelve."

Now the tall blonde boy took charge. "We study English since we five years old. It required in school." He spoke slowly and properly, trying to impress us. The yellow fuzz on his cheek glowed from the candlelight behind him.

I turned toward Carla. "I can only speak a little French. What did you study in school?"

She put up her hands, "Like, I barely got through French two. These kids are good."

At this point, a large, blonde man stood up behind the boys, raised his hand to stop the conversation and indicated to the tall, blonde boy to step into the aisle.

The congregation rose as the organ bellowed a tune and one hundred voices sang in German, *Jesu Joy of Man's Desiring,* all in four-part harmony. The priest flowed down the aisle, white robes swirling, carrying his miter high, followed by one acolyte swinging incense, and three others in unisex robes. The bass notes in the organ shook my body; my eyes wandered to the massive altar where a carving of the Virgin Mary held a crucified Jesus, red stains flowing from his chest, one of his arms lying limp across her legs, his face frozen as if he had found eternity.

When the Mass began, the priest spoke in Latin, and the congregation responded reflexively. I let my mind wander to thoughts of Bill, home, and my dreams about Europe. Carla nudged me as though I'd been sleeping.

After ten minutes, the priest climbed up a rounded, wooden staircase to his pulpit, a perch hanging over the darkened congregation, separating him from us. In German, he began the sermon. The blonde boy who had returned to his seat next to Carla began scribbling a few words in English and handed the words to me: *My father not let me talk, but I write you a translation.* I couldn't read everything the boy wrote, but he kept writing the words: "Sinners. Hell. Repent. Death. Jesus forgives."

Never had I experienced such a condescending, stentorian voice as that of the priest. The audience appeared to be bored, but nodded when the priest stopped to ask a rhetorical question.

I began squirming in my seat until Carla put her hand on my shoulder. The three boys laughed at my discomfort. They seemed to be unfazed by the sermon, probably a weekly occurrence for them.

The rest of the service turned into a mindless hum for me. The damp cold made me shiver, the tired wrinkled faces of the congregation took on a death pall, the priest's voice echoed as though he were speaking from a tomb. I tried to keep my thoughts away from Bill, Vietnam, death.

I closed my eyes, so I didn't have to look at the bloody Jesus, and tried recalling the beauty of the mountains, the soft caress of the wind, the sound of my skis gliding on the snow. My head ached as though it were pressed in a vice.

Once we'd escaped outside, the three boys led Carla and me to a street lamp. Again, the blonde boy took command, "Hi, I'm Wilhelm. This is Stefan and Gunter. Welcome. We be your guides this week. You here for the World Cup race, yah?"

I sighed and said, "I hope we didn't get you in trouble with your parents."

"Nein, nein. They be happy we have new American friends." He jumped up and down.

Carla stepped forward, "Hey, Lia, we'd better get back to the inn as it's almost nine. Remember, we turn into pumpkins at nine." She puckered her forehead, knitting her heavy, dark eyebrows together, and started walking through the light dusting of snow.

"Okay, we walk you back," said Wilhelm.

Then, the smaller, dark-haired Gunter said meekly, "We meet you tomorrow and help you with your skis?"

I smiled, thinking how jealous the others would be if Carla and I had our own ski porters. "Of course," I said. "We'll meet you at 12 outside the Oberstaufen Inn. Auf Wiedersehen." I giggled, struggling to get the last words out. Carla and I, now compatriots, waved good-bye to the three urchins who disappeared into a snow-covered alley.

Back in my room, Becky chastised Carla and me. "Coach told you not to be out late. Where did you go?"

I felt put out that Becky thought she owned us, "Hey, we just went exploring and wound up in church."

"In church? Why there?" said Becky, angrily.

Carla broke the tension that was building like an avalanche.

"It was my idea. We saw the people going to Mass, and I used to go to a Catholic church with my parents."

I entered the verbal brawl, "Yeah, and I used to go to church before ski racing took over my life." I squared my hands on my hips to show my frustration at her questioning.

Becky sat down on her bed. "Okay, let's not get heated about this. Tell me more about what you discovered. I'm curious."

Carla sat down next to her and said, "Well, like, I thought it might be cool to see what the villagers do at night. Most stores were closed, so we followed a group to the church. We didn't understand anything the priest said."

I flopped onto my bed, "Yeah, and all he talked about was sin, death, repentance, and forgiveness. At least that's what our new friends told us."

"What new friends?" asked Becky, shifting her position, obviously uncomfortable.

"Well, we met some cute boys—yup, twelve year olds—who tried to translate for us. They did get in trouble with their parents though," I said, wagging my finger. "I hope Coach Ryan won't be angry." I laughed.

"I'll bet their parents thought we were being too forward," said Carla, giggling at the idea that we'd already gotten in trouble.

"So, let me get this straight. You went to church. Got some boys in trouble. Then you got their parents mad at you. What did coach tell you?" said Becky, furling her eyebrows.

"Hey, we didn't break any rules," said Carla, trying to minimize the problem.

Sensing that there might be a confrontation coming, I decided to change the subject. "Hey, Becky, have you ever been to church?"

Becky turned to me, "Interesting question. Yes, I, too, was raised Catholic. But when my brother died from polio in 1955, my mother stopped taking us to church." Her face looked pained as she fidgeted with her pajamas. "Now I can't accept any of their teachings."

Neither Carla nor I knew what to say. Finally, I said, "I'm sorry. You never told us about him. Do you want to talk about it?"

"Not really," said Becky. "Anyway there's not much to say about it. He got a fever, went to the hospital, and never came home. My mom blamed God for his death."

"What did God have to do with it?" I asked naïvely.

Becky shook her head, "Well, my mom had to blame someone."

A long silence ensued before I probed more, "So who or what is God? Does anyone want to answer that?"

Carla yawned, " Isn't this getting a little too heavy for this time of night?"

I laughed, "No seriously, I'd like to know what you think. I've got my own ideas. I just don't get the idea of Heaven and Hell. I think God is in each one of us, and you know, that thing we call conscience when you feel guilty, that's the voice of God. He's also in every aspect of nature, in every leaf, mountain, and waterfall."

Becky listened and then said slowly, "Well, when I was a Catholic, I thought God was in Heaven, that He was a strong force of good that oversees our lives. I absolutely have a problem with Hell, though." She stopped. "I'd like to think my brother's in Heaven with God." She shook her head, "I just can't accept how the Catholics treat women. You know the rest of the Catholic doctrine."

Carla began to grow restless. "Great, let's solve all the world's problems tonight. I'm going to bed. See you guys in the morning." She left through the door that connected the two bedrooms, adding, "Please keep it down."

I shrugged at Becky, saying, "Wow, we must have pushed the wrong button."

"She'll talk about it when she's ready," said Becky. "Let's hit the hay. We're all tired. We've got a big day training tomorrow afternoon, right?"

I changed into my flannel pajamas, my favorite blue ones, and snuggled next to the cold window. A crescent moon started sliding behind the mountain like a deflated balloon.

CHAPTER 35

Preparations

A ray of sun woke me at 6:30. I struggled with my heavy comforter, trying to shield my eyes, but the blast of light burned through my eyelids. I wiped away a sandman, coughed, and placed my chin on the window sill. I marveled at the alpenglow that moved down the white slopes of the Bavarian mountain; tall, black pines climbed to meet the sun, a scene out of the Black Forest in *Grimm's Fairy Tales*. I whispered to myself, *I'm really, really here.*

Quietly slipping out of bed, I braced for my crisp morning run, piling on my USA warm-up pants, wool hat, parka, and gloves. I became a walking American flag. Downstairs, pans clanged in the kitchen, a tired night clerk lifted his head from the desk, awakened by the squeaking of my sneakers on the tile floor. Outside the air glinted, pixie dust reflected the sunlight. I shivered, the thermometer outside the hotel read minus 15. Then I realized that this must be Celsius.

Germany, Oberstaufen, Hitler—these words echoed in my brain as I pranced through the narrow streets. I started recalling my father's stories about World War II. He'd been in the 10th Mountain ski troops that landed in Pisa, Italy in 1945. Trained to push Hitler's army out of the Italian Alps, my father told of one particular battle on Mt. Belvedere. Although he rarely spoke about the decimation of his friends by German gun fire across the valley from Riva Ridge, he did tell me about his shoulder wound and his evacuation to Bagni di Lucca.

Even now he hated the Germans and Japanese, showing his disdain by refusing to buy any products from these countries, especially cars. I struggled to keep my thoughts away from Bill and Vietnam. *Had he arrived in Saigon? Was he safe? Had he been in any combat yet?* The thoughts burned like acid in my mind.

After an hour of running, I realized that I'd lost my way. The zigzag streets reminded me of lines in a crumpled piece of paper that had been flattened. I looked up to the mountains, trying to orient myself, but the rounded peaks stared blankly back. My panic rose fever-like, my heart flopping like a fish in my chest. I ran west toward the highest peak and stopped at the foot of a chairlift. A sign above the entrance to the lift read, "Wilkommen La Coupe du Monde."

Flags of many nations fluttered in the light breeze: the reds, yellows, whites and blues of Switzerland, France, Austria, Germany, Italy, Great Britain, Yugoslavia, Sweden, Denmark, Norway, Finland, and the United States. My heart began pounding in my chest with pride. Tears welled up in my eyes, and I struggled to hold them back the way I used to when I'd cry in a Disney movie. A voice called from the small hut nestled against the finish line. "Guten morgen." Out the door came the blonde, heavy-set man who had scolded the young boy, Wilhelm, in church. I nodded and responded, "Bon jour," and then blushed, realizing that this was the only other language I knew.

The stately man began to speak in German until he realized that I understood nothing. He, too, reddened and said in very broken English. "You. The American in church."

"Yes," I said. "I'm so sorry if I caused a problem." I stopped when the man raised his hands and shrugged his shoulders. I continued, "Okay, anyway. I'm lost. Can you tell me where … ?" I stopped mid-sentence, trying to think of how I might say this in French. "Où est Hof Oberstaufen?"

The broad-shouldered, tanned man smiled. "Ah, you lost." He pointed toward the direction of the church and beckoned me with his padded glove. I shyly walked one pace behind him as we wandered through the streets, past the white church, and ducked into an alley. I hesitated for a minute, remembering my father's admonition about going with strangers. To my relief, a white-hatted man, holding a tray of pastries, popped out from a narrow door, *"Guten morgen, Herr Mayor. Meuhten sie eine pastry, bitte?"* The mayor took two and gave one to me. I felt my mouth water even before I could take a bite of the strawberry delicacy.

"*Merci*, oh, I mean, *danke schön*," I stammered. How I wished I'd paid more attention in eighth grade language class when I had learned greetings in many languages.

"You're welcome," said my new friend. "*Ich bin Mayor Wilhelm Scherholz. Kommen sie.*" I now paced the mayor, step for step, like two comrades in arms. At the ironclad entrance to the inn, the mayor extended his hand, smiled showing his yellow, crusted teeth, and said, "*Auf Wiedersehen.*"

As I entered the foyer, Becky was descending the stairs, with Carla behind her, sliding down the railing, arms flailing like a rag doll. Becky announced impatiently. "Well, I thought you might of waited for me."

Carla broke in with giggles. "Well, you'll never get me to run in the morning, Little Miss Fitness."

"Be quiet you two." I said. "I … I just got lost in town. The mayor had to bring me home. In fact, he's the father of the little boy, Wilhelm, the one in church." I barely paused for their response before continuing, "Have you eaten yet?"

"Nope," said Carla, "We waited for you. Let's hurry. Breakfast closes in five minutes." We picked a new window table which held a small red carnation in a vase set on a lace doily. A blonde waitress, tiptoeing in a tight blue skirt, white top, and apron, walked toward us, balancing a basket full of fresh bread. Steam billowed through the cloth covering.

"*Meuhten sie coffee o tea?*" she said. Reading the confused expressions on our faces, she continued. "Oh, Americans. Would you like coffee, tea, or hot chocolate?"

Becky took the initiative, "I'd love some hot chocolate. Do you have whipped cream?" The waitress nodded.

"Please for me, too," I said, reaching for a roll now placed in front of me.

"Ditto, thank you," said Carla.

As the waitress turned to leave, all of us started to giggle. I nudged Carla, "Can you believe we're here?"

"Waaaaay cool," said Carla, her mouth full of a sticky bun.

Becky pushed back her chair before saying in her patronizing voice, "Okay, girls. Now you understand what a challenge it'll be to race in Europe. The first barrier is the language. Fortunately, the Europeans are not as limited as us Americans. Most of them have studied English since grade school. Only the older generations have trouble with English."

"So I discovered," I said, sitting up with authority. "The mayor could barely say anything in English." I started eating the bread while the waitress delivered the hot chocolate and left. Munching mindlessly, the three of us finished the basket of bread over idle chatter.

I finally announced, "I'm really hungry, when do we get to order?"

Becky laughed, "That was your breakfast. The ski team only pays for a continental breakfast."

"Geez, is this supposed to last until lunch?" said Carla, holding her stomach in protest.

"Yup, now let's go sharpen our skis and get organized." said Becky, shaking her head at our naïveté.

Later on, after a lunch of soup, salad, and more bread, we met up with Pammy and Tracy in the lobby. Coach Ryan joined us, puffed up in his US Ski Team parka. I stared at his gold embroidered name below the ski team logo. Balancing my skis and poles at my side, I fell in line with the other four at the inn's door, a group more impenetrable than a giant U.S. flag. I nearly fell over when the barn-like door opened into my back, and in strutted the three blonde boys from church. "Guten tag. We are here to carry your skis," said Wilhelm, saluting with his hand.

Carla and I burst into laughter, seeing the startled expression on our coach's face and the amusement in Becky's, the two expressions as contrary as the tragic and comic masks of Greek tragedy. Once outside the parade began; the three boys carrying two pairs of skis on each shoulder followed by us, six Americans. We walked in step, using our ski poles for balance. Merchants stepped out of their colorful doorways, shoppers stopped to admire our uniforms, and cars honked as our menagerie wended its way to the base of the lift. Carla, Becky, and I walked side by side, actually stopping once to get our footsteps in synch. Pammy, her long blonde pony-tail swinging, and Tracy, waving like a queen, walked behind Carla, Becky, and me. Dan brought up the rear, stern and attentive like a gander protecting his flock.

I felt ambivalent emotions—proud yet scared. Breaking the tension, Carla started the song that would frame our adventure, "Climb every mountain, ford every stream, follow every rainbow, 'til you find your dream."

All four of us joined in; our skiing version of the Bremen Town Musicians wending our way to the lifts.

CHAPTER 36

First World Cup Race

On race day at 6 a.m., I ran through the village, more focused and deliberate. I knew my way after three mornings of the same routine; however, now I had to add my pre-race ritual—a short jog, some stretches, some sprints, and snowballs thrown at a telephone pole. Superstitiously, I felt if I hit the pole once, I'd place in the top ten, twice I'd be in the top five, three times, I'd win the race. I couldn't remember when I'd started this tradition, but now I couldn't avoid it. I imagined Boast's face was on the pole; one, two, and boom! The third one connected like a grenade. *Yes, this would be a good day,* I thought.

At breakfast, Becky stood up and took charge. "Okay, you all," she said. "This is the real deal. We need to meet at the lift by 8 a.m. to get in a warm-up run before we check the course with Coach Ryan. We'd be better off to take another trail, so the officials don't think we're shadowing the course. They're very strict over here." Stopping as if recalling a nightmare, she continued, "Believe me, I know." I liked the way she was taking leadership.

Tracy tried challenging her, "Yeah, and what would they do to me if I did shadow the course?"

Becky sat down as she answered, "Well, in reality they could disqualify you." She paused as if not certain about adding the next remark. "Then again, you don't have to worry. You have connections." As Tracy blushed, the rest of us began a guttural laugh that took on its own life.

Nervously, I tried to change the subject. "Becky, have you heard anything about Wren?"

"Lia," said Becky sternly, waving her hand trying to dismiss the topic, "if I learn anything, I will tell all of you guys right away." Then pausing to collect her thoughts, "One of the hardest parts of racing World Cup in Europe is the lack of communication with the States." She put her hand to her ear, "You all know how hard it is to call home. The connections from the hotel—well, they're miserable, not to mention the cost. Europe is way behind us in phone service."

Carla broke in. "Yup, I tried to call Brandy to find out what was happening at Monmouth and all I got was static on the phone."

I said sheepishly, looking down, "I wouldn't even know how to pay for a call."

"I've got a deal for all of you." said Becky, pausing to diffuse the tension in the room. "After the race today, we'll call McElvey. He'll update us on Wren, and we can give him our results." She nodded as methodically as a mother bird feeding her fledglings. We finished our breakfast in silence, broken only by the rhythmic tinkling from the knives and forks, and then the scraping of the chairs on the floor.

"See you at the base of the lift" called Tracy, waving as she and Pammy left.

"Hey, Becky," I said, attempting to sound nonchalant, "I hate to bring it up, but it feels like we're not working as a team."

"Yup, I've seen this before," said Becky, in a soft yet commanding voice. She stood up, turning to add, "Once the races start, the team has difficulty looking out for the needs of each other. We become individuals racing against each other."

"Okay," broke in Carla, "so what do we do about this?"

Becky returned to the table. "Here is where it gets difficult. We do have to look after ourselves, make sure we have all our equipment prepared and get to our meeting places and to the start on time. But the group can help. Positive support is invaluable." Then looking to Carla and me individually, she warned, "We have to drop any frustrations and worse, gossip. I know you're uncomfortable with what you see happening. But we can't talk about it. We have to be quiet and respect our coaches' words."

I couldn't hold back a groan, "Uhh."

Becky stared me down, "Lia, we're here to race, not to be petty. Focus on the task. If you have problems, you can speak to me quietly."

I nodded, resenting the distance that was coming between us and pushed back my chair to get up. I didn't want her to see the tears filling my eyes.

"Okay, you all, let's go get 'em. See you at the lift in twenty," cheered Becky, trying to be upbeat.

On the road to the lift, I walked alone slowly, yet deliberately. I kept looking to my right and left for the boys, Wilhelm, Gunter, and Stefan. Soon I realized that they had probably gone to school. The sun lit the rooftops of the buildings, the white church blinding me, the freshly plowed snow squeaking under my feet. My skis and poles were unfolded wings resting on my shoulder.

At the base of the chairlift, I found my group assembled around Coach Ryan and under the multi-colored flags. Becky beckoned to me to hurry. "Where've you been? It is after 8."

"Sorry," I said, pulling up my parka sleeve to look at the time. "Wait a minute. My watch says 7:50. What's going on? Is this a joke?"

Becky, looking puzzled, said, "Lia, you're always on time. Did you drop your watch or something?"

"No, but I did leave it in the ski room overnight by accident." I gasped, remembering the cut on my finger when I was working on my skis and that I'd put the watch on the bench. A sharp pain radiated under my Band-Aid. "Do you think someone could have changed the time on my watch?"

Just then Boast came out of the timer's shack. He carried a pile of flattened red and white bibs. I saw him smile at Tracy. "Okay, here they are, just as I promised," said Boast. "I'm glad to see everyone's on time." The group moved to form a circle around Boast like a gaggle of wild turkeys gathering around the Tom for protection. Lia, you and Becky are in the first seed. Becky you're #5, Lia's #15. Both of you should have a fast course. I'm afraid that it will rut after the first fifteen. Pammy #21 and Carla #30. Tracy, my dear, the best I could get you is #60." He handed each of us our bib printed with the Evian water-logo, "*e*," the sponsor of this World Cup. "Please wear these on the outside of your parka at all times. They're your lift ticket, but more than that, this is how you'll be identified. Put them over your racing jacket at the start."

I slipped mine over my head and smiled at Becky as though we were one up on the rest.

"Where do you want us to meet you to go over the course?" said Becky, showing her leadership.

"Well, since I've got all of you here, let's go up now and side-slip the course," said Boast. He turned toward Coach Ryan. "Take them up lift one, then to Chair Five and start down. They can free ski after they've memorized the course."

I nudged Becky after we had both clicked into our bindings and strapped our safety thongs around our boots. "Beat you to the lift. I'll ride up with you," I said, stumbling on my own skis as I hurried.

We skated and poled as hard as we could and then snow-plowed into the roped corral where people were lined up like animals in a zoo. "Well, hello, Americans," said a familiar voice. I looked up to see Mayor Scherholtz checking the bibs. "Guten luck."

Sidling up to get on the lift, I winced when the chair banged the back of my knees. I turned, asking him, "Where are the young boys?"

"They will be at the finish," said the Mayor waving. "They have school this morning."

As the chair rose, looking back down the long line of chairs, I saw my friends side-stepping to the lift like penguins walking toward the ocean for the first time. Their red, white, and blue uniforms distinguished them from the Europeans, who had more traditional navy warm-up pants and parkas.

"Hey, Becky," I said, trying to adjust my helmet and goggles so I could see her. "I'm not feeling very confident. What's happening to me?"

"Well, my friend, this is a different show. The races mean much more to the Europeans than they do to the Americans. For many, this is their ticket to a better life."

"What do you mean?" I said, placing my pole straps over the safety bar.

"Well, in reality, skiing's their livelihood. Racers that do well on the World Cup circuit get money, and when they finish, the government may give them a hotel or auberge to run."

"Wait a minute. Aren't we supposed to be amateurs? You know, for the love of the sport."

"Ha, so you have bought into that fairy tale. No, racers are receiving money under the table all the time."

"Even the Americans? Won't that disqualify them from the Olympics?"

"Yup, but no one can prove it. Do you know the name Tony Franz, an Austrian?"

"Of course, do you think I'm dumb?"

"Well, rumor has it that he receives big money from his ski company, Alais."

I paused for a minute before I said, "What kind of kind of money are we talking about? One hundred? One thousand?"

"Try tens of thousands," said Becky adjusting her wrist straps in order to make a quick exit from the chair when it hit the top. The clanging of the chairs against the bull wheel stopped the conversation and both of us prepared for a quick slide down the ramp. I pushed into my first skating step to build speed toward the next lift. I tripped and fell, losing my ski, so Becky stopped to help me up.

Once on the next lift, I looked up to see a line of red and blue flags flowing down the trail. The course had brown snow fences along the side of the steep sections. Back on the lift, I continued the conversation, "Do you think that some Americans are receiving money?"

Becky held up her hand as if to stop the conversation. "This is where I have to stop talking. I've heard rumors but don't want to speculate."

"Are you?" I blurted. She put her fingers to her lips. I lowered my head and whispered to myself, "Damn."

Becky pointed to the course on the right. "Let's take a look at the course."

We continued the ride in silence. I felt a cold breeze cross my cheek. Then, a tuft of ice fell from the lift tower and banged the back of our chair. Below I saw Coach Boast standing at the starting gate with Tracy by his side. They were in deep conversation. I couldn't figure out how they'd beaten us up the lift.

As we slid down next to Coach Boast, one by one, a silence settled over us, as if there were a predator stalking the group. Boast nodded when, Carla, the last, came to a scraping stop. "Okay," he said. "Try to keep the conversation down and stay focused. You need to memorize the course as we side-slip down. Please no turning beside the gates." He stopped, looking around to see if we were listening. "Coach Ryan and I want to point out a few key gates where you'll need to start your turns early. Each one of you needs to pick a line that you think you can hold."

He turned his head toward Tracy who said meekly, "I've no chance." Boast stepped past us to console her, putting his arm around her shoulder. She continued whimpering, "What about me, Coach? Racing so late, my line will be miserable."

He pulled her toward him, and said, "I know, I know. We can't do anything right now, because your points are so poor. Just try to stand up and get a smooth run. I'll work on what we can do for you." He winked at Coach Ryan, conspiratorially.

On course, Becky and I stayed behind the rest, so we could work out our own line for the race. I didn't feel like sharing my thoughts with the others. Besides, we would be in the first seed, so our line should be chatter-free, cleaner than the others. I made sure to stay within earshot of Coach Boast, so as not to antagonize him. I felt my ski catch as I side-slipped through the gates and made a note to check the edges when I got back to the start.

An hour later, Becky and I arrived at the starting hut together, having enjoyed two exhilarating warm-up runs. I felt confident now that I had memorized the course and loosened my legs in the moguls.

Coach Ryan waited for us above the hut. He had boot-kicked a flat area in the snow for us to stand in, saying, "Lia, Becky, come over here. I want to rub some paraffin on top of your wax job. The temperature has warmed a little more than I'd planned last night when I waxed your skis."

Becky went first as she had to race first. I took off my skis and stood, resting them on my shoulders like two goal posts. Then, I remembered I wanted to check my edges. I rubbed my cut finger along the right inside edge. A nick flared like a scab. "Whoa, coach do you have a file? I have a huge problem in my edge."

"Lia, did you work on your edges last night?" asked Coach Ryan, showing impatience in his voice.

"Of course, Coach. They were perfect and sharp enough to cut me. They even took off the top of my fingernail." I showed him my bandage.

Coach Ryan finished with Becky's skis and reached for mine. As he felt the bottom, he said, "Wow, this could've cost you over a second on the course. You need to do better work next time." I wondered if someone had tampered with my ski.

A voice from inside the starting hut called out. "Forerunner, bitte." A tall, smooth-skinned, stork-like German skier stepped from the huddled racers and slid into the hut. He braced his boots against the starting wand. *Drei, zwei, eins, los.*" A spray of snow hit me like a cold slap on the cheek.

Becky moved down into position, followed by Coach Ryan. He started rubbing her thighs and whispering to her. I stood, mesmerized by the scene. I thought, *The show. Bill. Here we are.* I took off my silver helmet, bib, and parka and slid the bib back over my racing jacket.

After #14 left, I slowly side-stepped into the starting gate. Coach Ryan put his arm around my shoulder. Methodically, I first put the left pole strap and then the right around my wrists. Leaning forward over the starting wand, I tapped my ski poles together and jumped when I felt Coach Ryan's hand on the outside of my thighs, then the inside. He began to rub them, slowly, then more aggressively. With each stroke he came closer to my crotch. Then, he let his thumb rub against my privates. Before I could react, he stood up and patted me on the butt.

"Good luck, Lia," he said with a wink and stepped back out of gate. In a blur, I leapt out of the gate and heard in the receding distance, "Get 'em, Lia."

When I crossed the finish line, I knew I'd nailed a run. I'd carved my turns and hit them early, my skis had run fast as I tucked on the flats. At the finish line, I pushed my goggles up to see the results board and heard my time announced, "Lia Erickson, USA: One minute fifty seconds, two tenths and one one-hundredth. Becky skied over to me and said, "Move away from the finish, smartass. Great run."

"How—how'd I do?" I asked, trying to catch my breath, feeling disoriented. My legs ached, my finger throbbed.

"You're out of first place by nine tenths. You beat me by a second. We'll have to see, but I think you'll make the top ten."

"Wow, I knew I had a good one," I exclaimed, looking over Becky's shoulder at the board. The first three finalists were from

France—the two Jacot sisters and then Isabel Duhamel.

Becky pointed up to the course. "Lia," she said, "Pammy's on course. Here she comes."

I looked up to the timing clock and watched as the seconds ticked on. I felt confusion, dread, like a fungus growing in my brain, clouding my thoughts. *Would Pammy beat me?* I hoped for a minute that Pammy would fall. Or slip.

As Pammy slid across the finish line, the clock read one minute fifty-five seconds and two-tenths. Pammy skied over to us, raised her hands in the air and said, "I made it! I completed my first World Cup race!" She bent over her poles in exhaustion. The three of us skated toward a break in the snow fence to wait for Carla at #30. As the succeeding racers crossed the finish line, their times grew slower—most were at least two seconds from the leader.

"Hey, Becky. The course must be breaking down," I said with glee in my voice. I tried hiding my smile in my glove.

"Yup, I'm guessing the top ten will stand," said Becky. Just then an official with a red and black World Cup jacket came over and asked us to move back. He handed Becky a sheet of paper.

"What's that, Becky?" I asked.

"Just as I thought," said Becky, looking down at the single white sheet. "They've already printed the results for the first ten. You're in tenth, Lia. Great beginning!"

Carla then crossed the finish line and fell to the ground. "God, I'm tired. The course is hell."

Becky beckoned to her to get up and leave the corral. Carla checked out her time but had no idea how she had fared against the others. She skied over to us. "This is tough racing so far back. We never had to ski courses like this in the States."

Becky took charge, saying, "Okay, now we need to wait for Tracy. Remember what I told you—we're a team." We watched in silence as racer upon racer came down, the colors of their country glowing under their pinnies. The roar of the crowd, the clanging of the cow bells in support of racers, the drone of the announcer, all together put me into a daze. Around me the air hummed with cheers.

Just then, I saw three little boys break through the crowd, swarming to us four racers. Wilhelm came up to me and put out his hand. "We proud of you. Great job."

Before I could reply, I heard the announcer say, "#60 Tracy Languile is down on the course. There will be a ten-minute delay."

My heart raced and I gasped for breath. My first thought was, *So she can't beat me.* Then, I wondered whether Tracy could be hurt. Trying to look worried, I turned to Becky, yet inside I felt a smile and I saw that Becky, too, was wearing a subtle smirk on her face.

Becky broke the awkward silence. "I know Coach Boast will be right there with her, but we need to wait." No one spoke as we watched the next ten racers come through the finish line. The crowd clanged souvenir cowbells each time a racer crossed the finish line. More and more kids gathered around our skis. Little Wilhelm directed us away as he tried to protect us. After fifteen racers crossed the line, Becky turned to the group and said, "Well, I guess Tracy must of skied down another trail. Let's go back to the hotel and get some hot chocolate."

Now we four, like conquerors, grabbed our skis and, accompanied by our three German friends, started back into town. Wilhelm stepped in front and said "Bitte," indicating that the boys wanted to carry our skis. After handing them over, I took in a deep breath of cold air, stepped between Carla and Becky and put my arms over their shoulders. I'd never felt happier.

CHAPTER 37

Grindelwald, Switzerland

The team left Oberstaufen with the first alpen light, my favorite time of day. Outside the hotel, I squinted into the warming rays and hefted my ski bag and rucksack onto my shoulders, dreading the short walk to the waiting Mercedes taxi, which would deliver us to the train station. My stomach grumbled without breakfast. I craved the fresh pastries, which the manager had bagged for each racer but lay hidden in my boot bag.

The train ride to Interlocken, Switzerland, took six hours with no layovers. I felt nauseated by the clanging of the cars at the stations, the compactness of the seats, and the musty smell of wet wool. The six of us crowded into a small compartment with Coach Ryan, Tracy, and Pammy facing me, Carla and Becky beside me. Cramped by the window, my knees kept bumping Tracy's as we jockeyed for leg room. I tried sleeping as much as possible, but my mind kept reviewing my runs and how I could've cut my times. Fortunately, my tenth and eleventh finish helped me to lower my overall FIS points, a result that would move me up in the seedings for this week's giant slalom race in Grindelwald. I avoided thinking about the downhill that would start this week's races.

Across the aisle, a plump, ruddy-cheeked woman, wrapped in a black headscarf, kept staring at me and, when I looked up, she nodded with a smile. A toddler cuddled under the woman's arm, occasionally peeking at me. The woman gently stroked the girl's curly, white hair.

I remembered my mother and how I, especially when little, had longed for such a hug or a loving word, but she never knew how to show affection. I squeezed my brow, trying to drive the sadness from my mind.

After changing trains in Interlocken, we took a smaller one to Grindelwald that coursed over the legendary Bernese Oberland and slunk under the infamous Swiss mountains. I prodded Becky, "Hey look, there are the Eiger, the Jungfrau, the Monch."

"Who? What?" said Becky, rubbing her eyes. "What are you talking about?"

I pushed my nose to the oversized-glass window so that my refection became part of my face and pointed up. "Seriously, look. They're the mountains that make the top of Europe. Can you believe we're here?"

"You woke me for this?"

"C'mon have some respect. This is the mecca of mountain climbing and skiing. This is where people have died. In fact, an American died here last year while trying to climb the north face of the Eiger." I pointed to the two thousand foot cliff.

Pushing me away from her body, Becky yawned, "So?"

"No, seriously, this is where mountaineering history is made." Then, pausing as if to recall a story that started to form in my mind, "and mountaineering tragedy. Boy, do I love to read how men have tested themselves against mountains."

"Lia, sometimes I think you read too much. Just enjoy the scenery."

"No, listen. Learn. We're stepping into so much history here."

"Okay, tell me a story about all this," said Becky, shuffling her feet in order to sit up. I noticed Tracy and Pammy across from us had opened their eyes.

I began, trying to remember all the details of the famous climb on the Eiger. I'd just recently read it in a tourist brochure. "Well, I think it was in 1936. Four Austrian and German climbers decided to try the north face of the Eiger. No one had climbed it before. I can't remember all the details, but I know all of them died."

Becky looked me straight in the face, "All of them. Wild." She spoke so loudly even Coach Ryan leaned forward.

"I'm not sure of the details, but I remember that three were swept off the mountain by avalanches."

Becky, now absorbed, said, "So what happened to the fourth?"

"This is where the story grows bizarre. The fourth, I think his name was Kurz. Oh yes, Toni Kurz, he had to cut his line to free himself from his dead comrade who hung from his rope. He then tried to get down to a train window in the cliff."

"Right, yeah, this is some tall tale. A train window in the cliff?" said Becky, dismissing me with a wave of her hand. "Now, I know you're making up the story."

"No really, believe me, the Swiss engineers had carved a railway passage inside the face of the Eiger, so tourists could go up to enjoy the view. Every hundred yards or so, they cut openings in the cliff for air. Kurz tried to swing down to the opening where help waited."

"Sounds simple, so why didn't he just climb over and get out?"

"As I remember, ironically his line was too short because he'd cut it to release his dead friend."

"So, what'd he do?" said Becky, raising her eyebrows in disbelief.

I thought for a minute trying to recollect the rest of the story. I wanted to extend the story now that I'd gotten Becky's attention, plus Tracy, Pammy and Coach Ryan, sitting opposite us on a bench seat, also leaned forward to hear the rest of my strange tale.

I spoke louder, "Well, it gets more sensational. People were watching the events from down in the valley through telescopes." I curled my fingers and put them to my eyes for dramatic effect. "The weather had turned bad, so Kurz had to spend another night on the north face. In the morning, the crowd waited to see if he would move. Then, they saw two men lean out from the train opening in the cliff. The rescuers threw a rope up to Kurz so that he could attach it to his line and then swing down to the train opening."

"Wild, but you said he died," said Becky, sighing in confusion.

"Here's where the story becomes tragic," I said, realizing I'd full command of the group.

"Stop teasing us," said Pammy, throwing a glove at me.

"Ha, maybe I'll finish the story when we get to Grindelwald," I said. A long, plaintive whistle and a slowing of the engine spurred me to finish the story.

Somberly, as if in reverence, I said, "Okay, so Kurz tied his cut rope to the new rope and started to belay himself toward the open window. However, he had tied a knot that couldn't pass through his carabiner, so he stopped and hung down, just twelve feet above the two men who wanted to reach him."

Pammy raised her hand, "Whoa, what's a carabiner?"

"Oh sorry, a clip that attaches to a round hook pounded into the wall," I said, realizing that my friends had little experience with mountaineering. "Then, you slide your rope through the clip to hold you."

"Whoa, couldn't the two men climb out and get him?" asked Carla, now fully engaged in the story.

"No, the overhang made climbing out impossible, plus the weather had changed to sleet, glazing the rocky cliff," I said. "Anyway, night came. Kurz talked to his rescuers and told them his hands and feet were frozen. He said goodnight and then good-bye. He froze to death during the night. When people woke in the morning, they looked through the telescopes and saw his limp body hanging from the ropes."

"How sad. I wonder if this could happen nowadays" said Pammy, shivering as if freezing on the mountain.

"For sure—remember I told you someone died just last year on the mountain," I continued, smiling with pride that I could impress them with my mountaineering knowledge.

"Jeez, what would you say to your friends if you were dying?" said Carla, tilting her head in curiosity. "I'd laugh and say, what a ride."

"Let's hope this never happens to us," said Pammy with a nervous giggle. Thoughtfully, she added, "Do you think what we're doing is just as crazy? I sure do like the fame and celebrity I get from racing, but ... ," she flicked her hair, "when I'm done, I want to be a model."

I rolled my eyes and thought for a minute before I said, "Does anyone believe in fate? Why some things happen? Like in this tale, the best laid plans destroyed by one misplaced knot. The irony."

Becky, trying to calm the conversation, said, "Okay, English teacher. Irony, but I believe that we have some control— that we can prepare and take precautions." She looked pained. "Oh by the way, remember I told you we would call McElvey when we got to Grindelwald. I'd like to find out about Wren's ... " A train whistle drowned her last comment.

A cloud of smoke flew by my window and my head rolled from the jolt of the train. Coach Ryan jumped up from his seat next to Pammy, collided with the woman and child who'd just risen from their seat, and said, "Okay, grab your gear. Your ski bags will be unloaded by a porter and delivered to our hotel. Just make sure you see them come off the train." Raising his hands exuberantly, he hit the woman's head. "Welcome to Switzerland!"

Outside, I took a deep breath of the crisp, sapphire air. I grabbed Becky's arm as we descended the metal steps to the platform. I checked to my right to see my large, overstuffed, red ski bag come out of the baggage car. As I stood next to Carla on the clean, cement floor, my rucksack hefted on my shoulders, Coach Ryan said sternly, "Follow me. We can walk to the hotel." I looked up to see Pammy fall into Becky's arms as she tripped on the last step.

Once settled into the Grindelwald Hotel, a massive alpenstructure at the end of town, Becky and I decided to go for a walk to stretch our legs. Pammy, Carla, and Tracy chose to unpack, organize their skis, and rest.

The narrow streets obscured the view of the three mountains until we rounded a corner where four telescopes, cemented into a balcony, pointed up toward the tooth-like peaks. A metallic map showed me the rugged outline of each peak: The Eiger, 13,035 feet, the Monch, 13,123 feet, and the Jungfrau, 13,642 feet. In parentheses next to each name was the English translation, the Ogre, the Monk, and the Virgin.

Becky pointed to the sign for the virgin, laughed and nudged me, "Hey, are you still one."

I nodded and said, "So what about you?"

She laughed and gave me an ambivalent sign with her hand.

Uncomfortable, I decided to change the subject and pointed up toward the Eiger and said, "That's the place where he died." As I put my eye to the telescope to get a better view, I felt a hand on my shoulder. I jerked around expecting to see Becky and instead a deep voice said, "So you know the story of Kurz."

Stepping back in surprise, I brushed into the chest of a tall, smooth-cheeked man. His handsome sweep of dark hair gave him a boyish look. "What, who are you?" I asked. He smelled of cologne masking alcohol.

"Oh, I couldn't help but notice the two of you in your USA uniforms. You are American racers, oui? You here for the World Cup, oui?" said the man in broken English with a French accent.

Becky noticed my distress, moved closer to me and said, "Excuse me, but do we know you?"

"Not formally, however, you might know my name. I'm Pierre Duhamel, the ski writer for *Le Monde*."

I swallowed hard and stuttered, "The—the one who writes about the French star Duvillard and the races."

"Oui, mademoiselle. And now I have been asked to write about the American girls. One of you had a good showing at the first World Cup in Oberstaufen."

Becky said, "Thanks," looking around to see if anyone else was listening.

He continued in his sexy accent, "Now is one of you Lia Erickson? I have to write a profile on her for the next edition."

I looked to Becky for reassurance before I said, "Ah, I am." I'd never been interviewed by a foreign reporter and felt uncomfortable about the attention.

"Do you mind if I ask a few questions?" he asked, gesturing for me to sit on a bench.

I said, blushing, "I'd—I'd appreciate it, if you'd include Becky in your article, and …and maybe the rest of the team."

"Ah oui, no problem. But at the moment the French are more interested in you, this new, cute, blonde American girl who has exploded onto the racing scene," he said, smiling and rolling his hands in the outline of a curvaceous body. I blushed, but answered his questions and found myself embarrassed at how much he knew about me, and especially about Wren and Bill. Becky wandered away to give me space to talk.

❋   ❋   ❋

Back in the hotel, Becky and I ran to our room to find the rest of the girls showering and cutting each other's hair. Pammy sat straight up in a chair, allowing Carla to trim her shoulder-length locks. Tracy sat on the bed offering suggestions about the style.

Becky exploded into the room, "You'll never guess what just happened to us."

"What?" said Carla, turning and nicking Pammy with the scissors.

"Well, Lia, you tell them," said Becky, folding her arms with authority.

"No, you tell them. I'm embarrassed," I said, turning to look out the window.

Becky sat down and said, "Okay, but you will all have to get used to this. Well, a reporter for the French paper *Le Monde* interviewed Lia in town."

Pammy stood up from the bed asking, "You mean he actually wants to write an article?" Pausing and looking into the mirror, she concluded, "Did he take her picture?"

"Yup," said Becky. "But you need to know that Lia made sure to put in a good word about each of you."

Pammy grumbled, "Darn, you two always seem to get the best luck," as she stomped to the door.

Becky took charge again, "Enough. Jealousy doesn't help a team. In time, each of you'll have to get used to the press. That's a part of being on a World Cup team." She stared at Pammy and continued, "So you'll get all the press you want. Uh, and that should help you become a model one day." Becky rolled her lips in a sneer.

Pammy giggled as Becky continued, "We're no longer unknowns, thanks to Lia's great finishes in Oberstaufen. But enough, it's time we try to call McElvey, even though it's 10 at night in Monmouth. We need to know about Wren."

Tracy turned to walk out the door, "I'll see you at dinner." Pammy followed her.

Becky waved to Carla and me that we should gather around the bed as she picked up the phone. Talking to the operator, she said slowly, emphasizing each word as if the operator were deaf, "Please, bitte could I make a call to the States? The number is in California 966-4537. I don't know how to call. I want to make a collect call."

After a long silence, I heard Becky say on the phone, "Coach, coach. Can you hear me? It's Becky?" After a pause Becky told McElvey about the race and my successes. Again silence and she asked about Wren. I noticed a change in her composure.

She collapsed on the bed and began shaking the phone as she concluded, "Okay, I'll tell the rest. I'm so sorry. Good bye." When she hung up, she put her hands to her face and started to tremble more. She looked into our searching eyes before saying, "McElvey is proud of us. He says ski for Wren now. Her, her legs are pa … paralyzed."

My heart seized, I stood up and stormed out of the room, saying, "So much for precautions."

CHAPTER 38

Wrong Trail

With a new authority, his cockscomb of dark hair bouncing atop his head, Coach Ryan strutted into the crystal-chandeliered dining hall the next morning. Becky pulled out a carved chair next to her, indicating he could sit there.

"Good morning," he said, taking a bow as if he were a prince courting five maidens. Forcefully, he slid the seat toward himself and stood behind it. The grating sound on the floor made my head jerk back.

"Good morning," we answered in one voice.

"Okay, my girls, you all know you'll have three races here—a downhill, a giant slalom, and a slalom. The downhill will start in three days. For the first time, there'll be a combined result. You'd do well to stand up in all three. I'll know more after the coaches' meeting about your start order." He paused and turned toward me, nodding in approval. "Well, Miss Lia, you should get a great start order. You really improved your points in giant slalom at Oberstaufen."

Blushing with pride, I said, "Thanks, Coach."

Taking charge, Coach Ryan waved away my comment and continued. "You can free ski today, just make sure to have your US Ski Team parkas on. This is your lift ticket." Frowning, he looked at Carla, "Why are you giggling?"

Carla, slouched into her chair and said, "Sorry, Coach, but we really don't have any other parka to wear."

"Enough. Just make sure to be polite and ski on the trails. You'll be tempted to go off-piste. That's where the untracked powder is, but you can get lost or end up in another town," he said, and sitting down, he signaled to the waiter who brought over a continental breakfast of rolls, fresh bread, hot chocolate, and hard-boiled eggs. "You'll eat all your meals here. Now, this afternoon at two, we'll meet at the train station. You are lucky. We've been invited by Coach Boast and the boys' team to go to Wengen and ski the Lauberhorn, the boys' downhill trail, just under the Jungfrau cliff. The boys, as you know, are staying over there." He looked directly at Carla.

Munching on a croissant, I couldn't hold back and said, "The Lauberhorn. The toughest downhill on the circuit. You mean, we can ski it?" I waved my hands in the air with the giddiness of a child seeing Santa's presents under the Christmas tree.

"Yup," said Coach Ryan. "And best of all, the boys and Coach Boast will meet us at the top to join us. Remember you'll just be skiing it." He stood up, placed his hands on his hips, and spread his legs like a gunslinger. "Let me remind you. The course is not open for training. Plus, I don't think you'll want to go 90 mph. Leave that to the guys."

Our group nodded in consent and Becky offered, "Whoever wants to go explore our mountain this morning? I plan to ski."

"Count me in," I said grinning.

"Me, too," said Pammy and Carla simultaneously, turning to give each other high-fives. Then in unison they laughed, "Jinx until someone says your name."

Tracy got up and said, "You're just silly. I think I'll take the day off. I'll meet you at two. Is that okay, Coach?" She put her hand to her mouth to stifle a yawn.

"Of course," said Coach Ryan with a wink. "You'll find some fun shops in town."

The four of us walked through town, two by two, skis and poles crossed over our shoulders. I noticed the absence of cars, the relaxed meandering of the pedestrians, the street lights lit with Christmas decorations and thought, *the perfect Swiss village.* I must've stepped off the curb because I had to jump aside, startled by sleigh bells; I was almost hit by a horse-drawn sleigh. Two lovers in the back, bundled in red blankets, waved and then saluted me. "Guten morgen, Americans. Good luck in the race." I envied the blonde girl snuggled next to her boyfriend or husband.

I turned to the group, "Wow, we're famous. Everyone recognizes us."

Pammy looked puzzled, "Duh, remember we're wearing the red, white and blue parkas with the flag on the shoulder." I gave her a little playful push.

Carla said, "Enough, you two. We're lucky these people feel that way. I had someone boo me the other day when they saw my American uniform. He yelled, "Baby killers!"

I stopped and stepped in front of my friends. "I wonder how many here support our war in Vietnam? By the way, has anyone heard anything about what is going on over there?"

"Not much," said Becky, shaking her head. "Obviously, it's not such a big deal to the Europeans ... well except for that one man."

"Strange," I said, lowering my head in resignation. "Our friends are dying in Vietnam and no one seems to care." After a silence, I continued, "Do... do any of you ever think about Bill?"

Becky, who started walking again, slowly picking up the pace, said, "My friend, some things we can't change and probably shouldn't worry about. The war is one thing we can't control."

Sarcastically, I said, "Yeah right. I remember, just take precautions. I know." I thought to myself, *Maybe someday I can work to change that. After all, the kids in college in the US are protesting now.*

At the ski lift, I noticed that many Europeans had different ways of queueing up. A free-for-all took place at the entrance to the corral before the skiers entered the final corridor. The Swiss skiers waited patiently for their turn in line; whereas, the French had no problem stepping on the skis of the person in front before walking right ahead of the person. A particularly aggressive French man in tight Bogner stretch pants said, "Attention!" as he started walking right over my Rossignol GS skis. I put my pole out and said, "Excusez-moi, monsieur, but I think I'm ahead of you."

The Frenchman made a gesture of hitting the inside of his elbow with his other hand and continued on. There was a scraping sound as his edges crossed the enameled logo on my skis. I deftly placed my pole between his ski boots, causing him to fall into a man to his left. I winked at Becky and said, "Precautions," while indicating that we should continue. "Serves him right," I said. "There can be control in the lift lines."

Becky groaned before she said, "Hey, remember we're the guests here."

At the top, the group gathered to look around at the three hundred and sixty degrees of mountains. The treeless slopes and infinite horizon made me feel as if I were on a cloud, no sense of up or down. I whispered to Becky, "Looks like the handkerchief of God."

Becky yelled back, "Of God—give me a break," as she poled off toward a trail sign, "You'll never stop being a romantic, will you?"

I screamed into the wind, "Nope, not if it has to do with my Transcendentalists."

The four of us regrouped under a large black trail sign which listed five trail names in German, followed by their recommended ski abilities. I pointed my ski pole at the one that said Arleberg—Gesperrt. "Must mean expert, let's go that way," I said. "Let's see what expert means to the Swiss." I poled off ahead of my friends.

Relaxed, I skated toward the top of a ridge, where a narrow chute dropped between two cliffs. None of the other tourists were headed in our direction, but that didn't worry me. I waved my pole, indicating to my friends that I'd found the trail head. Two crossed bamboo poles with a sign draped over them said *Gesperrt*

again. "Last one down has to file the edges tonight," I said, dropping into the narrow chasm, throwing my skis from side to side in
the heavy powder, pushing piles of snow that sloughed downhill
like molten-white lava. The snow traveled faster than I did because of the slope's steepness. I struggled for balance as I continued my weightless free-fall, my skis rocketing side-to-side like a
metronome.

Tired, I pulled up under a rocky outcrop to watch Carla take off
next: a precaution against possible avalanches that I had learned
about in *SKI Magazine*. As Carla made her third turn, I saw a
jagged fracture-line break above her. Becky and Pammy, standing
above the crack, skied off to the side, screaming, "Avalanche!"

I cowered under the rocky overhang just as Carla tumbled
passed me, riding the top of the metastasizing snowslide. "Shit," I
whispered as I heard the train-like rumble. In slow motion, Carla
flailed, like a Raggedy Ann doll, head over heels. A spray of snow
splashed my face and melted down my spine. The white foam covered my goggles. I crouched, clinging to the nearby rock, waiting
for the slope under me to give way.

When the white shroud stopped, the vacuum of silence frightened me until I heard Becky's voice. "Are you okay? We're coming
down."

I yelled back up, "I'm ... I'm here. Can you see Carla?"

"I'm coming down. Stay where you are," screamed Becky. She
skied up to me and then pointed down. "We've got to help Carla.
Get going. Be careful; the snow's like cement."

Pammy cautiously joined us next to the buried Carla, whose
head and right shoulder were sticking out above the snow. "Hey,
guys. I'm stuck," said Carla, trying to make light of her predicament. She started to wheeze, "I ... I can't get a full breath."

"Whoa, that was a close one," said Pammy, her eyes as large
as two ski pole baskets. Becky and I undid our safety straps and
snapped out of our skis.

I yelled to Becky and Pammy, "Start digging! Carla's frozen in." We had to pound the white concrete with our ski tails and lift the chunks away. Carla's eyes rolled up, her head flopping to the side as she passed out. Pammy cradled Carla's face in her hands as I continued digging.

Once her chest was exposed, Carla took a big gulp of air, opened her eyes, spit, and said, "Ouch, you just hit my arm." I used my ski tail to dig around her.

Carla shook her head, saying, "Go slowly, I'm okay," totally unaware of how close she'd come to not breathing.

After we'd pulled her from her snow-coffin, we all sat down on our flattened skis, not speaking, spaced like sparrows on a telephone line. Carla spoke first, spitting snow, "Am I ever lucky! Jeez, that sure was scary. My first time fighting the white dragon."

"The what?" I yelled, confused by her lack of fear.

Continuing to spit snow from her mouth, she laughed, "Oh, I guess you haven't heard how we personify the avalanches. You … you English teacher."

I shook my head and patted her shoulder, "You can find a way to make light of just about anything."

Pammy finally found her voice, "I don't think we should tell Coach Ryan. We could get into trouble." She tucked her head between her knees as though trying to stop a nightmare from coming into her thoughts.

"I agree," I said. "Mum's the word." Then, falling back into the snow, I felt a cold, wet shiver run up my legs while the sun blazed through my eyelids, and added, "Does anyone remember the story of the great Buddy Werner? I think he died somewhere here in Switzerland in an avalanche after the 1960 Olympics." I paused to remember the day when I'd heard the news of his death at the Stowe Spring Sugar Slalom. I'd just completed my first junior race when the announcer stopped the race to tell the one hundred racers about the tragedy. That was my first experience with a skiing death. I continued in a somber voice, "We don't need a repeat."

Becky nodded in agreement, also settling back into the hard snow, and said, "Yup, I remember. He was the top American skier that year. In fact, I think he has the American record on the Lauberhorn downhill right here. He took the combined." She waited to see if anyone could remember, and then sitting up, she said, "Now let's go have some fun. I see a groomed trail just down below the chute."

When she skied up next to me, she whispered, "Sometimes I wonder if we are crazy to be doing this?"

I yelled over the wind, "Nope, life isn't worth it, if we don't live on the edge."

CHAPTER 39

The Lauberhorn

Becky, Carla, Pammy, and I gathered at the entrance to the train station under a sign that said, "Wengenalpbahn," just as a bell atop the cupola tolled two o'clock. Coach Ryan strutted toward us, his skis and poles balancing on his shoulder like a pitchfork. He beamed through his boyish freckles, looked up to the mountain and said, "Well done, girls. I'm glad you're on time." He looked around anxiously. "Where's Tracy?"

Becky stepped forward. "I don't know. Remember, we split up this morning. While we went skiing, she went shopping."

"Oh, righto," he said, trying not to look upset. "Did you girls have fun skiing?" A long silence greeted his question. Carla looked to me while I, holding my finger to my lips, looked at Pammy.

Becky, noticing our nervousness, broke in, "Yup, we skied some challenging terrain. One trail even said 'gesperrt.' "

"Holy crap! Did you say 'gesperrt'?" he said, throwing his hands in the air.

"Yup," said Becky, lifting her chin in the air in an act of pride.

"Do you know what 'gesperrt' means?" he said, his face reddening with anger.

"Sure, 'expert,' " said Becky.

"Jeez, are you stupid or what? No, 'gesperrt' means closed. Did you have any trouble?"

Another longer silence ensued before I stepped forward. "Well, Coach, we had everything under control and skied some great chutes." A sigh went up from the other girls.

Before he could challenge me, Tracy stepped from around the

entrance gate. "Hi, Coach. Sorry I'm late. I had to go back to the hotel to get my skis." Her face glowed with tan makeup and fresh lipstick.

"Okay, okay. Get on board. I'll buy the tickets," he said, flustered at our new independence. No one spoke during the whole trip up the side of the Eiger. The black granite wall looked even more menacing up close.

Getting off the train, I tripped on my ski boots. As I grabbed the railing, trying to balance my skis on my left shoulder, I heard Coach Ryan say, "Be careful. One never knows where danger is lurking." He snickered and pointed up to the face of the Eiger just as a dark shadow descended and clouds roiled around the shrouded peak. "Watch out for the ogre," he said laughing. "Oh, by the way, after we ski the race course with the boys, we've been invited to dine with them."

His grin made me uncomfortable, so I stepped closer to Becky to put on my skis. I saw the boys' team waiting for us in the distance, lined up along the edge of the course in a straight formation, rigid as soldiers at attention. Jason Lang skied out from the line of red, white, and blue parkas to put his arm around me. "What's the matter, babe? Remember me? You stayed with my family in Denver."

"How could I forget? By the way, how's your brother doing?" I said, stepping away from his arm.

"No idea. That hippie draft-dodger is probably in Africa by now," said Jason disdainfully.

Happy not to respond, I turned my attention to Coast Boast who stepped forward, his weathered face ruddy from the cold wind. "Welcome, girls. Yup, the boys have been excited to see you. They want to show you the downhill. Then we can all eat at our inn." He looked to each girl individually before his eyes rested on Tracy. "You'll look great. Please ski cautiously. The course crew is still setting up the safety fences."

Each boy then skied over to one of the girls as if choosing a dance partner. Pete Timmons moved over to me, pushing Jason away who then moved toward Carla. Dennis Albright, a strong downhiller from Seattle, slid next to Becky while the youngest and most glamorous boy on the team, Scott Forman, sidled up to Pammy. I noticed that no one moved toward Tracy Languile, as if she were the forbidden fruit.

In pairs, we danced down the trail, snaking, chasing, jumping, flowing, gliding, and circling until we stopped on a snow-covered road that crossed the trail. I pulled up behind the lineup of red, white, and blue parkas and looked out over the valley. A darkness had descended on the village, but the peaks glowed like wedding candles. Pete said to the gathered group, "Now this drop off is the Hundschop—our first challenge. We have to hit our pre-jump perfectly."

I laughed derisively, thinking of Wren, before I said, "Yup, perfectly. Take precautions." Becky gave me a scowl.

The group took off again, led by Pete. Like a slinky descending a staircase, we followed each other, lowering ourselves into egg-shaped tucks on the flats. Often the boys had to snow plow in order to keep from riding up the girls' tails. We cruised the Kernen S turns, standing up to slow down.

At the next stop by a railway tunnel, Pete said, "This is the Wasserstetcher Tunnel. Scary because of our speed." He raised his chin proudly, "Yup, as fast as 80 mph."

I'd never seen a downhill go under a tunnel and said "Whoa, this makes our downhills seem like cakewalks," I cringed, looking into the darkened shaft.

After a long flat section, the trail dropped off again, and Pete stopped the group in the middle of the steep pitch. Just as the last of us pulled up, he pointed to the hard snow and said, "This is the famous Haneggschuss, where we can hit speeds close to 90 mph." An audible sigh came from each girl.

Jason quickly stepped forward, lifted his goggles and said, "So now you'll have some respect for us. We're the kings of skiing." He put both thumbs up in a display of confidence. "The course can take as long as two-and-a-half minutes. By the time we get to the end called Stump Alley, we are ready to vomit from pain."

Giggling, the group continued to follow one another, descending into the village, into the darkness and cold. Pete and I left the group when we found a small trail between two shepherd's huts. A sound of laughing led us to a gathering of children, sliding on wooden sleds. I stopped to watch, causing Pete to cruise in next to me. The hand-made sleds with curved front rails and woven seats were very different from my red Flexible Flier, a wooden sled with metal runners and an actual handle bar. In Vermont, I used to slide down Brook Road face-first, my nose three inches off the ground, after a new snowfall covered the dirt road, always at night so I could see the headlights of the cars coming up.

We left the innocent kids by snow-plowing down a narrow path between two stucco chalets. Cows hung their heads out the basement doors, munching and watching. I pointed to a brown Swiss with horns, "Hey, Pete, why do they keep the animals in the bottom of their houses? Doesn't it smell?" I wriggled my nose, remembering the smell of cow dung from my neighbor's barn in Vermont.

"Yup, it smells, but the animals do provide some warmth for the building. Everything is more compact here. A more frugal way of life." He pointed toward a side trail and took off. "Try to catch me." We skied past houses, slalomed through yards where the house lights cast rectangles on the new snow.

A brown and white Bernese Mountain Dog jumped out from a gate, barked and ran back inside. "Watch out for the dog," yelled Pete. I stopped and tried to lure the dog out from under the house. He peeked out, his dark brown shaggy coat rippled in the wind, the white cross on his chest glowed, but obediently he ran back in when a chunky, scarf-covered woman came out to check on the commotion. At this moment, I remembered my own dog, Sheba, who loved to chase me while sledding down Brook Road, her legs flailing. How I missed my simple life in Vermont, now so far away.

At the bottom of the hill, we found part of our group gathered near a dying pine tree. Coach Boast skied over to me and beckoned to the rest of the group to hike up, indicating for Tracy to sidle up to him. He smiled, put his arm over her shoulder and said to the group, "Okay, let's go have dinner. The girls can use Jason's room to freshen up. Dinner will be at 5."

Hoisting our skis on our shoulders, Pete and I left the group to walk through the village of Wengen. The quiet, snow-covered streets spoke of a time without cars. We marched down narrow brick-lined alleys, past wrought-iron lamp posts garnished with Christmas wreaths. A buttery glow from the display windows in the shops lit our way. *A perfect Swiss village, a Christmas-card world,* I thought.

Horses not only pulled sleighs with tourists, they pulled the sleds carrying produce and retail goods. Men, bent like mules, lugged the supplies into the small shops. I stopped in front of a bay window where I heard the song, *Edelweiss,* tinkling from a music box in the well-lit shop. I laughed, "Hey, Pete, this could be a scene from 1771, 1871, or 1971—nothing's changed."

Pete smiled before he said, "Lia, you're right. Remember, Switzerland has never had a war. It's always remained neutral. So, all has remained the same."

"Oh, yeah. I studied that in World History," I said proudly.

"Yeah, how lucky for its people. They never suffered from the bombing during the World Wars." He held his skis at his side like a soldier at attention.

I pointed to the trellised window displaying miniature toy shepherds, cows and carved music boxes resting on a white pad of cotton. "Wow, would I like to get one of those for Bill." I moved over toward the window, pointing to an open box with a detailed scene of a shepherd and lamb. Next to it lay an old leather book entitled, *Manfred,* by Lord Byron. "What's that got to do with all this?"

"Well," said Pete, raising his head in a superior manner, "I think Lord Byron used this town for the setting of his long poem— something about a very troubled, dirty old man." He grimaced as if trying not to remember the story and changed the subject, "Would you like to go in?"

"No, actually, I'd better get back to the hotel. I don't want to miss the group. Hey, how do you know all this literature stuff?"

"Lia, you know I was an English major at WU."

"Great. Did you know that when I'm done with this ski team, I think I want to study English in college, too?"

"Not a bad idea. For sure, you do like reading."

"After that, I want to become a writer." I paused and looked away, afraid to see his reaction. "By the way, what room did Coach say we were to meet in?"

"He said you could use Jason's. Number 33. I want to go into this shop and look around. See you at dinner. The hotel Parker is just around the corner. You can't miss it."

I looked around the hotel entrance for my friends and then realized that they must have gone ahead while Pete and I had been window shopping. I left my skis outside in the ski rack, kicked the snow off my boots, and entered the large marble foyer. Slipping on the polished white surface, I found a chair where I took off my ski boots. I set them next to a pile of boots near the hotel elevator.

Taking the elevator to the third floor, I followed a sign to room 33 and knocked. Jason opened the door and said, in mock surprise, "Oh, welcome. What are you doing here?"

"Oh, I … I thought we were supposed to change in your room," I said, as Jason moved behind me and grabbed the door.

"Well, yes. I guess the others haven't come in yet," he said slowly, once more looking into the hallway. "Come on in. The bathroom's next to the closet." He closed the door, locking it.

I was uncomfortable, but I took off my parka, and before setting it on the bed. I said, "Maybe I … I should wait downstairs until the rest come."

"Not to worry. I'll just step outside and find them."

I went into the bathroom, took off my warmup pants but kept my jeans on, washed my face, my underarms, and brushed my hair. The warmth of the water burned my chilled cheeks. A smell of Aqua Velva cologne came from the medicine cabinet. Reaching to turn off the water, I knocked a razor to the floor and picking it up gingerly, I spotted a condom wrapper in the wastebasket.

I opened the door to find Jason sitting on his bed in his underwear. "Hey, what are you doing?" I said as I edged toward the hallway door.

He put out his hand, grabbed my arm, and jerked me down on the bed. "Okay, little Miss Priss. The guys and I have a bet. The guys bet that I can't get you to kiss me. C'mon just one little kiss. You've the reputation of being a nun."

I struggled. Jason threw his muscular body over mine. I tried to protest, but he cupped one hand over my mouth. "Shh. No one knows you're here. The guys and I planned it. The girls have gone to another room with Coach Ryan."

I twisted my head, so he couldn't put his lips on mine. "Okay," he said. "So you want to play rough. I can play rough, too." He grabbed my crotch and squeezed. I tried to kick, but he put his powerful legs over mine. I felt my pant zipper break, his hand thrust into my underwear. He now had one hand over my mouth, holding my head down and the other started exploring my private area.

Violently, he started pushing two fingers into me. He poked and squeezed. "Tell me now that you don't enjoy this." He continued. I felt a soreness between my legs and then a warm moist trickle.

Pushing his hand away from my mouth, I sunk my teeth into his cheek. "Ouch," he said, jumping back, holding the bite mark. "Christ, are you trying to hurt me?" He raised his hand as if to hit me, but instead settled down on the bed laughing. "C'mon, Lia, I was just playing. I didn't hurt you."

"Leave me alone!" I yelled, instinctively reaching to snap my jeans back on.

"Okay, okay. But if you try to tell anyone, I'll say you came to my room willingly and attacked me. Who's going to believe you?"

"You bastard—I'll tell your coach."

"Yeah, right. You do that. Do you want to get kicked off the team? Remember, you came to my room."

I stopped, thought, looked around the room, grabbed my parka and warmup pants, and slammed the door as I left. Outside the room, I knelt to the ground, tears warming my cheeks. *Who'd believe me? Had I done something wrong?* I wiped my eyes with my parka, stood, and wandered down the hallway looking for a staircase, not wanting to face anyone on the elevator. I turned left, right, backtracked but couldn't find any exit signs—just a maze of narrow corridors snaking in every direction. Finally, I saw a small door with a red light over it. I jumped into the dimly lit staircase and stumbled down the narrow metal steps.

In the foyer under a brass chandelier, Becky stood talking to Coach Ryan. I waited at the bottom of the stairs until Becky looked to me. Discretely, I waved her to come over. Becky's jaw dropped when she saw my distress. "What's the matter? We've been looking for you?" she said, furling her brows together with impatience.

"Uh, please, I need to talk to you," I said, turning my head so others couldn't see my panic.

"Lia, can't it wait? Coach wants all of us in the dining hall right now—for pictures. *Le Monde* is here to do an article on the whole US Ski Team." She grabbed my arm and led me into a large room with linen-covered tables. In front of the fireplace stood both the boys' and girls' team, bounded on each side by a coach. The burning wood smelled like sulfur.

Off in a corner, I saw Coach Boast talking to the reporter from *Le Monde* whom I'd met under the Eiger and who now looked even more disheveled. Two cameras hung from his neck, swinging as he staggered to keep his balance. The two kept looking at me as they conspired, which made me even more nervous. They appeared to be exchanging some money.

Coach Boast stepped forward and said angrily, "Lia, we almost took the picture without you."

Then Jason stepped forward, "Hey, Lia, why don't you come stand next to me? I saved a place for you."

CHAPTER 40

Night

Back in my bed, I pulled the duvet over my head; I was afraid to talk to Becky about Jason's attack, worrying she'd think it was my fault. To calm myself, I turned on my flashlight and opened my journal. Earlier on the train ride back from Wengen, she must've wondered why I was so upset, because I'd barely spoken to her, and at the hotel, I'd raced to my room, instead of joining the others in the ski room. Maybe tomorrow I'd tell her after the downhill training, but right now I had to find a way to get through the night.

Knowing I couldn't write about my anger as someone might read my journal, I began to reread my entries. Each page contained memories about Monmouth, about my dreams, about Bill. Each brought a small joy, until I came across a poem about my life with my dad, which caused me to chuckle cynically at my former naïveté, at my trust in a divine order, at my innocent optimism.

The Thin Line

Between my home and church wanders
A brook road, muddy, rutted, steep,

Jeez, I thought, *how idealistic, but I did love walking Brook Road to the village.*

Two miles, a thirty-minute walk in silence with my father.
A yellow pencil-light bathes the water
The breeze stirs a new hope in me.

I remembered how my father loved the walk down the pine-covered road on Sunday mornings, especially after my mother had died. Just the two of us.

> The water flows from its mountain womb,
> Carves a path over granite boulders,
> The birches, beeches, pines and maples
> Shade the spring trillium.

I tried to recall why I'd used the flower trillium. Oh, yes, in my Transcendental journey I had wanted to allude to another trinity—nature, the divine, Man.

> Leaving my father's side, I choose the less-traveled route to
> the steeple;
> Down the middle of the stream, hopping
> Over boulder mazes and under log bridges,

I remembered the balance required in order to jump from stone to stone, much like running a slalom course.

> I stop, listen to the unknown force that strums the branches.
> A different scripture, a natural sermon from the mount.
> A message along the thin line
> Where heaven and earth recline.

Every week, in the fall and spring, before and after ski season, I looked forward to these walks with my father. I think he went because of the home-cooked meals that the church-community provided; plus, he basked in the female attention and, as a singer, he loved to belt out the hymns. On the other hand, I'd stopped believing in the Christian God after my mother had been killed in the car crash, and instead, I'd turned to nature and writers such as Emerson, Thoreau, and Wordsworth for solace.

Also, I'd felt guilty that, while she was alive, I'd been disrespectful to her, intolerant of her drinking binges. In a small way, I'd blamed my father and myself for not being able to stop her alcoholism.

Now Jason's abuse had caused me to relive similar feelings of guilt, of loss of control—a psychic dark-place, a vortex from which there was no return.

Could Jason be right? Had I brought this attack on by going to his room? Was I guilty? Had I been set up by the other boys? Had Pete Timmons been part of this scheme? Would I get kicked off the team if I told someone? Would everyone turn against me? Who could I trust—my teammates, the coaches?

To quiet my mind, I read the poem again. I pictured the brook, the moss-covered stones, the watery vapor that roiled out of the small waterfalls and settled into the quiet pools.

"Hey, Lia. Aren't you going to bed? We have to start training tomorrow," moaned Becky impatiently. "Stop being so selfish and go to sleep."

"So sorry, I've had a bad night," I said, turning off my flashlight and setting my journal on my bedside table.

"Well, tell me about it in the morning. I need my sleep."

"Okay, night."

"Good night," said Becky, emphasizing the good.

I tossed in bed for an hour, listening to the snow against the window and Becky's shallow breathing before I decided to get up and go work on my skis. Slipping on my jeans, I remembered that that the zipper was broken, so I threw them in a pile by my bed and put on my sweat pants. I ran my fingers through my gnarly hair and tiptoed out the door.

Once in the hallway, I squinted to get used to the dimmed lighting. The red-carpeted stairs felt soft on my sock feet, quieting my steps. At the front desk, a swarthy night-man nodded as I explained, "Just going to work on my skis." He grunted something and resumed shuffling his paper work; however, I felt his eyes on my back as I turned toward the basement door.

At the bottom of the stairs, the narrow hallway, leading to the ski room, stank of ski wax as I followed it around two corners. A dim light escaped from a partially closed door on my right, where I stopped in order to listen to two voices coming from the room. Although whispers, they sounded familiar. I held my breath, so I could hear what was being said.

"Okay, Dan. So you want a cut. I should of known you'd get wind of this."

The other voice said, "Righto! Tracy's dad, Jack, told me before we left for Europe. Did you think it'd be—?" A sound of shuffling feet muffled the last words.

I knew instantly that hearing this conversation between Coach Boast and Coach Ryan could get me kicked off the team, yet I lingered, pressing my head toward the door jam.

Lowering his voice, Coach Boast continued, "Okay, did he tell you how much money he was offering?"

"No, but he told me he'd make it worthwhile for the coaches."

"Ah, coaches? Damn, I guess the cat is out of the bag. How much do you want now?" said Boast. A long silence ensued.

Finally Coach Ryan demurred, "Okay, don't get angry. Put your fists down. I just want my cut. How much did he offer?"

"Oh, now you want me to tell you specifics."

"Well, you'd better or I'll go to the team's Board of Directors."

After a long pause, Boast said, "Well then, I'd better let you in on the deal. Tracy's dad, Jack, has offered me $30,000 if I can get her on the Olympic team."

"Shit, 30?"

"Yup."

"What will you do with the money? Give it to the team?"

Boast laughed, "Um. I've thought of other options. What if we split it? I could use your help in making this happen."

"Could we get in trouble over this?' said Coach Ryan in a slow, uncertain voice.

"Not if we don't talk. Jack said he'd put it into whatever account I wanted."

"I'm in, but how are you going to make this happen? It's not like you can lower her points," said Coach Ryan.

"I'll have to work on this. She's been skiing well. I've some thoughts. Let's go to bed now."

I backed away from the door when I heard footsteps coming toward me. Ducking into a darkened room across the hallway, I slipped behind the partially closed door. Cobwebs crossed my mouth, but I held my sneeze. I put my hands to my sides, still as a statue. Fear squeezed my heart. A metal clanging from the furnace broke the tense silence, allowing me to shift my position. For two minutes, I held my breath until I heard the two men step into the hall. A door slammed behind them. The schemers continued the conversation in a way that made me confident they didn't suspect anyone had heard them.

"See you in the morning," said Coach Ryan. "I want to check on the girls' skis and make sure that they've sharpened their edges. I'll wait to wax in the morning. I've heard there's a storm coming."

"Night, Dan. Let me know if you can think of any more options."

"Later. I'm beginning to like this coaching job."

I listened for Coach Boast's footsteps go up the stairs and for Coach Ryan's to go down the hall. After ten minutes, I edged along the hallway to the stairs, a splinter from the rough pine wall jabbed my thumb. I sucked on the blood from the wound while I tiptoed up the wooden steps like a spy in the James Bond movie. At the top, the night clerk didn't even look up from his work. I looked around, fearing someone else might be in the vestibule.

An outside light glowed through a mist of falling snow. My childhood, my dreams, seemed far, far away like a country I could never return to.

CHAPTER 41

Day

"Hey, wake up, kiddo! You've been moaning in your sleep all night like a baby cow bellowing for its mother," said Kathy, shaking my back.

Rubbing my eyes to get a big bugger out, I said apologetically, "You've no idea. I've been having nightmares."

"Do you want to talk?"

"Not yet. Yesterday was hell." I squeezed my eyes, trying to keep out the light and felt a massive ache in my head.

"I thought so. You really shut down last night. By the way, did you go out after I went to sleep?"

"Yup."

"That explains it. The door was partially open when I woke up. Someone could of come in and attacked me."

"Sorry." I shook my head, hoping everything had been a bad dream.

"Okay, okay, calm down. Let's get up. We've got downhill training today even though it's snowing."

"Hey, do you think the coach will be mad if I stay in bed? I feel awful."

"I'll tell him you're sick."

"Thanks." I pulled the covers up and listened to Kathy dressing. Her routine helped me relax. I heard the water flow, her toothbrush splash, the toilet flush, and then her bureau drawers squeak. I imagined how she dressed: first her bra, her turtleneck, her underwear, long underwear, socks, stretch pants and finally her sweater. I even heard her hairbrush twisting in her brown snarls. "Damn," she said, "I hate the frizz that I get over here. The air is so humid."

The door creaked open and as she left, she said, "Get some rest. There's some aspirin in my toilet kit if you need it." Her motherly tone reassured me. The doorlock turned, helping me doze off to cadences of the hissing radiator, the clacking pipes and the ticking snowflakes against my window, a repetitive tap like small moths flickering against a lamp.

Then the pain hit. I grabbed my forehead, struggling with the down comforter that trapped me in its feathers. I looked down between the sheets and that's when I saw it: a red spot. *What the heck?* I thought. I'd already had my period. What's going on? My crotch ached, my legs hurt, my head pounded. Hand-over-hand, I crawled out of the bed, along the floor and into the bathroom like a drunk with a massive hangover. The smell of Kathy's deodorant and hair spray shrank the room in its feminine odor. Pulling myself up to the sink, I splashed water on my face and then looked in the mirror. A tired, wrinkled face with dark blotches under its eyes stared back. My hair stood straight up, matted. My mouth opened in horror.

Stumbling back into bed, I tried not to think about the pain. *Should I tell Kathy about Jason? Would Kathy tell Coach? Would I be sent home? Who could I tell about the coaches' plot? How could I get out of this nightmare? Whom could I trust?*

Like a person falling in an avalanche, I'd never felt so helpless, my head spun, my lungs gasped for air, my hands quivered. I took deep breaths the way my mother had taught me while sitting under her Buddhist prayer flags and finally dozed off, dreaming of going home to Vermont, where my father waited at the door, his shock of gray hair sweeping to the right and his craggy teeth glinting in the sun. Home. My sheepdog, Sheba. I ran toward her, arms outstretched, but when I went to grab her, she vanished. I screamed, "Dad, help me!"

"Hey, Lia. Wake up, you idiot," said Kathy who had come in the room with Carla and Pammy. She shook my shoulder. Carla sat on my bed and started rubbing my back. "Hey, slow down. We're here!" I opened my eyes, painful holes that felt as if someone had thrown mud on them.

"Hi, guys, I guess I had a nightmare."

"Holy cow, I guess so," said Pammy. "Do you want us to get the coaches?"

I sat up and stared right at Pammy in panic, announcing, "No, never. I've had it with them."

"Whoa, slow down," said Kathy. "What's gotten into you?"

"If I told you, I'd get kicked off the team," I said cautiously, adjusting my pajama top.

"Try us," said Kathy angrily.

I thought for a moment before I felt the swirling motion again. "No, I can't right now. Maybe later. I'll see you after skiing. I'm going to take a shower. K?"

By the time I got dressed, the others had left for the downhill course. I put on my ski pants for breakfast so that no one would ask me why I wasn't training. Before leaving the room, I grabbed the phone to see if I could call the States.

"Bitte, USA." I paused and heard an English-speaking voice. "Yes, please can—can I make a collect call to the USA?"

The hotel operator answered, "Where to?"

"Vermont. Number 529-9520."

"What room are you in?"

"Number 24."

"Your name, bitte?"

"Lia, Lia Erikson."

"One moment, bitte."

I heard bell tones, then ringing, then an operator with a Vermont accent. "Waitsfield, Vermont. Jenny here." Ah, good old Vermont where I knew the operators.

The hotel operator said, "A collect call from Grindelwald, Switzerland, for a Stan Erikson, bitte."

Holding my breath, I heard more ringing on the phone. I pictured our black house phone next to the sink. At this time of night, probably three in the morning, I knew my dad was still in bed, but he might hear the ring. The operator said, "No one is answering."

I jumped into the conversation, desperate, "Please, please, keep letting it ring. I know my dad will wake up." The phone rang six more times. I could put my hand through the intervals between seconds. Finally, I heard a fumbling and a groggy "Hello."

"I have a collect call from Switzerland," said the Swiss operator. "Will you accept the charges?"

"Yes. Hello, hello, Lia," he said, panicking.

"Dad, dad. I'm here." I could hardly speak through my tears.

"What's wrong, Lia? You know it's three in the morning here. Aren't you supposed to be training for the downhill today?"

"I'm not feeling well, Dad. I want to come home."

"Okay, it's natural to feel homesick. Aren't your friends treating you well?"

"They're fine. It's...it's the coaches."

"Remember what I told you. Respect."

Hugging the phone, I sat down on the edge of my bed, my covers falling to the floor, my shoulders slumping as I pushed the phone closer to my ear. "I know but ... " I couldn't finish, so I decided to change the subject. "Dad, have you heard from Bill? Any news?"

"I know he's just north of Saigon in a place called the Iron Triangle. At least that's what his mother told me."

I didn't even know that Dad knew Bill's mom. "What's the news from the war?"

"Not good, Lia. There's been heavy fighting and many casualties. Bill's a second lieutenant, you know, so he'll be in the thick of it." His voice trailed off as if he wanted to say more.

I held my head, trying to keep the phone to my ear. My chest felt as though it had been hit by a giant snow ball. "I can't hear you very well. I'll call again."

"No, Lia, save the money. Miss you and good luck."

"I love you." I held on to the phone, hoping he'd reciprocate, but then I heard the click. I don't ever remember a time he'd said I love you.

Skipping breakfast, I decided to go out into the storm and see whether I could find an English newspaper; maybe one that would have more news about Vietnam. Now all my problems seemed small compared to Bill's. Outside, the heavy snow floated down like saucers, each crystal unique until it hit the ground where it melded with the whole and disappeared. I thought, *how small, how simple. Just like us. We think we're special, but we're just part of a bigger picture or, worse, pawns for someone else's pleasure.*

Around the corner at the pharmacy, I saw many papers lining the racks, but they were in German, but then I spotted a black and white picture of the US Ski Team on the top fold of *Le Monde*. Jason's face stared in a taunting manner, as if he could see out of the picture. Picking up the paper, I read the headlines, "Equipe de Ski des E-U Prête à Succéder."

Next to the picture, I saw a more familiar newspaper, the January 10, 1971 copy of the *New York Times*. I pulled it from the rack and walked over to the shopkeeper. I had no Swiss francs, but he was more than pleased to take my American dollars. I held out three ones; he returned a few coins.

Folding the paper into my parka, I trudged back to the hotel. The snow seared my face like a file, wet my cheeks and made my head pound more. My eyes blurred, I tripped twice. I turned right down an unfamiliar street, enticed by the odor of confectioneries baking. A tourist sleigh slid by and the young driver, dressed in a heavy fur hat and coat, didn't even slow when he passed me. A young couple strolled by, arm in arm, so wrapped in each other's gaze that I had to step off the curb to avoid them. An old woman, walking a poodle, forced me into a doorway—even the dog didn't stop to notice me. I hurried to the hotel, letting the snow stay on my cheeks and nose, so as to form a mask. I didn't want to be recognized by or talk to anyone.

Entering the hotel, I saw my reflection in the glass door; a white shroud covered my whole body, even my face. I slipped passed the clerk who didn't look up. After taking the elevator to the second floor, I dropped my boots inside my room, where the fresh snow melted onto the wooden floor, and feeling soaked to the bone, I slipped into bed and opened the paper to an article about Vietnam. The caption read, "We will stand firm" under a picture of President Nixon. Another picture showed three American GIs, faces smeared with black, standing over a small body of a North Vietnamese soldier who looked no older than ten. The article went on to talk about the fighting to the north of Saigon, about the tunnels dug by the North Vietnamese, about the casualties, and the number of North Vietnamese killed. Another paragraph told of how UN Secretary-General U Thant no longer believed that Vietnam was crucial to the security of the West.

I tried imaging Bill in the picture with his rucksack, his M16, his canteen, his flak jacket, his helmet, his black boots and his radio. In the picture, the soldiers resembled overloaded turtles. I wondered how Bill would be changed from this experience. During my last year in high school, I'd heard a saying, "War is betrayal, betrayal of the young by the old, of idealists by cynics, of troops by politicians."

I fell asleep, holding the paper. In my dream I was falling off a cliff; however, the snow at the bottom kept receding, so I never hit. I woke to a knocking on my door. A voice called my name, so I got up, slid on my sock feet to the door and unlocked the latch. Outside the day clerk, a young blonde boy-child, held a telegram, a blue and white striped envelope that said Western Union.

I took the envelope, and turning it, I read the name next to mine, Sarah Emerson, Bill's mother. Sitting on the bed, I opened the envelope carefully so as not to rip any part of it and read the words in capital letters: "BILL WAS KILLED BY FRIENDLY FIRE TWO DAYS AGO. MORE LATER. NOW YOU MUST SKI FOR HIM. MY LOVE, SARAH."

CHAPTER 42

First Downhill

Loud giggles filled my room as Becky and the others returned from training. "Hey, Becky, please, please, ask everyone to stay for a moment. I need to tell you all something," I said, patting the bed for Carla, Pammy, and Tracy to sit next to me while I handed Becky the telegram. No one said a word as Becky read the three sentences aloud. An air-sucking silence filled the room. My eyes darted from each face, looking for some reaction.

Finally, Becky, taking her hands from her face, took the initiative. "Okay, okay. Listen we need to regroup. This, this … " She groped for the right word. "This sucks."

Carla, wiping her eyes, mumbled, "Why? This isn't fair. He was such a good guy. By the way, what's 'friendly fire'?"

Shaking, I said, "I—I don't know? Sounds like an oxymoron."

Tracy just stared at me, a wide-eye expression that revealed no emotion. "What's an oxymoron?" I shook my head in frustration.

Pammy, gagging on her words, said, "First … first Wren's paralyzed, now your friend Bill's killed."

Angrily, looking directly at Becky, I asserted, "I thought we could control things in our lives. Now I feel that we're all pawns in someone else's bigger game. The question is whose?" The image of the two coaches conniving in the basement flashed through my thoughts.

Immediately, Becky put her fingers up to her lips and looked right at me, "Calm down. You still have some control." She looked down as if not truly convinced of what she was going to say. "Yup, I know what you're going to do, what you have to do." Her eyes looked right into mine. You are going to do what Bill's mom asked. You are, no, all of us are going to ski for him."

I snapped, "That won't bring him back!"

Becky put her hands up in front of her to stop the questions. "Look, I've been in this game longer than you have. We get hurt, we get setbacks—yes—and we can get killed." She paused letting us digest this information. "A fact of this sport and, in fact, of life. But we don't have to be victims. To the point, we're also a team." To emphasize her words, she stomped her feet. "We help each other. We're here in Europe to become the best we can. Yes, we'll support each other. Some of us will make the Olympic team, but let us all be able to say that we will have tried." Her chin jutted out in defiance. She broadened her stance. "We've sacrificed a lot already just to get here. Now we must pull together even more." As she said this, she turned directly to Tracy.

Just then the door opened and Coach Boast strode in with Coach Ryan at his side. "I just heard the news about Bill from Lia's dad. He sent me a telegram saying that Lia had also heard. Is everyone okay here?"

No one said a word; the radiator hissed; a door slammed. I stood up and yelled, "I can't believe he's dead!"

"Okay, Okay," said Coach Boast. "I know you're angry at me for cutting him from the team." He shook his head, searching for words. "However, my job is to create the best team I can for the World Cup races and then for the Olympics next year. It's a fact of life. Many boys are being drafted into the army. I can't protect everyone."

"But Bill?" I said, turning my back to him.

"Lia, we're here to ski. You can take some time off if you want, but you do need to stay on task. If you want, I can pull you from the downhill race in three days, but you do need to get the downhill experience. European downhills are much more demanding than our American ones." He looked to each one of us individually before continuing, "Please speak to me in private if you want to pull out."

He left the room with Coach Ryan at his side. I closed my eyes, remembering Sugarloaf, Damien, and the pressure to race even when grieving. Turning to Becky, I said, "I guess that means that the race goes on."

She challenged me, "Yup, Lia. If you want to go home, I'm sure Coach Boast will make the arrangements. He'll probably replace you with one of his younger protégées to give her experience in Europe, but probably not Stephanie."

I sat down in thought and then responded forcefully, "Do you think I want to give up my chance for the Olympics? Bill wouldn't want that."

Carla stood up directly in front of me, "That's the fighting spirit! We're a team. One for all, all for one." She raised her hand as if holding a sword like the three musketeers.

Pammy rose from the disheveled bed and put her arm around me. 'I'm with you, too."

Tracy slowly got up, walked over to Becky, and said coyly, "Yup, I agree with Coach Boast."

✳　✳　✳

For the next two days, we all trained on the downhill, rarely speaking about Bill, except to remember the fun times at Monmouth. In quiet moments, I pulled out his picture in my wallet.

The long course proved to be more challenging than the downhill in Vail. The lack of trees at such a high altitude made judging and setting up for the gates difficult. To help with the flat lighting, the race officials had set pine boughs along the side of the course and blueing in the middle. The contrast of blue on white helped me anticipate the rolls and dips. I used the distant peaks for markers to establish my line. However, my heart wasn't in the training. My pre-run proved to be my worst showing yet on the team: even Tracy beat me by one second.

On race day, clouds rolled in, slamming the face of the Eiger. The valley filled with a wet mist, the course became icy. With start number 25, I'd already decided to just cruise the course, not trying for a great time. This decision took the edge off my run.

On course, when I hit the second pre-jump, I missed my landing and fell on my back, sliding into the snow fence along the side. More embarrassed than hurt, not wanting to face my coaches and teammates, I stayed up on the hill until the last racer, number 80, went by. I followed this timid racer down, arriving at an almost deserted finish line.

The crowds had dispersed. No one seemed to care about the last contestant, a girl from Japan who'd even snowplowed just before the final turn. I skied up behind her, patted her helmet, and said, "Good job. You finished standing up."

The young girl pulled her goggles up onto her helmet and said through her tears of fear, "Arigato." I looked around for the girl's teammates or coaches. No one stepped forward from behind the barrier.

I said to her quietly, my arm over her shoulder, remembering what Damien had said and trying to reassure myself, as well as her, "Courage isn't the absence of fear—it's doing your best despite it." I'm not sure she understood me, but she nodded as I stooped over to help her take off her skis. Simultaneously, the two of us hoisted our skis onto our shoulders. I put my hand out, indicating that my new friend should go ahead of me through the exit gate. I turned in our two pinnies to an official who seemed more distracted by a reporter talking to him. I looked around for my parka, hoping that the coaches had left it at the finish line. No luck. Then, I pointed down the road toward the village.

Side-by-side, models in our tight racing suits, not saying a word, we walked toward the inns, occasionally stopping for school children who asked us to sign autographs.

At the main crossroad in the village, the Japanese girl pointed down a side street and said in broken English, "My room."

I pointed straight ahead, saying, "Mine. Good luck, see you later." I bowed and walked on ahead, feeling good that I'd turned a disaster of a day into one where I could help another.

Back in the hotel, the day clerk handed me a note. "Lia, meet the team in the wax room before lunch at 12. Coach Boast." I looked at my watch and realized that it was already 12:10. Lugging my skis through the hallway, I stumbled down the two stairs. The pounding of my hard plastic boots on the pine stairs echoed through the cavernous space.

"Hey, slow poke," said Becky as I entered the wax-encrusted room. "Where have you been? I waited awhile for you at the finish line."

"Uh, I fell and stayed up on the course until after the last racer came down."

Boast turned, scowled, and gestured for me to sit on the bench. "Okay, now we're all here. Lia, I'm glad you're okay. Rough day, huh!"

"Yes, sir," I said, trying to avoid his eyes.

"Okay, now that we've finished our first downhill. I'll bet you're all tired. Becky and Tracy, great job. You beat your pre-run times." He grinned with the authority of a commander who had planned and successfully executed a secret attack on the enemy.

Coach Ryan jumped in. "Not only that. Those two held their tucks through the last four gates and picked up extra time for the final runout. Great conditioning."

"Thanks, Coach, for that astute observation," said Coach Boast. "Okay. Tomorrow, the giant slalom will begin at 10. Please meet at the start at 8:30, so we can side-slip the course together. Tonight, after you prep your skis, leave them by the furnace, so Coach Ryan can wax them."

"Coach, when will we get our start bibs?" asked Becky.

"Ah, I actually have them here. We had a coaches' meeting last night about start orders. I had to pull a few strings for some of you."

I sat up as I knew that I would be in the first seed for the giant slalom, my event. At least, now I would get some respect from the coaches and my teammates.

"Let's see. Starting in the first seed at number 10, Tracy," said Boast. A gasp came from the group as Tracy jumped up to get the bib offered by him, bumping me with her knee

"What?" said Becky. "How'd she get that number?"

"Remember, I said I had to pull some strings. Coaches do have some prerogatives," he said, glaring at Becky's challenge to him. Becky sat back down before he spoke again. "Becky, you got lucky, number 16. Pammy, number 22 and Carla, number 30." Then he turned to me. "So Lia, you're probably wondering why you're not starting in the first seed." He handed me number 42.

I lowered my head, "Yes, sir." An emotional bullet went through my heart.

Coach Boast continued, "Well, I made an executive decision. I gave Tracy your start number and you got hers. I wanted to give her a shot at getting some good points."

"At what?" I said, feeling an anger redden my face. "How can you do that? Those are my FIS points. I earned them."

"Remember, Lia. The coach has the final say. I didn't think your heart would be in the race tomorrow, so I decided to give Tracy a chance."

I stood up, glared at Boast before turning to Becky, and whispered under my breath "Damn." Then in a louder voice I said directly at Coach Boast, knowing he wouldn't understand the lines from *King Lear*, "As flies to wanton boys, we are to the Gods, they kill us for their sport," and stormed out of the room.

CHAPTER 43

Race Day

Becky caught me in the hallway before I could get to the front door and run out into the dark. I wanted to get away, to be free to follow my own rules. She yelled, "Hey, you! Stop. I'm here. Settle down! It's going to be okay." I relaxed, moaned as loud as a death rattle.

Becky put her hand on my back. "Whoa, slow down, take a deep breath. Let's talk."

Trying to hold my breath, the sobs broke out again as if an invisible force were trying to exit my body. Tears rolled down my cheeks, wetting my turtleneck. "Becky, oh Becky … ," I held my breath and continued, "I can't take all of this."

Putting both her hands on my shoulders, she said, "It's okay, my friend."

"No, this isn't what I signed up for. I … I just wanted to ski, to race, to be in the mountains."

"I know, I know," said Becky, indicating I should sit down in the foyer corner.

"Why can't it be like Monmouth? We were safe there." She lowered me into a plush chair with red velvet arms.

"Shh, it'll get better." She sat down on the arm and reached for my shoulder. The weight of her hand made me feel more trapped.

"No, it won't." I pushed Becky's hand away. "Wren won't be well. Bill won't come back. And now Boast is taking my points."

"No, I can't change that or explain it." She paused, searching for the right words. "Maybe we need to find a belief in something greater than ourselves. Remember when you used to think there was a purpose to all this?"

I pushed against her and stood up. "Not anymore. If there's a purpose, I'd like someone to tell me what it is."

"Well," she said in a voice meant to soothe, "that we need to think beyond ourselves, our selfishness about our racing." She opened her arms as if to encompass the world. "We used to think life was simple: just work harder than others toward our goal and we would reach our dreams." She checked my reaction before continuing, "Remember McElvey used to say 'a goal is a dream with a timeline.'" She paused. "Yeah, now you're nodding. So, maybe we were wrong, maybe we don't have full control over our goals, dreams, and lives."

I continued to shake my head from side to side, "I can't accept this. I've worked too hard for all of this. Sacrificed too much." I started to walk in circles. "Seen too many people hurt. I thought I could ski hard, win, and that this would give all the injuries, pain, and disappointments some meaning. Yeah, in some way I could give meaning to my life, to Wren's, to Damien's, and now to Bill's"

Becky looked confused. "How does your skiing add meaning to their lives?"

"Hey, if I could make the Olympics, then all this would have been worth it. Remember, you're the one who keeps talking about the team. Weren't they part of our team?"

"Okay, I see. But what if you don't make the team? What if you get hurt?"

"Well, somehow, I also used to think that the journey, the work had a meaning of its own." I paused, looked toward the window, got up and moved toward the cold glass front door which held a rim of frost. I turned back to Becky, putting both hands up in a motion of surrender. "Now I'm wondering, what if...what if nobody or nothing cares?"

Becky opened her eyes in disbelief. "C'mon, we have to believe in what we're doing. We're role models, examples, leaders. We've been picked by the US Ski Team for a reason."

"Yeah, tell me about the reason. How much has your father paid to get you on the team?"

"What, where'd you get that idea? I've earned this place through hard work." Her eyes looked down. "What have you been hearing, anyway?'

"I'm not sure you'll be ready for this," I turned back to her with a smirk.

"Try me" Her cheeks grew red with anger.

"Okay, last night, when I went to the ski room to work on my skis, I overheard Coach Boast and Ryan talking."

"Okay, so ... "

"Well, they were talking about a payment from Tracy's dad. Something about a secret bank account if she got on the Olympic team."

"Yeah, right, as if you can buy your way onto the team." Immediately, Becky stopped and put her hand to her mouth.

"Yeah, so now you understand. Why do you think he gave her my points for tomorrow's race."

"Shit," said Becky. "Who can we tell?"

"Right, so now you want to get kicked off the team? How can we prove anything? My word against his." I shuffled my feet on the floor in frustration.

Becky pulled me into a corner away from the doorman. "Here's what we'll do. We'll ski our best, lower our points, and maybe, just maybe Tracy will be cut from the team. Remember, hard work. Let's do it for Bill, just like his mother said."

I shook my head. "Yeah, for Bill, but how will this bring him back? Why'd he have to go to Vietnam, why'd he have to die?"

"I don't know, Lia. You're confused right now. Anyhow, let's try to control what we can. Let's control this moment. Do our best, take precautions. Let's help each other." I was growing tired of her prefab-phrasing.

Just then Coach Boast strutted into the foyer and stood with his hands crossed on his chest. "Pardon the interruption." He stepped back when he saw the anger on my face. "I'm worried about you, Lia. Will you be okay to race tomorrow? You shouldn't race upset, or worse, angry."

I looked at him in disbelief. Ready to confront him, I walked toward him. "Coach, I'm more than ready. I can win from any position, if I ski my best."

He sighed, turning to leave and looking back over his shoulder, "I'll not tolerate disrespect. You know, someday you'll understand all this."

I waited one minute until he'd left the foyer, turned back to Becky and said in a mocking voice, "One day you'll understand all this. Right, when we go visit the bastard in his mansion on the slopes of Vail, Colorado. What a jerk."

"Slow down. You're not sure that he has a deal with Tracy's dad."

"Okay, let's go to our room. We have to race in the morning," I said, stopping the conversation.

Back in the room, we didn't speak again as we methodically put on our pajamas, brushed our teeth, and crawled into bed.

✳　✳　✳

The first ray of dawn woke me from my fitful sleep. I realized that I'd overslept, that I'd forgotten to set the alarm clock. "Hey, Becky, wake up. It's seven and we have to be on the hill by 8:30."

"Huh, wow, we must of been tired. You grab the bathroom first. I'll get dressed."

I got up slowly, looked straight at her, wagging my finger like a schoolteacher, and said, "You mean 'have.' "

She laughed, "That's my Lia. Now I know you're ready to fight."

We rushed to breakfast and saw that the team had already eaten and gone to the mountain. Grabbing a few rolls, we ran to get our skis in the wax room, scraped Coach Ryan's new wax job, snagged our pinnies, and headed out.

We ran through town as if a demon were chasing us. At the

lift, Becky stopped. "Let's put on our pinnies now, so we don't lose them."

"Great, now check out my start number 42. Tell me we don't know what's going on."

Becky put her hand to her lips, "Shh, we never know who's listening."

At the start of the course, we came upon our huddled American friends, Tracy next to Coach Boast, Coach Ryan rubbing the bottoms of Pammy's skis, and Carla climbing up, trying to warm up her legs. "Hi all," said Becky nonchalantly. "We overslept a little."

Coach Boast dismissed her comment with a wave of his hand. "Please follow the rules. Now it's time to focus and check out the course. It looks as though a fog is settling in. Note that the officials have put blueing along the middle of the course to break up the flat light."

I looked toward Tracy who happened to be brushing her pinnie, number 10. She sneered back at me.

The group snow-plowed the course in a line, like ants on a sugar-trail. Boast pointed out the hairpin turn, the fall away and then stopped at the side-hill where the lower part of the trail dropped toward a small cliff. He proudly said, "I asked the officials to put up a fence here. They refused, saying that you'll have completed your turn before this sidehill. Just make sure to edge hard before you enter this tough gate."

"Yikes," said Tracy. "They sure don't believe in safety here."

"Just complete your turn early and you'll be fine," he said. "In fact, racing in the first seed, you'll have a smooth course here. The later racers will get the chatter-marks. These can make your skis bounce, make holding the turn more difficult." He paused and looked up the hill toward me. "Please take note, young lady."

We all hurried down to the lift as the clock at the bottom indicated 9:30. Boast nodded to Tracy. "Time to head up," he said. "Be sure to take a few turns before the start. This could be your day. Take advantage of your start order."

I waved to Becky. "I think I'll go take a run as I've at least an hour before I start. Have a great run … see you at the finish."

I moved to the side, so my friends could ride up in pairs, Becky with Carla and Tracy with Pammy. I looked around for a single rider to share the double chair. A tan, Germanic blonde man stepped from the crowd and said, "Single, I'll share with you."

My heart raced as I sidled up to this Bogner-dressed man, his blue eyes capturing my attention. Excitedly, I took my seat on the lift as he said, "Ah, American? Good luck in the race."

"Where are you from?" I asked. I nervously tried not to look him in the eyes, but instead let my eyes rest on his Kästle skis. Every piece of his equipment was immaculate.

"Ah, I'm also an American, but I'm working in Bern for General Electric. I'm helping the Swiss build nuclear power-plants."

"Wow, how'd you get into that business?"

"Well, it's a long story, but I learned the nuclear industry when I worked in the Navy on the American nuclear subs. Have you heard about these ships?"

"Hum, I do remember about the Thresher that sank off Portsmouth, New Hampshire. It was a big deal for a while."

"Smart one. Yup. This was one of our first nuclear subs. We still don't know what happened. I lost many friends on that ship."

A silence followed as I didn't know what to say. I felt a heaviness in my head. Finally, I said, "I'm so sorry."

"Not to worry. That's the price we pay for pushing the limits of our knowledge. We all know the risk. We have to make sacrifices in order to move ahead, to gain better technology." His white teeth lit up his sun-dried face. "It's a team effort. Every event matters." I was intrigued.

I thought to myself, *Yup, we know the risks of the game we're playing.* The grating rattle of the summit cogwheel broke my reverie. I looked up to see the clouds roll off the top of the Eiger, its glistening granite on the north face stared knowingly into the valley. Poling off the ramp, I looked back to see the man waving his overstuffed mitten, "Good luck, American. I'll find you later."

My heart fluttered.

CHAPTER 44

New Friend

I had one hour before my start, so I skied to a trail away from the course for a warm-up run. Like a spy, I snuck into the woods to watch a few racers on course before Tracy took off. I hoped the others wouldn't see me hiding behind a spruce tree, as I didn't feel like talking to anyone.

At the start I saw Coach Ryan rubbing wax on Tracy's ski, the ski tail resting behind her back against her shoulder blade, a ballet-style stance. Becky and Carla were climbing above, jumping to loosen their legs. Pammy had her eyes glued on a Swiss coach above her.

I should be there, I thought. *Number 10 should be my number. Will my late start hurt my finish time? Will this affect my chances for the Olympic team? Does one change alter everything in the future?* I sucked in my breath, afraid to let my thoughts continue. *No, I'll ski harder, faster, and beat everyone.* My thoughts broke off when the start official announced, "Number 10. Number 10." I thought for a second, *I hope she falls. No, I can't wish that on anyone.* My thoughts raced. Kicking my skis around, I took off down a side trail. The feel of my skis on the compacted snow eased my mind. *This I know, this I love.*

More relaxed, I arrived at the start just as Pammy took off. I had no idea how my teammates had done, nor did I want to know. Coach Ryan yelled to me from his spot above the starting hut, his red, white, and blue parka barely visible in the heavy fog that had begun settling on the hill, snow melting into the air. He beckoned to me, "Lia, come up. I want to check your skis."

Carefully side-stepping up, I tripped on my uphill pole and fell sideways into the hill. Embarrassed, I used my pole to push myself up and continued toward him. Coach Ryan laughed at my clumsiness and then challenged me, "Just to let you know, Tracy struggled on the fall-away turn and lost time. She's three seconds off the lead. Fortunately, Becky is third and Carla is tenth. Pammy didn't put in any effort." He glared at me, "Do you think you can put in a solid run?"

I looked up to him "Sure thing. I'll cut the gates close."

"Bad idea, Lia," he warned, "I know you're angry that Coach Boast gave your points to Tracy, but the course is filled with chatter-marks now." I'd never seen his face so stern. "Your best bet is to just ski the course and try and post a reasonable time." He looked down the hill to avoid my eyes. "I don't want to see you get hurt." I sensed concern, a doubt in his voice.

"Okay, Coach." Sidling up to him, I asked, "Do I need to change my wax?"

"Nope, the course is plenty fast. Just ski and start your turns early."

I heard my number 42 called and surveyed the course one more time before I slid my skis up to the start wand. Off to the right, I noticed the American engineer, his mitten waving to me. My ski tips balanced precariously in the air as I edged them under the wand. I stomped my feet to loosen my legs, watching my tips vibrate. I clicked my poles together as I carefully placed them over the wand and dug the points into the snow. I gripped the handles hard, first left then right, in rhythm to the count down. "*Fünf, vier, drei, zwei, los.*" I kicked up my heels and blasted through the start wand, my adrenaline spiked.

Hitting the first turn with more speed than I expected, I started my next turn early. More chatter marks, more ruts, more jarring of my teeth. My lower ski slid out at the next turn, so I leaned hard to throw my weight on my uphill ski. I hadn't seen a course this rutted in years.

The tails of my skis continued sliding as I headed into the turn before the side-hill gate. I recalled coach's warning, but I couldn't complete my turn before I hit the fall-away slope. My left ski caught a rut, my weight shifted downhill. In slow motion I felt myself headed toward the cliff. I tried jumping one more time to detach my weight from the edge-catching ski, to re-center my balance, but my ski continued straight ahead.

I launched into the foggy air, flipped forward and then saw some tree branches below while still cartwheeling like a pile of laundry tossing in a dryer. Landing hard on my back, I bounced and flipped again before sliding into a tree stump. Cautiously, I moved my head, lifted my arms, and pushed on my legs. All seemed to be moving. I looked up into the fog to see a tanned man in a red parka leaning over me. "Are you okay, miss? Don't move."

I sat up to prove I could move. "I'm okay." I felt dizzy, even a bit nauseous. "Just let me rest for a minute."

In a daze, I sensed others arriving. Another ski patroller pushed a toboggan beneath my left foot. He gestured that he wanted to lift me onto the sled, but waving him off, I stood up. "I'm okay, no toboggan, nein!" I yelled, spitting snow from my mouth.

I looked around for my skis and saw they were far above me, sticking out of the snow. As I started to walk up to them, another man grabbed the buried skis and slid down to me. "Okay? Your skis. You okay?"

Annoyed, I insisted. "No problem. Please give me my skis. I'm fine." I didn't want to arrive at the finish on a stretcher, imagining how Tracy would delight in that.

Kicking my left foot into the binding, I felt a twinge in my ankle. *Oh no*, I thought. *I hope I didn't sprain my ankle.* I adjusted my poles, waved off the first-aid helpers, and skied down the rocky hillside, dodging even more stumps. A quick right-hand turn helped me find my way to the race course. I stood on the trail side, brushing snow from my pinnie and my goggles, all the time cursing Coach Boast and Tracy. Then, I stopped and looked up the hill into the snow-eating fog, into the void, realizing I could've been seriously hurt … like Wren.

At the bottom, my friends waited for me. Becky came up as I skied around the finish area into the crowd. "Whoa, Lia! We were worried. We'd heard you were hurt."

"No problem. I just couldn't hold the side-hill with all the chatter marks. I guess I tried to ski too fast … " I said, letting my words trail off.

Carla came up next and, putting her arm over my shoulder, asked, "You okay, my friend?" She brushed some snow off my pinnie, "You look like a snowman."

"Yup, just a bit sore."

Pammy emerged from the crowd but didn't get too close. She smirked, "I guess we all had a tough time today. Only Becky and Carla posted good times."

In frustration and anger I looked around, "So where are Tracy and Coach Boast?"

Becky stepped forward to diffuse the mood. "They headed back early. Tracy had a bad run and he felt she needed time to herself."

"Yeah, to herself," I said. "So why'd he go with her?"

Just then the good-looking American engineer stepped from the crowd. "Hey, American, how about getting some hot chocolate with me? Sorry about your fall."

I looked to Becky for approval. She smiled, "Go ahead. You need some time away from us. Here, I'll take your pinnie back. See you at dinner."

Untying my pinnie, I pulled it over my head, and skied off toward the mysterious, handsome, square-jawed man. Not turning to acknowledge my friends, I looked up toward the Eiger where a patch of sky had appeared; the fog clouds were lifting.

I pulled up next to the six-foot man who reached out with his mitten. "Hi, Lia, my name is Rob, Rob Attelfelner."

"Oh, nice to meet you. How'd you know my name?"

Rob pulled out a sheet of paper with the start order. "See here, I found your name on the start order, #42."

I giggled. "Of course." Hesitating, I asked, "What else do you know about me?"

"Well, actually I've been following your results since you got to Europe. You know you've gotten some pretty good press. You're definitely one of the top Americans. You've lowered your FIS points, for sure. What I couldn't figure out is why you are skiing so far back in the order. Your points should have put you in the first seed."

Pulling off my helmet and goggles, I shook out my blonde hair, "Now that's a long story. I'll take you up on the offer of hot chocolate."

He reached for my skis and hoisted both mine and his effortlessly on his right shoulder. I felt small next to his large gray parka, yet I also trusted his gentle manner. I looked up to him, "Thanks, you did that so easily."

"Yup, I lift weights when I'm bored. That's what I used to do in the Navy."

"Navy, oh yeah, I remember. You said you were in the subs."

Walking toward town, I noticed that I needed to take two steps to his one. The silence between us was awkward, so I struggled to find conversation. "So where're we going?"

"Oh, I thought we'd go to Rudi's. I assume that you don't drink. By the way, how old are you?"

I hesitated, answering, "Well, I'm almost nineteen."

"Oh, good, we can get a hot chocolate," he said with a wink.

I enjoyed the silence that grew as we walked through the town. He had to lower my skis to let a woman and her child pass, the mother nodding a thank you while smiling at me. A small boy, pulling a sled, stepped to the side to let us go by. A shopkeeper nodded to me, saying, "Guten abend." I felt like a tourist, not a racer. No one knew that I was an American, no one knew my relationship to Rob. We were just a good-looking, blonde couple out for a walk. The fog continued to lift and the afternoon sun spun a golden light on the buildings. This fairy tale village came alive, just like *Brigadoon*.

Rob headed toward a stucco building where a ski rack stood outside and carefully placed our skis next to each other, "You okay if I leave our skis here? We can trust everyone in this village. I've been coming here for years."

I nodded. Rob took my arm and led me into the building where the aroma of *glühwein*, pastries, and hot chocolate mingled. A piano tinkled from a smoke-filled corner and after a few notes, I recognized the tune, *Climb Every Mountain*. I started to hum, causing Rob to join me with his bass voice. We sang the words in English, causing the felt-hatted piano player to beckon to us to approach the piano. Together we led the rest of the customers in song. At the end, the pianist jumped up, saying to Rob and me, "*Danke schön.*" He pointed to a table and said, "Mein pleasure. You make a beautiful couple."

Rob pulled out a wooden chair for me and then sat across the plank table. He removed the beer list and menu from the middle, so he had an unobstructed view of me. His look bored into me as he said, "Ah, music, the invisible thread that joins us." My heart flipped, I swallowed and returned his gaze. He continued, "Hey you, you look lost in thought … are you okay? Are you hungry?"

Regaining my composure, I blushed, "Nope, just a hot chocolate will do. Thanks."

He beckoned to the tanned waitress who wore her dirty-blonde hair in pigtails. He spoke German words to her that I couldn't understand. She nodded, smiling and winking at me.

He broke the silence. "Okay, Lia. Do you want to talk about the race?"

"Not really. Let's just pretend we've met on vacation. Sometimes it's fun to get away from the team, the racing, and be a real person."

"What do you mean real person? Aren't you a real person on the team?"

"Well, I sometimes feel as if it's a masquerade, a show, someone else's life. I wonder who I'd be if I weren't a ski racer."

"What do you mean—who you would be if you weren't a ski racer?" he spoke slowly.

"Well, you have to understand: my whole life has been ski racing, my whole identity is caught up in this image. Most people don't even know the real me, just my talents on the slopes."

"I still don't get it. Aren't you proud of who you are?"

I started to get more comfortable with him. "To tell you the truth, I don't know who I am. If I didn't have skiing, I don't know who I'd be. For sure I know that all this skiing, fame, and press is so transitory, even fake compared to … " I couldn't finish.

"You've lost me. Let's try again. What would you be doing if you weren't skiing?"

"I'd be in college studying English. I'd be exploring Emerson, Whitman, Thoreau- -yes, even Shakespeare. I'd be joining clubs, writing for the school paper. I wouldn't be trying to beat others. I wouldn't be living in a dangerous dream."

"Wait a minute—dangerous dream?"

"Yup, this ski racing is a crazy world, a narcissistic world where people get hurt, killed."

"Hey, people get hurt and killed in real life, too."

"Oh, you have all the answers. I guess I'm confused, but I'm also tired of being a pawn for others."

"Now we're getting somewhere. For whom are you a pawn?"

I told him about Coach Boast, Tracy, my dreams for the

Olympics, Bill, Damien. He listened without asking questions.

When I finished, he grabbed my hand. "Lia, you have to continue your quest. Right now, this ski racing is your journey. When you finish, and you'll know when the time is right, you can go to college, you can write, you can expose the corruption."

He paid the bill, pulled out my chair and turned to me, "And I'll find you then."

CHAPTER 45

The Confrontation

Coach Ryan spread out the colorful map of Europe, flattening it on the breakfast table. His finger traced our route through the Alps as he explained how we'd catch the afternoon train back to Interlaken, onto Liechtenstein, over to Innsbruck, and finally up to Bad Gastein, Austria. I marveled at the line of mountains, the rivers—Europe before my eyes—mythical names like St. Anton, Kitzbühel, Zell am See, ski areas I'd heard about from my dad.

Coach Ryan said sternly, "Please try to be packed by eleven. We need to be at the train station by 12:30. Coach Boast planned this trip so that you could sleep some on the train or at least get some rest."

"Hey, coach," said Becky with a smirk, placing her hand over her mouth. "I'm running out of room for my trophies. Where am I supposed to put them?"

"Once again, Becky, the team's proud of you. Congratulations on your 1st place in the combined. And Carla, good job on your tenth. You've both improved your FIS points."

A silence fell over the group, before Carla opened up. "So regarding our points, I hope that we all get to keep our own points from now on, so we can race in the appropriate seed."

Not expecting this confrontation, I turned to look out the window, hoping that Coach Ryan didn't think I'd put Carla up to this. The last thing I needed was for him to be mad at me. He glanced at the other girls who were nodding in agreement, except for Tracy who had covered her face with her hands and he answered, "Carla, that's an inappropriate comment. The coaches will always have the final decision." I'd never seen him so annoyed.

"Sorry, Coach, but morale on the team is rock-bottom. We need to trust that everything will be fair," said Carla, emphasizing the word "fair." I'd never seen her so serious and down.

"What seems fair to one might not be fair to another," he growled under his breath.

I couldn't hold back anymore, "Coach, if you want to make changes to the lineup, then maybe you should speak to us individually, not just announcing this in a group meeting at the last minute."

Trying to regain control, he snapped, "Hold it, young lady. Enough from you."

I took the croissant in my hand and squeezed it into crumbs. The yeast smell calmed me.

Becky stood up, brushed some crumbs from her jeans, and threw her hands in the air. "Okay, team, enough. To the point, we've had some individual and some group successes here in Grindelwald. Let's not dwell on the past, but instead let's move to the future. I'm going to pack."

The scraping of chairs on the oak floor sounded like a herd of cows racing out of the barn. I looked back to see Coach Ryan, red in the face, beckoning to Becky. She touched my shoulder. "See you in the room. I'm going to talk to him for a minute."

I saw a devilish smirk on Tracy's face, her brows furrowing, and her tiny teeth flaring in a fake grin. I let my sock feet slide along the floor toward the dining room door, just as Carla came up behind me. "Let's meet in your room," said Carla softly, "we need to talk."

I made sure the door closed behind Carla as we entered my room. I sat down in a chair at the desk, moved my journal to one side, while Carla sat on the edge of my bed. She started the conversation, "Okay, so you got screwed here in Grindelwald."

I looked up and gave a caustic laugh, "Yes, in more ways than one."

"What do you mean?" asked Carla.

"Forget it. I spoke to Becky. Enough said." I bit my lip, so I wouldn't show my emotion.

"No, seriously, you're not the same Lia I remember at Monmouth. What's going on?"

"Well, let's just say I'm getting cynical, disillusioned, angry."

"Duh, that's obvious … what's happened?"

"You know: Wren, Bill, Tracy, Boast. Nothing has gone as planned."

"Hey, that's life. Get over it. Remember, life's not about how you fall down, but how you pick yourself up."

"Well, let's just say I'm getting sick of picking myself up."

"Okay, okay. But we've three more races to go here in Europe. Let's reset and get some great points."

"Sure, so Boast and Ryan can take them from me again."

"Hey, trust Becky. I think she's going to confront Coach Ryan about the points."

"Well, if she does, she may be off the team."

"Do you think they'll send home our top racer?"

"Yup, and give her points to Tracy."

"Hmm, maybe you have a point. Let's wait for … "

The door burst open and Becky came in like a plume of smoke. "Shit, shit, shit." I'd never heard her use such language.

Carla jumped up and closed the door, saying, "What's gotten into you? You're supposed to be the calm one, the mediator."

Becky sat down where Carla had been sitting. "Well, the coaches know we're upset, but they don't care. Coach Ryan says their job is to get the best team they can for the Olympics. Age is important."

I stood up and said, "What's age got to do with it? We're all the same."

"Well, he thinks that since Tracy's the youngest, she needs an opportunity to get some points."

I turned in a full circle on my sock feet. "Okay, then let her work her way up the way we have."

Becky got up and pushed me back into my chair. "He thinks that Tracy doesn't have time before the team is chosen in March. That's why they gave her a chance with your points."

"Yeah, and what did she do with them? She blew it. Plus, I almost got hurt racing from the back." I grabbed my ankle that had begun to swell since my fall.

Becky threw her hands up and glanced toward my ankles. "Yeah, because you didn't listen to Coach. You skied too fast for the course conditions. You need to cool it."

I let seconds pass before saying, "Let's stop here. We've started to fight with each other. What's happening to us? We used to be so close, to work together. I'm going to pack." I started to open my dresser drawers.

Carla left quietly, subtly nodding to Becky. I grabbed my suitcase, threw it on the bed, and began pulling my clothes from my bureau. Becky sheepishly asked, "Do you want to talk?"

"Nope." I was afraid I'd start yelling at her.

CHAPTER 46

Train to Bad Gastein

I jumped backwards when the train whistle blasted in my ear. My teammates and I stood side-by-side, waiting for the through-train to Bad Gastein, Austria. I hated the fact that, because of budget constraints, we had to catch the cheapest ride to the next race. Balancing next to the tracks, juggling my boot bag, breathing the heavy afternoon fog, I felt like an immigrant searching for a new home. Church bells bellowed to each other like cows in the field. Nobody spoke.

Coach Ryan nodded toward the last car, "Hop on and find a seat. We have got a five-hour train ride, but fortunately we don't have to change cars. Keep your boot bag close to you—you can re-place your skis but not your boots." A few people on the platform pointed, smiling as they recognized our US Ski Team parkas.

I waited while my friends clambered up the high steps, each bag knocking the person behind, before tossing my bag up on the metal grill, then climbing up and dragging it step over step. Inside, I looked for an empty seat, found one in the back, gestured to Becky that I wanted to be by myself and slipped down the aisle to the last seat, a gray-padded bench with a wall behind. Looking back, I saw Becky grab a front seat with Carla, while Pammy sat with Tracy. Coach Ryan also stopped toward the front, looked around before stepping over an older woman to take his place be-side a young blonde woman, who looked up adoringly. *Does he know her?* I wondered.

I sighed as I carefully placed my boot bag under the seat. My bulky parka rolled easily into a ball to form a pillow. *Ahh, five hours of sleep, no talking.*

The train began filling with skiers in addition to men with business suits, balancing fedoras on their heads. Each time a new person stepped through the entrance, I looked away, hoping not to catch an eye, hoping not to intimate that the seat next to me was free. I spread my parka on my seat so it appeared taken.

Two blasts of the whistle and the train car tilted forward; I knew I would be alone. After a quick glance out the window, a final, long look at the acne face of the Eiger staring through the fog, I shivered, stretched out my legs, and settled against my parka, closing my eyes in relief. *Jeez, this has been a long week,* I thought.

I reviewed the awards ceremony the previous night when Becky had proudly marched up to receive her first place medal in the combined. In a half-sleep, I thought: *Yes, the Europeans have begun to take note of us. No longer can they dominate their own races.* During the ceremony I remembered the American flag draped in one corner. *Why'd I still get goose bumps when I saw it?* As the Oompah Band played the US national anthem for Becky, I had mouthed the words "The bombs bursting in air." *How violent! How many times had Bill heard the anthem before he died—died for his country. Would they play it at his funeral? His funeral. When would that be? Where would that be?*

Angry voices woke me from my daymare. A man and a woman toward the front were yelling at each in a language I couldn't understand. Suddenly, the woman, her head covered in a shawl, stood up and crawled over the man. He followed her, yelling, *"Juden, Schmutzigen Juden."* The woman, with anger reddening her cheeks, her lips trembling, fumbled hand over hand toward the back of the car. Her right shoulder slumped from the weight of her brown wool bag. I looked up into the woman's eyes as she came to a stop in front of my seat. Nodding to the woman, I pulled my legs off the seat and moved over, gesturing that she could sit next to me. She barely acknowledged me as she settled her large rump into the seat. A strong odor of wet wool and unwashed underarms hit me. *Whoa, this could be a long ride*, I thought.

The woman pushed her overstuffed bag under her seat, smoothed her skirt over her knees, looked at me, saying, "Danke schön."

I smiled, raised my hand in submission, and said. "Sorry, I don't speak German."

In a German accent she said, "No problem. I speak English." She paused, looked around the cabin, before continuing. "Are you from America?"

"Yes, how'd you know?"

The woman pointed to my parka, crumpled by my shoulder, the American flag on the sleeve standing out like a billboard. "Yeah, a lucky guess."

"So what happened over there? Why'd that man yell at you?" I asked, trying to make her feel comfortable.

"Well, it's a long story. Do you want to hear?"

"I ... I guess so. We've a long train ride ahead. Where are you going?"

"I'm taking the train to Innsbruck. I have family waiting there for me." She smiled proudly. "Where are you going?" She emphasized the "you."

"Oh, I'm going to Bad Gastein, I'm racing on the American World Cup ski team."

"Oh," she paused and her lips turned down. "American skier, I see."

"Why do you look like that?"

Stopping, she took off her shawl and let her long brown hair, streaked with gray, flow over her shoulders. She swept her fingers through her strands to break up the knots and tangles. "Well, do you really want to know?"

"Yup, I might as well learn about you. Where are you from?"

"Dresden. Do you know Dresden?" As she spoke her German accent increased.

"Well, sort of, I think so."

"I have lived there since before the war."

"War, what war? Do you mean Vietnam?"

The woman looked puzzled before saying, "No, the war." The woman emphasized "the" as if there'd never been any other war. "World War II."

I became curious as I hadn't ever talked to anyone except my father about the Second World War. "What were you doing during the war?" I asked, quieting my voice in deference.

"Well, I was seven years old when Hitler invaded Poland in 1939. My family felt safe because we lived in Dresden, you know in Germany. My father worked in the china factory. Have you heard about Dresden china?"

I thought about the Dresden hot chocolate set that my father had inherited from my grandmother, its cobalt-blue background overlaid with Wagnerian opera scenes which I couldn't understand except for Tristan and Isolde, a tale my father loved to tell. The woman nudged me, "I asked if you had heard about Dresden china?"

"Well, yes. My family has some. By the way, I'm Lia. What's your name?"

"Greta."

"Nice to meet you."

"Mein pleasure."

"So what was it like to live in Germany during Hitler?"

"Did you hear what that man called me earlier?" I pretended I hadn't and shrugged my shoulders. The train jerked around a corner, pushing me into her while blowing its whistle.

"Ja, well, I am Jewish. So now do you have any questions?" Her face tightened.

I gulped, looked at her, and panicked. Finally, I found the words. "Forgive me for asking, but did … did you go to a concentration camp?"

"No, I didn't, but my twin sister was not so lucky … " She paused, " … neither were my parents." She seemed very comfortable relating this, as though she had told the story many times.

"A twin sister. What happened to her?"

"Lia, I don't know." Greta settled back, looked out the window before continuing. "I just remember the day that the Gestapo came for us. I had been wearing a yellow star as had all the Jews on our street. However, when my father heard the Nazis were coming, he pulled the patch from my jacket and sent me out the back window, saying, 'Run to the Borst house. They know you will be coming. Do not look back, do not ask questions. Just do as they tell you and you will be safe.' "

"What…, what happened to your parents and sister? What was her name?"

"Hilda, her name was Hilda. I don't know. No one knows where they were sent. Rumor had it they went to Sobibor."

"What's that?" I asked, nervous to hear the answer.

"I think you know; you are just afraid to hear it said. It was a concentration camp. Have you studied about concentration camps in your American schools?"

"Of course, why I've even read *The Diary of Anne Frank*," I sat up proudly.

"Well, then you know few survived. I do not know what happened to my family, I expect they died right away."

"Aren't there any records?"

"No, only information gathered from survivors. My parents and Hilda had their names listed only once. Steinberg. On a train inventory from Dresden." The train slowed and whistled at a crossing, so I couldn't hear what she said next. The trees outside flicked shadows through the window, creating a strobe effect. I felt as if I were in a time machine. Then, the shadows became faces, ghosts trying to speak to me, their mouths opened and closed. I blinked and turned back toward Greta.

"So, Greta, what happened to you?"

"The Borsts were an unusual Germanic family. They adopted me as their own. They had lost a daughter my age to the influenza, so they gave me her name and papers. Why? I even dressed in her old clothes. Mama Borst loved me from the day I came into her home."

"Didn't the neighbors ask questions?" I wondered how a family could keep a Jewish girl so openly.

"No, everyone saw how happy Mama was and went along with the conspiracy. I like to believe that in their hearts they did not approve of what the Nazis were doing. The problem was that no one spoke up against the Jews' deportation. Many pretended that they did not know what was happening to their former neighbors and friends. They were told that we were being sent to work camps."

"So, how long did you live with your new family?" I looked out the window at the bucolic scene of cows hunkering in the pastures. The Alps behind rose into jagged peaks.

"Until 1945 when the bombs came."

"What bombs?"

"Oh Lia, you never learned, did you?"

"Learned, learned about what?"

"The fire-bombing of Dresden." A silence settled over the two of us like a fog: Greta, wanting to guard her words and I, not knowing what to ask, wondering what she meant.

"What's a fire-bombing? Who did it?" I fidgeted.

"My child, when you get back to the States, go study, go learn. You Americans are not always the good guys."

I sat up straight, "Hey, I know that. Look at what we're doing in Vietnam." Then, an image flashed across my mind, a photograph from *Life* magazine of a child, her head swaddled in a bandage, her arm in a splint, naked, her face burned like bacon from the napalm, one open eye trailing a tear, her expression of terror. I asked cautiously, "Did we drop a lot of bombs the way we're doing in Vietnam now?"

"More, Lia. The Americans flew many planes. Their goal was to wipe out Dresden, a cultural center of Germany." Again, her voice trailed off. She looked around the cabin, fearful that someone might be listening.

"What happened to the city?"

She paused, searching for an analogy, "I'll bet you have seen photos of Nagasaki and Hiroshima, ja?" She crossed her flattened hands.

"Of course, we bombed those two cities, so that Japan would surrender. They turned into ashes."

"Right. But I'll bet you have never seen pictures of Dresden." I let my mind wander back to the Dresden china and the scene of Tristan imploring Isolde to die with him.

"Nope."

"Well, the bombing came so fast that the whole city went up in flames. The firestorm sucked all the oxygen from the air, from the buildings, from the basements." I felt her stare. "People vanished, bodies melted into the stone, the stone became cinders, and the cinders blew into dust." She sounded as if she were reciting a poem.

I shuffled in my seat, moving closer to the window before asking, "How did you survive?"

"Papa Borst had a food locker under his home: a place to store dry food and water. He had built it during the war in case the Russians invaded. We could live there for three months if needed."

"Wow, you stayed down there during the bombing?"

"Yes, we only heard the blasts, sometimes the screams."

"When did you come out? What did you see?"

"Ah, words are inadequate to describe such horror. There was no city, just ashes, crumbled buildings and the smell of smoke and burned flesh. A few dogs and cats had survived. Who knows how? Slowly, survivors emerged from the ruins like rats coming out of their burrows. No one spoke. No one smiled."

I looked down the train toward my friends who appeared to be sleeping. Coach Ryan was chatting with the blonde as though the two were lovers. He kept touching her shoulder.

"Is this why you hate the Americans?"

"I did not say I hate you. In fact, I love so much your idealism, your hopes, but not so much your actions." She paused, then smiled. "You probably wonder why my English is so good. Well, I have been traveling in America for the last two years, trying to educate Americans about the atrocities of Dresden. You Americans are so self-righteous about your laws and government."

I felt for a minute that she was accusing me, and said, "Yes, but not all the time. You probably know that there are some who aren't happy with American foreign policy right now." I recalled the college protesters. "In fact, I've friends who're protesting the war in Vietnam."

"Well, of course, Lia, these are exactly the groups I have been speaking to. They see the folly in war." She reached into her jacket and pulled out a clipping from *The New York Times,* showing her addressing a group of students at the Berkeley campus in California.

I fumbled with the article, smoothed it, and studied the anger in the students' faces, their long hair, their raised fists. She continued, "Not many will listen yet, just the young ones, the ones who have to go to war." She shook her head in resignation.

I remembered Bill, his submission to his orders. I didn't want to bring him into the conversation. "I know. I've friends being drafted." Suddenly the shadows were again rushing by the window, their open-mouthed faces became one: Bill's face, his toothy grin, his shock of dark hair, his Monmouth halo.

"But worse Lia, you do not see the prejudice in your own country."

I jolted upright. "What..., what prejudice?" Just as I protested, I noticed Tracy get up, climbing over Pammy, glancing at Coach

Ryan, and heading toward the bathroom in the front of the cabin. He quickly got up and followed her.

I felt Greta's hand on my knee as if to stop my protest. "Look how you treat the Negroes. Do they have full rights? Look how you treat the immigrants."

Confused at this accusation from her, I stuttered "Why..., why, we're trying. Remember President Johnson passed the Civil Rights Amendment in 1964."

Greta smiled the elusive smile of the Mona Lisa. "Finally, Lia, look how women are treated—no equality."

I thought of my mother who'd never had a job, did not go to college, my father wanting her to stay home to raise me. She died, drinking her depression away. I put my hands to my temples, my head hurt. I wondered if I'd been an accomplice to my mother's unhappiness, if I hadn't supported her enough. Looking straight into Greta's eyes, I asked, "How can I change this? I'm only one person?"

"Ah, yes, Lia. And if each person were to say, 'One word does not make a book,' then there would be no books." I nodded, as she continued. "Prejudice is a chronic condition. It cannot be cured, just treated. You cannot change history, just use it."

I looked up to see Coach Ryan return to his seat and put his arm around the blonde. Greta continued, "Lia, think about it. If you do not speak up, then you are part of the problem. Someone has to be first." Her voice grew louder, as though she were addressing a group.

Just then, the train whistle blasted twice. The conductor came through the cabin. "Innsbruck. Innsbruck." Greta stood, pulled down her ankle-length skirt, grabbed her bag from the floor, and extended her hand. "Good luck, American. I hope you can use what I told you." She stopped, before lecturing me one last time. "Remember, the arc of the moral universe is long, but it bends towards justice." She smiled, seeing my confusion, and finished,

"Martin Luther King, Jr." She paused, pointed her finger at me and said, "But you must help it bend."

Turning down the aisle, she pulled her shawl over her head: a walking ghost who disappeared into the seemingly unrepentant crowd.

CHAPTER 47

Sexual Identity

At every bend in the track after Innsbruck, the mountains became more rounded, more feminine. The train pulsated through the valleys, creaking, swaying, whistling, clacking. I let the rocking motion put me to sleep, but the image of Greta and her dead twin Hilda haunted me.

Later, I woke to a baby crying, the acrid smell of a man's cigarette, and the conductor checking passports and tickets. I yawned, stretched my cramped legs, and then smiled, realizing thankfully that I'd caught some sleep and that just maybe Greta had been a bad dream.

A pain in my bladder reminded me that I'd not used the bathroom or eaten for over five hours, so I welcomed the conductor's call, "Bad Gastein, Bad Gastein, la prochaine arrêt, nächste Station, next stop." I got up and walked toward the front of the car, stopping to put my hand on Becky's shoulder, who smiled, and then on Carla's head, who playfully batted my hand away. "See you in a minute," I said, happy to be back with my friends.

Standing on the Bad Gastein train platform, I looked toward the mountains, a more domesticated gathering of Alps, covered with pine trees that flowed down their flanks like black curls of hair. Pink ribbons from the sunset painted the peaks, and lace-like clouds flitted above. In contrast, massive buildings penetrated the mountain valley, fortresses of dark hotels and shops. Nothing quaint here. I remembered how much I hated cities.

Accidentally, I tripped, falling into Coach Ryan.

He protested, "Ouch, watch where you're going! You just stepped on my foot."

"Sorry," I said, looking away. "I just woke up." I noticed that his streetlamp shadow cast a stain on the new-fallen snow.

Becky yelled impatiently, "Hey, Lia, hurry up; the taxi's waiting. Coach will get your skis and bags. Just bring your boot bag."

"Okay, slow down. Remember, I needed to use the bathroom." I said, rubbing my eyes to clean some grit.

Becky stamped her feet impatiently, "Please get in the taxi, or you'll be walking to the hotel that's around the corner." She pointed to a black Mercedes and a stern-looking, blonde Germanic man standing by the passenger door. He extended his hand to me, a huge, brutish, animal paw. Ignoring the hand, I placed my boot bag on the ground and crawled into the back seat next to Carla and Pammy, while Tracy chose the jump seat, facing us. Becky slid into the front next to the driver and said, "Hotel Elizabethpark, bitte."

I felt comfortable huddled next to my friends, but Tracy's glare, her curled lips, her eyebrows lowered, and squinting unnerved me. She seemed to bite her lower lip.

"Here we are, hotel first-class, for the first-class Americans," said the driver dryly.

Crayola-colored flags waved above the marble entrance. A glass door swung open and a young blonde boy stepped out stiffly, smoothing the front of his gray Tyrolean jacket. The stiff collar supporting his head made him look like a mannequin. I giggled at this boy who tried to comport himself like a man.

Inside the hotel, I felt overwhelmed, seeing all the women's teams from Austria, Switzerland, and France gathered in separate corners. *Wow,* I thought. *We're all staying in the same hotel for the first time. I wonder if they'll welcome us.* Just then, a member from the Austrian corner stepped over to Becky and gave her a hug. "Bienvenue, ma petite amie. Ca va?"

"Bien Annie, come meet my friends," said Becky, grabbing Annie's elbow. "These are my teammates, Pammy Siemans, Lia Erikson, Carla Kluckner, and Tracy Languile." The dark-haired Austrian girl extended her hand to each one of us. "Je m'appelle Annie, Annie Hecker." She paused and searched for her words. "I …I think you do not speak French. Quel dommage. Anyway, welcome to Bad Gastein. Home of the famous spas and, of course, the World Cup giant slalom."

Becky stepped forward and took charge, *"Oui, et si je me … "* Becky paused looking for the correct verb, *"…souviens bien de cet androit, vous avez gagné cette course l'annee dernière."* She smiled, pleased at getting the sentence out. Immediately, she turned to me and smiled, "Annie won here last year."

Annie laughed and said, "Très bien, Becky. Certainment. *Mais, vous avez gagné la quatrième place, n'est-ce pas?"*

"Oui, j'ai eu de la chance." Becky's modesty made Annie snicker. She turned to me, "Annie helps me avec mon francais."

I envied Becky that she'd learned a little French during her former ski team travels to Europe. I made a mental note to practice my high school French as often as I could while here.

Just then a tall, horse-faced person wearing an Austrian parka brushed past me and headed for the hotel bathrooms; I looked up to see if it went into the men's or woman's toilet, but the figure disappeared behind a column.

The door-boy took our bags and directed us to our rooms, which I again shared with Becky. By this point, I felt warm and safe with her, who now seemed especially interested in me. Becky pointed to the small bed by the window, indicating I should enjoy the view, "Well, my friend, I've been on the European tour once before, and I've never stayed in such a beautiful hotel. We must be doing something right for Coach Boast to spring for so much money. Or Tracy's dad … ?"

I put up my hand and said, "Let's not go there now. So this is how the Europeans travel," I patted the lace on the bed, admired the realistic oil paintings of the Alps hanging on the walls and the plush oriental rug set on the floor.

Becky grinned, "Yup, remember they're the superheroes in their respective countries. Other than soccer, skiing is the main sport over here. Hey, by the way, who's one of your favorite female sports heroes?

I thought for a moment. "You know, Becky, I don't think I have any female heroes."

"What, no heroines?"

"Well, first there aren't many professional female athletes." I scratched my head. "Unless you include the Greek mythological heroes. I could say I always liked Athena, or maybe Atalanta. Remember, she could beat all the boys in running." I paused, realizing no one had ever asked me that question before. "Come to think of it, I've never had a female coach either. So, who's your favorite heroine?"

"That's easy. There's a woman in Monmouth, Andy Mead Lawrence. She won two gold medals in the Olympics ... " she paused, "in 1956, I think."

"Are you sure she's a girl? Sounds like a boy's name."

"Yup, I guess her real name is Andrea. Anyway, she actually grew up in your part of the world, Pico Peak in Rutland, Vermont. I'm surprised you haven't heard of her."

"Nope, haven't. But I'll definitely try to look her up when I get home."

"Actually, numbskull, she lives in Monmouth now, so I'll introduce you to her when we get back," she added, beginning to unpack.

Nodding in agreement, I watched her methodically lay out her underwear, blouses, and pants on the bed before asking her, "Do you think much about Monmouth and home?"

"Yup, always. But I try pushing the thoughts from my mind.

Traveling is hard, especially as we get to the end of this tour. We've one more stop in Maribor, Yugoslavia; then we'll be back for the American World Cup races."

"Whew, what a relief that'll be. This four-week tour has been tough. I feel as if I've gotten out of shape, put on ten pounds, and lost touch with everyone. No one told me how isolating this trip would be," I said, leaning over to pull down the duvet on my bed.

"Welcome to the world of ski racing. Your teammates are now your only friends; your coaches are, well I guess, your parents." Slapping me on the butt before, she laughed, "Or your lovers."

I stepped back, confused by this familiarity and wondering what she was referring to. I tested her, "So you've been noticing the intimacy between Tracy and Coach Boast."

"Of course, fortunately Boast is in Kitzbühel with the men's team at the moment."

"Right, at the moment," I said, sneering.

Dressing for our first dinner, I put on clean wool slacks and a blue turtleneck, the usual team outfit.

"Let's get gussied up tonight and put on some lipstick and rouge," said Becky, handing me a bright red tube. "I'll do your hair, if you'll do mine."

Coach Ryan was waiting for the five of us to gather before he led us to our table under a gold chandelier in the formal dining room. A svelte, fifties-looking man in a blue blazer and gray flannel slacks greeted us at our table. His salt and pepper hair was swept to the side in a Kennedyesque fashion and his skin seemed untouched by the weather—for sure he was a man with a case of 'affluenza'. Coach Ryan turned to us, "Now that we're all together, I want to introduce David Solomon. He's the chairman of the board of the US Ski Team."

"Hi, Becky," said David, extending his hand. "I'm pleased to hear about the leadership you've been taking with this young team. Also, congratulations on your results." He politely stepped forward to shake our hands while saying each name without any introduction. I was surprised at how easily he connected names with faces. When he came to me, he held my hand tightly, placing his other hand on top. He whispered, "Good work, Lia." Leaning closer, he continued. "If you have any issues or concerns, please speak to me."

Becky broke in, "Thank you. So, are we staying in this grand hotel because we've been doing so well?"

David stepped back, caught off guard by her direct question. "Well, actually, Becky, this hotel upgrade is thanks to a parent's beneficence. As you know, the ski team is always on a tight budget." He glanced at Coach Ryan and gave him a conspiratorial wink.

"Who?" asked Becky.

"I prefer not to say. But do enjoy your comfort." Looking to me, he added, "Be careful with all the pastries that they offer after skiing!" He then turned back to Coach Ryan. "Thanks for the opportunity to meet the team. I have to go to a meeting now." He left, striding out with the authority of a president.

During dinner, Coach Ryan briefed us on the schedule for the following day: up at 6:30, on the hill by 8:00, giant slalom training all morning, then free-skiing in the afternoon, or visiting the town. Curfew always at 9 p.m. He reiterated the chairman's warning about the pastries, adding that the hotel served them every afternoon. He mentioned that some of us had been putting on some weight.

When we finished our three-course meal, Becky stood up, asking, "So, anyone interested in exploring the town? There's a wild waterfall in the center." We raised our hands, even Tracy. "Well then, go get your parkas and I'll meet you in the lobby in ten."

Once again the door-boy held the glass door with a deferential bow, and I envisioned him breaking into the song, "I am sixteen going on seventeen." I started humming the tune as I stepped into the streetlight. Gleefully, Carla joined in.

Tracy jumped in front of us. "Why are you always singing? It seems like you make fun of people with your songs."

Becky stepped forward to put herself between Tracy and me. "No Tracy, you don't understand; we sing because we're happy. Happy to be skiing. Happy to be together. We do this all the time at Monmouth."

To support Becky, I said, "Music is the invisible thread that joins us at Monmouth."

"Yeah, well, and about Monmouth: I'm sick of hearing about it and how great Justin McElvey is." She stopped, waiting for our reaction, and then added, "And I ... I think you're rude to Coach Boast sometimes. You seem to be comparing him to McElvey all the time." I'd never seen her so angry, as if she were hiding something.

An awkward silence accentuated the rift forming between us. Only the traffic sounds in the street broke the tension. "Okay," said Becky, "Enough. We need to work together and enjoy tonight. During my last trip here, I saw the team start to break apart at this point on the tour. For sure, tensions grow as we become more competitive, even adversarial with one another." She hesitated, looking directly at me, "We need to be mindful of what we say."

To change the subject and get the group moving, I pointed to the street sign, "Who was Kaiser Joseph? The name sounds medieval."

"No idea," said Carla. "Who cares about the history. He was probably someone from a war or empire." She pretended to hold a gun on her shoulder and began goose-stepping.

Pammy turned away from the group. "I'm going back. You're all getting nasty. I'm tired. I'm going back to my room and call my mom. You know, she once was a ski racer."

"I'll join you," said Tracy. "I don't like being in groups anyway."

"Yeah, but one-on-one suits you fine, doesn't it?" said Carla sarcastically.

"What do you mean?' challenged Tracy, squaring to Carla.

"Like you don't think we haven't noticed all the time you spend with Coach Boast," said Carla. Tracy exploded, turning right into the bell boy. He fell back into the glass door, clunking his head, while Tracy pushed past him, not saying a word.

Becky turned on Carla and me, "Okay, okay. Enough. No more nasty comments about others. Let's go check out the town. We need some down time." She began walking up the hill toward a large building.

"Yeah, like you haven't noticed what I've noticed, "said Carla, stepping in front of Becky.

"Look, we've all noticed about Boast and Tracy, but what can we do about it? Do you want to get kicked off the team?" said Becky, throwing her hands up in disgust.

I looked at both of them. No one dared speak. Carla smirked, continuing, "So, do you smarties know why we're staying in this grand hotel?"

"Of course," I said, trying to dispel the tension. "David Solomon said a parent had given some money."

"Yeah, do you know whose parent?" said Carla. She smiled, believing that none of us knew the answer.

I put my hand to my mouth and noticed that Becky had done the same. I said, "You've got to be kidding. You mean ... "

"Yup, Tracy's dad."

"Shi ... " said Becky.

Without talking, we walked toward the center of town, turning down the narrow side streets, tripping on the cobblestones as we window-shopped. Inside one window stood a naked, blonde mannequin; a towel with a sign in front of her private parts that said, SPA, MASSAGE. I stopped so suddenly that Becky actually ran into me. "What's this? Is this a town of prostitutes?" I asked.

"No," said Becky. "Bad Gastein has a history of spas. Back in the 19th century, people came here to take radium baths in the thermal pools and then have massages … "

" … Radium?" I interrupted. "You mean the stuff that makes nuclear bombs?"

"Well, sort of. Do you remember studying about Madame Curie, the scientist who discovered radium? Well, she came here once and discovered the element in the water. She and others thought it could cure sickness."

"Yeah, cure you like in killing you," said Carla, rolling her eyes.

Becky, shaking her head, added, "Hey, I took a thermal bath here last year. Some of them don't have radium. In fact, this would be a good thing for us to do tomorrow after skiing. It might relax us." She thought for a moment. "Yup, we could use that." Carla and I nodded in agreement.

I looked back into the window, checking out the frozen sex-object, and saw a person's dark shadow reflected there. "Hello, Americans," said a deep voice. I turned, falling into the down parka of a six-foot creature, the same figure I'd seen charging into the bathroom earlier. Behind it stood three Austrian skiers.

"What the heck? What are you?" I said, gasping for air.

"Hi, Bernadette," said Becky calmly. "To what do we owe this visit from the Austrian team?"

"Well, we want to welcome your new teammates to our country and to our World Cup race," said the gruff voice. I noticed her chin, her rough complexion masked by thick make-up. Her horse face, straggling dark hair, and bushy eyebrows belied the fact that this was a woman. This she/he Austrian didn't fit the stereotype of either sex. I backed away into the store window, bumping my head against the glass.

Becky laughed, "Well, thank you, Bernadette. We look forward to seeing you on the mountain. Now, we're off to find the waterfall. Could you remind me where it is?"

"Of course, just take two lefts and you'll find it under the bridge. Be careful: people have fallen to their deaths down there," she said, laughing at our naïveté. "Auf wiedersehen."

Becky pointed at Carla and me, gesturing that we should take off immediately. Walking in step, I asked. "So what was that about? Who's that she/he monster?"

Becky rolled her eyes, "We don't really know. All we know is that it's been winning all the girls' downhill races in Europe. It weighs about 200 pounds, is 6 feet tall and dresses like a man."

"What? Is it a man racing as a woman?" asked Carla, pulling at her crotch.

"Who knows," said Becky. At the moment there's no checking of sexuality that I know. Each country monitors its own athletes. There's talk that there may be chromosome testing for the Olympics next year."

"Why would a man want to race dressed as a woman?" I asked.

"Duh, stupid" said Carla. "Money. There's big money in ski racing here in Europe."

The sound of the waterfall drowned out Becky's next comments. I saw her lips moving, just as a wet spray glanced off her face.

The pounding of the water, the coldness of the mist made me anxious. I wanted to call out, to tell someone the truth about the corruption I was witnessing on our team, on the World Cup tour, even though it might end my chances for making the Olympic team.

CHAPTER 48

Writing

That night, settling into my duvet, I did what I always do when confused: I grabbed my journal, discovering that I'd only written a few entries since Oberstafen.

While listening to the comforting sounds of Becky brushing her teeth, I reread my descriptions of the German countryside, the people, the church—*such innocence and optimism*, I thought. Wow, had I learned much since that entry. I used to look forward to writing in my journal; however, after Germany I'd grown disillusioned, overwhelmed by my experiences to the point that I'd avoided writing.

Now, rereading my last entries, I realized the process had become more like taking the lid off a box to find another box inside. The layers of intrigue confused me.

Determined to unravel the recent events, I picked up my pen and began writing: *January 20, 1971 Bad Gastein, Austria. Today we arrived in this city of spas, Kaisers, and World Cup skiers. I met David Solomon, the suave, confident Chairman of the Board of the U S Ski Team, who looks more like a financier than a mountain man. I wonder why he's here? Also, I met Bernadette Schmidt, a most frightening man/woman, a member of the Austrian team.*

Our team seems to be falling apart as we grow more competitive with one another. I'm changing, becoming short-tempered, lonely, and frustrated—also I'm losing my physical conditioning. No one told me how hard it would be to race in another country.

The bathroom door squeaked open, warning me that Becky had finished, so I set down my journal and looked up into her concerned, blue eyes. She cautioned me, "What're you doing? Don't you know that anyone can read your journal? Be careful what you write in there." Playfully, she knocked the blue cover of the cloth-bound book, "Don't get too personal."

"Not to worry. I'm not writing about you, but then again, do you have something to hide, do tell me?" I laughed, picking up the book.

She paused and softened her voice. "Maybe we all do. You know you must be careful about some topics."

"Yeah, like what?"

"Oh, I think you know."

"No, tell me."

"Okay, about Boast and Tracy, for one."

"What would happen if I did write about them?" I picked up my pen as if to start writing.

"If Boast found your journal, he'd find a way to send you home. No one's indispensable."

"Okay, what other topics are verboten?" I smiled smugly, "Like my German?"

"Good job. Well, don't write about David Solomon."

"Hmm, why?"

"I'm not sure why he's here. It's weird; he's never come around before. I've got the feeling that he's looking for something."

"Right—like Boast and Tracy."

"Or something else." A new anxiety grew in her voice.

"What do you mean?"

"I'm not sure I should get into it."

"Try me."

"Well, remember the big Austrian woman who told us where the waterfall was?"

"Yup."

"Well, rumor has it that she is a he and that the Austrians have been cheating."

"Do you mean that the team knows she isn't a she?" I laughed, uncomfortable with the strangeness of this situation.

"Yup."

"What do they have to gain?"

"Well, for one FIS points, but also money, sponsorships."

"Who would want to do that?"

"Have you ever heard of transsexuals?"

"Nope."

"Well, some people feel they have been born as a male in a female body. They would rather be the opposite sex."

"Now you're creeping me out. Why?"

"Who knows? Hormones? Family dynamics?"

I held up my hand to take time to register what Becky was saying. Pulling the covers up to my chin, I continued, "I'm not sure I want to hear more about this. This is way too strange."

"Oh, Lia. You're so naïve. Don't you know anything?"

"I'm not sure what you mean."

"Well, for starters, what do you know about homosexuals, lesbians, and gays?"

Again, I put up my hand, shrugging, "Not much. I'm not sure I've met one."

Becky shuffled over to my bed and sat down. She put her hand on my arm and looked straight into my eyes. I squirmed back toward the window, "What are you doing?"

She then moved her hand to my forehead, letting it slid to my cheek with the back of her hand. The silence between us felt as if an avalanche were about to start— an outpouring of emotions, feelings, pain that I didn't want to hear. I pulled the covers over my head. "What are you talking about?"

Pulling the covers back down, so she could look into my face, she said, "Okay, I'll be honest … I'm a lesbian. I've slept with other women."

I sat up, "So why are you telling me this now? What am I supposed to do?"

"I know you're probably uncomfortable with this, but I needed to tell you. You met Annie Hecker today. Did you see how she looked at me?"

"I'm not sure."

"Well, she 'likes' me. The Europeans know that I'm gay."

"Okay, but what does this have to do with me?"

"Because, well, you're my friend and something might happen."

"Like what?" I pushed back into the window.

"Like, I might invite her to our room. I don't want you to tell anyone."

"Becky, you're my friend. I wouldn't tell on you. I don't want you to be kicked off the team."

"Good, but I don't trust anyone on our team. Not even Carla. I'd never knowingly put a teammate in an uncomfortable position."

I struggled with my words, remembering when Becky had slapped my butt and all the times she had asked to room with me. Nervously, I asked, "You don't think I'm gay, do you?"

"Lia, sometimes we don't know ourselves. Sometimes it just happens."

"Well, I'm not. I like boys." I struggled to find just the right words. "In fact, I almost 'slept' with Bill. Did you know that?" My voice grew angrier, "But I feared getting pregnant."

"So guess what, Lia? I've slept with boys. They just don't do it for me; I guess I was born different."

"Okay, so I'm not worried that you'll attack me. But, are … " I stuttered, worried at how she'd interpret my next words, " … are you attracted to me?"

"Yup."

I felt nauseous, the phlegm building up in the back of my throat, my head started to swim. I pushed her off the bed onto the floor. As she landed on the oriental rug, there was a knock at the door. "Hey, you guys. Go to sleep! We can hear you in our room." I wondered what Tracy had heard.

Becky opened the door, saying, "Well then, you'd better come in." Tracy stepped forward, looking as though she'd just caught a mouse in a trap.

"Yup, I heard you two talking … the walls are really thin," she said, rubbing her hands together.

"Okay, so what did you hear?" asked Becky.

"Enough … enough to send you home."

"Oh my God!" I said. "You heard everything!" I felt as though the lid was off the box and another box was inside.

"Well, let's say, I won't talk, if you won't talk," said Tracy.

Becky challenged her, "Talk, talk about what?"

"I think you know. Why do you think David Solomon's here?"

I decided to take the pressure off Becky who'd grown red in the face from either from blushing or anger. "No, we don't know why he's here."

"Have you heard any rumors about why we're staying in this grand hotel?" Tracy asked, grinning.

Becky pushed Tracy in order to create some distance, so I stepped between them. "Of course," said Becky. "Someone's parents."

"Yup, and whose?" said Tracy, challenging her.

Becky shrugged, "Ah, I don't know. Maybe yours?"

"That's what I thought," said Tracy, her voice rising. "And if they did?"

"So you're not denying it?" screamed Becky.

"Hey, don't you enjoy being in this great place? After all, now you can be closer to your European girlfriends," she smirked.

Becky lunged at Tracy. I grabbed Becky's night gown, ripping it and leaving her breast hanging out, like a soggy fried egg. She quickly covered it with her hand and then pulled the torn material around it. "Shut up, you bitch!"

"Hey, nice talk," said Tracy, pleased that she'd been able to rile Becky.

"Okay, so do you want to tell us what you have been doing with Coach Boast, as though we don't already know?" Becky demanded, putting her right finger into the circle made by her left finger and thumb. She let the one rub inside the other. "A little fucky, fucky?"

"Nice talk. Butt off. My business is my business."

"Not when it affects our team. Not when it gets you seeds that you don't deserve. Not when it gets you preferential treatment," said Becky, putting her hands on her hips defiantly.

I giggled, realizing the irony in her accusation.

Tracy stepped forward and raised her fists, saying, "Ha! So who are you going to tell? I've the goods on you. If you talk about me and Boast, then I'm telling the coaches and David Solomon what I heard tonight. Then, who'll go home?" She stormed out the door. I looked up at Becky who stood like a punch-drunk boxer waiting for the bell.

Becky turned to me. "Do you want to talk about this or can you keep it quiet?"

"I'm so confused! I'm not telling anyone anything, and I'm certainly not going to write about it in my journal. I guess this is our secret. It's sort of like toothpaste."

"What?" said Becky. "Toothpaste?"

"Yup, once you squeeze it out, you can never put it back in." I smiled, fancying myself a writer. Maybe in the end that was all I'd get out of this trip to Europe—a story, a fat, juicy one.

Becky said, "Well, Tracy's one up on us now. I'm not sure how this'll affect the team. Let's sleep on it and talk in the morning. We have to run some practice GS runs tomorrow, so rest up."

Discretely laying my journal under my pillow, I settled my head on top of it, wanting to protect what I'd written, but more importantly, needing time to clear my thoughts. I shivered, thinking what I'd find if I opened the final lid of the black box.

CHAPTER 49

Panic

On the next morning's jog to the waterfall, the street ascended like a mountain trail, steep, bumpy, and twisty. Halfway up, a Mercedes splashed my pant leg with slush, forcing me to turn off Avenue de Kaiser. Winding through the narrow side streets, I stopped in front of a plate-glass window bearing the Swiss bank logo UBS. My worried and tired reflection leered back at me; my blonde hair stood up like a crown of crystal thorns. Shocked, I realized I'd forgotten my hat. I started running again.

The uneven cobblestones became slippery and the wet flakes, dripping down my lashes, blurred my vision. Every muscle ached in the act of waking up. The wind, pushing the snow ahead of me, guided me. Finally, at the top I heard a deafening roar— the waterfall.

Taking a deep breath, I climbed on the iron railing to get a better look, locked my heels into the filigreed-metal, and leaned out into the swirling mist, endorphins coursing through my body. Flakes of snow fluttered past and disappeared into the vortex, crystals merging with the foam, ending yet never-ending.

My thoughts whirlpooled in my brain. *Who was David Solomon? Why was he here? What did he know about Boast and Tracy? Is he part of the collusion? Does he know about the money to Boast? Does he know about Becky? Should I call my father? Would he listen?* Then, I remembered my last call to him when he called me insolent.

The bestial thunder, a deep roar as if the water were striking a membrane in the earth, grew louder when I closed my eyes. I thought about the disappearing snowflakes: *my father had taught me that each flake, a unique crystal, was formed around a piece of dust; no two alike, they existed for less than three seconds, but in total they could create glaciers, streams, waterfalls. Are we, Becky, Wren, Bill, Carla, Pammy, Tracy like snowflakes—all unique with a dream that would disappear? Would our bond, our playfulness, our song dissolve? Who had warned me this might happen? Or could we build something greater than ourselves?*

The wind, created by the pounding water, pushed a strand of hair across my face. To clear my mind from the turmoil, I kept my eyes closed and focused on the diverse sounds: music created by the thrumming of the cascading water, the lapping of water on rocks, the contrapuntal sounds of side streams, and finally the bass drone of water deep beneath the ice. I imagined Nature as the conductor.

Confused and scared, stepping back, I jerked off my gloves, unzipped my parka, reached for the inside pocket and found Bill's picture. I held up his face, and taking one last look at his smile, his sweep of dark hair, I kissed his lips and tossed him into the swirling cataract. Ironically, he floated up, up into the void.

A tug on my back made me slip. Grabbing the railing with my bare hand, I panicked, gasping as my chest fell back over the railing. A cold spray from the falls splashed my cheek, making me push back hard against the hand. "Who's there?"

A glove clutched my parka, pulling me away from the railing, while an Austrian voice yelled, "Don't jump!"

Surprised, falling into the arms of a slight, dark-haired woman, I said, "Annie, Annie Hecker. What're you doing here?"

It was a moment before Annie spoke, "Why, I followed you from the hotel. I had stopped by to see Becky and she told me you were leaving for a run. She asked me to catch you, to let you know the downhill pre-runs have been canceled for today—too much new snow." She looked into the abyss. "What are you doing?"

My words were lost in the thunder. "Well, ah … ah, I just wanted to get a better look at the falls. I guess I like a little risk."

"A little?" said Annie, not thoroughly convinced. "You looked like you would jump."

"No, I just like to test myself. You know the adrenaline rush."

"So relax, there are no pre-runs today. The officials want to boot-pack the course," She looked joyful, "That is why I take off for home."

"Home, where's home?" I asked, confused.

"Why, here, in Bad Gastein. Top of the hill." She pointed above the falls. "Would you like to come back with me ... for breakfast?" She hesitated, then added, "I know mein Mutter would love to have an American visitor."

"Wow, sure! I've nothing to do until the lifts open." I shuffled my feet. "If you're right, then I could go free-skiing later today." I paused, wondering about her timing, about her motives, and said, "What a minute, how will I be able to talk to your parents? Do they speak English the way you do?"

Annie giggled, "Lia, just because you Americans don't know German doesn't mean we Austrians don't know English. Why my father, the Baron, is a banker. He is required to know three languages— French, English, German. I, too, had to study English and French in school. Also, my whole family traveled to England for a year while my father was in banking school."

My eyes opened wide. "Cool."

Annie nodded, continuing, "Okay, that's a yes—right? Yah, maybe after breakfast, we can go skiing together." I nodded in affirmation. Annie pointed up the hill. "Race you." She swiveled on her heels, brushed against me, forcing me against the railing, and headed up the hill.

"Okay, I'll catch you," I laughed.

Like two projectiles, we sprinted toward the highest part of the town. Occasionally a shopkeeper would put down his snow shovel and wave. "Guten morgen, Annie." Everyone knew her, even schoolchildren stepped off the sidewalk to let us pass.

I turned to her, "Hey, you're sure famous here." She snickered and sped up. Her feet doubled-timed my pace.

At the top of the hill, she put out her arm to stop me and pointed to a large chalet set back from the road, nestled under an overhanging cliff. "Come, come this way. This is mein home." The width of her smile announced her pride.

CHAPTER 50

A Home-Cooked Meal

I caught my breath at the sight of her iconic two-story villa with an Austrian flag hanging over the front door, black shuttered-windows balancing on each side and the white-washed foundation glowing like fresh milk.

"Oh, Annie, how beautiful—just as I dreamed," I exclaimed, stepping up the stone walkway. My eyes wandered up and down, finding a coat of arms with a sword and shield, a cowbell by the red wooden door.

"Ja, this has been in my family since my great-great-great-grandfather was given the farm in 1750." She smiled like a mother introducing her newborn. "Can you believe this was once a small farm outside of town?" Grimacing, she pointed to the five-story high-rises across the street. "Now look." Then, she beckoned me inside, "Any friend of Becky is a friend of mine."

Stepping onto the polished pine floor, I smelled the fresh-baked bread, "Should I leave my sneakers outside?"

"Of course, meine Mutter would be angry if we get one drop of snow on her floor." Her Austrian accent became stronger.

I placed my wet sneakers on a wooden tray and slid into the living room. The penetrating eyes of a stuffed mountain goat followed me; two crossed swords glinted above the stone fireplace; the smell of leather from a sofa draped with a crochet throw reminded me of my father's chair in our living room. Two oversized portraits hung behind an oak dining table set back in the far corner. The man's prominent nose seemed disproportional to his size; the women's rounded checks shone as if they'd been rubbed raw.

Annie watched my expression, "So how do you like my grandparents? Funny-looking, huh?"

I laughed, "You mean the goat?"

'Hey, careful, mein grandfather shot him. He is a chamois."

"Cool! I can't believe that your family has owned this land since before America became a country. I ... I feel so insignificant," I said.

"Ah, you Americans. You have so much to learn. You are so arrogant. Why, I will bet you even think you can win the Austrian World Cups the first time you race here," she said, poking me and pointing to a glass trophy-case behind the couch.

We walked toward the silver plates and glass vases that grew brighter from the glow of the fireplace. I leaned closer to break my reflection and read the inscriptions on the trophies: Hahnenkamm 1960 - Karl Hecker, Lauberhorn - 1962. "Wow, Annie who won these?"

A deep voice from the back of the room made me jump back, "Mein Bruder." I turned to see a statuesque, blonde young man, his chin as solid as the man's in the portrait, walk into the room. His high cheeks, ruddy from a life in the mountains, lifted into a grin.

"Wow, your brother won these." My hand cupped my mouth in amazement. "What an accomplishment."

The man said, "Ja, what an accomplishment. He was mein older Bruder." He looked down, continuing, "Too bad he didn't live to enjoy the fruits of his labors." He made a motion across his neck with his hand.

"Oh, Kurt, why are you so negative?" said Annie angrily.

Kurt put his hand up to stop Annie, "You know, Karl never did get much of a ... " He struggled to find the right word. " ... a financial reward, despite all his successes in the races."

"Okay, but he got national recognition," said Annie, looking back into the trophy case.

"Not much good it did him. He died in an avalanche right

after his wins." The two glared at one another as if they'd had this argument many times.

A heavy-set woman, her gray hair pulled back in a bun, waddled into the room, and after wiping her hand on her apron, she extended it, "Enough, mein Kindern. Annie, please introduce me to your guest." Her smile accentuated her rosy cheeks.

"Mutter, this is Lia Erickson, an American in the race. She's a friend of Becky."

Annie's mother checked me up and down, head to toe. "Ah, Becky. Well, wilkommen, Lia. Please stay for breakfast." No one said a word until she finished, "No practice today, ja Annie?" I marveled at how good her English was.

"*Ja, Zu viel Schnee*," said Annie.

"Annie, do not be rude to your guest. Please speak English," said the mother.

"Mutter, too much snow. Ha, can you imagine? No training because we have too much of a good thing." Annie pointed for me to sit on the couch while Kurt went to put more wood on the fire. He leaned well into the hearth, an opening big enough to swallow his body. I couldn't help but admire his tight buns and strong quads. The fire roared to life, its red blaze throwing a warm glow over the room.

"Hey, Kurt, were you ever a racer?" I asked, trying to start a conversation. I ran my fingers through my wet, blonde hair flirtatiously.

Annie settled in next to me, bumping my wet pant leg. "Racer, he was better than mein Bruder, Karl," she exclaimed proudly.

"Wow, a family of racers," I said, shaking my head in wonder.

"Well, let's say we had to live up to Karl," said Annie.

"What, what happened to him?" I looked over to the trophy case again.

"Lia, he liked risk, like you." Annie shook her head, "So after the 1962 World Championships, he … "

"Enough," said a loud, bass voice. I looked up into the bluest eyes I'd ever seen. A six-foot man with broad shoulders, a barrel chest and cropped beard, towered over the two of us. "Annie, please introduce me to your guest," he bellowed.

Annie stood up in embarrassment. "Mein Vater, excuse me. This is Lia, Lia Erickson, an American racer."

"Wilkommnen, Lia. Please, don't get up," he roared.

I stood up anyway so as not to feel so overpowered by this man's presence. I felt I'd run into a boulder that was ready to roll down a hill. "Nice to … to meet you, too," I stammered, extending my hand. His firm grip made me draw in my breath. He settled into an oversized leather armchair and drew out a pipe. Tamping the end, he struck a match and sucked on the pipe until a small flame sprang from the bowl. No one spoke during his virile exercise. The acrid smoke curled about the room, making me cough.

To break the silence, Kurt, leaning against the mantle, said, "Papa, maybe our guest not like smoke."

I sat back in my seat and said, "No problem. My mother used to smoke. I like the smell."

Another silence as a sweet smell of bread wafted in from the kitchen. Annie stood and swept her hand around the room. "So, Lia, what do you think of Austria?"

"Now Annie, what kind of question is that?" said Baron von Hecker.

"Well, Papa, Lia is an American. American women are different from us. They can speak their mind. Do what they want."

"Do you mean that you can't, mein Vogelein?"

"No, Papa, you let me ski race, you let me travel. But Lia, she … she can go to college. Ja, and she can have a job." She spoke with the impatience of pent-up emotions.

Kurt moved closer, waving his hand to push the smoke away and to redirect the conversation. "Annie, we have had this conversation before—enough."

The Baron stood up and raised both his hands. "Now, Kinder, please stop. No arguing in front of our guest. Why don't you girls go help meine Marie with breakfast."

Annie grabbed my arm and led me into the kitchen where her mom was cooking. Glazed strudel lay on the counter, eggs gleamed from a frying pan, and coffee percolated in an aluminum pot. I marveled at the cleanliness of the wooden counters and darkness of the oak cabinets. I'd never seen such a large kitchen, such copper pots, so many herbs dangling from pine beams.

Annie's mother moved with the dexterity of a surgeon as she pushed one pot from the stove and moved the strudel to the side, all while flipping the eggs. Her apron was stained from years spent in the kitchen. A hiss came from the coffee pot.

"Nein, go sit at the table. All is ready," said the mother. She motioned for us to move back to the oak table where four blue place mats rested, four red napkins lay curled in silver napkin rings and the heavy silverware spoke of a family history well beyond the present. I'd never seen such a legacy, like a museum.

The mother rushed in with an extra place setting, putting it next to Annie's seat. The silverware clanged like swords as she placed them next to the napkin. The Baron gestured formally for me to sit. "Bitte."

Kurt took the seat beside me and smiled at Annie as if to say, "I won." The Baron took his seat at the head, scraping his chair as he pulled it in.

The mother returned again, carrying a plate of eggs and the strudel. I tried standing to help, but the Baron put up his arm. "Bitte, you are the guest." Neither Annie nor Kurt stood to offer help to the Baroness as she returned to the kitchen. She came back with the coffee pot, again placing it in front of the Baron.

Demurely, she moved to her end of the table, pulled out her carved armchair and sat down. "So, wilkommen again," she said. "Before we eat, a little prayer, bitte" When they all bowed their heads, I did the same. The Baroness spoke in a hushed voice. *"Pater, wir danken fur das Essen ... "*

I could not understand the rest, so I looked around, waiting to see who would move. The Baron started passing plates filled with eggs and strudel. My mouth watered at the aromas of yeast, sugar, and butter. I hadn't had such a breakfast since I'd left the States and I'd never in my life experienced such a warm feeling of food, family, and home.

"So, Lia, how do you like the World Cup circuit?" asked the Baron, looking straight into my eyes.

I stuttered, "Well—well, sir, it's new. It's a bit overwhelming."

"Ah, what do you mean?" said the Baron, looking confused.

"Well, I try hard, but not everything works out the way I think it should." I looked around to see whether anyone would agree with me.

"What do you mean?" he asked, frowning in puzzlement.

I looked at Annie to see whether I should continue. Annie's smile reassured me. "Well, sir, I tried hard, but then my coach gave my FIS points to another American racer."

"Ah, so you think you deserve those points. You think they are yours," said the Baron in the tone of a judge handing down a verdict.

"Well, yes—I skied hard, risked myself to get them," I insisted.

"Lia, do you think everything should be fair?" asked the Baron looking at each person at the table. He pulled on his beard, awaiting an answer.

"Well, yes ... " I said, hesitant to challenge him.

Annie interrupted before I could finish. "Papa, remember this is Lia's first time in the World Cup."

Then Kurt interjected, "Oh, Lia, don't you know anything about ski racing?" He looked around the table to see whether he should continue. "The whole system is corrupt. Each person takes as much money as he can!" He threw up his hands in disgust. "Grow up!"

"What, what do you mean … ?" I said, struggling to finish my sentence.

"I mean that it is all about money—money for the coaches, money for the racers, money for the manufacturers."

All the heads were nodding in agreement now. "No, no this can't be true," I protested.

"Hey, Lia," said Kurt, raising his broad chin. "I'm a salesman for Kneissl now. I am finished with racing." He paused and looked toward the trophy case. "I could never be as good as my brother." He raised his voice, "But guess what? I make more money than he ever did." No one said a word.

Finally, I asked, "What do you mean?"

"Well, dreamer. I get paid by the ski company to get racers under contract. If they win a race, they get one thousand marks. And their representative gets five hundred. Guess who their representative is?

'Who?" I said, shaking my head in wonder.

Kurt paused and looked into my eyes. "Duh, their ski coach. Why, even your coach Boast gets a take for every race that his racers win or place on our skis."

I remembered the time Boast had tried to push Kneissl skis on me, but I'd never liked the skis as they were too stiff. Kurt nodded, acknowledging my epiphany. "Yup, he gets a take on each race. Now how do you feel?"

I felt nauseous. I looked at Annie who nodded in affirmation. "Lia, open your eyes. Nothing is as you think it is," said Annie.

The Baron held up his hands. "Enough, mein Kinder, poor Lia has the optimism of a young American. We have seen too much here in Austria." He pushed his chair back and put down his fork. "Lia, continue to work hard. You will reap some future benefits. Some joy in your love for the sport."

Kurt broke in with a slight giggle. "Ha Papa, that's where I differ with you. Look at Karl. He worked hard, won races, and died in a fluke avalanche. What was his reward? I say, take what you can get every step of the way," He waved his hand in front of his face to dismiss the other's views.

The Baroness stood up. She pushed her chair back and raised her hands to quiet the table. "Our poor guest, she now hears us argue. I pray to God that you keep your thoughts to yourself. And God bless our Karl who is now in the arms of our Lord. Whatever you may think, there is a divine justice. God will grant the good life everlasting." She made the sign of the cross on her breast.

I turned to Annie who was starting to fidget. This conversation had gone too far.

Finally, Annie lifted her napkin defiantly, "Justice, man-made or God-made. Who knows the answer? We have to live our lives according to our hearts, our loves, our dreams." She winked at me, implying no more discussion.

I nodded in agreement, "I just want to ski, enjoy my friends, and try to get to the Olympics."

The moment was interrupted by the chime of the grandfather's clock, followed by eight gongs. Kurt waited for the bells to stop and said, "Well, a toast to the success of our new American friend, Lia." He raised his coffee cup and nodded to each family member. Then he turned to me, "I hope to join you and Annie skiing today."

For the first time since I'd left Monmouth, I felt the universal constancy of family and friends, like a boulder that could not be moved by a waterfall or glacier.

CHAPTER 51

Paradox

Struggling to keep my balance in the tram car while holding my skis upright, my ski edges knifing into my cheek, I squinted out the window at the fog-enshrouded cliff, a frightening fortress fifteen feet away. Right after the Hecker family breakfast, Annie and I had returned to the hotel to grab our skis, tell Coach Ryan and Becky where we were going, and then catch the cable car to the top. We hoped we might get some first tracks in the upper bowls. The ski patrol had announced that all trails were open, but urged care in the fog at the lower levels.

Looking back toward the city of Bad Gastein, I marveled at the contrast between this elite spa-resort in Europe, with its hot springs, gourmet restaurants, and luxury hotels and the rugged Alps and waterfalls. My new friend Annie nudged me. "Hold your breath, Lia. Right now," she said, fighting the sway of the tram car.

"Why, what are you … ?" I said, but stopped when the tram car, crawling up the side of the cliff, broke over the edge, out of the clouds, into a blinding white light. The sun glinted off the treeless snowfields, while above floated a seamless cobalt sky held up by encircling, jagged peaks. Time ceased.

"Welcome to my world," announced Annie, sweeping her hand 180 degrees in front of her. I loved how her "w's" became "v's." "In summer, I hike and help Franz tend his sheep, and in winter, I wander with my skis. Look up, there is the Stabneckog, above is the Kreuzkogel, over 2,600 meters, to the right is, uh, the Graukogel" She looked deeply into my eyes. "Heaven on earth,

313

ja?" Her Austrian accent had definitely grown stronger. The names intrigued me.

I shivered, realizing I was being welcomed into the world of an Austrian celebrity, one from a family of champions. "Cool, Annie! This is all I would ever need to be happy." I whispered, nodding my head, "You're so lucky." I looked again. "Thanks for inviting me to ski." Feeling free from the team stresses, I looked down on the tops of the white clouds and whispered as if in prayer, "Yes, this is my sanctuary, too, my snow sanctuary—my place where my physical and spiritual worlds become one."

Annie looked puzzled, "What did you say? I ... I think I know what you mean."

Before I could respond, another passenger on the tram turned and looked at us, "*He jeder, Annie Hecker ist hier.*"

I heard the murmurings of the other skiers and looked down to see a little girl stepping forward to say, "*Tour Autogramm, bitte.*" She extended her small ski tip toward Annie, and someone else handed her a pen. Nervous giggling spread through the tram car.

Annie stooped, hugged the small child, and scribbled her name on the ski. She whispered to me, "This is how I started ... I got the autograph of the famous Toni Sailer."

A clanging of metal, a slowing of the cab, then a banging of the car against the rubber guards, let me know that the lift had arrived at the top. I lost my footing and bumped into Annie's shoulder. She reached out, "Careful, Lia, you're probably not used to funiculars. Remember even though we are safe in this cabin, there is always danger lurking outside. Nothing is as it seems." Pausing, she smiled wryly. "Always be prepared." I grinned awkwardly, unsure how to respond to this caveat.

The side door opened, the forty passengers squeezed out, each pushing one another in an effort to be the first. I slipped on the concrete floor, planted my skis on the tarmac for balance, held my breath as I flowed along with the crowd. I lost sight of Annie but stayed with the horde.

Once outside, after the group dispersed, I saw Annie standing near a rocky outcropping, stomping a flat place in the new snow to place her skis. She waved, "Over here! I try to stay away from the crowd."

I gulped in the cold, moist air, pulled my goggles over my eyes to lessen the glare, and kicked my way through the four feet of fresh powder. "Holy cow, what a free-for-all!"

"What is a free-for-all, do you mean free fall?" said Annie, giggling.

"No, a free-for-all, an American slang for uncontrolled mess."

"Ah, a *frei-fur-alle*?"

Placing my skis down carefully, I pushed one pole into the ground and lifted my ski boot in order to triple-bang the snow from the sole with my other ski pole. I delicately slid my boot into the left ski binding, toe first, and then repeated with my right boot, always the same, left to right. For some reason, I always felt in control performing this ritual.

"One can never be too careful with new snow," I cautioned Annie, "It could clog the safety binding, which could then release unexpectedly."

Annie looked into the distance "Ja, Lia, another paradox of the mountains—no matter how careful you are, you cannot plan for everything." She smiled sardonically before continuing in her reflective voice, "Once I was skiing above a cliff, when my binding released because of snow under my toe. I fell head first, sliding on my stomach with my arms in front toward the cliff. And to protect myself, I try to use my arms as a break. But I'd built up too much speed. I grabbed a bamboo pole that marked the edge of the trail where the cliff began. The pole snapped. I went over the cliff." She paused, "How do you say it? Head-over-heels and landed on my back between two rocks. I could have been paralyzed." She looked at me for my response.

The word "paralyzed" took me by surprise and my thoughts flashed back to Wren: *Was she still at the hospital? Could she use her legs by now?* I said slowly, "I know exactly what you mean."

Annie poked me, saying, "Enough of the scary stuff, let's go have fun. Follow me." She flicked snow off her ski tips into my face as she cruised past. "Let the dance begin!"

I followed her tracks over a steep drop, braiding her rhythmic turns. We were skiing a knife edge, a shoulder where the wind-blown snow dropped down on both sides. Carefully, I made sure to shorten my turns, control my speed, and to stay exactly in Annie's slipstream, turn for turn, the way two colorful monarch butterflies chase each other through the still air.

My legs began to burn, but she just didn't stop. Loose snow billowed against my chest, swaddled me in white curds, forcing me to lean back to prevent my tips from diving. Annie's tracks descended the side of the ridge. Following her, I made larger turns, which let me know that the slope was not as steep. I thought, *For God' sake, stop, Annie! I can't keep up.*

Finally, far below me, Annie's red parka came to a rest. Feeling confident, I left her path, made two sweeping arcs to slow down, stopped below her, and looked up. A delayed crystal wave flowed over both our boots. I closed my eyes and felt myself melt into the sun's rays.

Annie, clicking her poles together, shook her head, and said, "Hey, wake up! Fun, ja? But remember to stay in my tracks. Even though this looks easy, avalanches can come from above for no reason." She gazed up the slope with a long, silent stare. "I always stay away from the avalanche chutes." She pointed up to a couloir topped by an overhanging cornice.

I collapsed into the powder, trying to relieve the ache in my legs. Feeling my heart pounding against my ribs, I gasped, "I … I guess I'm not in as a good shape as you are."

"Ha, my friend. One of the problems of World Cup racing—no

time to work out. I struggle to keep up my, uh, fitness. This is why I free ski without stopping."

I continued wheezing like a horse before finding enough breath to ask, "So where are we skiing today?"

"We'll work on skiing the north facing slopes where the powder will stay lighter, drier. There will be few trail markers, so stay close to me. Let's head up to the Kreuzkogel, hit some steeps."

Once again I was bathed in a rush of adrenaline, the elixir of risk-taking. I felt confident in Annie, a friend who knew these mountains like the top of her ski. She cruised over my buried tips, waving, "Come, let's play in the snowfields of the Lord, as mein Mutter calls them." She looked over her shoulder and laughed. "She says, 'Nature is God's art.'"

Happily, I hopped up, brushed the snow from my pants, and pushed off with my poles. A hawk cruised below, playing in the updrafts above the cloud-covered valley.

CHAPTER 52

Birthday Party

Two hours, six runs, and numerous falls later, Annie, after checking her watch, pointed to a mid-mountain chalet at the bottom of a run. "Let's ski down for lunch. Franz, my friend, is the chef there." Impishly, she smiled. "We'll get a free meal."

Annie led me to an outside table set for five next to the railing. She pulled out a wooden chair and pointed for me to sit. "Bitte, you take the one that has the view. Beautiful, ja?"

"Oh, Annie, I've never seen such open slopes, even at Monmouth. Amazing, and here in the Alps we're sitting at a table with a tablecloth and napkins." I ran my hand over the red-checkered cloth and picked up the glass in front of me. "Incredible! You even have real wine glasses up here."

"Ja, and you will have some schnapps with me. Remember, in Austria you can drink at 18 years."

I started. "Holy cow, I'm nineteen years old today! Wow, Annie I forgot … this is actually my birthday. It's January 26, right?"

Just then, from around the corner of the building appeared Becky, Carla, and Kurt, singing "Happy birthday to you." Kurt changed the lyrics into German while Annie joined in with her clear, soprano descant, also in German. Becky and Carla stopped singing and Kurt and Annie continued, in harmony, but with new words:

> Hoch sollst Du Leben
> Hoch sollst Du Leben
> Drei mal so hoch

Schön sollst Du warden
Schön sollst Du warden
Drei mal so Schön.

Then they sang the tune once again, but this time in English:

High should you live
High should you live
Three times so high

Beautiful should you live
Beautiful should you live
Three times so beautiful.

My eyes wandered from friend to friend—from Carla's shining brown hair to Becky's eyes closed in perfect serenity, to Annie's smile, slight as though she were just getting the point of someone's joke, to Kurt's handsome grin, and then slowly from mountain top to mountain top —peaks that fit into peaks like lovers, the ridges resembling straddling thighs—and finally to the lace of fog below. As he kept singing, Kurt's eyes wandered up the slope to the Kreuzkogel. His eyes were searching like a St. Bernard's looking for a lost person.

When the serenade ended, I asked, "What's up there?"

"Oh, nothing. I just thinking," said Kurt, obviously lost in thought.

Annie broke in. "Well, Lia, since we're all friends, I'll tell you. Up on that slope, that—that is where Karl died ... " Tears swelled her eyes. "In an avalanche. It happened on a day like today, new snow, sun, and no wind. Perfect conditions. Karl had skied off before Kurt." She turned toward Kurt to see whether she should continue. He nodded back. "Karl was so confident in himself. He'd just won in Lauberhorn and in Kitzbühel and ... " She stopped, choking up.

Kurt broke in. "Ja, skiing in new snow is like skiing in an hour glass."

"What do you mean?" asked Becky, joining the conversation.

Kurt took charge to teach us. "Well, you know, with an hour glass, the sand piles up slowly, grain by grain into the bottom, makes a pyramid."

"Yes, what's your point?" asked Becky confused.

Kurt continued, "Well, you never know at what point, what time, the sand will break away and the whole slope will slide." He made a rubbing motion, one palm across the other.

Annie added, "Ja, Karl was set up for disaster, not by his inexperience, but by his experience. Another of the mountain paradoxes. He thought he could conquer everything."

Feeling a blend of pride mixed with horror, I realized how vulnerable Annie and I'd just been. "But ... but, didn't we just ski that slope?" I shook my head in disbelief.

"Jah, Lia. But we took precautions, staying high on the rib. Remember. The slope, if it slides, will slide under the cornice," she added with conviction.

I noticed her Austrian accent growing stronger.

Kurt interrupted in an angry voice, "Ja, I did the same, I stayed high on the wind-blown ridge, but Karl wanted the fresh powder in the chute. I tried to warn him."

Annie shook her head in an attempt to ease Kurt's guilt. "Hey, Kurt, do you remember Papa saying once, "He who is brave in daring will be killed, and, uh, he who is brave in not daring will survive." A long silence ensued—the same quiet found when one holds one's head underwater in a swimming pool.

Kurt, shaking his head, summed up the conversation, "Now the final irony. Once you have experience, once you accept the danger, once you know you are—how do you say it—vulnerable, then you will get hurt. Game over. Get out." I looked back up the hill and thought of Damien, of Bill, of Wren. *Their game was over.*

Kurt stood up and bowed to me, "Well, let's not ruin your birthday." He raised a glass of schnapps the waiter had just poured,

"To our new American friends and to Lia. Happy birthday and remember, always eat dessert before your meal." He laughed in a low guttural noise that took me by surprise. I ran my fingers through my corn-silk hair, seeing my reflection in his sunglasses. I felt sexy.

With joy, I held my glass forward and let each person clink it before drinking the bitter liquor. I said slowly, "All so beautiful, so ephemeral—just like a snowflake."

Becky took charge of the group. "Let's order, think about good things, and then go skiing."

Carla agreed, "Wow, Kurt and Annie, will you show us your mountain after lunch?"

A deep voice broke into the group, "Guten morgen, meine frauleins," and I looked up into the eyes of a dark-haired, red-cheeked man, his rotund waist supporting an apron. His smile—furrows creased like the bark on an ancient tree.

Annie, recognizing my surprise, announced, "Wilkommen Franz. Diese sind meine Freunds, Becky, Carla, and Lia," pointing to each of us as she said our names.

Franz reached out an oversized-calloused hand to each of us, saying, "Wilkommen, ein Freund von Annie ist ein Freund von mir." He took extra time with my hand, and kissing it and adding in heavily-accented English, "Happy Birthday. Mittagessen ist auf mir."

Blushing, I looked around for a menu. Annie said, "Not to worry, Lia. Becky and I have chosen my favorite lunch for you. Chicken strudel, Austrian potato dumplings, and linzer torte."

Kurt laughed, "Ah, Annie, are you trying to fatten up your American friends, so they won't race as well? Ha, good plan."

"Shh, Kurt. No, this will be our energy for success in the races," said Annie firmly.

A small waiter, with smooth cheeks like a ten-year old, brought out the first course of dumplings. Annie nodded to me to try it, "So, Lia, this is not usually how we train. But for you, enjoy. Look around. Over the mountain lies Salzburg, home of Mozart. "She pointed at the largest peak. "Once home of the Von Trapp family. You Americans made them famous."

"Wow, right over there. You mean they had to climb over mountains as high as these to get to Switzerland, to safety?" I said open-mouthed.

Annie scolded me, "Ja, if you want to get away from persecution, from imprisonment, from death, you would do anything, wouldn't you?" Her voice turned a bit condescending. "When you get to Maribor, Yugoslavia, for the next race, you will learn about a communist country, a place people would do anything to leave. Then you'll understand."

Feeling uneasy, I tried bringing the conversation back to my home. "Did you know that one of the Von Trapp children, Werner, is my neighbor in Vermont? His mother, Maria, brought the whole family to Vermont after the baron died. She thought the hills resembled those in Austria. In fact, Werner's children, Maria's grandchildren, go to my school."

"Ah, we have more in common than we thought," said Kurt with a flirtatious wink.

Becky broke in, "Hey, Lia. Why didn't you tell me that when we were singing all those 'Sound of Music' songs? I guess we'll never know everything about each other." She winked at Annie.

The waiter picked up our plates and brought the next course. Annie announced, "Now, this is meine favorite, chicken strudel. Smell the onions, mushrooms, parsley, and basil."

I played with the sour cream dabbed on top of the square filo pastry. "Whoa, lots of rich food."

Carla broke in, "We'll ski it off this afternoon. I think Annie and Kurt will lead a merry chase around the mountains." She rolled her eyes.

"Ja," said Kurt. "Try to catch us. Remember we're the invincible Heckers." He laughed and looked up to the overhanging peaks.

After we finished the chicken strudel, Franz arrived with the Linzer torte, topped with candles. An older man, dressed in lederhosen and playing an accordion, stepped from around the corner. The group sang *Happy Birthday* once again while Franz placed the cake in front of me. He stepped back, waving his hands in the manic frenzy of an orchestra conductor.

At the end Annie said, "One thing we share—the love of singing, especially at birthdays. Blow out the candles, Lia. We wish you a successful life on the ski slopes, filled with new friends."

I gathered my breath, wishing this snowflake-moment would never end, and blew out all nineteen candles at once. Suddenly, I jolted, remembering that I'd not saved one to grow on. Smelling the almond pastry filled with raspberry jam, I pressed the knife into the torte, before passing each piece around.

The jovial accordion player played polka music, inspiring some of the other diners to dance. Kurt jumped up, swung around the table, offered me his hand, bowed, and asked, "Bitte, will you dance with me?"

Blushing, I stood up and stumbling on my ski boots, I took both his hands. He swung me into the group of dancers, leading me with his strong arms, one leg pressing between my thighs, forcing me to follow his quick steps, spinning me until the mountains became a blur.

I tightened my hold to keep my balance, so he leaned down to whisper in my ear. "Don't worry, follow me, one-two, one-two." His bulging arms picked me up and swung me, lifting my heavy ski boots from the deck.

With my heart pounding, I tried to focus on the floor to keep from getting dizzy, when I noticed that our two liquid-shadows had become one.

CHAPTER 53

Maribor

"Damn," yelled Coach Ryan. The car skidded, bounced off a snow bank and threw me into Carla.

With my heart pounding, I looked up to see the snow-covered road barely lit by the cone of the headlights. We were in a rental car making our way to Maribor. Frantically, Coach Ryan kept clicking from low to high beams, hoping to spot the snowbanks through the veil of cotton-ball flakes. I felt as if I were in a washing machine, spinning, tumbling. Finally, he pulled over, demanding, "Becky, check the map. This can't be the fastest way to Maribor."

The road south to Yugoslavia had crossed the southern Alps and wound through farm fields and villages. Unfortunately, we'd gotten a late start because of the storm. To compound the problem, the Mercedes wagon we'd rented came with a roof rack but no studded tires.

Becky traced a road on the map with her finger, asking, "Have we passed Klagenfort or Volkermarkt?"

"Not sure," said Coach. "Damn, I can't even read the road signs or anything." He opened his door, stepped into the blinding snow, scraped the windshield, cleared the headlights and, after brushing the sticky snow from his jeans, slid back in next to Pammy.

Pammy turned toward Tracy, who was sitting next to her in the front, "Oh, you're so wet. Yuck."

To further irritate her, Coach tilted his head toward her lap and brushed the snow from his thick hair into her crotch, "Ha, enjoy the moisture." He sneered. "Such prissies." He dropped more snow in her lap as he bent to turn the ignition, "Guess

324

we've no choice but to continue to the next town." A silence filled the cab. I felt my pulse speed up in time with the throbbing wipers.

He continued driving cautiously with Pammy and Tracy squished next to him. Once again trying to catch some sleep, I snuggled between Carla and Becky in the back seat. My thoughts kept returning to the last two races in Bad Gastein: *Annie had been right. The Americans did well. In fact, I'd been the top American and had captured a fifth in giant slalom and a fourth in slalom. The downhill had been canceled. My best World Cup results to date. I recalled my runs, effortless, flawless. Was it that Kurt had been watching? My FIS points kept dropping, so I felt sure I would be in the first seed in at least the slalom in Maribor, unless … oh, yes, now the Olympic team seemed closer than ever.*

Becky pushed me, "Hey, wake up sleepy head … you've been dozing for an hour."

I rubbed my encrusted eyelids, "Uh, oh, I was just thinking about Kurt."

She leaned into my ear, "Okay, talk. Did you go out with him after the awards ceremony?"

I sat up, caressed my two prize medals in my pocket, smooth as polished stones. My thoughts returned to my walk to the dais to shake the hand of the mayor of the Bad Gastein. Kurt had been waiting in the aisle when I returned to my seat. I answered her, "Well, yes and no."

"What do you mean?" Becky asked as I realized the others were listening.

"Well, he did walk me back to the hotel. I was too tired to go out, plus … " and, I said this louder, " … I didn't want to miss my curfew."

"So you think he's cute?" asked Carla, getting into the conversation.

I didn't want to tell them that I had fallen for him, his accent, his love of the mountains, his carefree attitude. He was unlike anyone I'd ever met. I said slowly, "Maybe."

"C'mon, spill the beans," said Becky, growing impatient.

My heart pounded as I remembered the kiss he'd given me in front of the hotel. I could still taste his minty breath. "Okay, enough, yes, I like him."

Becky then put her hand on my knee, giggling, "I saw you kiss him at the hotel."

I elbowed her and put my finger to my lips, "Shh, enough!" and looked to the front seat to see if they'd heard.

The grinding of the brakes stopped the conversation. "Shit," screamed Coach Ryan. The car was skidding side-to-side like a jack rabbit darting away from a fox.

Becky screamed, "Watch out!" With a thud, a large, wooden gate banged onto the car's hood. Spotlights blazed, washing the front and back of the car, lighting us as if we'd just escaped from prison. The car bucked once more, my head slapped the front seat, Becky's head hit my shoulder, and I heard Carla's head crack against the side window. Then quiet.

A pounding on the driver's window caused me to look up. A brown-uniformed guard was pointing a machine gun at the car and motioned for Coach Ryan to open his window. Two more guards jumped in front of the car, their machine guns aimed at the windshield. I ducked.

"Easy," said Coach Ryan, carefully opening his window while holding his other hand in the air. He nervously said, "Americans, we're Americans." He pointed to the US flag sewn on his parka. The guard gestured for him to step out.

Becky started to open her door. Coach Ryan commanded, "Not now Becky. Stay in the car. I'll handle this." His stern worried voice trailed off as he stepped out into the blizzard.

No one spoke during the thirty minutes that Coach remained inside the primitive, wooden guard house. He returned with some papers and a new road map and gave them to Pammy, while he tucked his wallet into his pocket. "Ahh, sorry, girls, I took a wrong turn and entered Yugoslavia from different direction. Anyway … " he laughed, "we're okay, nothing a few dollars couldn't fix. It's only twenty minutes to Maribor." He paused, trying to compose himself. "Guess they've never seen Americans trying to escape into Yugoslavia." Our soft giggles crescendoed into a nervous chorus.

As the engine roared, my thoughts went back to a Christmas when my mother had welcomed a group of Hungarian refugees who had fled a communist country. I remembered, *December 1956 in Vermont: my mother had agreed to welcome a family of Hungarians, a mother, father, and three-year-old boy into our home. She had picked them up at the local church on Christmas Eve. They'd escaped during their revolution, traveling three days in a snowstorm to cross the border between Hungary and Austria.*

She had told me that when the revolution erupted, many had fled the invading Russian soldiers. Even though she'd tried to explain who'd been on what side, I didn't understand. Why would a government want to kill a child? She explained that this particular family, along with some others, had been led out by a Hungarian rebel group who knew the mountains.

During their journey, the mother sedated her son for the sleepless, snow-bound trip. The father had strapped the drugged child on his back, stopping every two hours to make sure his son hadn't frozen any limbs. At the border in an open field, the family had been fired on by Hungarian guards; two in the party had been killed.

What a Christmas our family had that year! This new family couldn't speak English and were so traumatized, they wouldn't leave each other's sight. The little boy cried non-stop.

But then again, that was my mother, always looking out for others and neglecting me in the process.

The sound of cars honking and Coach Ryan's asking for directions to the hotel brought me back to the present. An officer, holding a machine gun and dressed in a brown and red uniform, pointed toward a massive iron bridge straddling a frozen river. "Drava, Stari Most," and then pointed left and then right.

Coach Ryan nodded as though he understood and turned to us, "Not to worry. We'll go over the river and head toward the city center. I know the hotel has a red-tiled roof. Coach Boast told me so."

I looked into the evening light to see that every building in the city had a red roof.

Carla poked me, "Right, he knows the way. Should we revolt?"

I put my fingers to my lips. "Funny, I was just thinking about revolutions. How do people find the courage to revolt against authority, against their government—to take up arms, to die, and for what?"

Carla was angry, "Fighting is hell. Ask my dead parents. Remember, I'm a refugee."

"Wow, I guess you are even though you were adopted by Americans," I said.

She leaned toward my ear, whispering, "In fact, if I make the Olympic team next year, after Sapporo, I'll go to Rome." She looked around the car to see if anyone had heard her secret. "I want to find what remains of my family." A palpable silence ensued.

I decided to break the awkwardness. "Hey, does anyone know anything about Yugoslavia, other than it's communist and the president is Tito?"

Becky turned and scolded me in her sing-song, condescending voice, "You know the problem with you Lia, you're too curious. You want to know too much. We're just here to race."

"Thanks Becky," said Coach Ryan. "I couldn't of said it better." He paused, wanting to get in the last word before we got to the hotel. "But seriously, do remember that you're in a communist country and you won't be as protected as you were in the European countries. You know, America can't rescue you if you break the laws here."

"What...what do you mean?" I asked.

"I mean just what I said. This country has a dictator and a different set of laws than we're used to. Just follow the rules," he said, shaking his right finger, his voice taking on a new urgency.

The car pulled under an overhang and a valet opened the driver's door. "Wilkommene, Rennfahrer," he announced in a Yugoslav accent. Each of us jumped out like kernels of popcorn from a kettle.

Tracy said to Coach, "Boy, am I sick of this crew." After a silence, she stammered, "Ah, is … is Boast coming here?" I'd never seen her look this worried, this frightened.

"Yup, he'll get here tonight for the seeding meeting," he answered with a glare.

Tracy moaned, lowering her head into her hands.

He continued, "Now girls, go to the front desk … I'll meet you there with your room assignments."

I grabbed my bulky, blue boot bag that the valet had set on the curb. Wearily, I trudged into a modern, sparsely furnished foyer, "Wow, this looks brand new. Not much history here."

A slim young man wearing a black bell-boy suit and hat stepped forward and in broken English said, "Welcome. Well, you Americans. I hope you have time visit our beautiful city. It restored since the war, even our Franciscan Church and castle." He smiled, obviously pleased with his English.

To my surprise, Coach Boast stepped out from the shadows, a Cheshire grin on his face. "Welcome girls! But I don't think you'll have time for sightseeing. In fact Coach Ryan and I've decided that you should stay near the hotel for your own safety." He glared at Tracy.

I looked to see Becky's reaction as she stood in amazement, staring at Coach Boast. "How'd you get here before us?" she asked.

"Easy," he said. "I took the train. I should ask, what took you so long?" I didn't like the way he turned toward me, sneering, his brow puckered, as if he had devious thoughts, his eyes roaming up and down my body. "Oh by the way, good job in Austria, Lia."

No one spoke. Finally, to break the silence I answered boldly, "Thanks. You'd better ask Coach Ryan about what happened on the way here." My friends snickered.

CHAPTER 54

The Communists

After dinner, Carla and I walked back to the elevator where Coach Boast was sitting in a black plastic chair, working on some papers, maybe the seeding for the races. He looked up, slowly letting his eyes check me out and chortled. I backed away.

Upstairs, we stopped outside my room. I said a little anxiously, "Hey Carla, my first time rooming alone. How come?"

"Who knows why the coaches chose who rooms with who?" she said, impatiently.

"You mean, with whom," I said, wagging my finger like a teacher.

"Hey, Miss English teacher, like I'm getting tired of you correcting my English. Anyway, as I was saying, I'm finding the randomness of so much travel upsetting." She walked into my room, looked around at the spartan furnishings, and flopped onto my metal bed. The springs creaked as if it had been hastily assembled. Casting her arm in a semi-circle, she continued, "Look how bare this place is. I guess we're not first class for the next three days."

I looked around searching for anything that resembled a home, warmth. There wasn't even a rug. I said slowly, "Something's changed. Tracy seems scared and Boast looks angry. And he's giving me dirty looks."

I started to unpack, tossing my toilet kit on the dresser. My Gillette razor slipped out and clanged on the floor, causing me to bend down and put it back on the dresser.

Carla gave my butt a playful nudge, "Hey, Lia, would you like to go for a run with me later? I need to …"

" … Thought we were grounded?" I interrupted.

"Well, we'll just go around the block."

"Okay, go get your sneakers on. I'll meet you in the lobby in ten. I won't tell if you won't. " I paused, "Wait a minute, you're rooming with Tracy. Do you think she'll tell Boast?"

Shaking her head, she left, while I continued the tedious task of unpacking. I, too, had grown tired of this suitcase-living, packing, and unpacking. My dirty clothes smelled like a barn, so I threw them in a pile next to the door. I had just one pair of underwear left and no clean socks. Hanging my racing suit in the closet, I searched for a laundry bag. Did I ever miss Monmouth, where I could wash my clothes every night!

Downstairs in the dimly lit lobby, the bellboy stepped from a shadow, saying, "Caught you. So, where you go?" He looked at Carla and me, smiling, "I must to watch for this, yah."

I reached into my pocket for some American ones. "Here, I'll bet you can say you saw nothing."

He pushed my hand away, whispering, "Better, I go with you. I can say I not here." He motioned for us to follow him. Carla and I walked nervously behind his black uniform.

Outside, away from the front entrance, I stopped him. "Wait a min, what's your name and where're you taking us? In fact why is your English so good?" I was becoming suspicious, just like Nancy Drew, my favorite female protagonist when I was a kid.

He turned to me, putting his hands on his hips, and said defiantly, "Novak. And our second language in Maribor is English. To get job in tourism, I has to know English. I learn twelve years." He smiled proudly and began walking.

"Okay, but I'm beginning not to trust anyone," I said, turning to Carla for affirmation.

"Right." She shrugged, her ski team parka puffing up over chin.

Novak answered, "Hey, I on your side. Don't worry me. Yes,

I dream of go to the States, yes and study someday. Do you know our President Tito? Though we still a communist country, he—how do you say it—let go travel bans here." Pausing to see whether we understood, he continued, "You probably don't know, but he go to America 1963 and actually friend your President Kennedy."

I shook my head. "I'm sorry. I don't read much about your country." Thinking I heard footsteps behind us, I looked back.

He stopped, extending his hand. "Well, if I be guide, you, you trust me. You look nervous. So what you names?" he asked.

I grabbed his hand. "Lia here and this is Carla." Carla, blushing, lowered her head.

He added with a generous bow, "Nice to meet you. Now me show you our most special place in this city."

The three of us walked into a foggy town center, air as thick as heavy cream, moisture that I could almost cup in my hands. He made sure to take the small back-streets, avoiding the lights. Suddenly, he ducked into an alley and indicated for us to stand quietly. A street lamp turned the mist into custard. He whispered, "Shh, we not be out this late." Running his hand along a windowed, red stone wall, he pushed occasionally against a pane until finally one swung open. "Ah, here it is. My especial entrance."

I felt an adrenaline rush as though I were about to discover a stash of gold and said, "Wow, you even have secret openings."

He answered, letting his eyes dart up and down the street, "Yah, remember we communist country. Police everywhere." He glanced back, ran his hands along the stone wall before crawling through the narrow opening and into a stone passage. We followed.

I bumped my head against an overhanging piece of granite. "Ouch."

He put his finger to his lips, "Shh."

I nodded an OK and then heard a faint chanting that echoed down the hallway; the granite walls magnified its beat. The singing, as it grew louder, saturated the air, lubricated the rough walls, hummed up through my feet to my bones, became part of my blood, turned into my blood, continuing up into my brain. I closed my eyes, my lips starting to vibrate as though I were going to join the chant, but I didn't know the words.

We didn't move until he poked me, indicating we should duck through a low-hanging door, and, one by one, he pushed our heads down. We entered a cavernous, half-domed room filled with the scent of burning candles. I sneezed.

Colorful banners hung from the walls, and at the far end, gleaming like a barricade in the candlelight, stood a gilded-stone altar, supporting a gold crucifix that held Christ's defeated body, head bowed, blood flowing from His bare, pierced side.

I whispered to Carla, "I've never understood why some religions like to worship such a morbid sight— a tortured, dead man." She nodded.

Ten brown-robed, hooded monks circled the altar in a scene right out of the Middle Ages. Not one looked up when we entered; they just kept chanting. Their hands folded together in prayer. Again, Novak held his finger to his lips. I held my breath, realizing we'd come upon some sort of centuries-old ritual. I leaned against the cold, granite wall, which probably contained memories of lives, of sufferings in each mortared crevice.

Again, I closed my eyes to let the harmonies, the words Christus, Domine, Sanctus, flood into my ears; the dankness of the stone dampened my back. I trembled in fear, realizing that for these oppressed people, maybe just maybe, religion was what had saved them. This Christian faith somehow helped them to feel they had some control over their lives, or their deaths.

After ten minutes—but what seemed an eternity to me— Novak signaled for us to return through the narrow doorway. In the hallway he said, "This the first year that Tito allow us to worship openly, but we scared, yah. The monks, they meet secret to practice their Gregorian chants." He smiled like a master spy who'd just discovered the Holy Grail. "You in the bottom of the famous Franciscan Church. Builded in 1300."

Carla, dropping her jaw wide open, exclaimed, "I've never heard such beautiful music. Do they memorize everything?"

"Yah, they have to," said Novak. "Remember for long time if we practice religion, we not get government jobs. Welcome to our communist country." He rolled his eyes and then let his head sink in an act of despair.

I looked up and down the narrow corridor, "Holy cow, could we get in trouble being here?"

"Well, we not get caught," he said. "Trust me, I move in this city at night for four years. Now follow me," he beckoned.

We left the church through the same window. Novak slowly closed the glass pane and signaled for us to follow him. Climbing over low walls, up narrow alleys, he finally stopped and pointed toward an iron fire escape. I heard the sound of my feet skidding on the wet cobblestones as I stopped abruptly. "Now come meet my friends. They study at university." A thousand invisible clicks let me know that the fog had turned into an icy drizzle.

I backed off. "I'm not sure we should. These are guys we don't know."

"Come on Lia," said Carla. "What's happened to Miss Nonconformist, to Miss Adventurer?" She laughed at my reluctance.

"Okay, but just for a minute."

I climbed up behind the others, grasping the icy metal as the fire escape swayed and creaked. In the lead, Novak knocked four times on a window. The casement opened and a dark-haired, bearded young man poked his head out. *"Novak, da li stc? Koli su vam doneo?"*

"Da, imam nekih americkih takmicara."

"Ono sto neki?" asked the voice softly.

335

"Americans," replied Novak impatiently. "Let us in."

I stepped over the window sill and pushed past Novak into a small dorm room where three unmade beds were set against the walls. The rank smell of liquor made me turn to Carla, whispering, "We'd better go. This isn't good." I saw at least six liquor bottles on a small chest.

Novak stepped in front of me, holding out his hand. "No worries. My friends want to meet racers. We all excited about the World Cup here." Three six-foot boys stepped into the light and held out their hands. Their sallow skin made them look very tired—one had a minefield of acne.

"Okay, so now we've met your friends. I want to go," I pleaded.

Novak looked at his friends and back to us, holding up his hands in frustration. "Okay, but you give them your address, so they write you. One day, they hope leave here and say they know an American." He reached onto a small wooden desk and grabbed a pen and paper. "No problem. Your address help them leave one day."

I looked at Carla who shrugged. "Okay," I said. "I'll give you my address." I took his pen and made up a fake address in Burlington, Vermont.

The taller boy, frail-looking wearing wired-rimmed glasses, stepped forward and took the paper from me. He held it to his chest as if it were a life vest. "If I ever leave, I let you know. Maybe one day we not be a communist country." He looked at the address again, "You Americans, you so lucky. You travel where you want, study what you want—um—read what you want." He put his head down; his voice cracking.

I coughed and blushed in embarrassment, grateful for what I had. Turning to Novak, I asked to have the paper back, so I could write down my real address. Returning it, I said, "Hey, we need to leave. Thanks for the tour."

I crawled back through the window and down the fire escape, my feet slipping at one point so only my hands held me from falling. No one spoke until we were back safe in our hotel, or thought we were.

CHAPTER 55

Boast

"See, I tell you we make this adventure," announced Novak, standing guard at the hotel entrance while Carla and I tiptoed through the foyer. I prayed the night clerk wouldn't look up until after we had gotten into the elevator.

As we stepped out on the third floor, Carla put her finger to her lips, whispering, "See you in the morning. What tales we have to tell!" I watched Carla's silhouette disappear down the darkened hall, feeling the invincibility that comes with successful risk-taking, and then quietly slipped the brass key into my lock, only to find it was already unlocked. Safely inside, I carefully closed my door with both hands and reached for the light switch.

Turning back, I saw a man's silhouette against the window. I screamed. "Who are you?"

Coach Boast stepped out of the shadow. "Ha, Lia. I saw you and Carla leave. So, I decided to wait up for you," he said, rubbing his hands together.

"How'd you get in my room?"

"Not a problem. Remember, I'm the head coach."

"Okay, so I went out. Big deal."

"Don't be rude," he said, stepping closer to me, "Well, young lady, it is a big deal. But then again it doesn't have to be." He reached for my shoulder. "We just need to talk a bit."

"You creep! Have you grown tired of Tracy?"

"Enough. Someone's been talking to David Solomon. I want to know who?"

I pulled back, more frightened than I'd been in the Yugoslavian students' room. I'd never been so close to him—his acne-scarred cheeks turned red, his breath reeking of liquor.

He pulled me close to him, "I've been wanting to do this for some time. You know I've the power to put you on the Olympic team. Just trust me and do what I want." Pausing, he put his right hand on his crotch. I saw that he'd exposed himself. "Then, you can have what you want. Don't fight me." Pulling me against his chest, he forced his lips toward mine, trying to kiss me, "You know you want this."

I pushed him away and fell back into the dresser. Instinctively, I let my right hand run across the wooden top until I found my razor. Clenching the blade, I scraped it across his cheek. Blood oozed to his chin as he fell backward.

He reached up to stop the red flow, "You fool. Now see what seed you'll get in tomorrow's race."

"Ha! The draw's already been made. You can't hurt me."

Frantically, he grabbed my hand holding the razor, pushing it across my eyebrow—a gash started leaking immediately. "One word about this and you'll be on your way home—no Olympic team. Remember, you were the one who broke the rules. You went out at night." He shoved me away and stormed out.

He turned back at the threshold, "And by the way, I'm done with Tracy."

I slumped to my bed, feeling helpless, still clutching the razor with one hand and let my head fall onto my chest, feeling the blood trickle into my turtleneck.

CHAPTER 56

My Room

Dazed, I stumbled to my feet to turn off the light, fell back onto my pillow, and pulled the comforter over my head, my body aching for release. My sobs became tears mixing with the blood that stained the white pillowcase. Trying to make myself invisible, intangible, insubstantial, I curled into a ball, moaning and calling for my father, my home, my mother, my bedroom, my books.

I stopped, held my breath, upon hearing the door squeak open. "Lia, Lia, are you okay?"

I recognized Carla's voice and raised my eyes above the comforter like a child trying to hide from her parents. "Do, do you know what just happened?" I muttered, my voice shaking.

"No, but I did see Boast storm out of your room, so I thought I'd check on you."

"What—what did he look like?" I asked, confused and scared. I put my hand over my eyebrow to hide the cut.

"He looked angry and he held his hand to his cheek." Carla put her hand on her own cheek, making a rubbing motion as though she were trying to wipe something away. Slowly, she approached my bed, sat down, and took my hand.

I thought for a moment. *Should I tell Carla? Who was at fault? What had he been trying to do?* "Carla, Boast tried to attack me," I mumbled, turning my head away.

"What?" Carla stood up. "You're crazy. He wouldn't do that."

"No, really. He also threatened me."

"Lia, you're making up a story to try to get out of trouble."

"No, it was … " I couldn't finish my words. "I think I cut him with my razor."

"Holy cow! Like, this is nuts. What's his game?"

"I'm scared. He threatened to change my race seed again tomorrow." I wiped my hand over my face, trying to make sense of the last ten minutes.

Carla grabbed my hand again, turned it over in the dim light. She said with concern, "Hey, you've got blood on your face, on your hand. What have you done?"

Just then the door squeaked again and a soft voice called, "Is everyone okay here?" I looked up to see Tracy was there in her flannel pajamas, pink cotton with tiny roses dotting the front. She closed the door softly and stepped to my bed. "Can I join you both?"

I turned away, "No, you're the problem. We don't we want to talk to you?"

Tracy slid back, "What—what do you mean?"

I looked at Carla for approval. "Should I tell her?"

Carla sat on the bed again, "Okay, let's have at it." She punched the air with a boxer's fist.

I sat up. "Well, Tracy, we all know that you've been slinking around with Boast."

She broke into tears. "Hey, he's been so brutal. I had no choice." She put her face into her hands and her shoulders sagged. She looked defeated.

"Yeah, right," I said.

"No guys, "He promised I would make the Olympic team, if I just did what he wanted."

Carla pushed Tracy away from us. "So you slept with him to get what you wanted?"

No one spoke. The radiator crackled, footsteps sounded in the hallway. I put my non-bloody hand to my lips, and slipping out of the covers, I crawled over to the door. I rested my head against the wooden panel. "Shh."

Tracy fell to the bed sobbing, "No, you all don't understand. Now I'm pregnant."

I jerked my head back from the door, incredulous, stood up, and moved back to the bed. Instinctively, I slapped Tracy's face, screaming, "You deserve it." My bloody hand reddened her cheek. I yelled louder, "You've tried to hurt me every chance you could."

A silence ensued like the quiet after a massive thunderstorm. Softly, she started to apologize, "Hey, stop! I was afraid he'd pick you over me. You have it all: looks, talent, brains." She looked down, afraid to continue her confession. "He always said if I didn't do what he wanted that he'd pick you, Lia. He said you were beautiful." She looked me in the eye. "And now ... now I don't know what to do," she stammered, "I'm—I'm so scared." Her eyes pleaded for help.

Carla sat down next and caressed Tracy's back like a mother, saying slowly. "How do you know you're pregnant?"

"Well, I haven't had my period for two months."

"Jeez," I said. "What a mess."

Carla picked up the razor on the floor. She rotated it in her hand, slowing to inspect the blood on the edge. "Okay! So, what can we do about this? If we tell, we're all off the team." Moving to the window, she asked, "Does anyone know why David Solomon, the chairman of the board, came to Bad Gastein? Do you think he suspects something?"

I'd never felt so hopeless, so unsure. Puzzled, I raised my hand, "Hold on. How about we call McElvey in the morning? Maybe he can help us out." I suddenly had an image of a Clark's nutcracker, of his lesson on mutualism.

Carla shook her head, "No one'll believe us." She looked at Tracy, "Unless you go to the authorities." She emphasized the "you," glaring at Tracy.

Tracy stuttered, "I ... I couldn't. I don't want to lose my chance for the Olympics."

I smiled, then laughed. "Yeah, and how are you going to prepare for the Olympics with a baby? Did you ever think about that?"

Tracy, putting her hand over her stomach, said through her
sobs, "John wants me to get an abortion. He said if I don't, he's
done with me."

"You mean Coach John Boast knows you're pregnant?" I
choked, emphasizing his first name.

"I had to tell him," said Tracy.

"An abortion?" said Carla. "That's illegal ... you could die."

"John says he knows someone in the States who can do it,"
said Tracy, sounding like a child who trusts her parent's authority.

"This is too much information," I said. "What deception, dis-
honesty, what a disaster!" My anger was building like a wall of snow
ready to break loose. I raised my hand, saying loudly, "I'm reporting
all this tomorrow to Mr. Solomon. I don't care now if I'm kicked
off the team. Enough is enough." I felt the frustrations of the past
months breaking loose. Turning back to Carla, I said with new confidence. "Let's go to bed, focus on the race. We'll handle this tomorrow." I pointed toward the door. "I need my sleep. Good night!"

I made them get up from my bed and forcefully walked them
to the door. I opened it, carefully peeking out to see if anyone
was in the hallway. As they left, I whispered, "We'll all be okay."

Once back in bed, my brain churned, my thoughts tumbled
unconnected, my sanity unraveling like the threads in my knitted ski hat. *Bill, dead. Why couldn't he be here? McElvey, what
would he think? My dad, would he listen to me or scold me? Was
making the Olympic team worth all this? Wren, still in the hospital. Was I really prepared to end all this by telling Mr. Solomon?*

I became more confused, my thoughts, swirling like snow
in a storm. I tried to remember the peace I'd found when skiing the slopes with Kurt: braiding turns, snow crystals flying
in my mouth, up my nose, imploding on my goggles. Rhythm,
rocking. Then the snow under my skis let go and I felt a wind

pushing me forward, my feet flying over my head; I tumbled, gasping for breath. Suffocating-snow stuffed up my mouth. Finally, quiet, silence.

CHAPTER 57

Last Race

An aggressive pounding on my door woke me. Rubbing my eyes, I hoped I'd dreamed last night's attack, but my throbbing eyebrow convinced me otherwise. The door opened inviting in a smell of eggs, bacon, and fresh bread. Becky entered, saying, "So you don't bother to lock your door anymore? Someone could come in and hurt you. Time to get up, sleepyhead." She looked at me huddled under the covers. "What's up?" Suited up for the day's slalom, she came closer. "I had to wake Carla and Tracy, too."

"Ah—thanks," I said, sitting up slowly. My knuckles continued cleaning my eyes, trying to get rid of the blur. "Ah, we, I—I had quite a night." As I looked around the room, I tried to orient myself. "What time is it?"

"Six-thirty. You have to be dressed, ready by seven, you know, so you can eat and get to the slope. The slalom starts at 10. Guess you won't get your good-luck jog this morning"

"Whoa, I really slept. What a nightmare."

"Up and at 'em! Hey, by the way, you got the number one start today, you lucky devil."

Devil, I thought. *Am I in hell? What does she mean?* "Did you say number one?"

"Yup, you earned first seed from your results in Bad Gastein and then got a lucky draw. Get going. Maybe you'll be the first American to win a World Cup race." She grabbed my pillow, pulling it from under my arm and smashing it against my face. She jumped back seeing the blood on the cotton and screamed, "What happened to you? You've been bleeding."

Before I could answer, the door opened and Pammy looked in, her long blonde strands rippling across her face. She said accusatorily, "Ha, what were all of you guys doing last night? Lia, you look as if an avalanche rolled over you. Tracy and Carla are a mess, too."

Shaking my head, "Ah, you guys wouldn't believe it if we told you. Let's talk after the race."

Pammy moved forward to prod me, "Okay, slowpoke. Now get going. This is going to be a day for the Americans!" She grabbed Becky's arm, and they marched out. Pammy laughing said, "One for all and all for one."

I stumbled to the door and locked it. In the bathroom, I threw off my pajamas and jumped in the shower. The cold water forced me to step out quickly: European hotels weren't like American ones which had instantaneous hot water. Waiting for it to warm up, I leaned toward the mirror. Two black bags swelled under my eyes, my hair stood up straight, but before I could examine my eyebrow cut, my reflection disappeared into the steamy glass. I tried wiping the condensation from the mirror, but my image kept fading into the fog.

Once in the warm shower, I scrubbed the blood from my cheek, my hair, and let the water flow down my face and between my breasts. The warmth took the sting from my cut. I hoped Boast hurt, too. Relaxing in the hot water, I bent to a full stretch, hands to my toes, loving the caress of the warm water down my butt crack. I stretched forward to pull my hamstrings, and then did a half rotation of my torso. Relaxing, I felt less stressed. *Maybe Becky was right. This could be my day. Everything could be resolved today.* I decided to win the race, gain the attention of the press, and tell the world my story. They'd have to believe me then.

In the dining hall, feeling powerful in my racing outfit, I walked toward Coach Ryan and the four girls who were immersed in chatter at a window table. Their eyes ran up and down me as I moved toward the last empty chair against the wall. The conversation stopped. I felt a sharp pain on my hand as it bumped the hot radiator. My eyes wandered from Becky to Pammy to Carla and to Tracy. No one spoke. Then, Carla put her finger to her lips. She whispered, "Later. Let's focus on the race now."

"So where's Coach Boast?" I asked, turning around to see if he might be at another table.

Coach Ryan, looking handsome in his blue team sweater, smiled. "He's getting your pinnies. You heard that you're number one, right?" He tapped his finger on the table. "Great job, Lia."

Tracy looked down, so I couldn't see her reaction; however, I caught a slight affirmative nod of her head. Carla clapped her hands together joyously, saying, "Cool! Good work … you can be the first to make the Olympic team. Just have two clean runs." She winked, realizing she had finally said what we'd all been thinking for four weeks.

I let the words "Olympic team" reverberate in my mind like the Gregorian chant from the monks. I thought, *Maybe, just maybe, this is the calm at the end of the storm. An image of a snow crystal flashed before my eyes. Maybe life is like a snow crystal—many sides, many refractions.*

Ordering a full English breakfast, I listened to Coach Ryan discussing the wax he'd put on our skis. The plan was to get all of us qualified for the second run, so he asked that we not go for broke. He wanted each of us to lower her points. Then, when we returned to the World Cup races in the States, we could bring these FIS points with us, giving other American racers a chance at lowering their points using ours as a standard. For some reason, he felt he needed to emphasize this to me, so he repeated himself, "This means you, Miss Risk-Taker. Don't go for broke just because you've got the number one. Save something for your second run." He stopped and added, "No falls, please."

I nodded thinking, *so now the point of the team was to bring lower FIS points back to the others who were eagerly awaiting our return. There would be two more World Cup races in the US: one at Sugarloaf in the East and the other at Heavenly Valley in the West. I had other plans.*

After breakfast we joined Coach Boast at the base of the chairlift. He was obviously distraught, pacing, a Band-Aid on his check. I smiled, "Tough time shaving, huh, coach?"

He turned, glaring, "You're lucky you got number one. Here, take your pinnie … no more from you. Okay?" Going over to Tracy to give her a pinnie, he attempted to put his arm around her.

"Please, please, don't touch me, Coach," she said, trying to assert herself. He stepped back and looked at her and then turned to me to learn whether we'd colluded. His surprised look told me he realized that we must have been talking.

He put his hand to his chin, squaring his eyebrows as if to attack me, but then stepped back. "Whatever is going on here, I'll have none of it." He looked each in the eye as he handed out the rest of the bibs. "You understand everything rides on this race. Stay focused." I felt the threat, a palpable presence like a vacuum trying to suck out my spirit. How I wanted to say something, but Carla grabbed me, putting her finger to her lips.

A shout from the gathering crowd at the lift entrance brought me back to the moment. "Go, Lia. Go, Carla." I turned to see Novak and his friends pressed against the turnstile. Novak yelled, "Hey, Lia. The guards no let us up. No cheer you. Good luck." Then I saw a six-foot soldier shove Novak back with his machine gun, a military weapon at the entrance to a ski lift.

At the top I took off my parka and tied my pinnie over my team sweater. *Number One. If only I could finish number one in the race!* I skied next to the slalom course that appeared to have four rolls and three side hills. A sheet of blue ice shone in the half-light at the last hairpin turn, just before the final five-gate flush. Becky signaled for me to stop beside her, so the two of us could silently sidestep up the course together. I loved this quiet time: studying the hill, memorizing each turn, planning my line, visualizing where to start each turn, where to edge, where to unweight my skis. After every four gates, I stopped and looking down the hill, I closed my eyes and moved my hand, tracing the line of an imaginary skier. I knew today was my destiny. Just like at Sugarloaf, these were my Buddhist prayer flags. This would be my defining race. Afterward, with confidence, I would tell all to David Solomon.

A slight breeze blew up the hill, caressing my cheek.

Resolutely, I skied the first run perfectly, leading the pack by one second. I just needed one more solid run to win the combined time, to be in control.

On the second run on the top of the course, I watched the forerunner take off. The grating of her skis indicated that the course would be hard and fast. Looking down the slope to where my teammates stood together, I saw Tracy smile at me, and then I saw Carla's arm go around Tracy. Becky put her thumbs up in the air. Pammy did a wiggle with her hips as if to say "stay loose." A photographer stepped in front of my teammates and started snapping pictures. Feeling their energy, I smiled. I now understand that this race would be for me and for them. My points could become their points. I finally understood how a team could be separate, yet together.

"Racer ready," announced the starter. I set my poles over the wand, rolled back into my boots to start rocking with the count down. "Five, four, three, two, one, go." I kicked up my heels, felt the wand spring against my boot top, poled and skated to the first gate.

A roar from the crowd told me that I'd hit the first knoll with speed, each turn linked to the next. My knees pulsated, my edges touched the snow lightly, my eyes flowed ahead of my turns. I had to bang a gate away with my hand when I cut the pole too close.

Carrying more speed than I anticipated, I forced myself to hit my turns earlier, trying to hold the fall-line, my knees working like pistons while my upper body remained still. I edged hard on the sidehill, stepped up around the hairpin turn and dove into the flush.

A blur suddenly stepped out of the crowd, a flash went off in my eyes, I looked up to see what had happened and lost my balance on the ice, catching my ski tip on the third gate of the last flush. One leg went into the air while the other edge caught in the snow; my ankle twisted, my knee pulled from its socket just before I hit both my shoulder and head on an ice patch. A sharp pain ripped up my leg, a pain so intense that I screamed, "Oh God!" I slid to a stop at the foot of the photographer—he kept taking pictures. I tried keeping my eyes open, but a blackness thankfully took away the all-consuming pain.

✳ ✳ ✳

A bright light woke me. I heard a muffled voice asking, "Are you awake, Lia?" The gurney under my back felt hard and cold. The sheet over my body was doing little to keep me warm. Shivering, I heard Becky's voice and felt her hand on mine, "Lia, Lia, wake up."

I opened my eyes but couldn't tell whether it was her face or McElvey's. A disembodied voice whispered, "Stay a little."

"Uh, what happened?" I asked.

I blinked, looking into Becky's brown eyes. She said, "You broke your ankle, a compound fracture. The doctor has okayed an emergency operation. He finally got hold of your dad."

"What? Oh, the pain," I said, grimacing. A nurse pushed Becky aside to give me a pre-op shot.

Becky moved closer and leaned down, forcing me to focus on her wavy, brown hair that caressed my cheek. She pushed her strands from my ear and whispered. "Not to worry, my friend. Tracy has told me everything. After the race, the two of us went immediately to Chairman Solomon about her problem. Coaches

Boast and Ryan are being sent home on the next plane to answer to the US Ski Team board. They can't hurt you anymore." She paused and leaned closer to my ear, laughing, "Snowflakes are such ephemeral things, but look what they can do when they stick together."

I nodded in a hazy affirmation. She continued, "Yeah, and more good news. Your dad told the doctor that Middlebury College has offered you a scholarship for the fall ... you can become the writer you've always wanted to be while your leg heals!"

I nodded, letting out a drug-induced laugh. "Guess I'll have plenty to write about."

The nurse moved behind my gurney, but Becky put up her hand to stop her from pushing it toward the operating room. She smiled slightly as if just getting the point of someone's joke, saying, "Oh, and one more thing. We called McElvey. Wren can move her legs."

My cheeks relaxed into a smile as a gentle wind caressed my forehead, a stir emanating from the blurry-white surgical doors that had just opened.

A Reader's Guide

Lia Erickson, an aspiring world cup skier racer, must confront danger in the mountains, her fears of downhill speed, and the loneliness of ski racing while competing in California, Colorado, Germany, Switzerland, Austria and Yugoslavia for a place on the U.S. Olympic ski team. In her coming of age story, she, a naïve eighteen year old, discovers that she must build her own moral system and learn to trust her teammates while grappling with the corruption of two predatory male coaches. Mentored by a supportive teammate, Lia finds the courage to tackle all her nemeses.

QUESTIONS AND TOPICS FOR DISCUSSION

1. What did *Snow Sanctuary* teach you about the challenges for a young female in the world of ski racing?

2. What are Lia's fears and wishes?

3. In what ways do you identify with Lia?

4. What themes are similar in Shakespeare's *King Lear* and in *Snow Sanctuary*?

5. How does the setting in the Sierra Nevada's change Lia's attitude about her vulnerability? What does Lia learn from the writings of John Muir?

6. Why is the image of knitting important to understanding the relationship between the girls?

7. What role does war play for each of the characters?

8. How does the setting in the European ski resorts change the relationship between the girls on the US Team?

9. To what extent does Lia's journal help her understand her growing sense of injustice? How do the writings of Thoreau and Emerson fortify her final decision?

10. What do we learn about Lia's backstory and her life in Vermont?

11. How does Lia relate to the boys on her team and to the male coaches?

12. Compare and contrast the coaching styles of Justin McElvey and John Boast?

13. Does Lia's relationship with her father help or hurt her?

14. Lia's meets many strangers who teach her lessons. How does the naval officer help her in a moment of confusion? How does the Jewish woman on the train influence her final decision?

15. Ski racing is a solitary endeavor, yet in order to compete on the World Cup tour the skiers have to learn how to work with their teammates. What does Lia learn from Kathy and Annie about the importance of team? How does her relationship with Tracy change?

16. Lia has never had a normal home life, so when she joins Annie in her ancestral home in Austria, she is transformed. What are some of the lessons she takes from this short gathering?

17. The different venues in each country teach Lia life-changing lessons. Compare and contrast the settings, especially the final adventure in Maribor, Yugoslavia.

18. Spirituality and religion are on-going themes. How does Lia's attitude about religion differ from those of other characters.

19. How would this story be different if the protagonist were a male ski racer?

CPSIA information can be obtained
at www.ICGtesting.com
Printed in the USA
FSHW01n0626030818
51130FS